# DUO # 1

## VIGILANTE

## THE CONSULTANT

Two novels by
**Claude Bouchard**

DUO # 1 VIGILANTE/THE CONSULTANT

All rights reserved

Copyright © 2009 by Claude Bouchard

This book, or parts thereof, may not be reproduced, in any form or by any means, without written permission from the author excluding the use of short excerpts for review or promotional purposes.

This is a work of fiction. Names, characters, places and incidents are either the product of the author's imagination or are used fictitiously. Any resemblance to actual persons, living or dead, events or locales are purely coincidental.

Published by Claude Bouchard

ISBN 978-0-9812790-4-6


ORIGINAL PUBLICATIONS

VIGILANTE

Copyright © 1995 by Claude Bouchard
Published by Claude Bouchard
ISBN 978-0-9812790-0-8


THE CONSULTANT

Copyright © 1996 by Claude Bouchard
Published by Claude Bouchard
ISBN 978-0-9812790-1-5

BOOK # 1


**VIGILANTE**


A novel by
**Claude Bouchard**

## Prologue

The old man was drunk again. That usually meant trouble.

The boy backed away into the recesses of the attic, his secret place, as he called it. There, he would be safe as long as he remained quiet because the bastard turned violent when he got drunk.

The youngster worried about his sister though, who had arrived ten minutes before their stepfather had. He had heard, then seen her through the ventilation grill set in the ceiling of her room but she didn't know he was there. Nobody knew about his secret place. They never used the attic.

"Where the fuck is everybody!" the old man hollered angrily as he plodded up the stairs.

The boy could hear the stupid drunk bounce off one wall, then the other as he stumbled upwards. Laying flat on his stomach, the youth quietly started inching back towards the ventilation grill. Doors could be heard slamming open and closed in the upstairs hallway. He reached the grill and peered down through it at his older sister, wishing that there was some way he could magically beam her up to him, like they did in Star Trek.

She was seated on the bed with knees gripped under her chin, huddled in the corner and trembling with intense fear as she stared at the door. She visibly stiffened as the footsteps approached, causing a nauseous wave to wash over her brother as he secretly but helplessly watched on. The footsteps stopped on the other side of the door and silent seconds went by, serving only to increase each sibling's private terror.

'Please go away! Leave her alone!' the boy pleaded in his mind, biting his knuckles to keep from screaming.

At that moment, door crashed open, causing his sister to jump with fright.

"Howya doin, girly?" their stepfather snarled with a leering smile. "Didn't ya hear me callin?"

"I, I was studying," she stammered in a thin voice. "I didn't hear you. I'm sorry."

"Where's your mama, sweetie?" he slurred, approaching her.

From the safety of his hideout, the boy could now see the old man through the grill.

"She's-she's out, I guess," the girl replied, trying to sound confident but not succeeding. "But she should be back real soon."

The old man smiled again, more of a sneer, as he wavered slightly.

"And that little shit brother of yours?" demanded her stepfather. "Where's he at?"

"I-I don't know," she mumbled. "No one was home when I got here."

"So it's just you and me, huh, kiddo?!" he mused, scratching his stubble thoughtfully as his cold bleary eyes wandered over her body.

"I'm sure Mom will be back real soon," she repeated tearfully as she shrunk into the corner, shivering with terror.

The old man grinned at her for a few seconds, then stepped back and pushed the door shut.

As he returned, he started unbuttoning his trousers and retorted, "Well, girly, real soon is just not soon enough for me today. You're just gonna have to fill your mama's shoes!"

The boy rolled away from the grill, not wanting to see what was taking place. His sister shrieked and several slaps were heard amidst a muttered "Shut-up, bitch!" Covering his ears, the youngster cowered in the darkness and silently wept with frustration. But, what could he do? He was only ten.

After a minute or two, the boy heard the bedroom door below swing open and slam shut and everything grew quiet. With tears in his eyes, he crawled forward and once again peered down through the grill.

Their stepfather was gone but his sister was still there, lying on the bed, whimpering and shaking uncontrollably. Her dress was ripped and he could see her exposed breasts, scratched and bruised. Her left eye, just above the cheekbone, was already starting to swell from when the pig had hit her and the sheets were spattered with blood.

He began to soundlessly weep once more as he vowed that he would get even when he was big.

### Chapter 1 - Tuesday, June 25, 1996

8:00 p.m. Sandy was at school, her last night of the spring term and would not be home for a while. She had mentioned that she would be going for a drink or two after class with a few fellow students to celebrate the completion of another semester. She would therefore most likely not be home before midnight. She never was on such occasions as she enjoyed these mini social events.

With Sandy out, he was alone for the evening but this had never proved to be a problem in the past and this night would not be any different. He was a big boy and could always find a way to occupy his time.

He pulled on some black Levi's and a dark t-shirt, slipped into his black Reeboks and laced them securely. Leaving the bedroom, he descended to the main floor, headed for the foyer closet and retrieved his black leather jacket. No studs or chains, just black leather. He slipped into the coat and donned a black baseball cap. Dark, reflective aviator glasses completed the ensemble.

Examining his image in the mirrored doors of the closet, he flashed himself a grin and murmured, "Perfect, as usual!"

It was time to go.

After setting the security system for the house lights and alarm, he picked up his small canvas bag and hopped down the short flight of stairs leading to the garage.

Once there, he hesitated for a few seconds as usual, tempted to use the Corvette, all black and waxed and shiny. But no, that would be too conspicuous, and frankly, not practical. Sighing, he climbed into the mini-van, turned the engine as the garage door opened, and sped off into the evening.

\* \* \* \*

She was sitting at the bar of her favourite watering hole, somewhat frustrated thanks to the two jerks that had been ogling her and flashing their stupid smiles.

'Why can't a girl blow off some steam in peace after a tough day like guys do?' she wondered, annoyed.

She hoped that the two idiots would get bored and look elsewhere. After all, she hadn't done anything to attract their attention. She was just trying to relax after a hard day at the office.

"Another Caesar?" the bartender offered, interrupting her thoughts.

"One more," she replied curtly, glancing towards her antagonists.

"Don't let them get to you, Eileen," the beefy barkeep suggested understandingly, nodding in the direction of the two suits. "Just a couple of schmucks, that's all. Ain't no way they're gonna bother you while I'm around!"

"Thanks, Alain," she responded, flashing a grateful smile. "And, anyways, you're right. They **are** just a couple of schmucks and all they did **is** look at me. I guess I should just accept that I'm a looker!"

"And a modest looker at that!" laughed Alain as he went off to fix her drink.

Before Eileen realized it, the third drink was nearly gone and she was actually feeling better. The two shirts and ties at the end of the bar were engrossed in the sports news playing on the big screen T.V. and seemed to have lost interest in her. They didn't look like bad guys anyways; probably married, with kids. Simply a question of excited hormones; men were like that. All you had to do was confront them, mention their wives, and they couldn't look you in the eye if their lives depended on it.

Some good rock'n'roll was playing in the background, Springsteen, mid-seventies. The place was filling up, even if it was only Tuesday night. But after all, it was only 8:45 and this was one of the more popular spots downtown. Many, like her, worked late and needed to wind down a bit before going home for a few hours of sleep and starting all over again. Ah, life in the fast lane, living in the 90's, work, work, work.

She drained her glass and although tempted to have another, decided against it. She was driving, plus, she had an important presentation to make in the morning. She signalled the bartender, paid her tab and left.

\* \* \* \*

He pulled onto a side street off Sherbrooke and found a parking spot with little trouble. It was still early and crowds did not tend to flock downtown on Tuesday nights.

Cutting the engine, he climbed out and engaged the car alarm. One could never be too careful on these streets; which incidentally was why he had come here in the first place. A few minutes of searching at best and he was confident that he would find some action. At least, this was what he hoped.

\* \* \* \*

Eileen had been lucky enough to find a parking spot on Aylmer, just one short block from the bar. She didn't particularly like this area in the evening but, then again, no sector of the downtown core could be considered completely safe once darkness set in. Drunks, junkies, the homeless and gangs had slowly but surely taken over night-time downtown during the last fifteen years. Crime rates had risen drastically and the city administration's efforts to curb them had failed miserably; life in the 90's.

As she rounded the corner, Eileen heard the clatter of steady, rapid footsteps coming down the sidewalk behind her. She quickened her pace and her car was in sight.

Reaching her vehicle, she threw a glance over her shoulder while she fumbled in her purse for her keys. The two suits from the bar were heading towards her.

Frantically, she tried to unlock the car door but before she could get the key in the lock she felt someone press up against her and firmly grip her waist.

"Pretty early to head home, sweetheart, don't you think?" the voice whispered from behind. "Why don't we go for a drink somewhere?"

Although frightened, she turned to glare at him, the younger one, and firmly shot back, "I'm not sure your wife would appreciate that!"

Grinning over his shoulder at his older buddy, her aggressor mocked, "Isn't that sweet!? The young lady is concerned about my old lady!"

Turning back to her, he snarled, "Maybe you're right, bitch! Maybe we don't have time for a drink!"

With that, he grabbed her around the chest, pinning her arms, while covering her mouth with his other hand. While his older accomplice kept watch, he proceeded to half drag, half carry her struggling form towards a dark alley close by.

Once into the alley, he threw her to the pavement in the corner formed by two brick walls. Eileen started to scream and he rewarded her with a slap across the mouth.

"Keep that up sweetheart, and this evening may become unpleasant!" her attacker hissed threateningly.

Leering at her maliciously, he unzipped his pants and moved in on her as she cowered in the corner in terror. At that moment, her aggressor heard a sudden gurgling, gasping sound behind him and turned to find his older accomplice lying on the ground, legs flailing as he clutched his throat.

As he stared in stunned, uncomprehending silence, he noticed a dark pool rapidly forming around the older man's head. Looking up, he realized that another man stood a few feet away, a long, thin knife in one hand and a baseball bat in the other. In the dim light, he noticed that the blade of the knife was stained and dripping. His buddy had now ceased moving and lay lifeless on the ground.

The stranger calmly crouched down over the body and carefully wiped the blade on the dead man's jacket. He then pressed a button on the knife's handle, causing the blade to disappear and slipped the weapon into a pocket.

Returning to a standing position, he turned his attention to Eileen and spoke.

"Miss, I believe that you should be on your way. I am truly sorry for any inconvenience these gentlemen may have caused you and I **promise** they won't ever do it again."

Speechless and in tears, Eileen rose on shaky legs and bolted down the short alley to the street. Within seconds, the gunning of an engine was heard, followed by the car's tires screaming off into the night.

The stranger, wielding the bat, turned towards the younger assailant who was frantically struggling with his pants zipper.

"Now my friend," he announced with a deadly smile. "It's my turn to have some fun!!"

## Chapter 2 - Wednesday, June 26, 1996

6:00 a.m. Chris Barry awoke to the opening lines of Etheridge's "Come to my Window" playing on the clock radio. Quickly, he turned off the alarm to avoid waking his wife who slept peacefully beside him.

He gazed at her and thought, as he had many times before, how lucky he was to have her. If anything, she was more beautiful now than she had been when he had first met her fifteen years earlier. Back when she was eighteen.

With a sigh of contentment, he climbed out of bed and tiptoed into the bathroom adjoining their bedroom, closing the door quietly so as not to disturb her.

Theirs was a good life and Chris was proud of what he had accomplished to date.

Following high school, he had felt that studies weren't as important as money was so he had headed for the labour market. After having held a couple of clerical jobs however, he had soon realized that if he wanted more, a further education would in fact come in handy. He had therefore enrolled at a local university and following several arduous years attending night classes, had obtained his degree in business administration. Now, at the ripe old age of thirty-four, he was Executive Vice President and Chief Operating Officer of CSS Inc., preceded only by Walter Olson, the company's founder, President and CEO.

CSS Inc., which was rapidly becoming the leader in computer security and related investigations, had been founded by Walter a number of years ago. Initially operating under the name of SecurInvestigations Ltd., its origins had been as an investigation and security firm, offering its services to corporations with internal crime problems. In addition, it had supplied security services for public events such as concerts and conventions.

Although the firm had gained a respectable reputation in its field over the years, changing times had gradually rendered prosperity an elusive objective. Faced with dwindling revenues due to growing competition and altering markets, Walter Olson had been attempting to identify diversification possibilities to give his company the rebirth it so justly deserved. That had been eight years ago. That was when Walter had met Chris Barry.

Chris had approached Walter on a cold call to offer his services. He had explained to Walter how limiting his business to the saturated niche of conventional investigative services was stifling, if not adversely affecting its growth. He had spoken of rapidly changing technology in the corporate world and of new opportunities for white collar crimes, thanks to the ever increasing use of computers. He had elaborated about viruses, record falsification and embezzlement possibilities which worsened on a daily basis due to the growing information highways. He had talked about the ease with which computer buffs with criminal minds could enter systems via modems and modify records to suit their needs. He had, in effect, described a market of computer security and investigations which was there for the taking.

This was an area which Walter, an old-timer, knew nothing about. However, the young man sitting before him obviously knew what he was talking about and presented his ideas with tremendous energy. Maybe this **was** the way to the future.

Walter had little to lose as his company was going down at a rapid pace. In addition, there was something about this Barry fellow, the way he exuded confidence that stroked Walter in just the right way. On a whim, he had offered Chris a job.

Within two years, annual revenues had increased tenfold, from twenty million to two hundred million. After five years, the company by then known as CSS Inc. (Computer Security Services), had surpassed the billion dollar mark in sales and had gone public. Revenues for the current year were expected to exceed 3 billion dollars.

Although the firm continued to offer investigative and security services, its success in recent years was clearly owed to the world of computers. Under the skilful guiding hand of Chris Barry, a security software division had been formed, with Chris personally handling all facets including recruiting activities, hiring only the best young minds.

CSS now boasted the reputation of leading the way in the field of systems security, counting among its clients such giants as Bombardier, BCE and American Express as well as many government agencies, both in Canada and the United States. Eighteen months earlier, the company had completely revised the systems security for the police departments of Montreal and a dozen other communities in the surrounding areas. Similar contracts were currently in the works with Toronto, Calgary and Vancouver as well as with a handful of major American cities.

Walter was an honest man who believed in rewarding for jobs well done. For Chris, this had represented a rapid ascension to the number two spot in the company, accompanied by the salary, stock options and other perks which went hand in hand with such a high level position.

'Yes, this is a good life,' Chris thought as he turned off the shower. 'Health, money, power, and my amazing wife, to share it with!'

He quickly dressed and kissed his still sleeping angel before leaving for his 8:00 a.m. meeting. He was confident that this morning, they would wrap up the contract with a fourth major bank in as many months. Yes, this was a good life.

\* \* \* \*

When Lieutenant Dave McCall arrived, the alley had already been cordoned off and several uniformed officers were standing guard to keep the growing crowd of curious onlookers away from the crime scene.

From the street, one could see what appeared to be two bodies in the alley, both covered with sheets. The large brownish-red stains also apparent on the concrete pavement made it obvious that the victims had most likely not succumbed to natural causes.

After briefly surveying the site of Montreal's two most recent murders, McCall approached Frank Bakes, who had taken charge of the scene pending his superior's arrival.

"This one's pretty messy, Dave," Bakes announced grimly as his boss strode up to him. "One got his throat slashed, which isn't too bad. The other one though, makes keeping your breakfast down somewhat of a challenge. Definitely the worst beating we've seen so far. Poor bastard musta got whacked with a pipe or something a hundred times. Good thing he had ID cuz I don't even think they could have depended on dental records to identify him. The son of a bitch smashed his face!"

"Were they punks again?" McCall asked tersely, staring down at the sheet covered victims.

"No," Bakes shook his head in puzzlement as he gestured towards the bodies. "That's what makes this one strange; two guys in suits and ties. Preliminary checks indicate no records. Card key passes identify them as employees of Heritage Mutual, some insurance company."

"Could it be a mugging gone bad?" suggested McCall as he crouched down and raised the sheet to examine the first cadaver.

"Nope. Doesn't look like it." disagreed Bakes, shaking his head emphatically. "They both still have their wallets loaded with credit cards and cash. If you're gonna go to this much trouble to rob a guy, you might as well finish the job."

"Who found the bodies?" McCall enquired, dropping the sheet back in disgust over the first victim and heading towards the second.

"Owner of that restaurant," replied Bakes with a mischievous grin as he pointed. "Came out to throw some trash into the dumpster. He ain't feeling too good right now!"

"I'll guess that we don't have any witnesses?" asked Dave, already knowing the answer.

Frank shook his head. "I have a couple of uniforms ringing doorbells, asking if anyone heard or saw anything weird. They haven't reported back yet."

"Alright," sighed McCall through clenched teeth as he stared at the second corpse, the battered one. "I'll let you finish up here. There's not much I can do anyways."

He took one last look before covering the victim's mutilated face then glanced up at Bakes as he spoke. "Try to get your report to me by tomorrow morning so I can add it to our impressive collection!"

There was no mistaking the sarcasm in his voice.

Dave McCall could not remember a time when he did not want to be a cop. He was convinced that it was a hereditary trait, following in the footsteps of his father, grandfather and great-grandfather. It was in his blood.

Upon completing high school at the age of seventeen, he had enrolled into the three year Police Technology programme in Lennoxville. He had then gone on to complete a graduate degree at McGill University with majors in law and criminology. He could have passed the bar and become a lawyer but Dave McCall wanted to be a cop and nothing else. It was in his blood.

He had joined the force at the age of twenty-four, right around the time he had married Cathy. They had met when she was four. He had been five. Best of friends over the years, they had realized by their late teens that they were in love. Today, they still remained best of friends.

From the onset, Dave had worked hard to prove himself and by the age of twenty-eight, he had made detective and was working homicide. It was obvious to his superiors that Dave was a superstar and that his ascension through the ranks was far from over. Now, only three years later, he was completing his first year as lieutenant heading a special division of homicide with a dozen detectives reporting to him.

Located in an old office building on Cypress just off Dominion Square in downtown Montreal, the Special Homicide Task Force Centre did not resemble the typical police station. A receptionist, rather than a desk sergeant, greeted visitors and uniformed officers were rarely found on site. Barring the two holding cells at the back, the place could have been mistaken for the offices of any given business.

Just as untypical as its locale were the affairs in which the Task Force was involved. McCall's division concentrated only on the bizarre, high profile and extraordinary murders which took place in his fine city. In addition, his team was often called upon to lend a hand in similar cases outside its official jurisdiction.

Approximately six months earlier, two days before Christmas, this most recent series of murders had started. Although the majority had occurred in or near the downtown sector, a few had taken place in the suburbs.

To date, the slayings had all had two points in common. For one, the victims without exception had all been known to the authorities; gang members, pushers, pimps and the like. Secondly, all had died by one of two means. Either their throats had been viciously slashed or they had been bludgeoned to death with a club of sorts.

As Dave made his way back to the office, he considered these two latest killings and agreed with Frank Bakes that they were puzzling. Sure enough, the methods of execution matched the others though this particular beating had been exceptionally brutal. However, these two victims were not bums. Neither even had a record of an outstanding parking ticket. Apparently, they worked for an insurance company; managers or sales reps, based on their attire. Their wedding bands indicated that both were family men.

Thus far, the choice of targets had suggested the work of some nut-case vigilante, saving the innocent from the trash of our society. But if that was the case, why had these two ended up on the killer's selection list? Either the presumed pattern had been a coincidence or these latest victims were.

It was possible that some other wacko had decided to copy-cat the Vigilante. God only knew, the press had been talking enough about this rash of murders over the last six months; especially that idiot, Ron Henderson, from the **Gazette** who practically praised the Vigilante whenever another execution occurred. "If the cops aren't taking care of the garbage on the street, at least somebody is," was the reporter's clear message.

But did such a person, this Vigilante, even exist? To be honest, even Dave's division had no specific evidence linking any of the murders to date. All they had was a hunch, a gut feeling. But that instinct was strong enough to convince McCall that these last two victims had fallen prey to the person responsible for all the other deaths.

He had a serial killer on his hands. Unfortunately, after eighteen murders, he did not have anything that even faintly resembled a lead.

\* \* \* \*

Walter Olson whistled cheerily as he strolled into the CSS executive board room and dropped into his usual chair at the head of the mammoth conference table.

Seated comfortably at the other end, feet crossed on the table and sporting a huge grin, was Chris Barry who had already shed his jacket and loosened his tie while Walter had escorted the five top executives of Century Bank on their way out.

The meeting had gone extremely well, with Chris effortlessly presenting the final sales pitch and Century Bank signing the contract. CSS Inc. would replace the computer security systems in each of Century's 625 branches and would handle all of the bank's future investigative work.

"What the hell do you need me for!" Walter bellowed, beaming at Chris. "Do you realize how much money this company would save if it didn't have to pay my huge salary?!"

"All I do is present the deals you so wisely come up with, Walt," Chris responded with a serious air. "If the customers are lining up to buy our services, it's because you built a damn fine company. You started this place so if it weren't for you, it wouldn't exist! I'm just the humble messenger."

"Bullshit, Barry!" Walter guffawed. "What are you sucking up for this time? Another raise or another stock option?!"

"Both!" Chris winked.

"I figured as much." chuckled Walter, shaking his head in despair. "Now, we just signed another major deal, plus, it's 11:00. Scotch time!!"

## Chapter 3 - Thursday, June 27, 1996

10:14 a.m. Dave McCall sat in his office, swamped by the ever growing collection of files and reports related to the Vigilante case. However, his attention was not currently directed at the ominous piles of paperwork which surrounded him. He was much more interested in Ron Henderson's front page article in that morning's **Gazette,** entitled **VIGILANTE, OR JUST A KILLER?**

Immediately below the headline was a rather vivid colour photograph of the previous morning's crime scene. Obviously, some photographer had shown up before the bodies had been covered and had made excellent use of a mighty fine zoom lens.

The article started by relating the details surrounding the two most recent murders allegedly committed by the supposed Vigilante. It then went on to describe the various killings over the last half year, all eighteen, highlighting the similarities linking them. Henderson concluded his story by stating that the two latest victims were not known criminals as others had been in the past. In fact, they were both insurance salesmen who had been with the same firm for a number of years.

Had the Vigilante grown tired of targeting the bad guys? Was he (or she?) now looking for greater thrills? This was a definite twist from journalist. His numerous articles over the last six months had valiantly cheered the Vigilante's efforts all while criticizing the police's attempts to fight crime in the city.

As McCall finished going over the article for a second time, Tim Harris, one of his top detectives, rushed into his office without bothering to knock.

"Dave! Maybe it ain't much, but it's the most we've had so far!" he uttered breathlessly, thrusting a printed sheet at his boss. "We just got a message on Eazy-Com from the Vigilante!"

> THE PAPERS ARE WRONG. I DO NOT KILL FOR PLEASURE. ONLY THOSE WHO DESERVE IT PAY THE PRICE.        VIGILANTE

It *wasn't* much, but it was **something**! Since these murders had started popping up, they had not had one clue. Nothing! Now, this wacko had suddenly decided to open up the lines of communication with them. This message might very possibly be the first of many.

Better yet, it was also possible that the wizards down at the Computer Centre might be able to track where the e-mail had come from. Maybe this was more than they thought, maybe, their big break. Perhaps the Vigilante had finally made a serious mistake.

"Call Thompson at the Computer Centre!" Dave excitedly ordered. "Tell him I need his two best men here in an hour! And tell everyone that NOBODY is to breathe a word of this to ANYBODY! I don't want the press getting a hold of this and scaring our friend off! That's it. Go!"

\* \* \* \*

10:21 a.m. Ron Henderson typed away in his cramped cubicle, working on an article for the next day's paper, when his PC suddenly beeped. The small flag shaped *EC* icon appeared in the corner of the screen, waving back and forth, indicating he had an incoming message on Eazy-Com.

Moving the cursor to the flag, he clicked the mouse to immediately access the contents of the transmission. The usual *EC* logo quickly filled the screen before fading away to reveal the message it concealed underneath.

> YOU ARE WRONG, MY FRIEND. THE GENTLEMEN WERE TRYING TO RAPE SOME POOR SOUL. I WOULD NOT KILL FOR NOTHING. F.Y.I.
> THANKS FOR YOUR PAST AND, HOPEFULLY, CONTINUED SUPPORT.    VIGILANTE

Dumbfounded, Henderson stared at the screen as he slowly whispered, "Son of a bitch!"

Quickly, he moved the cursor to the *Sender* icon and frantically clicked the mouse several times. The screen went blank. Nothing. There was no return address.

"Son of a bitch!" he repeated softly, both awed and terrified. "What do I do? What do I do?!"

He considered going to his editor but quickly decided against it. The boss would insist on printing an article about the e-mail and, as a result, the cops would get involved. The wiser thing to do was to wait and see if the Vigilante sent him more messages. If the sender was truly **the** 'Vigilante', this could be the start of an incredible relationship.

Yes, he decided, he would keep this to himself. In a day or two, he'd think up an angle to write an article about rumours or reliable sources regarding the rape possibility. He'd let the Vigilante know that he was still on his side. It was in his best interest, possibly for more reasons than one.

\* \* \* \*

Having completed a demanding semester with a heavy workload, Sandy had suggested she might go spend a couple of days at her mother's cottage in the Laurentians. Decompression, she called it. He had agreed, but only after she had promised to be back for the week-end. She had solemnly vowed to return by Saturday afternoon and make up for her absence in a big way at that time.

So it was Thursday night and he was on his own. He watched a little television for a while but lost interest within the hour. Goddamn reruns. Bored, he went into their study, or 'the office' as they affectionately called it, where he retrieved his notepad from his attaché-case.

Returning to the living room, he settled comfortably on a couch and flipped open the screen of the compact but powerful computer which automatically came to life. He keyed in his password, followed by several security codes and quickly found the directory he was looking for.

Selecting the file named **PROSPECTS**, he began to scan through the data bank, looking for something to do and, within a few moments, his selection was made. Highlighting the chosen item, he transferred it to another file appropriately entitled **SETTLED**.

He now had plans for the evening.

\* \* \* \*

Computers had never been Dave McCall's forte. Fortunately, his work required little use of such machines and, when it did, he had twelve people reporting to him, many of whom couldn't function without the damn things. In addition, when things got too technical, he could also count on Thompson and his band of geniuses from the Computer Centre. After all, they were the best.

Unfortunately, this time the best had not been able to trace the origin of the Eazy-Com message. Although Thompson and his team did what they could to keep up with rapid technological change, public sector budgetary cuts and cost controls in recent years had somewhat slowed their efforts. As one of the whiz kids had explained to Dave, equipment and software was being developed and perfected everyday. What was great today was obsolete tomorrow. As a result, keeping up was practically impossible.

Bottom line was, with the tools and technology available to the Computer Centre, they had not been able to trace the source of the e-mail.

Whenever Dave McCall grew frustrated, angry, or both, he had the habit of pacing slowly back and forth in his glassed office with hands clasped behind his back, glaring harshly at nothing in particular and muttering to himself. Through experience, his staff had come to recognize Dave's 'walks' as a clear 'Do Not Disturb' sign unless the disturber was the bearer of good tidings or critical information.

Dave was 'walking' when Harris stuck his head into the doorway.

"Smile, Boss! There may be hope yet! Thompson's on 217 for you."

Grunting in response, Dave returned to his overflowing desk and dropped wearily into his chair before picking up the phone.

"Yeah, Bob. What can you do for me this fine evening?" he asked in a tired, pleading voice.

Thompson laughed. "I can try to save your ass again, as usual! Listen, I understand that we weren't able to track that message for you. According to my boys, it seemed to come out of nowhere. Good news is I think I know someone who **can** help you. A buddy of mine back from my days in night school. *He* was smart, went into the *private* sector and now, he's a goddamn millionaire. Goes by the name of Chris Barry and he pretty much runs CSS Inc."

"CSS? Sounds vaguely familiar," commented Dave.

Thompson explained. "They're the ones who re-designed our systems a year or two ago and they also look after all our computer security. These guys are true systems specialists and they're really up on the latest technology. Hell, they make it! Anyways, Chris and his people have helped me a few times in the past and I'm sure that he'll be happy to give us a hand once again. I've left him a message late this afternoon so I should hear back from him sometime tomorrow. I'll have him give you a shout once I've spoken to him."

"Thanks Bob. Great! I'll look forward to hearing from him."

Hanging up the phone, Dave leaned back into his chair, a hint of a smile on his lips. He had great faith in Thompson who, in turn, seemed to have great faith in this Chris Barry fellow. Maybe, just maybe, there was hope yet!

\* \* \* \*

As he got ready for the evening, he thought about Tuesday night once again. It continued to bother him.

Sure enough, he had come upon other crimes in progress in the past and had handled them, without prior planning. However, Tuesday night had been different. This time, there had been a witness and she had gotten a good look at him; a very good look.

Maybe she wouldn't talk, he reasoned, trying to reassure himself. After all, he had saved her life or, at the very least, prevented her rape. However, people were funny sometimes. You did them a favour and yet, they turned on you.

He had actually seen the whole thing unfold.

Having just stepped out of the mini-van and set the alarm, he had spotted her as she rounded the corner. The two jerks in suits had been following close behind and had moved in on her as she had hurried for her car. One had grabbed her and dragged her into the alley while his elder cohort had just stood and watched with a stupid grin on his face.

Scanning the area, he had quickly confirmed the absence of any other onlookers and had hurriedly followed the trio into the alley, pausing only to memorize her plate number. One could never have too much information.

Into the alley, things had been almost too easy. The older guy had just been standing there, watching and drooling like a goddamn idiot while playing with himself via his pants pocket. Consequently, the man had not heard a thing coming and a fraction of a second was all that had been required to eliminate him.

To that point, the terrified young woman had not even noticed this welcome intrusion. Her young assailant had had all her attention. But when he had spoken, she had looked at him, intently. Just for a moment, because she had left quickly. But she had looked at him.

Once she was gone, her aggressor had pleaded a bit, but not for long. The first blow with the baseball bat had knocked the wind out of the bastard and within fifteen seconds, he had been unconscious. Although the man had been dead after half a minute, the vicious clubbing had continued for a while, fuelled by the vivid image of a sister, victimized so many years before.

He didn't regret what he had done on Tuesday night. Giving these subhuman sons of bitches what they deserved never bothered him. Quite the contrary, it satisfied him, however temporarily.

But the witness bothered him. He would have to speak to her.

\* \* \* \*

Jimmy Green basically lived for Thursday nights. Thursday was payday which meant cash to go to *Charlie's*, drink and play some pool. If he got lucky, he could get together with one of the bimbos that hung around the bar and get laid. Otherwise, his wife was back at home for that. It was win-win either way.

Tonight hadn't been the best of Thursdays. He'd played eight-ball for a couple of hours but had consistently lost and was down fifty bucks. As far as women went, nothing of interest was happening at *Charlie's* on this particular night so by 10:00 p.m., Jimmy, slightly drunk and definitely horny, decided to cut his losses and go home. The bitch was probably sleeping by this time, but what the hell, she'd just have to wake up and tend to his needs. He paid his bets and bar bill and shuffled out to the parking lot.

As he unlocked the door of his pickup truck, a voice behind him quietly enquired, "Howya doing, Jimmy?"

He turned to find a stranger standing a half dozen feet away, clad in black jeans, a baseball cap and a black leather jacket. Although it was dark, the man wore sunglasses, the mirror kind. In his hand was a baseball bat, swaying ever so gently.

"Who the hell are you?!" Jimmy demanded in a surly tone, displaying more confidence than he actually felt.

"Why do you beat your wife?" the stranger asked softly, ignoring Jimmy's question.

"Listen, buddy," Jimmy growled, trying to fight the fear growing in the pit of his stomach. "I don't know who the fuck you are or what you're talking about! You just better get the hell away from me or I'll break your fucking legs!"

For a few seconds, the stranger just stood there, looking at Jimmy and smiling. He then raised the baseball bat and smashed it into the side of Jimmy's skull.

\* \* \* \*

As Frank Bakes pulled into his driveway, he glanced at the dashboard clock. 10:37, still early. What the hell, he had nothing else to do and was on the later shift in the morning.

He backed his mini-van back into the street and headed for the local video store. He'd rent a movie or two to pass what remained of the evening.

## Chapter 4 - Friday, June 28, 1996

Carl Denver loved computers. He remembered being twelve years old and buying his first, a Commodore Vic 20, with the money he had preciously saved from his paper route. His stepfather had always bitched at him about it, telling him that he was wasting his time, that he would never get anywhere in life playing his silly games on his stupid machines. But Carl had known the old man was wrong. What did he know anyway. All the horny louse had been good at was losing jobs, drinking and domestic violence.

His had not been the best of family lives but, in the end, Carl had faired nicely. After finishing high school, he had sought a job in the computer field and, thanks to his self-acquired in-depth knowledge of that fascinating world of zeros and ones, had quickly found a suitable programmer's position.

Although Carl had never furthered his formal education, he was a true genius when it came to bits and bytes and had quickly advanced in his career path. After having occupied several positions of progressive responsibility with a handful of employers over the course of eight years, he had joined CSS Inc.

The security software division had been in full blown expansion and hundreds of applicants had been lining up for a chance to join the re-born elite firm. At the time, Carl had been employed with Intelecturer Ltd., a software developer which specialized in educational programmes, earning $43,000 per year. One afternoon, he had received a call from Pierre Gaudry Consultants, a head-hunting firm which was on retainer with CSS; was he possibly interested in a career change with definite advancement possibilities?

Two days later, he had met with none other than Chris Barry himself and, at the term of their three hour meeting, Barry had offered Carl a job as senior programmer with a starting salary of $70,000 per annum. Needless to say, Carl had immediately accepted the position.

He had now been with the company for five years and, at the age of thirty, was earning over $100,000 annually as a senior development analyst. His work consisted mostly of identifying methods to access confidential, supposedly secured information. His job was to find ways to beat the system. He sometimes considered it ridiculous to get paid so well to do what he loved so much.

*  *  *  *

Cursing under his breath, Dave McCall stormed into his office, fighting the incredible urge to punch, kick or throw something. They now had number nineteen on their hands and, of course, to add to his pleasure, Henderson had the front page spot in the **Gazette** again, praising the Vigilante. Christ, the reporter was making this killer sound like a goddamn hero!

The body had been found around midnight in the parking lot of *Charlie's*, a low-life pool bar in the east end. The beating had not been too severe this time, less than half a dozen blows; broken ribs, a broken arm, and a couple of solid whacks to the head. One of them had done the trick.

The victim, Jimmy Green, a warehouse worker, was somewhat known to the cops in the neighbourhood, having been arrested several times in the past for disorderly conduct and disturbing the peace. One of Jimmy's favourite hobbies seemed to be getting sloshed and picking fights.

The police had also responded to a call to Jimmy's home about a year ago, when neighbours had claimed a big fight was taking place at his house and that he just might kill his wife. Things had been quiet when the police had arrived, although it had been clear from the disarray in the place that more than just words had been exchanged.

Jimmy's wife had answered the door when the uniforms had knocked and had quickly assured them that everything was alright. Jimmy was just drunk and she had done something to piss him off. She had obviously been crying and the right side of her face was red and slightly swollen. She had insisted that she was fine and had asked the officers to leave.

From where he lay sprawled on a couch in the living room, Jimmy had told the cops that he was sorry; they had just gotten into a little argument was all. The police had left and no charges had been laid.

Well, Jimmy's wife would not have to worry about his beating her any more. Someone had made sure of that; dead sure.

The cops had interviewed Mrs. Green for a couple of hours earlier that morning and were relatively certain that she was not involved in Jimmy's death. She had definitely not been the one to kill him. Three neighbours had been playing cards with her until 11:45 the previous evening while Jimmy's estimated time of death was 10:00. In addition, she was a rather frail slip of a girl and most likely not physically capable of delivering the forceful blows indicated in the M.E.'s initial report.

Tim Harris tapped on the door frame as he strolled into Dave's office, interrupting his boss' thoughts.

"We might have another lead relating to Tuesday night," he informed McCall as he hopped his rear onto the small conference table in the corner. "A student was walking home, just before 9:00, when he saw some lady run out of the alley and get into a car, a black Celica. She started up the engine and took off with the tires screaming for about half a block."

"Did he get a good look at her?" McCall demanded hopefully, hungry for some positive news.

"Not really," Tim replied, "Except that she was young, 25 to 30, well dressed, skirt and jacket kind of thing, high heels and had a decent body. The kid was surprised to see someone like her, dressed like that, running the way she was."

"Wonderful," Dave sarcastically growled.

"Hang on," Harris soothed. "It does get better. Our witness did happen to look at our lady's license plate when she took off. He didn't get the whole thing but clearly remembers TSN. Said that he's a sports buff so he didn't have any trouble remembering the letters."

"Any trace on the car so far?"

"Not yet," Harris shook his head. "Spoke to Reynolds at DMV ten minutes ago. He promised to get whatever he could come up with before noon."

"Did the kid see or hear anything else?" McCall pushed on.

"Nope. He was on his way home to change for a party after work. Walked back past the alley fifteen minutes later and didn't see or hear anything then either."

"O.K." sighed Dave. "Let me know how you make out on that plate."

As Tim left his superior's office, Joanne Nelson stuck her head through the doorway and announced, "A Chris Barry on 213 for you, Dave. You want to take the call?"

"Yes!" McCall exclaimed as he punched the number on the phone. "Mr. Barry, this is Dave McCall. Thanks for calling so soon. I presume that Bob Thompson filled you in on what this is about?"

"Yes Dave, he did," replied Chris. "I just wanted to touch base with you to let you know that we'll do whatever we can to help. I've always enjoyed doing this kind of work for Bob in the past; makes me feel useful. It's our feeble attempt at showing that we're not in business just for the money!"

"Well, I appreciate anything you can do for us, Mr. Barry. If there's anything I can help you with, let me know."

"Right now, Bob has supplied us with what information we need," Chris responded. "I've got somebody reviewing the data banks where all your Eazy-Com messages are stored. Plus, we'll be talking to some people at Eazy-Com for additional technical help. At first glance, the only record is that of the message itself. There is nothing that indicates its point of origin or the routing that was taken to get it from there to you. But don't worry. If there's anything hidden somewhere, my people will find it. They're the best!"

"That's good to hear, Mr. Barry," said Dave hopefully. "Once again, if I can be of any assistance, don't hesitate."

"I won't Dave. By the way, if we're going to work on this thing together, you're going to have to call me Chris. I don't function well under formality!"

"Sure thing, Chris," McCall smiled. "Thanks for the call. I'll be waiting to hear from you."

\* \* \* \*

As promised, Reynolds from DMV had supplied a list of vehicles with a TSN plate number to Harris before noon. He had also been thoughtful enough to include registrations under TSH, TSM and TSW, just in case the kid had seen wrong. If Harris needed any other TS plates, they could also be supplied.

Although the list was somewhat extensive, quite a few vehicles could be initially eliminated, simply on the basis of geography or vehicle type. Thankfully, Reynolds had also been kind enough to sort and print the information according to those parameters.

Tim was now concentrating on a short list which included only Toyota Celicas. There were twenty-two in all, nine with a TSN plate and, of these, six were in the general vicinity of the city. Of the six, only one was registered to a woman, an Eileen Baker living in upper class Westmount, just west of the downtown area.

They would have to pay a visit to Miss Baker.

### **Chapter 5 - Saturday, June 29, 1996**

Eileen Baker awoke around 9:00 on Saturday morning, feeling refreshed. She had slept well, a first since her ordeal of Tuesday evening. After getting the coffee going, she headed back upstairs for a shower, the events of the last few days still heavily dominating her thoughts.

She had not spoken to anyone about what had happened. After all, this was not the kind of thing you just casually chatted about. She had therefore been somewhat surprised when those two cops, McCall and Harris, had shown up yesterday after dinner.

They had started by questioning her about her whereabouts on Tuesday night and she had asked what this was all about. A witness, they had informed her, had seen her leaving the area where two murders had occurred and had noted her license plate number. That was how they had found her. Upon learning this, she had immediately admitted to her being there. Anyways, she had nothing to hide. Well, almost.

She had described what had happened, starting at the bar with those two jerks ogling her and ending with her close call with rape, only to be saved by a passer-by.

Could she describe what the man looked like? Unfortunately, no she couldn't. It had been getting dark outside and little lighting had existed in the alley. Anyhow, she had seen the man who saved her only for the briefest time. When he had spoken to her, suggesting she leave, she had not hesitated to comply. She had been more than happy just to get the hell out of there.

In reality, she had gotten a rather decent look at the guy, although the baseball cap and sunglasses had concealed his face to some extent. In responding to Harris' and McCall's questions however, she had limited her description of him to 'medium height and build, wearing dark clothes' and had volunteered nothing further. There was no way she would help getting him caught. If it hadn't been for him, she might have been the one to die.

The cops had thanked her for her time, asking her to call if she remembered anything else. She had agreed to do so, although she had no such intention.

As she was coming back downstairs, towelling her hair, the doorbell rang. She looked at her watch, 9:55; probably the paper boy. She tied her terry-cloth robe and headed for the front door, grabbing her purse on the kitchen table on the way.

She unlocked then opened the door and he was standing there, wearing blue jeans and an open collar shirt, no jacket. But the baseball cap and the glasses were the same. It was him.

"How are you Eileen?" he asked calmly, his tone friendly. He seemed relaxed, hands casually tucked in his jeans pockets.

"I-I'm fine, I guess," she whispered, a quiver of fear in her voice. "W-what do you want from me?"

"I was wondering if we could chat for a minute?" he politely enquired, "About Tuesday night? Can I come in?"

For a fraction of a second, she thought of slamming the door and calling the police but realized that she would not have the time nor the strength to do so.

Reluctantly, she stepped aside to let him in, gesturing towards the kitchen.

Nonchalantly, he strolled ahead of her and slid into a chair at the table.

"Nice place you've got here," he praised, looking around, just making conversation.

"Th-thanks. Would you like some coffee?" she offered, not quite certain how to handle a friendly visit from an assassin.

"Sure, if it's not too much trouble," he accepted, "Cream, no sugar."

She poured two cups and brought them to the table, her hands shaking slightly as she set them down. She dropped into a chair across from him and, gathering her courage, forced herself to look at him.

"Please don't be scared," he said softly, gazing back at her with a gentle smile. "I just wanted to make sure you were all right."

"I-I'm O.K.," Eileen replied unconvincingly.

"I also wanted to talk about your having seen me," he continued, pausing to try the coffee. "I trust you understand that I did what I did to help you. However, the police might consider that what I did is wrong. I'm therefore uncomfortable knowing that you could possibly identify me."

"I would never do that!" she blurted out, her sincerity obvious. "I'm grateful that you showed up when you did. You probably saved my life. Those animals deserved to die!"

"I'm happy you feel that way," he responded, relieved. "What I did was right. I need you to realize that."

His tone was not at all menacing and, strangely, she was starting to feel more at ease. They sat quietly for a moment, each contemplating this bizarre meeting with the other.

"How did you find me?" she asked finally, breaking the silence.

"I saw them grab you from your car on Tuesday. I noted your plate number before joining you in the alley."

"The police found me the same way," she commented absently. "Someone saw me take off and reported it."

"You spoke to the police?!" he exclaimed with concern. "What did they want? What did you tell them?"

"They asked about what happened. I told them," she replied reassuringly. "Then they asked if I could describe the man who helped me. I said I couldn't. It was dark. I couldn't see much. It all happened so fast and I was scared. I'm afraid I was not much help to them."

He nodded approvingly, an amused smile appearing on his lips as he relaxed. "This person who saw you; did he see anything else?"

"I don't think so," Eileen shook her head. "At least not based on what the police told me. They just said that he saw me leave."

Still smiling at her, he rose to leave. "Thanks for the coffee, Eileen. I apologize for dropping in unannounced. I just wanted to make sure everything was O.K. You be careful out there from now on. It's a crazy world we live in."

She followed him to the door, her fear by now having essentially disappeared.

He stepped outside, then turned towards her and, to his surprise, found her reaching out to offer a handshake.

"Thanks for helping me," she said quietly as she clasped his hand. "I owe you big time!"

"Thanks for your support, Eileen," he grinned, squeezing her hand warmly. "See ya!"

"You be careful too," she replied softly, almost shyly.

Tucking his hands back into his pockets, he hopped down the steps and started whistling "Here comes the Sun" as he strolled off down the sidewalk.

\* \* \* \*

Dave McCall returned from his jog around 10 o'clock and, since Cathy was gone shopping, he was on his own.

Following a quick shower, he got himself a glass of orange juice from the fridge, grabbed the morning paper and went out to the terrace. He enjoyed these Saturday mornings, when he could actually relax a bit and have some time for himself. Unfortunately, they were few and far between.

Laying the paper out on the patio table, he glanced at the front page as he settled into one of the comfortable chairs. The major headline referred to the recent G7 summit; although he liked to keep up on current events, politics were of little interest to him. As he started to turn the page however, his eye caught a smaller headline towards the bottom. **VIGILANTE VICTIMS WERE RAPISTS**. The by-line, of course, was Ron Henderson.

The article recounted that a reliable source had confirmed that the two insurance reps murdered on Tuesday had been attempting to rape a young lady whose identity remained unknown at the present time. Henderson stood corrected. The Vigilante had done another good deed for society where the police had failed.

"Little schmuck!" McCall muttered to himself as he finished the article, wondering where the son of a bitch had gotten his information.

* * * *

Carl Denver arrived at CSS headquarters at 11:00 on Saturday morning. He generally avoided working on week-ends, especially during the summer, preferring to spend his leisure time with his spouse. However, she was out of town and would only be returning that afternoon. He could therefore take advantage of this free time to fiddle around a bit with the Eazy-Com message which Chris had assigned him.

As far as he was concerned, this whole exercise was a waste of time. He knew from experience that it was relatively simple to communicate through a network like Eazy-Com undetected. With the arrival of the wireless communications era, portable computers and built in modems, it got easier by the day. A half decent hacker could even get into the data banks and erase information if required, without any fear of detection. All that one had to do was beat the security system to gain access to such a network unnoticed. And as Carl knew, beating a system could be very easy when one knew how. After all, he did it for a living.

* * * *

Just as Chris' feet left the diving board, he heard the telephone ring. By the time he emerged from the water, his wife was standing by the pool with the cordless in her hand.

"A gentleman by the name of McCall on the phone for you, sir!" she solemnly announced. "Will you be taking the call or shall I take a message?"

He climbed out of the water and gave her a hug as he took the phone, getting her quite wet in the process. Laughing, she dived into the water, hoping to splash him but missing.

"Hey there," Chris said into the phone. "How are you?"

"Fine, thanks," replied McCall. "I'm sorry to disturb you on a Saturday afternoon."

"That's O.K. I'm just with my wife," Chris commented nonchalantly, flashing her a big grin as she climbed onto the diving board.

She stuck out her tongue at him in a lovely grimace before diving again.

"I just wanted to let you know, Chris, that we received another message on Eazy-Com earlier this afternoon," Dave went on. "I didn't know if you had anyone working on this over the week-end. Just in case, I thought I should let you know."

"One of my geniuses, Carl Denver, was looking at some things earlier today," Chris replied. "I spoke to him around 1:30 as he was leaving the office. It's been a dead end so far with the first transmission. Maybe we'll have better luck with this new message."

"Do you want me to have a copy sent to you or something?" offered McCall, still lost in all this computer stuff.

"No," answered Chris. "Bob gave me an access code to your Eazy-Com data banks. I can tap in from here or from the office. Anyways, it's not the message itself that I'm really interested in. It's more how the hell it got to your place and from where."

"Well, once again, sorry to bother you on a Saturday," concluded McCall. "I'm just anxious to catch this guy. The press is having a field day with us. If you need me for something, you can reach me at home over the week-end or at the office on Monday. Have a good one."

As Chris cut the connection, he glanced at his wife in the pool where she lay on a mattress, wet and relaxed, eyes closed, soaking in some sun.

Having promised not to work during the week-end, he quietly picked up his notepad from the patio table, looking in her direction occasionally, to avoid getting caught. He flipped open the screen and began to softly key in the required access codes. In a moment, the Vigilante's latest message was displayed on the screen:

WHY WASTE PRECIOUS RESOURCES ON ME WHEN ALL I AM TRYING TO DO IS HELP. YOUR ATTEMPTS TO FIND ME ARE FRUITLESS. I WILL ALWAYS BE ONE STEP AHEAD. PUT YOUR EFFORTS TOWARDS THE REAL CRIMINALS INSTEAD.      LATER,
VIGILANTE

'Pretty cocky, that's for sure!' Chris thought, smiling as he read the message.

Looking up, he noted with relief that his wife had not seen what he was doing. Quickly exiting the system, he soundlessly closed the notepad before diving into the pool and splashing her grandly in the process.

## Chapter 6 - Monday, July 1, 1996

The funeral service for Jimmy Green took place on Monday at 10:00 a.m. A limited number of people were in attendance; Jimmy had not had many friends.

Jimmy's wife, Lisa, was holding up rather well. There were no tears and she seemed at peace. She was definitely better off without him. Sandy had spoken to her on Saturday after she had returned from her mother's. Lisa was shaken, but definitely not unhappy.

He had learned of Lisa and her wife-beating husband from Sandy. She and Lisa were both enrolled in the same programme and had attended a number of classes together. Lisa was sweet and smart and wanted to get ahead. Having come from a blue collar family, she had decided that she would make something more of her life. She and Sandy had immediately hit it off when they first met and had quickly become good friends.

Early on though, Sandy had detected that something was wrong. Lisa regularly had mood swings and often seemed nervous. Many mornings, she looked as if she hadn't slept and she rarely, if ever, was available on a social basis after class, not even for a quick cup of coffee. Many of the students got together following an exam or the end of a semester, to celebrate. Lisa never attended these functions.

Sandy had tried to bring this up with Lisa on several occasions but had received little response. Then about four months ago, Lisa had broken down and told Sandy all about Jimmy; the drinking, the cheating and most of all, the beatings. She was scared, tired and had had enough. Suicide was rapidly becoming an attractive alternative.

Sandy had calmed her down and tried to convince Lisa to leave her abusive husband but Lisa could not even start to consider that idea. She was frightened as Jimmy had often told her that if she ever even thought of leaving him, he would kill her.

Once Sandy had brought Lisa's plight to his attention, he had quickly started tracking details about Jimmy; where he lived, where he worked, where he played. Incredible amounts of data were available via the computer and related networks and accessing records was easy in his line of work. Most systems were simple to get into, with no risk of detection.

On nights that Sandy had classes or was off studying, he would go out and shadow Jimmy. That had been how he had found out about Thursday nights and Charlie's. Jimmy had turned out to be a creature of habit and far from bright. It had been easy.

He had made sure beforehand that Lisa would not be in any financial difficulty once Jimmy was gone. Jimmy held a union job with a decent life insurance benefit and pension. He also had taken out a personal policy of $50,000 several years earlier, bless his heart. All told, Lisa would receive close to $200,000. In addition, due to Jimmy's death and a mortgage insurance policy, the house was clear. All in all, Jimmy Green's violent passing was not a bad deal for Lisa.

\* \* \* \*

Shortly after lunch, Chris sauntered into Carl Denver's office at CSS where the latter, as usual, was practicing his favourite pastime; working on his computer.

"How are we doing with those Eazy-Com messages?" Chris curiously enquired as he perched on the corner of Carl's desk.

"Nothing so far," Carl replied, his eyes remaining glued to the screen. "I've been speaking to a few people at Eazy-Com and they're really intrigued. They agree that accessing the network illegally can be relatively simple for a computer buff. What they can't understand however, is how someone can send a message through the network without leaving a trace. As you know, their systems automatically keep records of all transmissions. With these messages; nothing! It's as if they weren't going through the network at all. The way I figure it, maybe the cops are typing these things in themselves to give the impression they've got some leads!"

"Could be!" Chris chuckled at the thought. "I'll suggest that to McCall and see what he thinks!"

"Anyways," continued Carl. "According to my buddies at Eazy-Com, if those messages went through their network, we've got a real wizard on the keyboard this time. I'll keep you posted if anything new comes up."

\* \* \* \*

Dave McCall was definitely not pleased with the progress, or lack thereof, of the investigation. Following six months of nothing, they suddenly had three leads; two in the form of computer messages from the killer himself and one from a witness who had actually seen the guy when he had so kindly saved her life. So far however, these three leads amounted to what they had had before; zip.

He was still waiting for some good news from the computer boys but it was slow in coming and initial reports held little promise. However, in Dave's mind, the girl might eventually lead to something.

When he and Tim had met with her, she had seemed sincere enough and had been quite cooperative considering what she had gone through. She had not even attempted to deny her being there. It was understandable why she hadn't gone to the police. When one went through what she had, one generally tried to forget the whole thing. However, she had remembered the whole thing, quite clearly in fact.

Although she had been in a state of shock and fright while Tuesday night's events had unfolded, her mind had been keen enough to record what was going on. She had described what had taken place that night quite fully, to the finest detail. Yet, when they had asked her about the Vigilante, she had only been able to give a flimsy, vague description at best.

Dave wondered if she was holding out on them. Maybe he'd drop by to see her one of these days, to jog her memory. Perhaps, with a little encouragement, she might manage to remember more about her hero.

\* \* \* \*

It was 11:30 p.m. and he was still busy at the desk in 'the office', working on some files on his notepad. Sandy came into the room, clad in nothing but a long t-shirt, and reached around his chest from the back, leaning down and kissing his neck.

"Working late?" she enquired softly, switching over to the other side of his neck.

"Not too late," he replied, tilting his head to one side to allow her better access.

"What are you working on?" she asked, unbuttoning his shirt to get at his chest.

"Just getting some files in order and setting up my schedule for the coming months," he responded, his concentration waning.

"Don't you ever worry about getting caught?" she questioned as her hands roamed, exploring his body.

"Constantly," he answered. "That's what keeps me alert. That's why I'll never get caught."

"You better be right!" she half-threatened, the ever roaming hands getting closer to their target. "Otherwise, you'll have to deal with me!"

"Yes ma'am!" he replied, no longer aware of what was on the screen.

"I'm going to bed," she whispered throatily, one hand lingering very close for a few seconds.

Pulling away, she sauntered teasingly toward their bedroom, removing her t-shirt as she went. He turned off the computer, turned out the lights and followed her.

## Chapter 7 - Tuesday, July 2, 1996

9:57 a.m. Dave McCall sat in the plush reception area at CSS Inc. headquarters, located on Viau, overlooking Maisonneuve Park. Chris Barry had called him earlier that morning, suggesting they get together to discuss the message tracings done to date. Although they had now spoken on several occasions, they had not yet met face to face.

Dave had arrived a little early, slightly before 10:00, but hadn't minded the wait. He had been served premium coffee in a real china cup, the overstuffed chair was extremely comfortable and the attractive young receptionist was a pleasure to gaze at. It was at times like this that he wondered why he had chosen to be a cop and work for the public.

'Stupid genes!' he thought, smiling to himself. Maybe, he hoped, Chris would be delayed.

"Dave, I presume," Chris called with a smile as he entered the reception area, unknowingly ending McCall's moment of pleasure.

"At your service!" replied Dave, rising to his feet as he examined Barry.

He had not really stopped to think about what Chris Barry might look like but the man standing before him was not what he would have guessed. The suit was made-to-measure and obviously expensive. He was young, early thirties at best, with dirty blond hair and perfect teeth. Approximately five-ten and one hundred seventy-five pounds, he seemed to be in fine physical shape. His most striking feature however, was his eyes; ice-blue, intelligent, powerful eyes. Chris Barry was an impressive looking man.

"Come on, let's go to my office," Chris invited, shaking his guest's hand.

He led the way down a short corridor to another large reception-like area, occupied by an equally attractive young lady, and into a huge corner office.

"We'll be more comfortable in the living room," he jokingly suggested, motioning towards a couple of large leather armchairs and divan in one corner. "Can I get you something to drink?"

"More of that wonderful coffee would be great!" McCall politely accepted. "You'll have to tell me where you got your vending machine. It sure as hell is a lot better than the one we have at the office!"

"We figured out how to program the thing!" Chris winked as he headed for the door. "Have a seat, make yourself at home. I'll be right back."

Dave took advantage of Chris' absence to examine and admire the man's office, located on the twelfth floor of the CSS building. The two outer walls were glass, allowing for an incredible view of the St-Lawrence River to the south, the Olympic installations across the way and the downtown area beyond to the west. A third wall was actually a huge bookcase, filled with volume upon volume from floor to ceiling. Four doors, including the one through which they had entered, were set in the fourth wall and a variety of plaques and paintings adorned the spaces in between the doors.

The tasteful decor was modern and expensive; white oak flooring, dark furniture. A large crescent shaped desk, placed diagonally before the glass walled corner, faced the mammoth room. A conference table, large enough to accommodate eight people comfortably, stood alongside one glass wall while a bar could be found along the other. In the corner opposite from the desk, the armchairs where he presently sat and a leather couch placed around a coffee table created a cozy little salon area; an impressive looking office for an impressive looking man.

"Sorry to keep you waiting," Chris apologized as he returned, carrying a tray loaded with a complete coffee service. "I had to find change for the vending machine!" he added, winking at McCall.

"No problem," replied McCall with a grin. "Nice place you have here. Maybe I should start learning to use these damn computers!"

They continued with small talk for a couple of minutes while Chris poured the coffee and then officially started their meeting.

"Well, let's get down to business," Chris said, leaning back in the comfortable chair. "We've asked our friends at Eazy-Com to review all of the transmissions which took place on the dates when the Vigilante messages were sent. Their system is supposed to record all information related to the sending of a message through the network. Not the message itself, mind you, due to privacy laws and all. What the system tracks is the sending and receiving addresses, the routing, meaning the switches, satellites, etc., the message went through, and the time and duration of the communication. Make sense?"

"Similar to what would be done by phone companies, right?" McCall suggested.

"Right," confirmed Chris. "Now the strange thing is there is no such record. Eazy-Com was baffled and so were we. Now, we are confident that the people at Eazy-Com are competent individuals and that they do their jobs well. But just in case we were wrong about them, we decided to quietly re-do the exercise ourselves."

"I guess you're not supposed to do that?" Dave stated more than questioned.

"It's not exactly proper, you understand," Chris continued with a smile. "But our intentions were honourable. Unfortunately, we didn't find anything more than they had. What it boils down to is this. The messages exist in your records. But that's it. Past that, it's as if they were never sent. We remain baffled."

"Can you explain that?" McCall asked, perplexed.

"There are three possibilities I can suggest," replied Chris, nodding. "The first; Eazy-Com's system has a flaw and does not in fact record all transmissions as it's supposed to. However, I wouldn't bet on that one. Eazy-Com is the most advanced communication network that exists today. Brilliant people, including some from this very company, were involved in its development and subsequent testing. It's some of the finest and most advanced computer work I've seen to date. The second possibility; your Vigilante has developed some even finer computer work which erases the message's path behind it, or bypasses the Eazy-Com computer. This is highly possible if we're dealing with someone who really knows systems. In our fight against viruses, we've seen, and even developed, programmes that do just that. Strong knowledge of communication networks would be required under this alternative however, because the Eazy-Com programmes are quite complex. An alternative to this option would be that he enters the data bank following a message transmission and erases the record. Different and much easier approach with the same end result. Option three, is the simplest. Your culprit enters the data bank where your Eazy-Com messages are stored. Types his message, sticks it in your inbox and exits the system. The deed is done; no traces on the network's system because the message never went through it."

"Could this be done easily from any computer?" asked McCall, confused.

"Nope," replied Chris. "Two options; your system must be connected to a communications network. We've already ruled out Eazy-Com as that network. Are you linked with another carrier; cable, telephone?"

"No, I do know that much," answered McCall. "All our external electronic communication is done through Eazy-Com."

"O.K. then; here's your second option. Someone is accessing your system internally and entering those messages."

"You're telling me the Vigilante is a cop!" exclaimed McCall indignantly. "Impossible! I've known these guys, worked with them, for the last three years! We've been busting our ass trying to get a handle on this psychopath for the last six months! There is no way in hell that he's a cop!"

"I'm just telling you what the possibilities are," Chris responded quietly. "I presume you want to investigate them all. I believe you wanted us to tell you where the messages came from, right?"

"I'm sorry," McCall apologized, calming down. "That wasn't fair. I just have a problem with the suggestion that one of my men might be the Vigilante. We've all put in so much time trying to solve this one. It just doesn't make sense, Chris."

"I understand," replied his host. "But you can't leave a stone unturned. Listen, Dave. We've done what we can with the messages you received so far and we'll do everything we can with any future ones that come in. In the meantime, there isn't much else we can do computer-wise. However, we **are** an investigation firm and we've grown this company's revenues one hundred and fifty times over the last eight years. That wasn't just luck. We do some reasonably intelligent work. Let us give you a hand."

McCall gazed thoughtfully at Chris, considering his offer. What did he have to lose? They had nothing after six months. His new friend, definitely a bright individual, eager to help and highly recommended by Thompson, was offering the vast resources of the country's fastest growing investigative firm. In addition, with the sudden, however slight, possibility that the Vigilante might be a cop, an outside source of help could prove to be extremely useful.

"Why not," Dave agreed, rising to his feet. "Mind you, I can't give you any kind of official status on the case. That's against department policy. However, I have nothing against a helpful ear, some friendly advice and a little unofficial help. There's more than enough frustration to go around. Welcome aboard!"

"Hope I can be of some assistance!" Chris grinned as both men shook hands.

\* \* \* \*

On his drive back to the office, McCall pondered Chris' suggestion. The Vigilante, a cop! He had difficulty accepting that but, it was possible.

What really bothered him was that only his team had access to the data bank. As a security measure, access to various parts of the system had been narrowly defined when the computer network had been revamped a year or so earlier. Traffic cops could not access murder records, nor could homicide simply tap in to review parking tickets.

He thought of each person working for him and could not even begin to doubt any one of them. They were his people, his team. Grudgingly, he accepted that he would have to put personal feelings aside and start digging.

Yes, it was a good thing that Chris Barry had offered to help. He, McCall, would most likely need the moral support.

\* \* \* \*

Following McCall's departure, Chris mused over his conversation with the lieutenant as well as the one he had had with Carl Denver the previous afternoon.

Of the options he had presented to McCall, his choice was number two. Having been personally involved with the development of Eazy-Com, he had no doubts about the efficiency of the network's systems, which eliminated the first option. As he didn't really buy into the theory that the messages had been entered directly into the data bank at McCall's office either, option three could also be discarded.

No, the police were dealing with an extremely intelligent and calculating individual. Someone who had committed nineteen murders to date without leaving the slightest of traces. Such a person would no doubt establish a method to send messages through a network like Eazy-Com without being detected.

Chris had many highly intelligent people working for him, all of whom had exceptional systems knowledge. Maybe the Vigilante worked for CSS! Maybe the messages were being sent from this very building!

The more Chris thought about it, the more he liked the idea. He could easily monitor the activity on his people's PCs if he wanted to. It was done occasionally for security reasons and attempting to identify the Vigilante certainly qualified as a security reason. He would have to look into this further.

\* \* \* \*

*He sat in the car with the engine running, waiting nervously in front of Taylor's convenience store. With the gear shift already in drive, he held the vehicle in place with his left foot on the brake while his right foot hovered just above the accelerator. He would be ready to get the hell out of there when the time came. At that moment, a blast from the shotgun exploded from inside the store.*

Carl Denver awoke in a sweat, his heart beating wildly in his chest. Breathing deeply to calm himself down, he quietly sat up in the bed as he glanced at the clock radio on the night stand. It was 2:50, Wednesday morning. He glanced at his wife and was relieved to note that she continued to sleep. At least this time, the dream hadn't woken her up as was sometimes the case. He hated having to fabricate stories to substantiate why he sometimes woke up screaming in the middle of the night. She never quite seemed to believe him anyways and he would never let her in on that part of his past.

It had happened sixteen years ago and still, the nightmare came back to haunt him on a regular basis. He had only been fourteen at the time and, all in all, had not been a bad kid. However, he had not lived in the best of neighbourhoods and most of the kids there had a penchant for crime. Gang fights, car hopping, drinking, drugs and B&Es had been regular pastimes.

Several of his buddies had participated regularly in such activities and on those occasions, Carl had stayed away. Oh sure, he had always been more than willing to get into the drinking and had been able to smoke a joint as well as the rest of them. He had even occasionally experimented with acid, mescaline and coke. But the real crimes, the stealing, the violence, he had kept at a distance. Mike and Eddy, his closest friends, had tried to convince him to tag along more times than he could remember, but Carl had always stubbornly resisted.

Then came that night, a Friday. They had been sitting in their 'clubhouse', an abandoned store, smoking hash and drinking a bottle of scotch which Mike had **found** somewhere. Carl was feeling great.

"Should we tell him now?" Eddy suddenly blurted, addressing Mike with a smirk.

Mike, a silly grin on his face, hesitantly replied, "I don't know. Maybe we should wait. Maybe he's not old enough yet."

"Tell me what? Old enough for what?" Carl curiously questioned while his two friends just sat there, grinning at him.

"Tell me what?" Carl impatiently insisted. "I'm just a year younger than you two fucks! What?!"

"O.K." Mike agreed, feigning reluctance. "I guess we'll tell you. Come out back, we have a surprise for you."

They proceeded towards the rear entrance of the building with Carl wondering what kind of surprise these two idiots might have in store for him. Upon reaching the alley, Mike and Eddy shouted, "Surprise!" in unison, both pointing to a navy blue Trans Am parked in the alley.

"Tonight, my friend!" Mike proudly announced. "You are going to learn how to drive!"

"I already know how to drive," Carl spat out sullenly, hardly bothering to look at the obviously stolen car.

"You call operating that piece of shit pickup of your step-father's, driving!?" Eddy cackled. "You probably don't even need a permit to drive that piece of crap, it moves so slow!"

"Fuck yourself, Eddy," Carl defensively suggested. "At least, it ain't stolen!"

"Carl, think about it," Mike pleaded. "Check it out! This is a CAR!!"

Carl forced himself to glance at the vehicle. It definitely was a CAR!

"Whose is it?" he asked helplessly, struggling to find a reason not to drive this dream machine.

"Some guy who parked it at the lot my cousin works at," Eddy answered glibly, moving in for the kill. "Guy's gone on vacation for two weeks so he don't need it. And he sure as hell ain't gonna report it stolen from Europe, is he?"

They had Carl where they wanted him. He could not argue of the danger that the cops would pull them over for driving a stolen vehicle. It wasn't officially stolen. Plus, it **was** an incredible car.

"O.K. Let's go for a ride!" Carl decided with a sudden burst of confidence. "And I'm driving!"

Amid hoots and cheers from his buddies, he climbed in behind the wheel while Eddy got in the back and Mike swung into the front passenger seat.

"Welcome to manhood," Mike solemnly declared, ceremoniously dangling the keys before his younger friend. "Start this baby up!"

Carl, grinning from ear to ear, nervously inserted the key into the ignition and, taking a deep breath, cranked the wondrous automobile to life. Closing his eyes, he savoured the moment, feeling and listening to the smooth rumble of the engine. This thing would move!

They pulled out of the alley and within minutes were cruising down Church Street with Carl trying to determine if this was not more exciting than his first sexual encounter a few months earlier with Easy-Suzy from school. It was a toss-up. The tie breaker would be once he got onto the highway to see what this machine could really do.

"Hang a left at the next light," Eddy ordered from the back seat.

"Screw that, Edward!" Carl challenged. "I'm driving, see!? And I wanna just cruise for a while!"

"Goddammit, Carl!" Eddy roared as they approached the intersection. "I just want to pick up some smokes at Taylor's! They got a brand that's cheaper than the rest! Turn already! We'll cruise after!"

"All right!" snorted Carl, slowing as they neared the light. "What the fuck's your problem!?"

"I just need some butts! That's all!" muttered Eddy, staring out the window.

They turned left on Hadley Avenue and two blocks further, pulled into the parking lot at Taylor's convenience store. Mike climbed out of the car and scanned the area as he removed his jean jacket. At the same time, Carl heard the sound of a long zipper opening behind him and, suddenly feeling uneasy, turned to see what was going on. In the rear seat, Eddy reached into a duffel bag, pulled out a sawed off shotgun and handed it to Mike who covered it with his jacket.

"What the fuck is going on!" Carl shouted, his stomach starting to churn.

"Shut up!" hissed Eddy. "You want everybody to hear you!?"

"I'm outta here!" Carl shot back, lowering his tone. "You guys are fucking crazy! You might kill somebody, or get us killed!"

"Nobody's gonna kill nobody," Mike stepped in to reassure their young friend. "The guns are just to scare them. They're not even loaded, Carl. Listen, all you gotta do is wait here with the engine running. We go in, place our order, we're back out in two minutes and we drive away. Nothing to it. It's all planned."

"I don't like this kind of shit!" Carl replied, finding it difficult to breath. "I'm fucking fourteen! I don't want to get busted at fucking fourteen!"

"Ain't nobody's gonna get busted, Carl," Eddy soothingly stated from the back seat. "You'll see. This'll be a piece of cake. Trust me."

"I still don't like this," mumbled Carl, resigning to the fact that he was about to participate in his first serious criminal activity. "You motherfuckers better not ever try to pull something like this on me again! Next time, I'll take off and fucking leave you there!"

"O.K. Carl, you're right," Mike conceded. "We shoulda told you ahead of time. We were just scared you wouldn't go for it and we needed a driver we could trust for our plan. We won't do it again. I promise. Come on, Eddy. Time's a wasting!"

"Back before you know it!" Eddy grinned as he climbed out of the rear of the car, obviously similarly armed based on the way he also carried his jacket.

They headed into the store and thirty seconds, which seemed like thirty minutes went by as Carl waited outside.

"This is crazy!" he whispered to himself, feeling progressively nauseous. "Goddamn fucking crazy!"

But he knew he couldn't let his friends down, although he promised himself to make them pay if anything went wrong.

As that thought went through his mind, a shotgun blast exploded from inside the store. Carl violently vomited, making a mess of himself and the interior of his wonderful stolen dream machine. He looked up and through a blur of tears saw Mike and Eddy burst out of Taylor's and frantically run towards the Trans Am.

As they reached the car, a girl in her late teens slammed through the store's exit and rushed towards them, crying and screaming. In her hands was a revolver, quite large, obviously of heavy calibre.

Eddy wrenched the door of the car open and dove head over heels into the back seat.

Mike followed and, although not yet completely into the car, screamed, "Go, Fuck, Go!!"

Carl jammed the accelerator into the floor and the car jumped forward, tires painfully shrieking.

As they raced passed the girl, she raised the gun and rapidly fired all six rounds. Both right-side windows shattered and several bullets ricocheted off the car in a shower of sparks. Miraculously however, none of the boys were hit and they sped off safely into the night.

The plan had not worked. Taylor, the owner of the place, had unfortunately not responded as expected to their request for the cash register contents. After bellowing, "I'm gonna kill you little fuckers!", he had reached under the counter, pulled out a handgun and aimed it at them. Mike had panicked and shot and Taylor had been dead before hitting the ground.

His daughter, Cassandra, who had been in the back store, had heard the explosion and had come running just as Mike and Eddy were exiting the store. In seeing her father, she had grabbed the gun from his hand and come after them but they had gotten away.

The boys were quite shaken by the ordeal and, of even greater concern, extremely scared of getting caught. The girl had seen them close up and would probably be able to identify them. This was no longer a simple robbery. This was murder.

They had dumped the car, along with the guns, into the river near Riverfront Park and walked home, dreading the unknown events which might befall them in the coming days. Carl had not stopped swearing at his two buddies most of the way.

The next morning, the story had been in the papers and on the news. By the evening, composite sketches had been made and were being presented to the public by the media. Although the rather vague sketches did not resemble them very much, the boys continued to worry.

Two days following the murder, Mike and Eddy, unable to deal with the pressure, had decided to leave town and head for Toronto. They had invited Carl to join them but he had bluntly refused. Unlike them, he had a mother who cared about him and, if he disappeared, the police would definitely become involved.

As they bade each other farewell, they had solemnly vowed never to speak to anyone about what had happened.

Carl looked at the clock radio again. 3:55 a.m. He was not surprised. Whenever he had the nightmare, sleep became a rare commodity afterwards. Resigning to his insomnia, he let his thoughts turned to Eddy and Mike, as they usually did following the dream.

He had run into Eddy, by chance, about four years ago. He had been in Toronto on business and was having a drink in a bar at Pearson while waiting for his flight. Eddy, who was also at the airport, had noticed him and had come over to chat. As is often the case when friends grow apart, times and interests had changed and neither had been comfortable with the other.

Mike, Eddy had told him, had died a few months earlier. He had been hanging around with a less than desirable crowd for a while and, apparently, had made somebody unhappy. Consequently, his body had been found in an alley off Yonge Street downtown. He, Eddy, was heading for Vancouver, having grown tired of Toronto. It was time to start a new life; again.

Carl dared another look at the time; 4:28. He rolled over, determined to get some sleep. He had a busy day ahead of him.

## Chapter 8 - Wednesday, July 3, 1996

9:42 a.m. Dave McCall exited the elevator and sauntered over to the highly attractive brunette at the reception desk of Griffiths & Donaldson.

"Good morning!" she gushed, with a smile which was much too sweet. "What can I do for you?!"

Avoiding the answer that his quick wit brought to mind, McCall courteously replied, "Hi. Eileen Baker, please."

"Do you have an appointment, Mr...?" the bombshell queried.

"McCall," he responded. "And no, I don't have an appointment. Please tell Miss Baker that I would like a few minutes of her time."

"Let me see what I can do," she replied coolly, efficiently playing her role of master of the gate.

She gestured towards a series of chairs off to the right, his cue to have a seat. Punching a few numbers on the console before her, she whispered something into the mike strapped to her head, eyeing him suspiciously throughout.

Following a ten minute wait, a good looking blonde appeared from one of the hallways which led to the reception area and approached him.

"Mr. McCall, I presume," she said with a stiff smile. "I'm Jessie Heft, Miss Baker's secretary. How can I help you?"

Holding off on another 'cute' response, McCall answered, "You can lead me to Miss Baker's office."

"Unfortunately," the blonde replied, "Miss Baker is extremely busy and has a very important meeting in..." she looked at her watch, "Exactly eight minutes."

"I see," said McCall, showing his disappointment as he stood. "I just wanted to say hello. I wanted to see how she was doing."

He was not sure if Eileen had spoken to anybody about her previous week's unpleasant experience.

"Eileen is fine," Jessie informed him, the tight smile still firmly in place. "She suggested I let you know that if she has anything else to say to you, **she** will give you a call."

"Well, I won't take up any more of your time then," said McCall, accepting that today would not be the day Baker helped him break the case. "Ladies, I thank you for your hospitality!"

He returned to the elevator, convinced more than ever that Eileen Baker knew more about the Vigilante than she was ready to admit. He would have to visit Eileen at another time.

\* \* \* \*

10:05 p.m. He sat in the mini-van, parked in a quiet residential district, with only the glow of his cigarette defying the darkness. Across the street, half a dozen houses down, lived his next prospect.

He couldn't go see him yet. The gentleman already had visitors but they would be leaving soon. Visitors never stayed long at this place. Just long enough to score.

The door of the house opened and two people emerged, crossing the street and heading his way. He watched them with growing disgust as they approached. They were kids, no older than thirteen or fourteen. Quietly, he climbed out of the truck and walked around to the back of it. They had not noticed him. He waited until they had strolled past and came up behind them.

"Freeze boys," he softly commanded. "This is the police."

The kids stopped in their tracks and started to turn towards him.

"No, don't turn around!" he ordered sharply. "Lean up against that car. Assume the position, just like in the movies."

The boys complied, leaning against the car, arms wide, legs spread.

"How do we know you're a cop?" one of them sneered, attempting to cover his fear with a degree of toughness.

"This proof enough for you, kid?"

He flashed a gold shield and I.D. card in the boy's face, holding it there long enough for the kid to study it.

"W-well, detective, sir. We haven't done anything wrong. We-we're just heading home from a friend's place."

"Empty your pockets on the roof of the car, please," he ordered.

"But sir!" the boy started to plead.

"Now!" he barked.

The boys obeyed and the quiet one started to whimper softly.

He sifted through their belongings on the roof of the car; wallets, keys, matches, small change, a pack of cigarettes; nothing illegal.

"I will give you one last chance to empty your pockets, boys," he quietly warned. "Then, I will be forced to search you myself. If, at that time, I find anything that I don't like, you will have the most unpleasant evening you have ever had."

The talker, admitting defeat, reached into his front jeans pocket and pulled out a small plastic bag which he placed on the roof of the car with a noticeably shaking hand.

They looked like good kids; most likely from upper class families, considering the neighbourhood. They had probably bought the shit with their allowance money.

"Have you boys ever done crack before?" he asked.

"N-No, s-sir!" the crier wailed.

The talker, who had grown silent, shook his head emphatically.

"I'm happy to hear that. This stuff will kill you. I can promise you that. I can also promise you something else. If I ever catch you doing something stupid like this again, you will have proved to me that you want to ruin your lives. That being the case, I will make your wish come true. I will personally make your lives so miserable you can't start to imagine it. Now boys, do I make myself perfectly clear?"

Both boys nodded with fervour while still assuming their spread-eagled position. He was not sure, but he thought one of them might have actually crapped in his pants. Good. They would be staying out of trouble for a while.

"Now, pick up your stuff and get the hell out of here! Remember, we have a deal!"

Only seconds were required for their belongings to disappear from the roof of the car. All that remained was the plastic bag. He watched them as they started to walk away at a rapid pace. Yep, the one on the left had definitely shit his pants! Three cars down, they started to run, fast. He chuckled a little, although it wasn't funny at all.

'Now,' he thought, 'Back to the business at hand.'

* * * *

Zack glanced at his watch as he closed and securely locked the door behind his two customers. 10:05. He thought about the two boys who had just left and realized how his customers were becoming younger and younger. But he didn't feel guilty. Hey, he wasn't forcing them to do the stuff. He was just a business man. Anyways, these kids were all spoiled little brats, coming from rich families. They were destined to have fucked up lives.

He had never expected that these little snobs would be so much into dope. His belief had been that only the punks in the low-life neighbourhoods needed the release. However, quite the contrary had turned out to be the fact, his customer base was widening on a daily basis and he was rapidly becoming a rich man.

Checking the time again, he decided to catch a couple of hours of sleep before going to the club. The real action only started after midnight anyways. He went upstairs to the bedroom, set the alarm for 12:30 and promptly fell asleep.

* * * *

His meeting with the kids had not been part of the plan and consequently, had delayed his schedule a little. But it didn't really matter. He was in no hurry and Zack wouldn't be going anywhere tonight.

Returning to the mini-van, he retrieved his small canvas bag, then crossed the street and headed for Zack's house.

He had come to know of Zack the same way he learned of many of his prospects; from the police's computer records.

Drug-related problems had been on the rise in this upper-class neighbourhood in recent months. A number of kids had been hospitalized due to crack or heroin overdoses, three of whom unfortunately had died.

Zack, who had moved into the area four months ago and was thought to be responsible for the influx of narcotics, was being monitored by the cops. However, the police had limited resources, Zack had rights, and until illegal activity could reasonably be established, he was protected by the system.

He reached Zack's house and, after scanning the street to ensure the absence of any curious onlookers, crept around into the back yard. The spotlight by the patio door illuminated the yard a bit too much for his taste; he twisted the bulb in its socket half a turn and the yard went dark.

Shortly after the boys had left the house, he had observed the lights go out, first on the ground floor, and a minute later, upstairs. That had been twenty minutes ago. He presumed, actually hoped, that this meant Zack was asleep.

He was pleased that the house did not have an alarm system. This, he had confirmed during an earlier visit two weeks prior, while Zack had been out. He had taken advantage of Zack's absence to study the layout of the house and therefore knew exactly where he was going.

He proceeded further along the rear wall where half a dozen steps led down to a basement entrance. On his last visit, he had taped and broken one of the four glass panels in the door and installed a new one using modelling clay rather than window putty to hold it in place. He smiled as he noted that his masterpiece had not been disturbed and most likely not noticed. Zack did not seem to use the unfinished basement nor this entrance very much if at all. With the help of his knife, he quickly scraped off the modelling clay, eased out the small pane of glass, reached in and unlocked the door. Pulling the door open on its quiet hinges; he had WD 40ed them last time, he slipped through, closed the door behind him and made his way into the house.

\* \* \* \*

Zack awoke, feeling somewhat groggy and confused. He didn't remember the alarm going off and wondered why the lights were on in the room. As he came more to his senses, he tried to sit up in the bed and realized that his arms were tied above his head.

"What the fuck!" he swore, trying, unsuccessfully, to move.

His legs were also tied. Now quite awake, he lifted his head and saw a man sitting on a chair, facing him at the foot of the bed, calmly reading a magazine.

"Good morning, Zack!" greeted the man, tossing the magazine aside.

It was 1:43 a.m.

"I gave you something to help you sleep a little," the stranger continued. "I hope you don't mind."

"What the fuck is this!" Zack retorted. "Who the fuck are you! What the fuck do you want!"

"Now, now, Zack," the man cooed as he smiled. "Are we always this cranky when we wake up? Guess you aren't a morning person now, are you?"

He continued, not bothering to wait for an answer. "I used silk scarves to tie you up so you don't have to worry. They won't leave any nasty burns like rope would!"

He had been quite happy to see Zack's big brass bed on his last visit. It made tying someone up so much easier.

"Listen, take what you want!" Zack offered, his fear mounting. "I got money, lots of it, hidden in this place. I even got a safe!"

"No, no, Zack," his uninvited visitor replied, shaking his head. "I didn't come here to rob you. I don't want your money. I came here to discuss a proposition with you. Here it goes. You make your living selling crack and smack to little kids, right? They fuck up their lives, some even die, while you get rich. Now, here's what I propose. I'll shoot you up with a massive dose of the garbage you put out on the street. You will die, knowing how those poor little boys and girls feel when they die. Net result, our society will have one less piece of shit to worry about. What do you think of my idea, Zack?"

"You're crazy, man, fucking crazy!" Zack shrieked. "This is fucking murder! You can't do this!"

He wrestled on the bed, trying to break loose, but to no avail. His visitor was obviously extremely knowledgeable in the art of tying people up.

The man stood up from his chair as he quietly responded to his prisoner's statement. "No, Zack. You see, you're wrong. I can do this. Watch me. I will."

Decisively, he walked to the door and picked up his canvas bag from the floor. Zack watched in horror and started to scream as the man removed a large syringe, candle and spoon from the bag and set them on a coffee table in the corner.

Shaking his head in silent disgust, the intruder calmly reached into the bag and pulled out another silk scarf. Moving over to the side of the bed, he skilfully squeezed Zack's jaw open with one hand and stuffed the scarf into his prisoner's gaping mouth.

"Quiet, Zack," he gently suggested. "You'll wake the neighbours."

Returning to the coffee table, he continued to prepare Zack's death, oblivious to the latter's whimpering. Within minutes, he was back at the drug dealer's side, armed with the full syringe. Zack stared at him, moaning with terror as tears streamed down his cheeks.

"Don't cry, Zack," the man softly encouraged. "I prepared you a special blend. Half heroin, half crack. You'll get a double rush!"

Producing a rubber tourniquet from his jacket pocket, he quickly wrapped it around Zack's arm and pulled it tight. After a moment of waiting, he inserted the needle into a prominent vein and depressed the plunger. Within seconds, Zack started convulsing. Twenty seconds later, he was dead.

"Too quick," the man sighed, gazing down at the body and wishing he'd caused his victim more suffering.

As an afterthought, he pulled out his knife and slit Zack's throat; his signature. He then picked up his belongings and, pausing only long enough to change his clothes, headed for home.

* * * *

Frank Bakes crept up the steps, silently unlocked the front door and slipped inside. A quick glance at the antique grandfather clock in the hallway caused him to frown; 3:15 in the morning. He had to stop coming in so late. Soundlessly, he moved upstairs and entered their bedroom where his wife lay asleep. Undressing quietly, being careful not to wake her, he gently climbed into bed and let his exhausted body and mind drift away.

### Chapter 9 - Thursday, July 4, 1996

It was 8:45 a.m. and Dave McCall, who sat brooding in his office, had already been up for five gruelling hours.

At 3:00, an unidentified caller had reported a disturbance on Belmont Avenue in Westmount and a patrol car had been sent to the given address to investigate. Upon their arrival, the officers on call had noticed nothing out of the ordinary, everything was quiet.

Normally, they might have simply left. However, this was the address of one Zachary Roberts, highly suspected by the police of selling crack cocaine and heroin. This being the case, they had rung the doorbell a couple of times but had not been answered. Upon venturing into the backyard, they had noticed a pane of glass from the basement door laying on the top step and radioed in for backup. They had then entered the home and, following several minutes of cautious search, had found Zack lying on his bed, obviously dead. Due to the gaping wound at his throat, McCall had been called.

Their unidentified caller had apparently also informed the press because, by 3:30 in the morning, crews from local T.V. and radio stations as well as newspaper reporters, including Henderson, were appearing on the scene. The story had been all over the morning news; Twenty unsolved murders, presumably committed by the same person, the infamous Vigilante, in just over six months.

However, the reports and articles had a surprisingly different tone to them this time. To date, Henderson had been the only clear supporter of the Vigilante from the press. But now, considering that the latest victim was a hard drug dealer with his prey consisting mostly of young teenagers, everybody seemed to view the Vigilante with a more sympathetic eye. One anchorperson had even suggested that the police might want to think about teaming up with this crime fighting phantom. At least, he got the job done.

Joanne Nelson called from her desk, breaking into McCall's thoughtful misery. "Dave, Chris Barry on 219. You taking it?"

He nodded and picked up the phone. "Howya doing, Chris?"

"Fine, thanks," Chris sympathetically replied. "Seems like you've got another one on your hands. It's all over the press this morning."

"Yup," McCall morosely responded. "And they're **all** calling him the good guy this time. Maybe we should offer him the Director's job!"

Chris chuckled politely and asked, "Does it seem like the same guy?"

"I think so," Dave hesitantly answered. "I just got a preliminary report from the M.E. It looks like the actual cause of death was a drug overdose. The throat was slashed after the fact. But, I think it's our man. He killed with drugs to prove a point to his victim. He cut his throat to leave his mark."

"Anything I can do?" Chris helpfully offered.

"Not really, not right now," McCall replied. "I'll let you know if something comes up."

"O.K., don't hesitate," urged Chris. "Anyways, the reason I was calling is I've got tickets for the ball game on Saturday afternoon and my wife is going to a bridal shower. I was wondering if you might be interested in going? It would give us a chance to get to know each other better which is something that's always proved helpful in my past business dealings."

"Saturday? Sure!" McCall accepted, his spirit brightening. "Cathy, my wife, is going to her mother's, a Tupperware party or something. Ball game sounds great!"

"Excellent!" Chris responded. "The game's at 1:35. Why don't you meet me at the office around 1:00. We can park there and walk over."

"Sounds good," agreed McCall. "If you're free afterwards, I'll buy dinner."

"Deal. See you Saturday."

## Chapter 10 - Friday, July 5, 1996

12:17 p.m. Eileen Baker hastened out of the air-conditioning of Les Cours Mont-Royal on Peel Street, home of Griffiths & Donaldson, and into the sizzling heat and humidity of July. It was a beautiful sunny day and the streets of downtown Montreal were alive with a colourful mix of street vendors, tourists and the usual noon-time crowd of office workers scampering about to get a bite to eat and complete as many errands as possible within an hour.

She hurried south along Peel towards Rene-Levesque Boulevard, on her way to a 12:30 lunch date with a possible new client. She reached the corner of St-Catherine and impatiently waited for a break in the heavy midday traffic.

"Hello, Eileen. How are you?" asked a male voice to her right.

She turned her head towards the familiar voice and greeted its owner with an icy smile. "Lieutenant McCall. What an unexpected pleasure."

The sarcasm in her voice was unmistakable.

"I came by to see you on Wednesday," McCall informed her with an innocent grin. "Unfortunately, you were busy so we didn't get to see each other."

"Yes, I have a very hectic schedule," Eileen testily replied. "In fact, I'm on my way to a lunch appointment right now. It was nice to see you, Lieutenant."

She started across the street and away from him but McCall followed, not ready to give up that easily.

"Do you mind if I walk with you?" he asked. "I'm heading your way anyways."

She allowed another cool smile as she responded, "You don't even know where I'm going."

"That's O.K. I'm just taking a random lunch hour walk," McCall explained. "Your direction is my direction!"

Shrugging, she replied, "If it will make you happy, Lieutenant. I'm only walking to the next block and I do have an appointment."

"Sure, no problem," agreed McCall. "Listen, I was wondering if you remembered anything else about the guy who helped you the other week. We would really like to speak to the gentleman, you understand, and to date, you're probably the only person who has ever seen him."

Her face tightened and she stared straight ahead, hesitating several seconds before responding. "I told you and your friend what I had to say when you visited me last Friday. I don't have anything else to add to that. Should something come to mind, I will not hesitate to give you a call!"

She darted across the street diagonally, heading towards Le Windsor, a landmark hotel which had been converted into luxurious office space several years before.

"I just want to make sure that you realize the importance of telling us anything you know," McCall stated quietly, still on her heels.

She stopped in front of Le Piment Rouge, located on the ground floor of Le Windsor, turned and, for the first time, looked McCall in the eye.

"I wish I could help you but I can't," she spoke slowly, putting emphasis on each word. "I have told you everything that I could. Please leave me alone!"

With that, she turned on her heel and hurried into the building.

McCall watched her go until she disappeared, then stuck his hands into his pockets and strolled back to the office as he contemplated. He would have to find some way to get her to talk because she knew more than she was telling. He was certain of that now. He had seen it in her eyes.

## Chapter 11 - Saturday, July 6, 1996

Chris and Dave had had a great time at the game, especially given the fact that the Expos had won 5 to 4, coming from behind and scoring four runs in the bottom of the ninth.

Although the two men had not known each other for very long, each had become quite comfortable with the other. McCall, for his part, listened in fascination as Chris recounted one anecdote after another about mammoth business deals and the incompetence of many of the business leaders in the world today. Chris showed equal interest when Dave spoke of the captivating world of murder investigations, from the tracking a killer and the satisfaction of seeing one go behind bars to the frustration of having one go free.

They were two different men from two very different worlds but had quickly developed a strong bond. In the short time they had known each other, they had become like old friends.

They were seated at a table at Le Joli Moulin, digesting their feast of steak and lobster while discussing the case of the elusive Vigilante.

"Just remember, if there's anything I can do, don't be shy," Chris reminded. "We have some excellent investigators whom we pay well, whether they're working on something or not. I'm sure I can spare a couple if you need anybody to do some legwork."

"I'll keep it in mind," shrugged McCall. "The thing is, policy doesn't allow us to sub-contract any investigative work. Plus, we'd get the union in an uproar if we did and, if the media ever got a hold of something like that, they'd rip us apart. Anyways, even if I wanted to throw a few things quietly your way, the point is, we don't have anything to go on right now!"

As he spoke, an idea suddenly came to mind. Though certainly farfetched, he didn't have much to lose.

"Maybe there is one thing you could do for me, Chris," he began quietly. "Those two guys last week, the insurance salesmen. As you know, there was a witness, the girl they intended to rape. Her name is Eileen Baker and she's an account executive with Griffiths & Donaldson, the ad agency. She got a look at our man. We questioned her about it but she couldn't really help us. I've had a feeling that she could tell us more than she did. I think that she's protecting him. After all, he did help her out in a big way. I've tried to get more out of her since we first met but she's not talking. I spoke to her yesterday afternoon and I could see it in her eyes. I'm sure she could help. Maybe you could think about this, see if you can find an angle to get her to open up. Maybe there's someway you can meet with her, get her to talk. I'm sure you're good at that kind of thing! Think about it."

"I'm in!" Chris keenly accepted. "I'm **sure** that I can arrange to meet with her easily enough. Griffiths and Donaldson has been trying to get a foot into our place for a few years. But, to get her to talk about what happened, I'll have to mention my involvement in this somehow."

"Guess you'll have to," McCall acknowledged. "Tell her you're my friend and that CSS is doing some computer work for the police department. That's the truth."

"Best way to go," Chris agreed. "Let me see what I can do. Do you have any documentation you can 'unofficially' supply me with that might help convince her how nasty this guy is?"

"Yeah, I can put something together for you."

"O.K.," said Chris. "Fax me whatever you think I need at the office. Here, the number's on my card. Only person who'll see it is Sonia and she's very discreet. Carl Denver and I will be visiting some customers out on the West Coast early next week but I'll get on this as soon as I get back."

"Hey!" McCall grinned. "I've a couple of people heading for Vancouver next week also. They're going to a seminar presented by the RCMP and the FBI. Maybe you can buy them a meal or two to help me control my expenses!"

"Are you kidding!?" snorted Chris. "With the taxes I pay, I've already paid for their trip!"

## Chapter 12 - Monday, July 8, 1996

Eddy had never regretted his decision to move to Vancouver. It was such a beautiful city. There weren't too many places in the world where, in the right season, you could play a round of golf in the morning, ski in the afternoon and be back for the club action at night.

The move to the West Coast had not only represented a change in geography but also one of lifestyle, for Eddy had ceased his criminal activities.

Upon their arrival in Toronto, following the fouled up Taylor hold-up incident, he and Mike had tried their hand again at armed robbery with more success than the first time. They had started small scale with liquor and convenience stores and soon had tried their hand at a couple of banks.

Mike liked to spend and usually blew his share of the take quickly. Eddy, on the other hand, put most of his money aside and had eventually saved enough to score a few good drug deals, which had allowed him to rapidly increase his bankroll. He'd also done a little pimping, which hadn't done any harm to his financial situation.

Although he had parted ways with Mike after a while and not subsequently seen him for several years, he had been shaken to learn of his friend's death. That was when he had decided to quit the life of crime. By then, at the age of twenty-seven, he had accumulated enough cash to invest into his own business and had always dreamed of owning a club and playing the boss. The time was right, he had decided, to pursue that dream.

To start fresh, he had gone to Vancouver where he'd bought a share of 'Aces', a little singles place downtown. He knew his partners were into the occasional shady deal but they did that on the side. The club itself was clean. Although he would never become filthy rich, his share of the profits allowed him to lead a very comfortable lifestyle with little required effort. At the age of thirty-one, he was looking for nothing more.

Whenever the weather permitted, Eddy liked to get up early and go jogging in Stanley Park. After an hour of running, he would sit to watch and listen to the city come to life across the harbour. On some mornings, when he was early enough, he got to see the sun rise over the mountains in the distance, always a wondrous spectacle.

Monday was one of those mornings. By the time he reached the point which extended into Vancouver Harbour, only the barest glimpses of daylight were apparent. He sat on the dew-covered grass, stretching his legs as he pulled a bottle of orange juice from the small backpack he always wore.

'Gonna be a great day!' he thought, looking at the sky.

Maybe Tony, a regular at 'Aces' who had become a friend, would be keen for a little round of golf. They hadn't played together for a while. He would call him when he got home.

Satisfied with his plans for the day, he turned his thoughts to the incredible landscape laid out before him. He gazed towards the mountains to the east, anticipating an impressive sunrise in the morning's cloudless sky. With his eyes fixed on the horizon, he absently opened his juice bottle and brought it to his lips. As he tilted his head back to drink, the baseball bat smashed into it, ending his life.

\* \* \* \*

Carl sat in one of the bars at the Richmond Inn, waiting for Chris to arrive so they could go for dinner.

After having flown in the previous day, Sunday, they had spent this day making courtesy calls to a handful of current and potential clients. Prospects were highly interested and required little convincing while actual customers were extremely satisfied with the firm's services. Therefore, their meetings had consisted of activities such as breakfast at the Vancouver Yacht Club, a round of golf at Quilchena and a mid-afternoon cocktail party, to name a few. The talk had been mostly about sports, music, movies and women and very little about business.

While Carl waited, he watched the news playing on the screen mounted above the bar. Although it was the second time he saw the brief report, he paid close attention, keen on grasping all the details.

The body of a man had been found early that morning in Stanley Park, having apparently succumbed to a violent head injury. Foul play was suspected and police were investigating but had no leads to date. The victim, identified as Edward Schaeffer, was co-owner of a downtown bar which was known to occasionally cater to members of Vancouver's underworld. Authorities were urging anyone who might have information about this crime to contact them at the 1-800 number which appeared on the screen. More details, the reporter promised, would be announced as they became available.

'Well, well,' Carl mused as the report ended. 'As long as Mike and Eddy kept their promise, I'm now the only one who knows our little secret!'

Feeling satisfied and content as he hadn't in a long time, he looked forward to a night on the town in one of North America's finer cities. He saw Chris enter the bar and stood to wave him over.

\* \* \* \*

In another bar across town, Frank Bakes and Terry McDonald, fellow cop and travelling partner, sat and watched the same news report.

"Same M.O. as the Vigilante case," Terry thoughtfully commented. "Think it could be the same guy?"

"Get real!" Frank scoffed. "We're 3000 miles away from home! Finish your beer, will you!? I'm starving!"

## **Chapter 13 - Wednesday, July 10, 1996**

Sandy constantly worried about her husband and his activities, even more so when he was out of town.

It was not that she disapproved of what he did. In fact, she encouraged and supported him. Her life had been affected by violence in the past and she had learned the hard way that the system could not, or did not, do much about it. Having also encountered violence when he was young, this was his way of making sure somebody paid, sometimes.

Over the years, she had offered to go with him on a few occasions but, each time, he had flatly refused. Although what he did was morally right, it unfortunately was also illegal and, should he ever get caught, he intended to assume full and sole responsibility for his actions. On this basis, he most certainly did not want her involved. Her moral support, encouragement and most of all, acceptance of what he did were all the help he required. Past that, he insisted on being on his own.

Financially, they were extremely comfortable with more than sufficient savings and investments for her to live on if anything ever happened to him. He had made sure of that. However, as he had told her many times in the past, she had nothing to worry about anyways for, he would never get caught.

She wandered around the house, looking for something to do to pass the time. She missed him when he wasn't near her and was always anxious for him to return. At least the waiting was nearly over. He would be home tonight.

## Chapter 14 - Thursday, July 11, 1996

4:15 p.m. Chris Barry left the office for his 5 o'clock appointment with Eileen Baker. He knew that by leaving at this time he'd be early but that was part of his plan. He always preferred to be the first to arrive at such meetings, believing that in so doing, the environment became his and allowed him more control over eventual outcomes.

Setting up the meeting had been easy. He had called her from the West Coast to enquire if they could get together upon his return, to discuss a business proposition. CSS did no television or radio advertising but they did run a large number of ads in a variety of business and computer magazines and newspapers. Although not from lack of trying, Griffiths & Donaldson had been unsuccessful in their approaches with CSS in the past. Eileen had readily accepted the unexpected invitation.

As he drove by the main gate and waved to the guard, he wondered how Eileen would react once she found out why he really wanted to see her. He highly respected people in general and blatantly manipulating them was not his usual style.

"Hey," he reasoned, trying to convince himself. "At least, I'll be swinging some advertising business her way!"

But, in the end, he was fairly certain that she would help out. Although not high on manipulation, he had an incredible knack for convincing people. That was how he had gotten to where he was today.

"Enough analytical thought!" he muttered to himself. "What you need is a little distraction!"

He hit the 'play' button on the CD player and within seconds was mellowly cruising towards his downtown destination to the sounds of 'Shine on You Crazy Diamond'.

\* \* \* \*

Eileen Baker still had difficulty believing that she was having drinks with Chris Barry, the second in command of CSS; even harder to believe was the fact that he had called her.

Henry Marshall, another account executive with G & D, had been trying to get into illustrous firm for the last three years, during which time he had not even managed to get onto their property. CSS was in the computer industry and to say that security was extremely tight was somewhat of an understatement. Without an appointment, one didn't get in and Henry had never gotten an appointment.

She had been brooding in her office following a particularly unproductive presentation and meeting with some top brass jerks from a major food packager. They hadn't appreciated her idea, claiming that it didn't communicate 'Farm fresh'. Jesus, the product was boiled, separated, processed, stuffed with additives and preservatives and canned. Six months elapsed between the farm and the final consumer!

The phone had rung but she had ignored it and a moment later, Jessie, her secretary, had knocked on the door and entered.

"Not now, Jessie!" Eileen had snarled.

"I think you should take this one, Eileen," Jessie had insisted.

"Why? Who is so important?" Eileen had shot back, glaring.

She was too hard on Jessie sometimes.

"Man by the name of Chris Barry. Says he's E.V.P. at CSS Inc. Says he wants to talk over some business possibilities with you."

Jessie had allowed herself a small smile, watching Eileen's expression transform from one of anger to one of sheer astonishment.

"Why me? CSS is Henry's prospect!" Eileen had stammered, obviously in shock but keenly interested.

"Told him that," Jessie had replied. "He told me that he wished to speak to Eileen Baker, not Henry Marshall. Shall I take a message or simply let him know that you're not interested in speaking with him?"

By then, Jessie's smile had turned into a smirk.

"Get out of here, you moron!" Eileen had responded, grinning from ear to ear. "Thanks Jess!"

"He's on 324!" Jessie had called out as she closed the door.

Barry had told her that he was planning some important increases in advertising volume which his marketing department could not handle. He wished to involve an outside agency, to get some new blood into the system. A few friends had recommended Griffiths & Donaldson, or more precisely, Eileen Baker. Was she available to meet on Thursday, maybe for a drink? She had willingly accepted. Henry was no longer speaking to her but that was no great loss.

She left the office and walked the four short blocks from Peel Street to Crescent, quite anxious to meet the great Chris Barry. If things went right, this rendezvous might just change her life forever.

* * * *

Chris arrived at L'Annexe at a quarter to five and requested a table on the far side of the terrace. From there, he would see Eileen approach the bar before she entered. Requesting that they be served only once his guest had arrived, he ordered amber Bacardi with Coke for himself and a Bloody Caesar, extra spicy, for Eileen. He had done his homework.

His watch read 4:59 when he saw her hurry up the sidewalk and to the restaurant's entrance. As she reached for the door, she noticed him watching her and froze for a few seconds, returning his gaze. He smiled and stood and she entered. Hesitating for a few more seconds, she took a deep breath, as if to sum up her courage, and marched determinedly towards him.

"Mr. Barry, I presume," she spoke demurely.

"Eileen!" he replied brightly, shaking her hand warmly. "How are you?!"

"Fine, Mr. Barry," she responded, glancing up at him. "How are you?"

"Never better! Please, have a seat," he invited, pulling out a chair for her. "And call me Chris."

The drinks arrived as he returned to his seat. He waited for the waiter to leave before speaking again.

"I took the liberty of ordering before you arrived. I hope you don't mind?"

"No, that's fine. I see you know more about me than I thought," she politely commented, gesturing towards her glass.

"Extra spicy!" he grinned. "I like to know who I'm dealing with. It's good business practice."

"I guess I can't disagree with that."

They sat for a moment in silence, waiting for the other to speak, some kind of unforeseen showdown. Chris won.

"So you want to do business with me, Chris," Eileen attempted a businesslike tone. "Why don't you tell me what it's about."

"Eileen, I got to where I am today by playing straight, so that's what I'm going to do with you," Chris quietly replied. "Now, what I told you about additional advertising and wanting to implicate an outside agency is true. G & D has an excellent reputation, as does Eileen Baker. I know. I checked. Therefore, if you want it, that business is yours. We can talk about the finer details afterwards."

She nodded wordlessly, waiting for him to go on.

"The purpose of this meeting however, the main reason, is not advertising," Chris went on. "I used that as a ploy to get you here and for that, I apologize. However, you probably would not have met with me otherwise."

She watched him silently as he spoke, growing uneasy as she wondered what he wanted of her.

"The police has requested the help of CSS in their investigation of the Vigilante murders," he continued. "We are responsible, primarily, of trying to trace some computer messages which the Vigilante has sent the cops through Eazy-Com. Any questions so far?"

She shook her head in response.

"I asked to meet with you at the request of Dave McCall, whom you've met," Chris explained. "Dave is a personal friend of mine. He believes that you may know more about the Vigilante than you let on. Dave hopes that, if he is right, I will be able to convince you to give a better description of the man."

"I can't do that!" she quietly exclaimed, her tone a mixture of adamancy and incredulity. "I-I really didn't get a good look at him! That's what I told the cops! I really don't think I can help, Chris! I swear!"

"Listen, I don't want to frighten you," he replied soothingly. "I just want you to do what's right. I'll help and support you in anyway I can."

He reached over and patted her hand before picking up a large envelope on the chair beside him and sliding it across the table towards her.

"Here's a summary of your interview with the cops as well as some other information related to the Vigilante case. Take the time to look this over. My card is in there as well. Call me once you've thought about it. If nothing has changed, I'll respect that. I'll get out of your hair and I'll make sure McCall and his boys do the same. But look this over, carefully, before you make your final decision. I promise I won't call you back on this. It's completely up to you."

She gazed at him and knew he was telling the truth.

"O.K.," she hesitantly agreed, "But no promises."

"Ball's in your court, Eileen. You decide if you play it or not. Deal?"

"Deal," she nodded nervously.

As he looked around to signal the waiter, he grinned and added, "Expect a call from Nancy Biron tomorrow. She's my Director of Marketing Services. Congratulations, Eileen! You've just cut a big deal for Griffiths & Donaldson! This calls for a celebration! Let's eat!"

\* \* \* \*

Carl Denver hit the 'Enter' key and the transaction was complete. As he did so, he suddenly thought of his step-father and involuntarily broke into a smile. The old man had definitely been wrong about the uselessness of computers. Just twenty effortless minutes had been required to make Carl another $50,000 richer.

Over time, especially since he had joined CSS, he had realized how easily money could be skimmed electronically. For example, every month, banks paid interest to millions of customers. A few minor changes to a couple of programmes and a fraction of each payment was re-routed to some dummy account. This dummy account was then emptied into a secured account in the Cayman Islands.

Thanks to networks like Eazy-Com and his system overriding skills acquired at CSS, such a task was relatively easy. And, with countless corporations and financial institutions to choose from, Carl had an extensive list of targets. He therefore never did one of his 'tricks' at the same place more than once. He didn't have to.

He knew that he could not go on forever but, then again, he had no intention of doing so. Sooner or later, he recognized that he would have to cease his activities, retire and disappear. And when that time came, Carl intended to be a very rich man.

### **Chapter 15 - Friday, July 12, 1996**

The west end section of downtown St-Catherine Street had changed drastically over time and unfortunately, not for the better. Once a well kept street, lined with posh boutiques, restaurants and respectable nightclubs, it was now home to strip-joints, peep-shows, amusement arcades and dollar stores. Drunks, junkies, pushers, pimps and prostitutes littered its sidewalks, completing the unpleasant decor.

This was Johnny B.'s world, his territory. Although only twenty-four, Johnny was King in the downtown sector.

Raised in a less favourable district of the city, just east of his now so-called kingdom, Johnny B. had grown up surrounded by crime. His father had been a two-bit addict who had spent more time in jail cells than at home. His alcoholic mother had been a hooker who usually spent her hard earned money on supporting her, and her husband's, respective habits.

By the time Johnny B. had turned twelve, he had already been involved in a variety of crimes including auto thefts, muggings and armed robbery. At sixteen, he had been pimping, with ten girls on his payroll. Now, at twenty-four, he was the unofficial Pimp King with some fifty girls walking the street for him. Another fifty, his classier dames, worked as call girls through his escort agency. Johnny B. kept 70% of the take, the girls got to keep the other 30%. All of his girls were young, some under eighteen, none over twenty-two.

Over the years, Johnny had clearly established his reputation in the area. On a few occasions, some of his girls had tried to hang on to more than their share of the take. Without hesitation, he had viciously demonstrated that 'One did not hold out on Johnny B.' His victims had served as examples to the others. In recent months, a couple of other pimps had tried to move in on his girls or his territory. Johnny had met with these individuals and, with the help of a tire iron, 'explained' that this was his kingdom.

Yes, Johnny B. was a man to be feared in this neighbourhood. Johnny B. was King.

\* \* \* \*

Sandy was spending the afternoon with Lisa Green and called to ask if he minded having dinner alone. She would stay over for dinner with Lisa and come home afterwards. That was fine, he replied. He had an errand to run anyways. He suggested that they meet for a movie later, for the 9 o'clock showing. It was Friday, after all. They agreed on what to see and where, and it was a date.

He left the office around 4:00 and drove around for a while, eventually making his way to Sherbrooke Street, downtown. Turning right off Sherbrooke onto Drummond, he rode halfway up the hill before veering left into the entrance of the underground parking garage of an apartment building. He inserted a magnetic card into the slot, opening the door before him and drove down three levels, to the visitors parking area.

He cut the engine and climbed out of the black Corvette, looking around to make sure that he was alone. It was only 4:25 so the place was deserted as he had hoped. Opening the trunk, he removed the small canvas bag which he had prepared especially for this occasion.

Not far from where he had parked were two doors, one marked 'exit', the other, 'maintenance'. He hurried to the 'maintenance' door, removing a key-like instrument from the bag as he went and quickly got to work. Within seconds, he was inside the small storeroom, the door securely closed behind him. He donned a pair of coveralls and then examined the remaining contents of the bag to ensure that he had not forgotten anything. Everything was there.

Opening the door of the storeroom just a few inches, he scanned the parking area for any signs of activity. Not a soul in sight. He left the room, locking the door behind him and ducked through the 'exit' door into the stairwell. He crept up one flight where he paused to peer through the small window in the door; nobody.

Entering the second level parking area, he headed directly for the spot marked P2-1017; he knew where he was going. The car was there, a silver-grey Mercedes SL convertible. He looked around one last time to make sure he was alone before crawling under the luxury vehicle and getting to work.

\* \* \* \*

Johnny B. was seated at a stage-side table at the Sex Cave, finishing his third Glenlivet. He liked coming here after dinner, for an hour or so, before going to do his rounds on the street. The girls looked good and occasionally, he offered one a job with his organization. They never accepted but were always polite in their refusal. After all, they knew who he was. He was Johnny B.

He looked at his Rolex and grunted when he saw the time. It was 8:25, time to go to work. He stood and the waitress automatically appeared. Slipping a folded fifty dollar bill deep into the front of her thong, he gave her bare behind a light, friendly slap.

"See ya later, doll!" he said, grinning. "Keep the change!"

Customers were forbidden to touch the girls; the club had strict rules about that. But he was an exception. He was Johnny B.

He strutted down the long narrow staircase which led to the street, preceded by Chuck, his bodyguard. Onto the sidewalk, he paused for a moment, surveying the surroundings through narrow eyes, evaluating the activity. It was a warm summer evening and a lot of people were out. Business would be good tonight.

Crossing the sidewalk to his car, which was conveniently parked in front of the club's entrance, he climbed in behind the wheel and started the engine as Chuck squeezed his bulky form into the passenger seat. Half a block down, the traffic light was red, so there were no oncoming cars. Johnny B. revved the engine and pulled out onto the street, spinning his tires in the process as he always did. He liked getting noticed.

He turned right on Union and then left on René-Lévesque as he headed for Old Montreal. A number of his girls worked this sector in the summer, especially around Place St-Jacques, which was crowded with restaurants, bars and a slew of prospective clients. Turning right on Beaver Hall Hill, he headed south towards the river, stopping at the red light at the corner of St-Jacques. With the exception of a car which had just turned onto the street at the top of the hill behind him, his was the only vehicle in circulation. Pedestrian traffic was also non-existent.

He always found amusing how this area could be so quiet, sandwiched between the active sector he had just left and the lively one he was going to. The light turned green and Johnny B. rapidly accelerated through the empty intersection and then decelerated just as quickly to turn left on LeMoyne. As it slowed, the Mercedes exploded into a huge fireball, sending bits and pieces of plastic, metal, flesh and bone flying through the air.

Two blocks behind the explosion, a black Corvette turned left onto Notre-Dame and headed for the cinema.

## Chapter 16 - Saturday, July 13, 1996

10:00 a.m. They were gathered in Chris Barry's office at CSS headquarters, present was Dave McCall, accompanied by his detectives, Tim Harris, Joanne Nelson and Frank Bakes as well as Bob Thompson from the Computer Centre. Since it was, theoretically, a 'day off' for them, all were dressed casually; jeans, t-shirts, running shoes. They had arrived a few minutes earlier and had been greeted by Sonia, Barry's secretary, who had shown them into the office. Chris, she had informed them, would join them in a couple of minutes.

The events leading to this meeting had started the previous evening at about 8:30 when a car bomb had exploded downtown, taking the lives of John Barrows, or Johnny B. as he had been called on the street, and Charles 'Chuck' Dunning. Barrows was a known pimp who ran a very profitable prostitution ring downtown whereas Chuck was Johnny's chief muscle and personal bodyguard.

Had the events limited themselves to the explosion, the police would have considered it to be a simple settlement of accounts. Johnny B. had controlled the downtown prostitution racket for a while and had a reputation of being somewhat violent with his girls as well as with any possible competition. However, at 7:00 on Saturday morning, another message had come through Eazy-Com to the police. Apparently, the Vigilante was at it again.

When McCall had called Chris about the message, the computer executive had suggested that they meet at his office to 'unofficially' discuss the case. Maybe an outsider's unbiased opinion could prove useful. McCall had willingly accepted the invitation.

Sonia came into the office with a tray of muffins and doughnuts, followed by Chris who carried the coffee. After laying the tray on the conference table, Sonia left the office, closing the door behind her as McCall started the introductions.

"Chris, I'd like you to meet Tim Harris and Joanne Nelson, two of my closest partners in crime. Bob Thompson, you already know, and that one, choosing the biggest muffin, is Frank Bakes."

Chris shook hands as they laughed and invited all to sit, gesturing towards the conference table.

As they settled into the comfortable chairs, McCall started, "Have you seen the latest message, Chris?"

"Nope, not yet," Chris admitted, flipping open his notepad as he spoke. "But I'm about to."

He continued to speak as he deftly worked the keyboard.

"When you called this morning, I contacted Carl Denver. He's in his office right now, working on some tracing possibilities. He'll be joining us when he's done. Here we are." The message appeared on the screen.

THE METHOD WAS DIFFERENT, BUT THE END RESULT THE SAME. NOW YOU NO LONGER NEED TO BOTHER WITH JOHNNY B. GLAD I COULD BE OF SERVICE.         REGARDS,
VIGILANTE

"At least he **seems** like a nice guy," Chris commented, drawing a smile from the others.

"Fact is, he does," McCall ruefully admitted. "I don't know what to make of this guy. As far as we know, he's only targeted people who, deep down, deserved what they got. Problem is, we have a system that's supposed to handle these things."

"Maybe he feels the system isn't working just right," teased Joanne.

"I'm sure he doesn't," McCall snorted. "Hell, I agree with him! But if I had blown away a punk every time I felt it was deserved, they'd have locked me up in a nuthouse for life a while ago."

"We'd also have a few less assholes to worry about!" Harris quipped.

They all laughed, nodding their heads in accord.

"I know you guys have been working on this quite extensively since it all started nearly seven months ago." Chris stepped in. "But I haven't. So, if you'll allow me, I'll ask a number of stupid questions which you've no doubt all thought of before and looked into. But maybe, just maybe, I might say something along the way that hasn't been considered."

"I don't see how it can do any harm," McCall agreed. "**We**'ve gotten nowhere so far. Fire away."

"O.K." started Chris. "Now, I've read about the different murders in the papers, but until recently, this whole thing was just of a passing interest to me. It was just news so I wasn't keeping track of events. Have you established any kind of timing or frequency? Does your man act only during certain times? Once a week? Only on odd days of the month? That kind of thing?"

"Not really," Harris shook his head. "It's been pretty random. Some took place on weekends, others on weekdays; some on odd days, others on even. The first and second were about a month apart; same with the second and third. Then, three or four happened in about two weeks; after that, nothing for close to two months. We had started to think he had quit. Then, during the month that followed, nine, pretty evenly spaced. Two more weeks with nothing; then the two insurance guys. Two days later, Jimmy Green. Six days after that, Zack Roberts. A nine day break leads us to yesterday with Johnny B. and Chuck, numbers 21 and 22 on the list. Do **you** see a time pattern?"

"Frankly, no," Chris admitted. "It may depend on his schedule. He might have other obligations, like a job. Were any of the victims worth paying for to have killed?"

"You mean that our killer might be a paid assassin? I don't think so," Joanne doubtfully replied. "They were mostly small-time, local hoods. No big organized crime people. If these were paid executions, the fees would be nothing for an assassin to get rich on. Plus, we never really found any connections linking any of the victims together. They were each doing their own bit to screw up society. I can't see that any one person could have possibly been directly affected by all the different victims to then pay a hit man to have them whacked."

"Methods of execution always the same?"

"Until last night, yes," Joanne continued. "Well, Zack Roberts was injected with a lethal dose of coke and smack. The throat was slashed afterwards, maybe as his trademark. Last night, with the bomb, was a new twist. But our man has done nothing so far that would indicate that he's a fool. Johnny B. always had at least one bodyguard with him. Getting at him with a knife or a club would have been complicated."

Chris pushed on. "But now we know that our Vigilante also has knowledge of explosives. Any luck on the bomb so far?"

McCall took that one. "Seems that it wasn't really complex. A one gallon canister of gasoline, half full, was fixed to the car's gas tank. Some kind of detonating device set off the canister. Canister set off the gas tank. The forensics guys are still looking into it, but they're pretty sure that the detonator was radio controlled. That would mean that our man must have been close by when it happened."

"That's nothing new," Bakes stated. "In fact, if anything, last night was probably the furthest from his victim he's been so far."

"Does that mean something?" Chris pressed. "Is he getting scared? Looking for methods which allow more distance between him and his targets?"

Shoulders shrugged around the table in response.

"What about witnesses?" Chris went on. "Did anyone report anything out of twenty-two murders?"

McCall responded. "There's Eileen Baker, whom you know about. To date, as you also know, she's been little help. The closest thing we have to a witness besides her is a kid who saw her take off in her car. He wouldn't have even reported that if he hadn't heard that two guys got murdered half a block from his place."

"But based on what Eileen Baker said, we can assume that the murders took place shortly after she left, right?" Chris queried.

"Actually, the first one, the throat slash, took place while she was there," volunteered Harris. "The guy was lying in his blood when she ran out of the alley. The time of death established by the medical examiner indicates that the other guy died shortly after."

"My point is," said Chris. "The kid walked right past the alley, probably while the second guy was being murdered. Maybe he saw something that he decided not to talk about."

"I doubt it," Harris disagreed. "Kid showed up of his own accord. Hell, we would've never known he existed otherwise. He volunteered his story without any pushing on our part. I'm the one he met with. If anything, he seemed excited to be part of this, not scared. He kept saying 'This is so cool man!' He walked by the alley as Baker ran out and got her license plate because he thought it seemed strange; walked by the alley again fifteen minutes later, on his way to a party. He practically seemed disappointed that he couldn't tell me more. Left me his name and number, just in case I needed his help."

"All right," accepted Chris, convinced. "So we have no witnesses, excluding Eileen. And therefore, we have no description, excluding Eileen."

"Speaking of Eileen, any idea if she'll get back to you?" enquired McCall.

"I can't promise anything," Chris replied. "But I have a pretty good feeling. I don't want to call her, at least not for now. I told her I wouldn't. If I break my word, I'll lose her trust. I want to give her some time."

"I agree," nodded McCall. "You met her less than forty-eight hours ago. Wait. Maybe she'll come around."

"I hope so," said Chris. "I think she can help. I'm not convinced that she's intentionally holding back anything. I do believe though, that if she really thinks about it, she'll remember at least a few more details. A little would be better than nothing at all."

A knock on the door interrupted their discussion and Carl Denver joined them, closing the door behind him.

"Everybody, this is Carl Denver," Chris announced. "Carl, this is Dave, Bob, Frank, Joanne and Tim." He gestured towards each guest as he introduced them.

"Have a seat," Chris offered. "So, what have we got?"

"Same as the others, I'm afraid," Carl gloomily replied, "Nothing."

They continued the conversation for a few minutes, concentrating the discussion on the computer aspects of the investigation, after which Carl excused himself to return to his office.

The meeting continued for another hour, sadly ending with a consensus that they were no further ahead than they had been in the past.

* * * *

Carl rushed back to his office, extremely troubled and worried. He had told Chris and the cops that, once again, there was no trace of the message, as had been the case with the first two. This time, he had lied.

Rather than bother his contacts at Eazy-Com, he had done the tracing himself immediately, knowing that Chris would ask him to eventually do so anyways.

He had accessed the Eazy-Com databank routinely, his mind much more on what he and his wife would do that afternoon than on the task at hand. This was easy work and he was confident, certain, in fact, that the result would be the same as the other times. There simply was no reason for it to be otherwise.

However, while scanning the Eazy-Com communication logs, he had found a record of the transmission; a complete record. He had nearly missed it, caught up in his daydreaming, but it had suddenly jumped out at him, a sender's address; 114.195.824//CSS.INC.427.

Dumbfounded, he had verified the message identification number and found it to match. This tiny bit of information, buried amongst hundreds of thousands of other bits of data, confirmed the transmission of the Vigilante message from CSS Inc. headquarters, PC number 427; His PC.

His initial reaction had been one of panic. How could this be? It was hardly possible! Something was terribly wrong and he was suddenly very afraid.

Feeling suddenly paranoid, he had hurried to close and lock the door of his office, not wanting anyone to come in on him. After a minute or two, he had regained a semblance of composure and had started to think a bit more clearly.

He would have to erase the record, that was a given. A thought flashed through his mind which gave rise to panic once again; backups. The message had been sent at 7:03 that morning and it was now 9:27. Nearly two and a half hours. It was possible that a backup had been made but there was nothing he could do about that. Maybe, he prayed, luck would be with him. After all, it was Saturday and he knew Eazy-Com backed up less frequently on weekends. Most likely, he reasoned, nobody else would verify with Eazy-Com, assuming that he had.

He had checked the time; 9:31. Chris had said that they'd be meeting with the cops at 10:00 which meant he had less than half an hour to erase the traces. There was no way in hell he could allow anybody to get a hold of this kind of evidence and start snooping around the systems at CSS, no matter what! He simply had too much at stake, too much to lose. Mustering all his energy and knowledge, he had gotten to work, doing what he did best.

\* \* \* \*

11:45 p.m. He started watching Saturday Night Live and quickly decided he'd be better off joining Sandy in bed. He turned off the television and headed upstairs, stopping in 'the office' before going to the bedroom.

Picking up his notepad on the desk, he proceeded to punch in a series of access codes, quickly making his way into the Eazy-Com databank. He needed to check again, just to make sure. There was no record of the message.

Smiling with satisfaction, he exited the system and went to Sandy.

## Chapter 17 - Monday, July 15, 1996

10:45 a.m. Following his initial meeting with Chris Barry nearly two weeks earlier, Dave McCall had begun the painful task of secretly investigating his own people. He had started with those less close to him, one by one, looking into their shift schedules and analyzing their daily reports, verifying their comings and goings on the dates of the murders. And one by one, he had been able to eliminate them as suspects.

If any one of them was involved, he or she would have to be acting as part of a team, not alone, and for the time being, he had no reason to believe that his Vigilante was more than one person.

In conducting his research, he had kept three individuals for last; Joanne, Frank and Tim, his closest detectives. Both Joanne and Tim had been easy to eliminate as they had been with him while several of the murders had occurred. Frank however, had been quite a different story.

McCall had doubted nothing before analyzing the shift schedules. Frank had been rather heavily involved with the case since its beginning and, in McCall's mind, had also been present while some of the murders had taken place. But as he had proceeded with his analysis, he had come to realize that he could not vouch for Frank's whereabouts on any of the murder dates. Not one. Frank had either been off duty or following up on some lead, alone. None of his daily reports placed him anywhere with a reliable alibi at the times of the murders.

To add to his troubles, Dave was also painfully aware that Frank had a favourite pastime. He was a computer buff. They often called on Frank's amateur services when a system bugged or a PC broke down.

Last of all, of the twenty-two murders, Frank had been the first from their division on the scene on twelve occasions. Two of those times, he had been off duty but happened to 'be in the neighbourhood' and had heard the call on the radio which he, like most other cops, left on nearly constantly.

But even after taking all of these factors into consideration, McCall had much difficulty even starting to accept that Frank might be their man. It just wasn't like him, just didn't fit. He did not have violent tendencies and always played by the book. Many a time, Frank had calmed down an angry cop where abuse of a perpetrator would have otherwise been the result.

It didn't make sense. This had to be the result of a series of coincidences or there had to be some other logical explanation.

Anyhow, with what Dave had so far, he was not ready to point a finger at Frank. Not yet. And until he had more, he would keep this to himself.

* * * *

4:00 p.m. Chris was busy at his desk, reviewing the final draft of a contract for yet another new customer, when Sonia appeared in the doorway, tapping on the doorframe to get his attention.

"Sorry to bother you, Chris. An Eileen Baker on the line for you. Says you're expecting her call?"

"Yep, I'll take it," Chris replied, smiling. "Thanks, Sonia."

She smiled back and closed the door on her way out.

"Hi, Eileen!" he called into the speaker. "How are you doing?"

"Fine, Chris. Thanks," she answered, sounding a touch nervous. "How are you?"

"Never better," he responded brightly. "I'm surprised to hear from you so soon."

'Well, procrastination has never been one of my weaknesses," she replied. "I've had enough time to think this over and I've made my decision."

Silence ensued.

Chris waited several seconds then gently prodded, "Do you want to tell me what that decision is?"

A few more soundless seconds went by before she hesitantly replied, "I-I'll do it."

"You don't seem sure, Eileen. I only want you to do this if you feel comfortable. That was the deal. If you aren't able to help the cops, so be it. They'll find other leads. They'll get him eventually."

"No Chris, I'm sure. I can't say that I'm quite comfortable with it yet, but I'm sure. I've gone over the file you gave me, several times. I'm convinced. I'll do what I can to help you. But there are conditions."

"O.K." said Chris. "What kind of conditions?"

"I remain anonymous," she answered. "I'll give the description, as required. The cops can do what they want with it. If and when they grab him, I don't have to identify him. If there's a trial, I don't have to be there, I don't have to testify. I do not want, I refuse, to face him. I just could not handle that. If that's not acceptable, then there's nothing more I can do to help than what I've already done."

Chris nodded approvingly. "McCall is really anxious to get a handle on this case. I'm sure that I can convince him to accept those conditions. If not, I'll tell him to forget about it. If he tries to get tough, I'll deny ever having spoken to you and I'll even withdraw this company's services. Like I said, I'm sure that I can convince him."

"I like your style, Mr. Barry," she smiled into the phone. "Oh, one more thing. This one's not a condition but more of a request. When I do meet with the cops, I would appreciate your being there. You know, just to make sure things go right and don't get out of hand. This whole thing is difficult for me and I'd like to know there's someone there I can trust. O.K.?"

"You've got it," Chris assured her. "I told you on Thursday that I would give you all the support and help you needed. I'm a man of my word."

"Great!" she answered with relief. "Where do we go from here?"

"I'll contact Dave and let him know what the deal is. I'll even throw in another condition. The cops are not to contact you directly under any circumstances. They must go through me and if I'm not available, they wait. I'll get back to you once I've spoken to him. Deal?"

"Deal," Eileen replied gratefully.

"If he accepts your offer, how soon would you be ready to meet him?"

"We might as well get this done while everything is fresh in my memory. Wednesday O.K.?"

"Wednesday's fine," answered Chris. "I'll set it up for 10 o'clock."

"Thanks, Chris," she said softly.

"No, my dear," he responded. "Thank-**you!**"

\* \* \* \*

Carl was still shaken by Saturday morning's events and continued to wonder how he had managed to sit there with Chris and the cops, lying to them, without breaking down. He had felt dizzy with fear, physically nauseous, but nobody had seemed to notice. He had been relieved to leave the meeting only five minutes after he had joined them. He would not have lasted much longer.

Since, he had checked the data banks several times, to make sure that nothing incriminating remained, but all was in order. He had heard nothing, directly or indirectly, from Eazy-Com either, and therefore presumed that no backups had been taken during the time that the transmission was on record. At the very least, if the message had been backed up, nobody seemed to have verified with the carrier.

He still could not begin to understand the record of the transmission. Either, he had been the victim of a very bizarre, inexplicable coincidence or somebody was aware of what he was doing and was playing games with him. He believed the second option to be much more plausible which meant that the situation had become dangerous.

He knew that he could not afford, could never accept getting caught. Maybe he would have to cease his activities and retire sooner than expected.

\* \* \* \*

5:42 p.m. Frank Bakes left work at the end of his shift, feeling uneasy. Although he couldn't put his finger on it, he knew something was wrong.

Throughout the day, he had gotten the impression that McCall was avoiding him. Sure, Dave had said his "Mornin, Frankie" when he had come in and bade him goodnight upon leaving but during the day, he had seemed distant. He had chatted as usual with some of the others, but had not once asked him, "How's it going?", or "Anything new on the streets?", as he typically did. McCall had a habit of keeping up to speed with the various cases handled by his department and regularly asked for updates; but not today, not with Frank.

Frank had gone to see McCall with a couple of questions after lunch and, although cordial, his boss had limited the conversation to the business at hand and no more.

Something was wrong and Frank could sense it. Did McCall know something? Maybe someone had seen him and talked.

Troubled, he climbed into the car, started the engine and suddenly felt weary, even a little ill. Tonight, he would stay home. Tonight, he would spend a quiet evening with his wife.

\* \* \* \*

McCall waited, parked on Stanley in a nondescript rental from Thrifty's, from where he could see the main entrance of his division's offices, half a block over. He had left work at five o'clock and switched his car with the rented Taurus he had parked a block away that afternoon. Now, he was about to start the unpleasant task of shadowing Frank Bakes.

He saw Frank come out of the building and head into the small parking lot to one side. Moments later, Frank pulled out, driving his wife's Corvette. Crouching low as his subordinate drove past, Dave then hurriedly veered in behind him to follow, drawing an angry horn blast from another approaching vehicle.

"Screw yourself!" McCall muttered at the rear-view mirror, "Official police business!"

Although traffic was still somewhat heavy, tailing the flashy black sports car was an easy task but after several minutes of driving, it became obvious that Frank was heading home.

11:47 p.m. With another massive yawn, McCall stretched his stiffened back and decided to call it a night. He had been keeping an eye on the Bakes residence for close to six hours and decided that Frank was not going anywhere tonight. The last lights in the house had gone out about forty-five minutes earlier and Frank was probably already comfortably in bed with his wife.

'That's where I should be too,' thought Dave guiltily, as he started the engine and drove home to his ever-understanding Cathy.

## Chapter 18 - Tuesday, July 16, 1996

Chris sat in one of the leather armchairs in his office, reflecting on the subject of Carl Denver. Carl had been acting very strangely lately, extremely nervous and jumpy.

Chris had first noticed it on Saturday when Carl had joined him and the cops. The young analyst's voice had been shaky and he had been sweating. Nobody else had seemed to notice but Chris knew Carl well enough to realize that something had been bothering him. Since, Carl had been moody and aggressive.

'Whatever it is, I'll find out,' Chris thought with a smile.

After all, he was EVP of a leading security and investigation firm.

\* \* \* \*

7:45 p.m. Dave was packing some reports into his briefcase, about to head for home, when the phone rang.

"Homicide, McCall," he answered.

"Man, are you hard to get a hold of!" Chris exclaimed.

"Hey, Chris. Sorry, I was out of the office most of the day, wasting my time in court."

"No problem," Chris replied. "I called a few times but I was in and out myself so I didn't leave a message."

"What can I do for you?" asked McCall.

"Ah, my friend," Chris brightly responded. "The question is more like, 'what can **I** do for **you**!' I got a call from Eileen Baker!"

"And???"

"She'll try to help, with conditions."

"What kind of conditions?" McCall enquired, already feeling in higher spirits.

"Anonymity, no involvement in identification when you catch him, no testimony when you take him to court. She's willing to do her 'good citizen' bit and give you a lead. However, she feels, and rightly so, that she owes the guy. She doesn't want to face him and doesn't want him to know she betrayed him. Frankly, I agree with her."

"Well," breathed McCall, elated. "It's not all that I was hoping for but it's much more than I was expecting. You're really good, aren't you!"

"I try," Chris modestly remarked. "By the way, she specifically asked that I be present whenever you guys meet her. She would also like all communication to go through me."

"I have no problem with that, Chris," McCall heartily agreed. "She obviously trusts you so your involvement can only help get more info out of her. Wow, this is good news!"

"Glad I could make your day," said Chris. "When do you want to meet with her?"

"It's getting close to eight so I guess I'll be reasonable. Tomorrow morning O.K.?"

Chris laughed. "Eileen has already agreed to tomorrow at 10:00, your place. I'll get in touch with her to let her know we're on."

"Excellent! I love you, Chris!" McCall exclaimed.

"Sorry, Dave. I'm married! See you in the morning."

McCall hung up the phone. A beautiful ending to a lousy day! He decided to make sure that his 'Vigilante team' would be present and available for Eileen's visit the next morning.

He punched the "Harris" speed-dial button on the phone and was speaking to him within half a minute. Yes, he would **definitely** be there. Moments later, Joanne Nelson was also confirmed.

He then called Frank Bakes and got his wife. No, Frank was not home, he was out helping a friend set up a computer. Yes, she would let him know, be in by 10:00. She would leave him a note as he had said he might be home late.

\* \* \* \*

Paulo Morretto stepped out of his limousine and strutted around the corner to the rear entrance of the apartment block, followed by Gino and Rupert. As he unlocked the door, he addressed his two goons.

"I may be a couple of hours tonight, boys. I ain't seen Cindy in a few months and we got a lot of catchin up to do!"

Grinning, he winked and disappeared inside. The two gorillas took their positions on either side of the door and settled in for a while.

Paulo Morretto was the son of Giovanni Morretto, founder, owner and president of the Morretto Construction empire. In addition, Giovanni also headed one of the most powerful organized crime families in the eastern half of the country. But Giovanni was growing old. Consequently, he had started transferring power to his first child and only son, Paulo.

Paulo was, and always had been, a tough, ruthless individual. Although Giovanni had always run the construction company on a fairly legal basis with respect to his competitors, his son had a different view of things. Paulo did not like to lose; he had to win.

As he became more involved in the construction company, Paulo increased the use of strong-arm tactics and intimidation to discourage others from bidding on projects he desired. Though most of the time, he was successful, once in a while, he encountered somebody who was not easily impressed by threats. Such had been the case with Angus Construction, in relation to a bid for the building of a condominium complex.

Since Angus had refused to back out, Paulo had decided to have a chat with Jeff Arnold, owner of Landmark Developments, the project's developer. If anything, Arnold was even less impressed with Paulo's aggressive attitude than Angus had been. As a result, the contract had been awarded to Angus even though Morretto Construction had submitted a lower bid. Paulo had been furious.

On October 29 of the previous year, Paulo had personally placed a powerful explosive device in one of the finished six-unit buildings and the force of the blast had completely levelled the three storey structure. Nobody fucked with Paulo Morretto. Unfortunately, unbeknownst to Paulo, one of the six units was already occupied and the blast had also taken the lives of a mother and her two kids, aged two and four.

An investigation had ensued and, by November 19, enough evidence had been gathered to place Paulo Morretto under arrest. The judge, who was quite familiar with the Morretto family's affairs, had denied bail and Paulo had been incarcerated, pending the outcome of his trial.

The prosecution's case had depended largely on the testimony of three witnesses, construction workers, who had seen Paulo enter and subsequently leave the ill-fated building shortly before the explosion. Early on, all three had positively identified Paulo as the man they had seen and had recounted corroborating versions of his arrival with a package and his leaving, in a hurry, without it. However, once into the trial, none of the three could quite remember who or what they had seen.

On July 15th, the previous day, the jury had declared Paulo Morretto not guilty, due to lack of evidence. Following eight months of prison life, Paulo Morretto was a free man.

After spending his first night of freedom at home with his wife, Paulo felt that it was time to get back into action. He had spent the morning at the offices of Morretto Construction, catching up with the business and the afternoon visiting a number of restaurants and bars which also belonged to the family.

Now, evening had finally arrived and it was time for his rendezvous with Cindy. Cindy was his current mistress and she supplied him with whatever he sexually desired. He, in turn, paid the rent for her lavish apartment, bought her whatever she desired and gave her $1,000 per week in spending money.

He reached the door of her apartment and knocked. When the door swung open, she stood there, wearing nothing but high heels.

"Oh BABY! Let's PARTY!!" he exclaimed as he entered, kicking the door shut behind him.

* * * *

The phone began to ring in the limousine parked around the corner of the building.

"Ah, Jesus Christ!" muttered Gino, pushing off the wall and heading for the car. "Why can't Paulo get us fucking portables!"

Yanking the door open, he slid behind the wheel as he reached for the car phone.

"Yeah, hello," he growled into the phone.

Nothing.

"Hello, you stupid fuck!" he fumed.

Still nothing.

"Jesus goddamn fucking Christ!" he snarled as he slammed down the receiver.

From behind, an arm suddenly wrapped itself around his neck, pinning him to the seat while a wet rag was shoved into his face, covering his nose and mouth. He tried to struggle for a few seconds but quickly succumbed to the effects of the chloroform.

"One down, one to go," whispered the man in the rear seat.

He hadn't killed Gino, nor did he intend to kill the other, Rupert, if he could avoid it. By the time he was done tonight, old man Morretto would probably have them executed anyways.

He peered up and down the small side street from inside the limo as he slipped his portable cellular back into his pocket. Nobody. Quietly, he opened the door and slid out onto the sidewalk. Looking like a homeless drunk, he walked quickly to the wall of the building, changing his gait to a stagger as he rounded the corner.

"Where the fuck is Gino?" Rupert impatiently grunted, looking up from his newspaper.

As he stepped forward to direct his attention towards the limo, a drunk, carrying the customary brown paper bag, tottered around the corner and headed towards him.

"S-scuse me, sir," the wino slurred.

"Fuck off!" Rupert warned. "I ain't got no fucking spare change!"

"No sir, wait," the drunk insisted. "Is that your car?"

He turned and pointed towards the limousine, reeling dangerously as he did so.

"Why you wanna know?" Rupert menacingly demanded.

"Cuz your friend, in the car," mumbled the bum. "He don't look good. Think he's sick."

Rupert hastened towards the limo, nearly knocking the drunk over in the process. Taking advantage of the bodyguard's proximity, the wino, with unexpected accuracy and strength, swung the brown paper bag into the side of Rupert's head. The bag contained the customary bottle; filled with crushed stone. The goon crashed to the ground, unconscious.

Hurrying back to the limousine, the drunk quickly scanned the area for witnesses but the street remained deserted. He popped open the car's trunk and returned for Rupert. Within seconds, the ape was properly stored away, peacefully sleeping. In the driver's seat, Gino, the other goon, was still out as he would be for hours. Neither man would be the cause of any further trouble this evening. Satisfied, the drunk returned to the building's rear exit, unlocked the door and entered.

With most everything he undertook, Paulo Morretto insisted on being in control. But when it came to sex, his ultimate thrill was being dominated. And having spent the last eight months behind bars, he was ripe for an ultimate thrill that evening.

He lay on his back on Cindy's king-size bed, his wrists securely handcuffed to the headboard. Cindy straddled over his naked body which was starting to show a number of marks and bruises where she had slapped and pinched him.

"Come on, baby!" Paulo pleaded. "Put it in you! It's been eight months!"

"I'll put it in me when **I** decide!" she snarled through clenched teeth. "You understand, motherfucker?!"

She slapped him again. He loved it.

"Sorry to bother you, ladies and gentlemen," a man's voice called from the bedroom door. "Miss, please get off Mr. Morretto and do not turn around. If you see me, I'll have to kill you."

Cindy froze, her naked body still straddled over Paulo.

"Get these goddamn cuffs off me, bitch!" Paulo shouted.

"Mr. Morretto, shut the fuck up!" their visitor curtly ordered. "Miss, I asked you to get off Mr. Morretto. I would like you to do so, now."

She climbed off Morretto and onto the floor as the man continued.

"Remember, Miss. Do not look at me."

"He's not even fucking armed!" Morretto screamed. "Turn around, look at him! Go call the cops! Get Gino downstairs, you fucking moron!"

"If you wish to live, Miss, don't listen to this asshole. I promise you, he will not hurt you. But if you don't do as I say, I can guarantee that I **will** hurt you."

Cindy did not turn around. The man picked up one of Morretto's socks on the floor and tossed it front of her.

"Mr. Morretto seems to like to scream and that bothers me. Stuff that in his mouth. Mr. Morretto, I strongly urge you to cooperate."

Both complied to his requests.

"Now, Miss," the intruder went on as he backed off into a corner. "I would like you to turn to your left and walk sideways to the door. Remember, you must not see me. Your life depends on it. When you get to the door, I want you to go to the pantry at the back of the kitchen."

She moved slowly sideways towards the bedroom door, staring straight ahead, obviously frightened. Into the hallway, she walked towards the kitchen, aware that he was following her. As she entered the kitchen, she glanced towards the right, at the knife block on the counter. The block was there but the slots were empty. Her fear increased. She continued towards the walk-in pantry.

"Please go inside," the man gently requested. "I will close the door behind you and jam it. You shouldn't be afraid. I will not hurt you."

She entered the small room and the door closed behind her, shrouding her in darkness. She heard a chair scrape across the floor in the kitchen, followed by a slight rattling of the knob as something was pushed solidly against the door. Not even daring to try the door, it just might open, she curled onto the floor into a ball, gripping her knees tightly to her chest and silently cried. She was extremely frightened.

The man returned to the bedroom and closed the door. Morretto had his back raised up against the headboard and was struggling frantically with the hand-cuffs, in vain. Regretfully, he had bought Cindy only the very best in furniture; heavy, solid oak.

"Don't worry about the girl," the visitor reassured him. "I didn't touch her. Her only crime has been to acquaint herself with a piece of shit like you. And don't worry about your two friends downstairs either. I hardly hurt them. They're just having a little snooze in that lovely car of yours."

Morretto stared at the intruder with angry eyes, but remained silent, due to the sock still stuffed in his mouth.

"As for you, Paulo," the man went on. "You, I will hurt. I was very disappointed to learn that you had been acquitted of your terrible crime. You see, the problem is, the system does not always work; which is exactly why I started my little hobby a while back. I had to make up for the system's failures. But Paulo, forgive me! Where are my manners?! I haven't even introduced myself! They call me Vigilante. You must have heard of me? Lately, I'm in the papers more often than you are!"

Morretto lay still on the bed, the anger in his eyes having changed to fear.

The Vigilante continued. "Back to the system and its failures. You see, your case was a failure. Allow me to explain. You planted a bomb last fall that killed a mother and her two kids. Now, in my book, that's wrong. Those people, that innocent family, had not done anything wrong and yet, you killed them. Logically, you should have been punished for your actions but you weren't. You see what I mean, Paulo? The system failed. But that's where I come in."

He paused for a moment as he produced a switchblade from his pocket and released the blade.

"I'm a fair man though, Paulo, no mistake about that. I could kill you slowly, cause you great pain and make you suffer for hours. But that would not be fair. You see, when you killed those three innocent people, you did not make them suffer. You did it quick. Boom! It was over. You are therefore entitled to the same treatment. No more, no less. Good-bye, Paulo."

Stepping over to the side of the bed, he grabbed Paulo's hair and slowly pulled the mobster's head back. He then raised the knife and plunged it into Paulo's throat.

It was getting late and the street was deserted as the drunk made his way down the sidewalk, wavering at every couple of steps. Stopping by a parked mini-van, he looked around to ensure that he was alone. Quickly, he unlocked the side sliding door and slipped into the rear of the vehicle. Inside, the floor was covered with a plastic sheet. He emptied his pockets and quickly removed his clothes, rolling them in the sheet which he stuffed into a plastic garbage bag. He donned a pair of blue jeans, sweater and running shoes, then climbed into the driver's seat, started the engine and headed for home.

On the way, he drove through a quiet alley and stopped just long enough to drop the garbage bag through the window into a dumpster.

He checked the dashboard clock; 11:38 and smiled. Sandy would still be up.

## Chapter 19 - Wednesday, July 17, 1996

5:28 a.m. Ron Henderson arrived at the office early, as was his usual routine. He liked coming in at this time, just to see what had come in on the wire services overnight. Often enough, he found something of interest which allowed him to write one of his controversial articles before the printing of the final edition at 6:00.

He strolled into his cubicle and put down his coffee, then turned on the PC. As the display appeared on the screen, he noticed the Eazy-Com icon flashing in one corner. He clicked the mouse and the message, which had come in just five minutes earlier, came into view:

> WE ARE SOMETIMES REWARDED FOR OUR LOYALTY. YOU HAVE EARNED AN EXCLUSIVE. PAULO MORRETTO IS DEAD, THROAT SLASHED. HIS BODY IS AT THE EXCELSIOR SUITES, #1219, HANDCUFFED TO A BED, HIS DOING, NOT MINE. WAS WITH HIS MISTRESS PLAYING SEX GAMES. BODYGUARDS SPARED AS WAS THE MISTRESS. HE HAD TO PAY FOR HIS BOMBING SINS. POLICE ADVISED ONLY MOMENTS AGO. THANKS FOR YOUR SUPPORT.
> VIGILANTE

Once again, Henderson checked for a sender's address but, as expected, found none. He looked at his watch; 5:33. He had less than thirty minutes. He hit the 'Speaker' button on the phone and punched the extension to the print room. While the line started to ring, he frantically started to type his article.

"Print room!" Ozzie, the supervisor, shouted above the ruckus of the presses.

"Ozzie! Ron!" Henderson yelled with excitement. "Save me a spot on the front page! At the top! No, not a long article. I don't have much information but it's big news! I'll get it to you in fifteen minutes!"

He didn't have time to verify if the story was actually true and he'd get his butt kicked, hard, if it wasn't. But he had followed up with some cop friends about the rape thing and, although they couldn't give him the girl's name, they had confirmed the story. Sure, he was taking a risk but he had a feeling that he could trust the Vigilante. After all, he was the killer's most vocal fan.

\* \* \* \*

At precisely 1:00 p.m., Chris drove into the lot adjoining the Special Homicide Task Force Centre and parked. As he climbed out of his car, he scanned the parking area in search of Eileen or her car but saw neither. He lit a cigarette and leisurely strolled back and forth as he waited for her outside. She would be arriving any minute and he had promised to support her throughout this difficult ordeal.

Early that morning, McCall had called him at home to request that their meeting be delayed a couple of hours. The Vigilante had scored again and he had to look into it. Yes, they were certain that it was him as he had sent the following message on Eazy-Com at 5:17:

> GREETINGS! THERE IS SOME GARBAGE TO PICK UP AT THE EXCELSIOR SUITES, #1219. PLEASE LET THE GIRL OUT OF THE KITCHEN CLOSET. DON'T WORRY, SHE DIDN'T SEE ME! I WOULD NOT LET YOU DOWN! ALWAYS A PLEASURE TO SERVE.
> LATER,
> VIGILANTE

When he had arrived at the office at 8:00, Chris had called Carl Denver and asked him to attempt a trace of the new Vigilante message. Carl had later reported that the trace had, once again, been unsuccessful.

\* \* \* \*

Dave McCall had still been at home when he had learned of the brutal death of Paulo Morretto. He had been in the shower, at around 6:15, when Cathy had come into the bathroom to announce that Tim Harris was on the phone.

Harris was calling from the apartment of one Cynthia Lewis, Morretto's girlfriend. Morretto was dead, the girl was in shock. Yes, definitely the Vigilante. He himself had tipped them off via Eazy-Com. It had happened somewhere around 11:00. No, the girl had not seen him. Bodyguards? Yeah, two of them and they were alive. One was still groggy, probably ether or chloroform. The other, they had found in the trunk of the limo, still parked outside the apartment. He was awake when they had arrived and was banging away and yelling from the inside. He had a nasty bump and gash on the side of his head. A drunk, he had said, was all he had seen. Hard to describe, had a big floppy hat pulled down over his head and shades. Yeah, they would question them further. They had spoken to the doorman at the main entrance but he had not seen anyone but residents enter or leave the building.

McCall, noting the address, had promised to join Harris shortly. He had then called Chris to inform him of the new message.

Upon hearing of the murder, Dave's first thought was of Frank Bakes.

*"No, Frank isn't home. He's helping a friend set up a computer. He said he might be home late."*

That was what Frank's wife had told him when he had called the previous evening, which bothered Dave tremendously. He should have chosen last night to follow Frank.

\* \* \* \*

Nauseous and utterly confused, Carl was not feeling well at all. Chris had called him that morning to inform him of a new message, requesting that he try another trace. Carl had verified and, sure enough, the record was there, same as the last one.

Once again, he had erased the data as there was nothing else he could do. He failed to understand why these transmission records kept appearing. He knew the Eazy-Com system inside out and it just didn't make any sense. Someone had to be playing with his head, playing a dangerous game. Somebody had to know something.

But who, and how? He had always been careful, always covered his tracks. He had **never** made a mistake, of that he was certain. So how could anybody know about him, about what he did?

Carl had thrown up three times that morning. He was becoming very worried and scared.

\* \* \* \*

McCall stomped back and forth in fury as he stared at the newspaper clenched tightly in his fists.

He had just reached the office after leaving the Morretto murder scene and on his desk was a copy of the **Gazette** boasting the headline.

### MORRETTO SLAIN BY VIGILANTE!!

Not surprisingly, it was the work of Ron Henderson.

"Goddamn little prick!" Dave hissed, trying to control his rage.

The article did not contain much information but what was there was fact. Where did the little sleaze get his information and how did he get it so quickly? Obviously, Dave surmised, somebody from this department had to have leaked the story and he had better not find out 'who' that somebody was.

He would have a serious talk with all of his people before the day was out. They were having enough trouble with this case; they really didn't need to be competing with the Morretto family to find the Vigilante!

Joanne Nelson poked her head through the doorway, interrupting his angry thoughts.

"Chris Barry and Eileen Baker are here," she timidly announced, aware of his mood. "Want me to go get them?"

"No," he barked before allowing an apologetic grin. "Thanks Jo. I'll go."

He was anxious to meet with Eileen to hear what she had to say and prayed that she would provide the much needed break they were looking for. The composite artist he had requested from Central Headquarters was ready and waiting as Dave hoped Miss Baker's visit would result in a viable sketch of their elusive killer. Last of all, he was quite anxious to see what Eileen's reaction would be when she was introduced to Frank Bakes.

Frank had not seemed at all bothered with the fact that Eileen was coming in. Quite the contrary, he had seemed genuinely pleased and excited which had served to comfort McCall to some extent. Maybe it wasn't Frank after all.

Following the customary greetings and offers of coffee, Dave quickly ushered his guests into his office, eager to get to the business at hand. It quickly became evident that Eileen was just as keen to get things over and done with.

She started by reiterating that it had been dark that night and that she had been frightened. She therefore hoped that they weren't expecting miracles.

Since her near rape, over three weeks ago, she had done a lot of thinking about the man who had saved her which had allowed her to remember a few more details about his appearance. McCall suggested that she start with the artist, after which they could chat if she felt up to it.

An hour later, the artwork completed, Chris and Eileen were escorted back to McCall's office. Though on the phone, he waved them in and motioned them to have a seat. After a minute, he completed his conversation and turned his attention to them.

"Sorry," he apologized. "Unfortunately, we're busy, busy, busy."

"No problem," Eileen replied as she handed him a sheet of paper. "As best as I can recall for now, that's your man."

McCall gazed at the color depiction of his adversary. Black baseball cap, very dark sunglasses, dark curly hair, Caucasian, male. Although the sketch was not extremely detailed, for some reason, the face seemed vaguely familiar. He concentrated for a moment, searching his memory, but he couldn't put his finger on it. However, by the same token, he was somewhat relieved. Though it did not outright exclude him as a suspect, the sketch bore little resemblance to Frank.

"You're pretty comfortable with what this looks like?" McCall asked, glancing briefly at Eileen as he spoke.

"Like I said when I got here," she shrugged, "It was dark and I was scared. And I only saw him for a few seconds. Taking that into consideration, yes, I'm comfortable with that drawing."

"Is there anything else you remember?" Dave pressed ahead. "Anything that might help us?"

"No, not really," was Eileen's quick response.

"His voice?" persisted McCall. "His clothes?"

"No, his voice was normal, nothing unusual. He was wearing dark clothes. A short jacket, like a windbreaker or something. Jeans, maybe. You know, not a suit and tie look. Much more casual."

Right on cue, a knock at the door interrupted their conversation and McCall waved in Harris, Nelson and Bakes. He had asked them to wait a few minutes, to let Eileen get comfortable, before joining them.

"Chris, you already know these guys," he said as the three detectives entered the room. "Eileen, I'd like you to meet Joanne Nelson and Frank Bakes. Tim Harris, you've already met."

He waited while she shook hands with each, watching her closely as she greeted Frank. No reaction whatsoever. Feeling better still, he went on.

"These three have been working the Vigilante case since it started back in late December. I just wanted you to meet them, Eileen, as you may be dealing with them in the future."

"Nice to meet you," Eileen politely addressed them before returning her attention to McCall.

"I believe that Chris informed you that I refuse to become the center of attention in this affair, right?" she firmly stated.

"Absolutely!" Dave reassuringly agreed. "I just wanted you to know that I'm not the only person you can contact if you have to."

"I see," Eileen stiffly responded, obviously becoming uncomfortable.

"Well," Chris stood as he spoke. "Unless Eileen has anything else to say, I think that we put her through enough for today. How about it, Dave?"

"I guess you're right," McCall admitted with resignation, recognizing that the girl suddenly felt cornered.

"I agree with both of you," Eileen announced rising to her feet as she looked gratefully at Chris.

"Mademoiselle, gentlemen, then we shall be on our way," Chris stated as he bowed slightly, thus formally ending the meeting.

"I'll be in touch," he added to McCall and they were leaving.

"So, anything?" Frank queried once their guests had left.

"At least, now we've got a picture," Dave answered, handing over the sketch. "It's not a Polaroid but it's the best we've had in seven months."

He gazed at Frank and continued to wonder about him.

\* \* \* \*

Into the parking lot, Eileen grabbed onto Chris' arm.

"Thank-you for getting me out of there! I don't know what I'd have done if you hadn't been with me!"

"I aim to please," he replied with a warm smile. "Anyways, don't thank me too quickly. It's my fault that you're in this mess."

"True," she nodded. "But it's the right thing to do so, thanks anyways."

"That was the deal," he reminded her. "You help me, I help you."

They reached her car and he waited while she unlocked the door which he gallantly opened for her. She slid in to the low seat and he pushed the door shut as she started the engine. A thought suddenly crossed his mind and he tapped in the window to get her attention. She lowered her window, gazing up at him as he spoke.

"By the way, Eileen. That envelope I gave you. It might be a wise idea to get rid of it. Not the kind of documents you want lying around the house."

With a grin, she replied, "I'm way ahead of you, Mr. Barry. I burned everything in the fireplace last night. Not to worry. See ya!"

* * * *

3:32 p.m. Giovanni Morretto shuffled aimlessly in the library of his Pierrefonds residence, a broken man. This was not a time to be working; it was a time to mourn. He was not taking the loss of Paulo well at all and still could not comprehend what had happened, nor could he accept it.

At the age of seventy-two, his health was not at its finest and this recent blow had hit hard. His doctors, family and associates remained quite concerned that he might have another heart attack. Having already suffered three in the last seven years, the doctors had been clear in explaining that the next one would be the last. He was not to get excited for any reason.

Gino and Rupert had just left, looking like sad puppies with their tails between their legs. They had spent the last hour profusely apologizing to Morretto, emphatically explaining how they had been ambushed, how they were not at fault. In response, Giovanni had assured them that he did not hold them responsible for the death of his son.

Perry, Giovanni's under-boss, closed the doors of the library behind the two departing men and turned towards his superior.

"Make sure they've told us everything that could be useful about this Vigilante cocksucker!" Giovanni quietly rasped. "Then, kill them, the stupid fucks! After that, find him. He's got to pay for taking Paulo's life."

## Chapter 20 - Thursday, July 18, 1996

He drove along the now familiar gravel road and slowed to turn into the barely visible opening among the trees. He appreciated the winding pattern of the narrow path as it headed downwards towards the lake and was certain that it had been designed as such for privacy. Coupled with the extreme density of the forest which surrounded him, within seconds, his vehicle was no longer visible from the road above.

After several hundred feet, the trees thinned and he could see the house and the lake ahead. Pulling up in front of the double garage doors of the impressive residence, he turned off the engine and got out.

He was alone, of that, he was certain. The owner only used this place on weekends and during his vacation. He surveyed the area and was quickly satisfied that he would not be disturbed. No other cottages were visible from this spot on the lake. The shoreline formed a small inlet which ended in a natural beach, directly behind the house and both sides of the beach were heavily wooded, making this a very private place.

Walking to the main entrance, he effortlessly unlocked it and entered, closing and relocking the door behind him. With no time to lose, he scanned the walls of the foyer, looking for the alarm pad. He quickly found it and punched in a four digit code. The red indicator immediately stopped flashing, replaced by a steady green one.

Moving into the house, he proceeded upstairs, studying the layout as he went; bedroom, bathroom, a den of sorts. It was a nice place; lots of space, ample rooms. He returned to the ground floor, examining the comfortable dwelling from where he stood in the living room. This level was open-air, with modern kitchen, dining area and living room all forming a large continuous L.

To his left was a door which opened to the garage; four-wheeler, mini-bike, snow-mobile. He strolled through the kitchen and headed down a spiral staircase to the basement and into a large game room, equipped with a billiard table, entertainment system, bar and easy chairs. Two doors, one on either side of the stairs, opened up to a storage area and a combination laundry/bathroom. A third door, set in the front wall of the basement, left him puzzled.

"Underground cold-room?" he wondered aloud, walking over to investigate.

He turned the knob and pulled, realizing with surprise how heavy the door was. Although, when closed, it looked like any other door, it was actually six inches thick, steel covered and fit with precise rubber insulation on all sides.

"Wow!" he breathed softly, looking through the doorway.

It was not a cold-room. Ten feet wide and eight feet high, the tunnel stretched horizontally about 150 feet deep. A wire cable, mounted on a pulley system, lined the complete length of the tunnel's ceiling. A folding counter blocked the access, six feet past the door. Cases mounted on the walls on either side of him housed a rather impressive collection of automatics, semi-automatics, rifles and handguns. The man had a private shooting range!

Heading back upstairs, he took one last look around before leaving, making sure he had properly memorized the layout. He left the house as he had come in, careful to re-arm the alarm and lock the door.

As he drove back up the path to the road, he thought approvingly about the house he had just visited. It was a nice place, secluded and that shooting range; that could come in very handy.

## Chapter 21 - Friday, July 19, 1996

3:15 p.m. Although nothing had really changed yet, McCall was encouraged with the recent developments in the case. Copies of his artist's rendition of the Vigilante had been made and distributed to all the precincts in the city and surrounding suburbs. He and Harris had met with Gino and Rupert the preceding afternoon and though Morretto's goons had not been much help, at least when Rupert had seen the sketch, he had agreed that it might be the guy.

Seated in his office, Dave was contemplating on whether or not to release the sketch to the media when his phone rang.

"McCall, Homicide."

"Lieutenant McCall, Lieutenant Honer from the Stanton station in Westmount."

"What can I do for you?" asked McCall.

"I may have something of interest for you," Honer replied. "We busted a bunch a kids this afternoon, drinking and smoking dope in King George Park. They were young, twelve, thirteen, so we hauled them all in to give them a scare. We had them broken up two by two in a few rooms, making them sweat, interrogating them. I start talking to two of them and they're really shitting in their pants. One of them suddenly breaks down and blurts out to his friend, 'We should have listened to that cop the night Zack died!' So I ask, 'Zack who?' and he says, 'Zack Roberts'. Then, I ask, 'What cop?' and he comes up with a story about a cop, gold shield, who had stopped them on the street, just after ten, the night Roberts got whacked. Cop took away their drugs and made them promise never to do it again. Now, the thing is, we had nobody in that area that night. That's a quiet neighbourhood. We'll have a patrol car do the streets every few hours, maybe, but not a detective roaming around."

"Could it have been a cop going home?" asked McCall, intrigued.

"Checked our records," responded Honer. "None of our guys live here. Can't afford it. I didn't check with Personnel at Headquarters but I doubt any cop would be living in this area. This is rich city."

McCall made no comment.

"Anyways," continued Honer. "It might be nothing, but I thought you might want to talk to these kids. There might be some connection with your case."

"You still got the kids there?" enquired McCall, holding the phone with his shoulder as he fumbled into his jacket.

"Yes sir! And they're not going anywhere until we say so. We want to make sure they never smoke a joint again!"

"Give me half an hour and I'll be there. Thanks, Lieutenant."

He hurried out of his office, calling out to Joanne on the way.

"Yeah, boss?" she turned to him.

He hesitated then replied, "Never mind. I got an errand to run. I'll be back in a couple of hours. Later."

It was best that he go alone. He had not spoken to anybody about Frank yet and Frank still wasn't in the clear.

\* \* \* \*

Frank Bakes' childhood had not been easy. Life at home had been difficult, with his mother working long hours at the local supermarket, mostly to support her boyfriend's alcohol habit. They had lived in the tough neighbourhood of St-Henri and Frank had learned early on how to take care of himself.

It was during his last year of high school that he had decided he wanted to become a cop and his application to the programme had been accepted. While he was completing his last year of college, he had met his wife-to-be, a rich girl. They had married during his first year on the force.

To date, Frank had been content with his life. He enjoyed being a cop, had his computers to play with and, thanks to ample old money investments from his wife's side of the family, was able to afford the finer things in life. He also had his secret pastime to keep him busy and, until recently, he had been certain that nobody was aware of that.

Throughout the week, Frank had continued to get that strange feeling from McCall and his uneasiness had grown. He had reviewed conversations they'd had, things they had done, meetings they had attended, looking for something he might have said or done wrong. He could find nothing.

He had been tempted to go to McCall and ask him flat out what the problem was but he hadn't for fear that Dave might tell him. And though he worried that McCall might know something, Frank couldn't figure out how that could be possible. He was always so careful.

He tried to convince himself that if Dave had any knowledge of his activities, he would have confronted him by now. However, he knew that his boss was first and foremost a good cop whose primary goals were stopping crime and getting justice. This being the case, Dave would only come forth once he had solid proof against him which would result in criminal charges, no more career....

He shuddered at the possibilities. His anxiety continued to increase.

\* \* \* \*

McCall had questioned the two kids at the Stanton station but they had not been able to tell him much about the 'cop' who had stopped them the night Zack Roberts had been murdered.

They had not seen his face as he had stayed behind them the whole time, insisting that they not turn around. Yes the shield and I.D. card had looked real. Yes, it was a gold shield. No, they did not remember the name on the card. They had been scared as hell.

McCall had taken advantage of the opportunity to give the boys a twenty minute lecture about drugs, addiction, prison and death, then thanked Honer for his help and left.

As he climbed into his car to head back downtown, he forced himself to think about Frank for a moment and immediately felt a burning queasiness in the pit of his stomach.

Frank lived in Westmount in this very neighbourhood.

\* \* \* \*

6:05 p.m. Carl's fear continued to increase on a daily basis. Highly nervous and edgy, he was holed up in his office, behind locked door where he worked furiously at the keyboard, cursing impatiently under his breath at the milliseconds required for the Pentium processor to execute his commands. A few more keystrokes and he was done.

With tonight's scam, he now had $3.8 million in the Cayman account. His goal was five million and he prayed he could make it but knew he would have to hurry. Soon, real soon, he would have to cease his activities and disappear because he was convinced someone was onto him. There simply was no other explanation.

He lit a cigarette, inhaling the smoke deeply in an effort to calm his frazzled nerves. After a moment, feeling a little more relaxed, he turned off his computer for the night. He was happy to get out of there and hoped that he could get his mind off things enough to enjoy his evening.

\* \* \* \*

9:15 p.m. McCall stopped the rented car a half dozen houses away from that of Frank Bakes, his sixth parking spot on the street over the last three hours.

This was crazy. He couldn't be constantly watching Frank single-handedly, yet, he was not willing to speak to anybody about his doubts until he was relatively certain that Frank was involved.

Wearily, he glanced at his watch again. 9:20. That was it. It was Friday, after all, and he did have a life besides his job. He started the engine and headed for home.

\* \* \* \*

9:30 p.m. He entered the den where he found Sandy curled up comfortably on a couch, reading a book.

"You going out?" she asked, looking up from her reading.

"Yeah, just for a bit," he answered, bending over to kiss her on the cheek.

"Coming home late?" she enquired.

"No, my dear," he replied. "I just have a little situation to resolve. I'll be back before midnight."

"Good," she approved. "I rented 'The Client' this afternoon. We can watch it when you get back?"

"Consider it a date!" he agreed.

There was nothing like their Friday nights together to rid him of the week's accumulated stress.

"Be careful, O.K.?" she quietly pleaded as he left the room.

Stopping in the doorway, he turned back and gazed at her with a gentle smile.

"All the time!" he promised.

\* \* \* \*

As is often the case with sensational news, the story had received extensive media coverage at the time the events had occurred. As is usually also the case however, the news had quickly grown old and the press and population had moved on to other scandals, forgetting about Margaret Slater and her abusive landlord, Peter Myers.

As the reporters had recounted, Mrs. Slater, a 72 year old widow, had been experiencing a number of problems with her apartment. The heating was inadequate, the wiring faulty and the plumbing in major need of repair. Several steps of the staircase leading down to her basement flat were broken, the wood having rotten through.

She had brought these problems to the attention of the owner and landlord, Peter Myers, on many occasions. On each of her visits, he had responded by verbally abusing and threatening the old woman. Finally, she had had enough and had submitted a formal complaint to the Rental Board.

Myers had been furious and had called Mrs. Slater, requesting that she come to his apartment to discuss the issue. Unfortunately, she had complied and, upon reaching the sixth floor, Myers had been waiting for her.

For starters, he had slapped the old woman in the face, delivering a blow of such force that it had broken her jaw. The impact had caused her to fall and tumble head over heels down the stairs to the landing below. Not yet satisfied, the enraged landlord had come after her. After kicking her several times, he had picked her up and literally thrown her down the next flight of stairs.

Thankfully, having heard the commotion, other occupants of the building had come out of their apartments and subdued Myers while someone called the police.

Mrs. Slater had been taken to the hospital with a slew of injuries; internal bleeding, a shattered jaw, cracked ribs, a broken arm, two broken legs and a hip fracture. Two months later, she remained in the hospital, in serious condition and the doctors were quite certain that she would never walk again. At her age, bones did not mend well.

Myers had quickly been arrested and arraigned. However, due to the over-crowding of the prisons and courts, his trial had not been scheduled to take place for many months. Since he had no previous record and his sole source of income was his apartment block, which he had inherited upon his father's death, the court was confident that Myers would not be in a hurry to disappear. He had therefore been released, without bail, on his own recognizance.

Due to his rather vile temperament, Peter Myers did not have many friends, which suited him fine. He didn't particularly like people to begin with and much preferred to be alone. His favourite pastimes were drinking beer and watching television, both of which he was practicing around 10 o'clock on Friday evening when someone knocked at the door of his apartment.

"What the fuck now!" he slurred as he dragged himself out of his easy-chair.

Taking a moment to steady himself, he was into his sixth beer since finishing dinner, he staggered uncertainly to the door. He opened it to find himself face to face with stranger, wearing a baseball cap and sunglasses.

"Whatta ya want?" he snarled angrily at the man.

The visitor grinned at him for a moment without saying a word then punched Myers square in the face, hard, with a leather gloved hand.

Casually, he glanced down the hallway in search of witnesses, but saw none. Satisfied, he entered the apartment and, after shoving Myers' legs out of the way with his foot, closed the door behind him.

The blow had knocked Myers unconscious for a few minutes and when he came to, his first realization was extreme discomfort. Lying on his side on the hardwood floor, his ankles and wrists were bound and had been pulled together behind his back. Something had also been stuffed into his mouth. His face felt wet and when he rubbed his chin on his shoulder, he left blood on his t-shirt.

Raising his head as best he could, he saw the man who had hit him, standing behind the couch, calmly flipping through a magazine.

Detecting movement, the intruder peered down at him and said, "Oh good, you're awake. I was hoping that you wouldn't sleep all night. I don't want to get home too late."

He strolled over nonchalantly to where Peter lay on the living room floor, gazing down at him with an amused smile.

"I hope you'll forgive me for tying you up and gagging you like I did," he politely apologized. "I realize that it's unpleasant. However, I have learned from experience that these things are necessary. It makes my job so much easier without the fighting back and screaming. You understand, don't you?"

Peter stared up at the intruder, sweat streaming from every pore on his body.

The man calmly continued. "I read an article about poor Mrs. Slater in the paper a little while back, and I must tell you, Peter, frankly, I was shocked! What you did was not very nice. Nope, not nice at all. I hear that she'll never walk again."

He paused to light a cigarette, playfully flicking the match at Myers. "In addition, one of her ribs apparently punctured a lung. Doctors still aren't sure if she's going to make it. Poor Mrs. Slater. Don't you agree, Peter?"

He watched Myers in silence for a moment, concentrating on finishing his cigarette before going on.

"Tell me, Peter? Did you ever fall down a flight of stairs? Or better yet, did you ever fall off a balcony from the sixth floor?"

Myers' eyes widened with fear but the gag, unfortunately, did not permit him to respond to the man's questions.

"I didn't think so," the man said, nodding knowingly. "There's no time like the present, don't you agree?"

He strolled over to the patio door and stepped out onto the balcony. Tossing his cigarette butt, he watched its glow drop six storeys to the paved parking lot below. Carefully, he examined the area behind the building for any signs of human activity but saw none. Satisfied, he returned to the living room.

"Time to go!" he announced, bending over his trussed up victim.

Peter began struggling as best he could as his assailant tried to grab him, adding difficulty to the latter's task. Stepping back, the man stared down at Myers with a look of exasperation.

"Now, Peter, you're being difficult!" he scolded. "We're not going to get anywhere with that kind of attitude!"

Pulling his leg far back for maximum force, he then swung it forth, kicking Peter hard in the abdomen, knocking the wind out of him. Meeting no resistance this time, he picked up his helpless victim, flung him over his shoulder and carried him out onto the balcony.

"Say bye-bye, Peter," he murmured softly before tossing Myers over the railing to his death, six storeys below. The only sound was a dull thud.

He returned inside and recuperated his burnt match from the floor. One could never be too careful. Following a quick self-examination for blood stains, none found, he left the apartment, making his way to the ground floor and to the mini-van parked two blocks away.

He would definitely have to send a message to the cops for this one. He wanted the credit for a job well done.

### Chapter 22 - Saturday, July 20, 1996

Gino and Rupert lazed comfortably in the rear of the well equipped fishing boat while Perry expertly piloted the craft along the small winding river.

They had had a meeting with Perry and Giovanni Morretto the previous afternoon to once again review the events surrounding Paulo's murder. Morretto had been insistent for details on the drunk's appearance as he had vowed to catch the heartless animal who had murdered his son. If at all possible, Giovanni intended to take the killer's life himself.
At the end of their meeting, Giovanni had suggested that Gino and Rupert take a couple of days off to relax. They had been through a lot that week, deserved the break and he had graciously offered the use of his fishing cottage, north of Sept-Iles; Perry would take them up there in one of the company planes.
The two goons had gladly accepted their boss' generous invitation, pleased that he did not hold them accountable for the death of his son.

The narrow river suddenly widened and they found themselves on a small lake in the middle of the wilderness. Perry cut the powerful engines and tossed the anchor overboard.
"Welcome, my friends, to the best goddamn fishing spot in all of North America!" he announced, beaming at his two companions.
Gino and Rupert gazed in awe, impressed by the natural beauty which surrounded them.
"Real, real nice!" Rupert softly commented as he admired the scenery. "Peaceful. Definitely a place to relax."
"Absolutely!' Perry enthusiastically agreed. "Nobody around for miles. Ain't a soul that will disturb us out here!"
Returning to the front of the craft, he pulled out a cooler from one of the storage bins.
"Anyone for a beer?" he called over his shoulder.
"Sure! Great!" his buddies accepted.
From the cooler, he extracted a revolver and turned back to face the two men.
"This is what happens when you fuck up on the job, boys," he calmly informed them before pulling the trigger, shooting each man twice in the head.

* * * *

Chris lounged by the pool, sipping a cold rum & Coke while reviewing a printout he had produced the previous afternoon. The report was a complete listing of the activities which had taken place on a selected number of PCs at CSS since he had started monitoring them.

Although much of it, being in computer code, would require some deciphering, he was knowledgeable enough to get an idea of the work which had been done. That is to say, when it was work! It never failed to amaze him how naive these incredibly intelligent employees of his could be sometimes.

Day after day, they designed sophisticated computer systems, the purpose of which was to track transactions, time data transmissions, measure efficiency; in short, record a user's every move. Yet, they never seemed to realize that they could be monitored by a similar system. Recipes, personal letters, financial records, computer games and various other non-business activities seemed to occupy at least a portion of their daily schedules. He would have to have a chat with his troops in the near future.

He had just had the time to scan a half dozen pages of the thick report when he felt a hand clutch the back of his neck.

"I thought we had a deal!" his wife growled scoldingly, tightening her grip as she spoke.

"What?!" Chris exclaimed, feigning innocence.

"Weekdays are the time to work, weekends are the time to play!" she reminded him.

Tossing the report into his open briefcase, he jumped to his feet and replied, "O.K., let's play!" before taking her hand and leading her back into the house.

### Chapter 23 - Sunday, July 21, 1996

"Nice shot!" praised Chris, watching the ball sail perfectly straight down the fairway, some 225 yards.

"I practice when I get a chance," was McCall's modest reply.

"That's strange," Chris replied, puzzled. "I thought that the official pastime for your kind was pigging out on doughnuts!"

"Screw yourself, sir!" Dave politely responded.

It was 7:12 a.m. and still fairly quiet at the St-Isidore Golf Club, where McCall was a member. He had called Chris the previous evening to invite him for a round of golf but, more so, for some conversation.

"Any further progress on the case?" Chris questioned as they walked along the fairway towards the green.

"Nope, not really," McCall replied. "Good news is we've now gone over four complete days without our friend acting up. Maybe he's decided to quit and wanted to finish big time with a wise guy like Morretto."

"I hope you're right," said Chris doubtfully. "But he's gone more than four days in the past."

"Yeah, I know," Dave glumly agreed.

They played their shots, both landing on the green, before resuming their conversation.

"Has the sketch helped any?" Chris enquired hopefully, lining up for his putt, going for birdie.

"Not yet. We showed it to one of Morretto's bodyguards. He had gotten a quick look at a drunk who smacked him on the head the night Paulo was murdered. The best he could do was say that maybe, it could be the guy. I'll probably pull the ape back in and put him together with my artist. Just to see what they come up with."

"Wouldn't you want to make the sketch public?" suggested Chris as he removed his ball from the cup. "I mean, there may be somebody out there who would recognize this guy."

McCall putted, making par, then replied. "I've been thinking about that. But I'm not sure if I should, for two reasons. One, there's the possibility that we scare him, which doesn't mean however, that he just quits. He might just become even more careful than he's been so far. Secondly, I wouldn't want him going back to Eileen. As far as we know, she's the only person who's really seen him. I don't want to put her in danger."

"I can't argue with that," said Chris, nodding in agreement. "She's been through too much already."

"So, my friend, that's where we currently stand. Twenty-three murders, hardly a clue and probable Mafia involvement now that Morretto's a victim," stated McCall. "Plus, I've got that son of a bitch reporter, Henderson, who takes pleasure in knocking our efforts every chance he gets while he publicly cheers on a serial killer!"

They walked in silence to the second hole. After both completing excellent drives, Dave spoke up again.

"Just between you and me, I've been looking into something which may relate to the case. I don't have anything concrete enough yet, so I'd rather keep it to myself. It could turn into more than just a lead but I still have some digging to do."

"Remember my offer, Dave," Chris reminded. "If I can give you any 'unofficial' help, let me know."

"I may just take you up on that real soon," McCall admitted, thinking of the difficult task of shadowing Frank solo.

"Seeing as we're vaguely confiding here," announced Chris. "I'll let you in on something too. I've been doing some work on a possible theory. Some quiet systems monitoring on the side. I don't know if it will go anywhere but I'll keep you posted."

They paused to play, McCall hooking into a sand trap, Chris slicing into a pond. They looked at each other and grinned. Golf was a game of concentration.

"Dave, have you ever looked into the possibility that this Vigilante might be active elsewhere, besides Montreal?"

"No, not really," McCall answered, a little surprised. "We do keep tabs of what's going on in other cities, but there hasn't been any pattern anywhere else like we've had here. Why do you ask?"

"Well, it's probably just a coincidence," Chris hesitantly replied. "I certainly wouldn't have even noticed it if I hadn't been involved in this case. While I was in Vancouver two weeks ago, I was watching the news before dinner one evening and they were talking about some guy who had been found dead in Stanley Park. Died from a blow to the head. I remember thinking, 'another one!' before realizing where I was. Like I said, it was probably just a coincidence. I just thought I'd mention it."

"It might be worth looking into, at least a little," McCall thoughtfully commented.

They walked and played in silence for a while, each engrossed in his own thoughts. Chris was thinking of Carl Denver while McCall thought of Frank. Both had been in Vancouver at the time the Stanley Park murder had taken place.

### Chapter 24 - Monday, July 22, 1996

I AM RESPONSIBLE FOR THE DEATH OF PETER MYERS. PLEASE FORGIVE ME FOR MY RECENT VARIANCE IN METHODS OF EXECUTION. I HAVE COME TO REALIZE THAT THE PENALTY MUST FIT THE CRIME. UNTIL THE NEXT TIME.
VIGILANTE

McCall gazed at the message and actually smiled, unable to hold it back. He had to struggle to not like the guy. The Myers case had enraged him when he had read about in the papers a few months ago. The sick bastard had deserved to die.

Leaning back in his chair with his feet on the desk, Dave mulled over a theory which had been slowly simmering in the back of his mind in recent days.

The crimes of some of the Vigilante's victims, such as Paulo Morretto and now, Peter Myers, had been well publicized. However, most of the others who had succumbed by the killer's hand had not been publicly displayed. Some had been in the process of being monitored by the cops but had not been arrested or accused of any crime, at least not currently. Then, suddenly, they were gone, thanks to the Vigilante.

The more McCall looked at this case, the more it became obvious that whoever the perpetrator was, he had to have access to privileged information.

This brought him back to thoughts of Frank. He had not discovered any evidence that concretely linked his subordinate to the murders. However, by the same token, he had not found anything that came close to an alibi during even one of the crimes.

He had tried following him twice so far, with no success, though he regretted not having stayed later on Friday. He might have discovered, once and for all, if Frank was their man.

He would just have to continue tracking him. It was tough, alone, but he still wasn't ready to ask someone else to do it. He still had too much respect for Frank. He would only be able to label Frank guilty when he, himself, was convinced that he was. Until then, this was a personal project.

Picking up the phone, he speed dialled Chris Barry's direct line to ask for a trace on the new message.

\* \* \* \*

Carl was busy analysing the specifications of the new security system for Century Bank when Chris strolled into his office.

"Hey there!" greeted his boss, closing the door before dropping onto one of the chairs in front of Carl's desk.

"Hi, Chris. How's it going?" Carl responded, putting down the specs.

"All right, I guess," replied Chris. "But I just got another call from McCall. The cops received another message for us to trace."

"Again!? Don't you think we're just wasting our time, Chris?" argued Carl, his frustration obvious. "I mean, this will be what, the fifth message we trace on this guy? We got zip with the four others! Why should this one or any others in the future, prove any different? At some point, someone's gonna have to accept that this guy knows what he doing! He's not going to do something stupid like leave his number!"

"I hear what your saying, Carl," Chris patiently replied. "But I also understand that the cops want to catch the guy. Say he starts getting nervous, or over-confident. Say he makes a mistake or decides after half a dozen messages that we've grown tired of tracing him and stops covering his tracks. That's why we have to continue. We have to show that we're smarter than he is."

"You're the boss," Carl replied grudgingly, a touch of sarcasm evident in his tone. "If that's what you want. But I still think that we're giving the cops too much of our time for free!"

"Maybe," Chris answered tightly as he stood to leave. "But until I decide otherwise, humour me!"

'Fine!' thought Carl angrily as he watched his superior walk out. 'I'll just keep on erasing the goddamn messages for the next two weeks. After that, I'll be done and gone! Then, whoever is playing these fucking games with me can play with himself!'

\* \* \* \*

Chris returned to his office with Carl and the man's recent change of attitude on his mind.

Ever since they had started working with the cops, Carl had been acting strangely. Could it be possible that the firm's top development analyst had something to hide? Obviously, these Eazy-Com tracings did not please him and he **had** been in Vancouver when that murder had taken place. It was much too early to paint a solid case but a number of pieces were starting to fit.

"Soon, very soon," Chris decided. "I will have to start looking into what dear old Carl is doing with his PC!"

\* \* \* \*

Like any respectable high ranking member of an organized crime family, Perry had more than his fair share of reliable police contacts. Therefore, not much effort had been required to obtain details on the progress and leads in the Vigilante case, which, to date, did not amount to very much.

The killer had sent a few untraceable messages through some computer network but these Perry was not overly interested in. The other lead the cops had however, seemed to hold more promise.

This Vigilante had apparently come upon a rape in progress a month earlier and had done in the two horny idiots. Of course, he had let the girl go.

With a little encouragement, Perry had managed to convince one of his cop friends to come up with a name. Eileen Baker. His friend had also given him a color copy of a composite sketch, the result of Baker's description of her saviour.

Seated in the comfort of his lavish office at Morretto Construction headquarters, Perry smiled as he scanned over Baker's data sheet. He didn't understand why the public complained about lack of results with the city's finest. As far as he was concerned, the cops did an excellent job; and made his life so much easier.

He promised himself to drop in on Miss Baker in the very near future.

\* \* \* \*

Ron Henderson was in heaven. Thanks to the help of his new friend, the Vigilante, his investigative tasks as a reporter had become so much easier in recent weeks.

He had to admit that the first message had frightened him a little. Sometimes these wackos could be extremely sensitive and come after you if you pissed them off and, in his line of work, pissing somebody off was a simple and common occurrence. However, his follow up story about the rapists seemed to have pleased the Vigilante and had apparently resulted in the latter becoming his buddy.

His editor had been somewhat worried with the article about Morretto's death, because Ron had not even gone to the scene. Ron had lied to reassure him, promising that he had solid sources with the police and that the story was legitimate. It had, in fact, turned out to be just that. The Vigilante had played straight with him.

Then this morning, while sitting in his cubicle, the PC had beeped, indicating an Eazy-Com message. It had been from his friend again.

Some guy by the name of Peter Myers was dead. Yeah, Ron had heard about that over the weekend. Some sleazy slumlord that had beat up a tenant awhile back. So the Vigilante had been the cause of death; Myers' penalty for harming an old woman; an eye for an eye.

Once again, the message had indicated that this was an exclusive, in exchange for his support. He, Ron Henderson, had unofficially become the Vigilante's press secretary, a role which he was truly starting to enjoy.

He finished typing the last lines of his latest masterpiece, his article on Myers, which would be on the front page of tomorrow's paper.

He was becoming the media envy of the city.

* * * *

Sandy was off to a self-defence class sponsored by the university, the type of activity he definitely approved of. He only wished that all the good people of this world could know how to adequately defend themselves while the criminals didn't. Then they'd really teach the bastards a lesson.

While he waited for Sandy to return, he kept himself busy completing his research on Gregory O'Shea, an upcoming prospect. O'Shea was employed by a major arms manufacturer whose principal client was the military.

He had learned of Mr. O'Shea by chance, from yet another prospect that he had handled several months ago, some punk gang member. The punk had had some extraordinary weaponry, one piece of which he had used in the drive-by shooting of a member of a rival gang.

Unfortunately, the foreseen target had not been the only victim of this act of violence. Sylvie Theriault, a young woman of twenty-three and soon to be mother of twins, had been standing on the balcony of her first floor apartment, waiting for her husband to come home from work. Three bullets from the automatic weapon had strayed and hit Sylvie, taking her life before her falling body landed in the rocking chair behind her. It was specifically for this reason that the punk had become a prospect.

He had gotten together with the punk, his purpose being twofold. Obviously, the scum-bag had to pay for his crime. The death of Sylvie Theriault could not go unpunished, that was a given. However, it was also quite important to determine the source of the weapons. The traffic of such killing instruments could not be allowed to flow freely on the streets.

Hoping to have his life spared, the punk had eagerly supplied a name when asked about the source of the arms. Unfortunately for the punk, his cooperation had not changed his destiny.

So all he had had to start off with was a name. Gregory O'Shea. But with a name and his computer, he was usually able to find vast quantities of valuable information, which had been the case with O'Shea. Driving records, tax returns, employment history, financial data, nothing was inaccessible with today's communication networks.

O'Shea's employment file indicated that he was Manager, Warehousing and Distribution with an annual salary of $68,000. Yet, in recent years, his net worth had grown to that of someone with several times those earnings.

His investment portfolio had ballooned quite extensively and eighteen months earlier, he had acquired a fairly large tract of land on which he had subsequently built a luxurious second home. Records showed that since, O'Shea had purchased a variety of expensive furniture, electronic equipment, a boat and several other recreational vehicles.

When he had tapped into O'Shea's PC at home, he had hit pay dirt, uncovering vast amounts of data confirming the man's illicit arms trafficking activities; records of transactions, customer names, delivery dates... He had even found the access codes for the security systems of the man's residences and place of employment.

Mr. O'Shea was a very methodical, well-organized person. He also wasn't very bright.

Had O'Shea been working for an electronics manufacturer, looting VCRs, or for an auto parts distributor, stealing mufflers, he would not have bothered with him. But O'Shea was stealing highly sophisticated and destructive arms and selling them for a profit. These weapons were subsequently being used to commit atrocious crimes; robberies, muggings, murders; the list went on and on. The Theriault family was still suffering greatly because of these tools of destruction.

Gregory O'Shea was not a good man and he would have to pay for his actions.

## Chapter 25 - Tuesday, July 23, 1996

### VIGILANTE FINDS SLUMLORD MYERS GUILTY

McCall stared at the headline, dumbfounded. Once again, Henderson's article accurately portrayed the facts of a Vigilante murder.

Over the weekend, the death of Peter Myers had been reported by the media, but no reference had been made to the Vigilante. Fact was, nobody had known that he was responsible. Following the 'chat' which McCall had had with his team the previous Wednesday, he was **convinced** that this information had not leaked from his department. His cops weren't that stupid, which could only mean one thing; Henderson had to have some kind of connection with the Vigilante. For all McCall knew, **Henderson** might be the Vigilante! The fool rooted for the assassin well enough in his goddamn columns!

He would have to invite Ron Henderson over for coffee and a little conversation to get to the bottom of this.

\* \* \* \*

Eileen Baker left the elevator and headed across the underground parking towards the section reserved for the management of Griffiths & Donaldson. As she approached her car, she noticed and admired an unfamiliar black Mercedes stretch-limousine parked in the spot next to hers.

Reaching the two vehicles, she squeezed into the tight space between them while digging in her purse for her keys. The driver's door of the limousine suddenly opened, blocking her path, and a large man climbed out. At the same moment, the rear door on the opposite side of the limo also opened, and a second man emerged, quickly circling the large automobile and coming up behind her.

"Good afternoon, Miss Baker," the second man politely greeted her. "Sorry to bother you. I was wondering if I could speak to you for a moment?"

"Who are you?" she asked uncomfortably. "How do you know my name?"

"I am a close associate of Giovanni Morretto," the impeccably dressed man answered, his tone friendly.

His response did little to reduce her unease. It was public knowledge that Morretto headed a major crime syndicate.

"You can call me Perry," the man continued suavely. "Now, you may have heard that Mr. Morretto has recently lost his son, Paulo. A great shame, you know, and Mr. Morretto is very saddened by his loss. He does not understand why somebody would do this to his son. Paulo was a little rough around the edges but never did anyone any harm."

He paused for a few seconds, gazing at her intently, his smile warm, yet sad, but his eyes cold and hard. "Mr. Morretto would like to meet with the man who did this. He would like the man to explain why he committed such an atrocious act."

"I-I'm sorry," Eileen stammered, her voice shaking. "I-I don't see how I can help you. Please, I have to go!"

"I understand that you saw the very same man not too long ago, Miss Baker," Perry reminded her, the slightest touch of menace to his voice, the smile cooler. "By chance, I happened to see the composite sketch which was made according to the description **you** gave. I'm sure that if you thought about it a little harder, you would remember more about this man. Am I right?"

"Please, believe me!" she begged, starting to panic and close to tears. "I've told the police what I could. You saw the picture. That's all I know! Please leave me alone!"

"I understand that you might feel for this man," continued Perry. "He did save you from an ugly situation. However, he has done something terribly wrong, this murdering of Paulo. I must insist that you help us find him."

"I-I swear, I can't help you!" Eileen sobbed, trembling with fear.

"I'll tell you what," suggested Perry, his smile turning to a sneer. "Why don't you think about this a little? I'm sure that if you do, you will realize that helping us is really the right thing, the **only thing** to do! Think about it, Miss Baker. I'll be in touch with you in a couple of days. By then, I'm **convinced** that you will remember more about the man."

He reached up and stroked her cheek softly, once. "Later, Eileen."

With that, he turned on his heel and returned to the still open rear door of the limo, disappearing inside while his thug climbed back in behind the wheel.

The engine roared and the car left with a slight squeal of its tires, leaving Eileen standing there, crying, frightened and helpless.

\* \* \* \*

12:17 p.m. Chris and Carl were seated at the conference table in the former's office, reviewing the conversion schedule which had been established for Century Bank. Sonia poked her head in the doorway, interrupting their discussion.

"Sorry to bother you, guys. Chris, Eileen Baker on the line for you. She seems upset."

"I got it, thanks," Chris acknowledged, going for the phone on his desk. "Hi, Eileen. Is everything alright? When? Where are you now? O.K. Listen, stay there. I'll be right over. Give me a minute to call McCall and then I'm on my way. Sure, just calm down. Everything's O.K. They just wanted to scare you, that's all. See you soon."

He cut the line and hit the speed dial identified 'McCall' on the phone, waiting impatiently for the connection.

"Hi, Dave? Chris. I'm really glad you're in. Yeah, I'm fine but Eileen Baker just got a real scare. Somebody from the Morretto family, Perry, he called himself, just had a chat with her in the parking garage at work. Threatened her if she didn't help them find the Vigilante. Yeah, he left, but promised to come back in a couple of days. Oh yeah, she's shaken up alright! I'm going over there right now. She's back in her office. Think you can do something as far as protection goes for a bit? O.K. great! Thanks. Talk to you soon."

He hung up the phone and noticed Carl picking up the various documents spread out on the conference table.

"Sorry, Carl," he apologized. "This is a bit of an emergency. We'll finish tomorrow, all right?"

"No problem, boss," Carl understandingly replied as he headed towards the door. "We were pretty much done anyways. I'll get the final copy together and see you with it once it's complete. You seem to have some bigger things to do right now."

"Thanks," said Chris. "I'll see you later."

He followed Carl out of the office, stopping only long enough to tell Sonia not to expect him back then headed for the downtown headquarters of Griffiths & Donaldson.

\* \* \* \*

3:36 p.m. Chris, along with McCall, Frank Bakes and of course, Eileen were scattered around the living room of the latter's home. She was much calmer now, the two double Caesars no doubt having helped to a certain extent.

"They were just trying to scare you," McCall attempted to reassure her. "To see if you knew more. But just in case, I'll have two cops keep an eye on you for the next few days, O.K.?"

Eileen nodded and stated, "I think I'm going to take a few days off and stick around here."

"Good idea," McCall approved. "That'll be even safer for you and tougher for those schmucks if they do decide to try something."

"Patrol car's here," announced Bakes from his perch by the window. "I'll go fill them in and be on my way, unless you still need me?"

"No problem. Go," McCall replied. "Thanks Frank."

"Take care of yourself, Eileen," Bakes encouraged, winking at her as he moved towards the door. "You'll see, everything's gonna be fine. Those guys won't bother you, especially if we have anything to say about it!"

She smiled gratefully at him as he left.

"Well, unless you want me to stick around," said McCall, standing, "I'll get out of your hair and let you relax."

"No, I'm fine, Dave. Really," Eileen replied. "I probably overreacted."

"Nothing doing!" McCall shot back. "You reacted fine, Eileen. Don't make it like you did something wrong here. These wise guys are the guilty ones. Can't even pick on someone their own size! Take care of yourself and, remember, there'll be two men here until I say otherwise. If you need something, feel free to ask them and if they can't help you, call me. Later."

She watched McCall leave and then looked up at Chris.

"You can go too, Chris. I've taken up enough of your time."

"You sure you're going to be O.K.?" he asked, worried. "I can call my wife and have her come join us for dinner if you want. I'm sure you'd love her. I do!"

"No, I'm all right," Eileen laughed. "Go. You've done enough already. I'm fine. Really!"

"Listen," Chris thoughtfully suggested. "If you want, you can spend a few days at our place until this all blows over. My wife's at home and you two could get to know each other. The pool's there, complete gym downstairs, everything you'd need to relax."

"Maybe," Eileen replied, her expression brightening. "I'll think about it. It might do me some good. Thanks."

"My pleasure," Chris smiled. "When I told you that I'd be there for you, I meant it. Anyways, you agreed to help so it's the least I can do. I'm sure that Dave's boys out there will be happy to drive you over. Let me know what you decide."

"You go on home and I'll call you after dinner."

"It's still early," Chris grinned. "You have more than enough time to pack a bag if you want. I'll wait for you."

"You sure it's no trouble?" she asked. "I don't want to impose."

"Not a chance. I swear."

"Give me fifteen minutes," she decided, scrambling towards the stairs. "I don't know what I'd do without you!"

"Probably lead a quieter life!" he chuckled in response.

* * * *

9:42 p.m. Giovanni and Perry lounged comfortably in the overstuffed leather armchairs in the library of the Morretto home. As he enjoyed his daily two ounce ration of Chianti, the old man fondly reminisced his departed son's youth, grateful for Perry's sympathetic ear.

The phone on the desk rang, interrupting the grieving father's nostalgic chatter. Perry started to rise from his seat but his boss waved him back down.

"Sit, sit," rasped Giovanni, standing stiffly. "I need the exercise. You don't."

Shuffling over to the desk, he noticed, with some concern, that the call was coming in on his private line. Not many people had, much less used that number.

Gesturing Perry over, he hit the speaker button and barked, "Morretto."

"Mr. Morretto?" the unfamiliar voice questioned.

"Who is this?" Giovanni demanded.

"This is the famous Vigilante," the voice calmly replied.

"You goddamn cocksucking motherfucker!!" Morretto screamed at the speaker, dropping heavily into the chair behind the desk.

"Now, now, Mr. Morretto," the voice said soothingly. "You mustn't get excited at your age. Bad for the heart. Now, listen carefully. I have something to say."

"Go ahead, talk, you lousy piece of shit!" Morretto hissed. "You ain't gonna be talking for very long! You're gonna die, you bastard!"

"Fine," the voice continued. "I'm going to die. So let me have my final words. Is your friend Perry there, Mr. Morretto?"

"Yeah, I'm here," Perry answered quietly from where he stood by the desk.

"Good," said the voice. "Because I wanted you to hear this too so listen carefully. Now, I admit, I killed Paulo but, I did it for a reason. Paulo took the lives of some innocent people and was getting away with it. In my book, that's not right so I acted accordingly. You don't agree with what I did? Fine. Then kill me. But leave the girl alone. She was nearly raped a month ago. That's how she was lucky enough to get to see me for three seconds in the dark. Then the cops harassed her. Now you guys. Come on! Lay off her! She's a victim."

"What's it to you, anyways?" Perry taunted. "You scared cuz she's gonna help us find you? And how do you know we spoke to the girl in the first place?"

"How do you think I got to where I am today, asshole?" the voice quietly enquired. "We all have our connections, Perry. All I'm saying is leave the girl alone. Trust me gentlemen, I'm serious."

"And what happens if we disobey?" Morretto sneered mockingly.

"First," the voice replied, "I will kill Perry. Then, if you persist, Giovanni, I will kill Maria."

"My daughter!" screamed Morretto, throwing his wine glass across the room. "You fucking low-life, I'm gonna kill you!"

"Leave the girl alone," the voice repeated slowly, a final warning.

"Mr. Vigilante," stated Perry, his tone deadly. "Prepare to die."

"Sure thing. See ya," the voice replied before the line went dead.

"Kill my daughter!" Morretto raved, pacing stiffly around the room. "I'll personally cut this fucker's balls off and shove them down his fucking throat!"

"Easy, Giovanni," Perry tried to calm his old boss. "Your heart! Don't get excited! Ain't nobody gonna touch Maria or anybody else. Don't worry. I've got things under control. This guy's a fucking coward, he ain't gonna mess with us. I'm gonna take care of him. Relax."

Morretto shuffled slowly back to his armchair and unsteadily sat back down.

"You better be right, Perry," he warned, his gravelly voice shaky. "You better be right! Maria ain't never done nothing to nobody! She doesn't deserve to die. Who does this fucking bastard think he is!?"

"Don't worry, Giovanni," Perry repeated soothingly. "Nothing's gonna happen to Maria. Trust me, all right?"

"Yeah, yeah," Morretto yielded, looking up fondly at his right-hand man. He didn't know what he'd ever do without him.

"Well, I'm gonna go," Perry announced, looking at the time. "Let you get some rest cuz it's getting late. Goodnight, Giovanni, and relax. Don't worry."

"Yeah. Thanks, Perry," Morretto smiled sadly. "Goodnight."

He watched his young assistant strut across the Persian rug which covered the floor of the mammoth room, calling out to him as he reached the heavy double doors.

"Perry. You be careful out there too. This guy may be serious."

"Ain't nothing gonna happen to anybody," the under-boss replied with an assured grin. "**Especially** not to ole Perry!"

With some effort, Giovanni pulled himself out of his chair and slowly plodded to the window, pushing aside the curtain to look out into the night. Outside, Perry hopped down the steps and, with his usual confident stride, briskly crossed the wide parking area to his car of the month, a Nissan 300ZX.

"These young punks with their fancy sports cars," Giovanni chuckled. "Gotta lie down to climb into the thing!"

He heard the engine start and watched as the car rolled down the circular driveway away from the house, slowing as it reached the street. The engine gunned and, as the car veered onto the road, it exploded in a brilliantly massive ball of flame.

For several seconds, Giovanni stared at the blazing wreck in shocked disbelief. He became aware of a ringing sound and realized that it was the phone. Reluctantly, he left the window and slowly, numbly, moved back to his desk where he eased gingerly into his big leather chair.

The phone's insistent ringing continued. As he picked up the receiver, he noticed, somewhat absently, that the call was coming in on his private line once again.

"Hello?" he rasped, softly, wearily.

"I warned you," the voice said quietly. "But you wouldn't listen. Now, do I have your word that you will lay off?"

"Yes," the old man whispered into the phone.

"Good," the voice gently replied. "Then so will I. Goodbye, Giovanni."

The connection broke and the voice was gone. Giovanni laid the receiver down on the desk and silently wept.

## Chapter 26 - Wednesday, July 24, 1996

11:47 p.m. Parked half a block from Frank's house, McCall slumped uncomfortably in his rental, amidst the empty coffee cups and hamburger wrappers and which littered the front seat. A lousy ending to a thoroughly crappy day.

He had started the day early, visiting the West Island residence of Giovanni Morretto, scene of the apparent assassination of Perry Gaglioni, Morretto's 'executive assistant'.

Morretto himself had been outside swearing at the cops, screaming of their incompetence and how all they could do was eat doughnuts with their thumbs up their ass while honest hard-working people were being murdered in cold blood. Eventually, the old man had nearly collapsed and thankfully, a young nurse had coaxed him back into the house.

After leaving the murder scene, he and Harris had spent the better part of the afternoon trying to track down Rupert, one of Paulo's goons, who had seen the drunk on the night of the younger Morretto's murder. However, nobody had seen him or his partner Gino since the preceding Friday.

At five-thirty, he had left the office to sit in his Thrifty special and wait for Frank's departure. Little had he known that Frank had chosen this particular day to work late and had not left the office until 7:00. To add to Dave's displeasure, his subordinate had not driven directly home, but rather, had zigzagged across town, making half a dozen stops along the way to run miscellaneous errands.

An hour after initially reaching his home, Frank had left the house again, with McCall trailing behind him. He had gone to a local convenience store for cigarettes and stopped off at a video rental place, returning with a couple of cassettes. He had now been back for close to two hours.

Weary, stiff and frustrated, Dave started the engine and headed for home, to Cathy.

## Chapter 27 - Thursday, July 25, 1996

Convinced that she was no longer in any danger, McCall had called off the police guard on Eileen Baker. Perry was dead and anyways, Chris had informed him that Eileen was spending a few days at his place with his wife to get her mind off things.

He appreciated Chris' help. Although the man's participation was purely voluntary, he took things to heart and really did whatever he could.

There had been no message, nor any indication from the press, not even Henderson, that Perry's death was the result of the Vigilante's handiwork. But McCall knew that it was. This being the case however, brought forth the unanswered question 'How had the man known?'

As far as Dave was concerned, the only people who had been aware of the specific circumstances surrounding Eileen Baker were Eileen herself, Chris, Frank and himself. They hadn't even told the uniforms who they were guarding Eileen from.

So who could he suspect? Frank? Painfully, Dave was starting to accept that Frank was a real possibility. He hated having to admit it but, he had to stop the Vigilante.

The sudden ringing of the telephone broke into his unpleasant thoughts and he answered to find Eileen Baker on the line.

"Everything all right?" he asked with a sense of urgency.

"Yes, yes," she quickly reassured him.

"Good," Dave replied, relieved. "What can I do for you?"

"Well, I tried to call Chris about this, but he's tied up in a meeting," Eileen began hesitantly. "His wife suggested that I call you directly. Anyways, you **are** a cop and you were very good to me on Tuesday, so I agreed to call you."

"I'm glad to see I'm making progress!" laughed Dave. "What's up?"

"W-well, it might be nothing," Eileen went on, still unsure. "But I've been thinking about that night, when I nearly got raped."

"Yes?" McCall prodded, wondering.

"O.K. Here it goes," Eileen, plunged ahead. "That night, just as I got to the corner of the street where I had parked, I noticed a, a little van kind of thing."

"A mini-van?" suggested McCall.

"Yes. A mini-van. That's what they call them. Anyways, I noticed this mini-van, parking. I remember thinking that this guy was lucky. I had looked for a spot for fifteen minutes before finding the one I had. Anyways, after that, those, those guys showed up and I stopped thinking about parking spots."

"O.K." McCall slowly acknowledged, not sure where this was going. "Is this supposed to mean something?"

"Well, when those guys grabbed me, there really wasn't anybody around," Eileen explained. "We went into the alley and suddenly, there he was. Maybe it was the guy who had parked the mini-van!"

McCall suddenly felt guilty for ever having doubted this wonderful soul.

"Do you remember what kind of mini-van it was, what color, anything?" he asked, trying not to sound too excited.

"I don't know too much about cars, Dave," she admitted. "But I know I've seen that kind of truck before. It's the one that sort of square at the back and steep in the front. You know which one I mean?"

"No, not really," he replied, realizing that this might not be as easy as he hoped.

"Wait!" Eileen suddenly exclaimed. "It's the one that, in the commercial, it goes down the Olympic ski jump! Then it goes back up in reverse. That's the truck I saw!"

"Chevy Astro!" stated McCall with a smile. He liked this girl!

"I guess so," she answered with a shrug in her voice. "I don't know what it's called."

"What about the color, Eileen?" Dave persisted. Maybe they were onto something.

"It was getting dark," she replied. "But I would say it was more of a dark color like brown or burgundy, maybe green. It wasn't white or some other light color."

"This is great, Eileen!" cried McCall. "This could really help! Even if it's not our guy, this might mean another witness. Maybe the guy you saw parking saw somebody or something!"

"Well, I'm glad I can help," Eileen shyly responded. "I'm sorry I didn't think of it sooner, but I've been pretty shaky since then."

"No problem," McCall reassured her. "Better late than never. I'm really happy you called, Eileen."

"Good," she replied, pleased. "I'll be sure to let you know if I think of anything else. Bye."

"Take care, and thanks," said Dave. "Bye."

He hung up the phone, looking happier than a clam. Then, just as quickly, the smile disappeared: Frank Bakes drove a mini-van; a burgundy Chevrolet Astro.

He could no longer afford to take his time with the investigating of his subordinate. He would have to do more about Frank in a hurry.

* * * *

Eileen slowly replaced the telephone receiver in its cradle and sat quietly with a troubled, thoughtful expression.

"What's the matter?" Chris' wife gently asked. "Why the long face?"

"I sorta feel sorry for him. That's all," Eileen replied softly. "I know he deserves to pay for what he's done. Chris convinced me of that. I just feel strange being involved in getting him caught."

"Don't worry about it," encouraged her hostess. "You're doing the right thing."

"I know I am," nodded Eileen with a sad smile.

\* \* \* \*

Ron Henderson fidgeted anxiously as he waited in the reception area of the Special Homicide Task Force Centre. He scowled, again, at the clock on the wall; 1:26. His patience was wearing thin. McCall had said 1:00 and now, the asshole was stalling him. Four more minutes, then he was out of there. After all, McCall was the one who had wished for this meeting, not him.

Dave McCall had called him on Tuesday morning, stating that they needed to have a little chat. When Henderson had enquired as to why, the cop had replied that he wished to discuss some of Henderson's sources of information. The reporter had informed McCall that his sources were confidential and therefore, he had nothing to discuss. McCall had responded with, "Thursday, 1:00 p.m. We'll meet in my office," after which the arrogant schmuck had hung up.

Henderson had seriously considered simply not showing up. However, he remained just a tad uncomfortable with his new found friendship with the Vigilante. After all, the guy killed people, violently, apparently as a hobby. The possibility that such a man was slightly unbalanced did exist. Also, the terms 'accomplice', 'accessory to the crime' and 'obstructing justice', however vaguely, rang in Henderson's mind. Maybe the lieutenant might have something to say that was worth hearing.

"Mr. Henderson!" McCall greeted, approaching his guest with extended hand.

"Lieutenant McCall," Ron coolly replied, rising from his seat.

As they shook hands, Henderson allowed himself to examine his host. He had seen the man in the papers and on the news on several occasions in recent years but the photographs and T.V. screen had not done McCall justice. The cop was definitely younger than he appeared via the media; early thirties, maybe less. And he looked intelligent. He no doubt had to be to have the job he did at his age.

Maybe he wouldn't be such a bad guy. Maybe they would get along.

McCall motioned for his guest to follow, continuing to speak as they went along.

"Sorry to keep you waiting," he apologized, sounding sincere. "We've got a case load that could keep four times as many people busy twenty-four hours a day! Unfortunately, we live in a violent world, Ron."

Stopping at a vending machine, he turned to the reporter. "Coffee?"

"Sure. Black, no sugar."

"You've obviously never had this coffee before!" McCall half-joked.

"You're drinking it at your own risk!" he added, handing Ron a cup of thick black liquid.

They continued on down the corridor and into the young lieutenant's office.

"Have a seat," invited Dave, gesturing to one of the chairs as he closed the door.

"Thanks," accepted Henderson, his tone cool and formal. "Now, what can I do for you, Lieutenant McCall?"

"Let's start by cutting the crap," McCall grinned. "Name's Dave and I'd like you to call me that. If you have no objection, I'll call you Ron."

"Fine by me," Henderson shrugged.

"Now," McCall continued, "I asked you to drop by so that we could play straight with each other. I'm not going to bullshit you and I hope that you don't bullshit me, O.K.?"

"Sounds fair so far," agreed Henderson, starting to believe that he actually **might** like this guy.

"Good," Dave went on. "Now, I may tell you some stuff that I don't want you to talk about. I'm gonna trust you not to use anything I say unless you check with me first. If I say 'No', you don't use it."

The journalist nodded in response as McCall continued.

"I think that you and I will get along fine, Ron. I'm not going to ask you to reveal your sources cuz I realize that you have a job to do. Anyways, with some of the information that you've had recently, it would have been likely that your source was a cop; one of my cops."

He paused for a second before, trying to read something in Henderson's expression but drawing a blank.

"If that had turned out to be the case, I'd have found out without your help and I'd have done some serious ass-kicking! But my cops know that. They're smart so they shut up. So I asked myself, if Ron's not getting his information from my people, where is he getting it from? I thought about it for a while, and I believe I found the answer. It was so obvious, it was funny."

Henderson gazed at McCall with narrowing eyes.

"You want to know where?" taunted McCall.

"Sure! Why not," replied the reporter with an uneasy grin. He certainly wasn't going to say.

"Eazy-Com," stated Dave as a matter of fact.

"Eazy-Com?" repeated Henderson, a well acted expression of puzzlement on his face.

"Eazy-Com," Dave confidently nodded. "You've recently been receiving messages from the Vigilante on Eazy-Com. Do you know why I believe that?"

"Can't say that I do," answered Henderson, suddenly feeling a bit warm. "Why don't you tell me?"

"With pleasure," McCall replied. "I figured, if our killer-friend's been sending **us** messages on Eazy-Com, why can't he be sending someone else messages as well?"

"Well, I'll be damned!" Henderson slowly exclaimed under his breath.

"Remember, Ron. You don't use this. We have a deal."

"Don't worry. You have my word," promised the reporter. "I'm just really impressed that you guys managed to keep this quiet to date. I guess you're all smarter than I've given you credit for!"

"Right up there above reporters!" McCall valiantly rallied. "Now, to date, we haven't been able to trace any of his messages. He erases the path on the network or something like that. I don't really understand computers. What I'd like to do is this. I'd like my computer guy, Chris Barry at CSS, to look into the messages you've received. Just in case our friend didn't consider it necessary to erase the traces of what he sent to you. Do you think we could do that?"

"I guess," Henderson replied. "But I doubt you'll find anything."

"Why is that?"

"I've received three messages so far," explained the journalist. "Normally, when you receive e-mail on Eazy-Com, you can click a 'sender' icon and the sender's address appears. If you want to reply, you just transmit to 'sender'. But, there was no sender address for any of the messages I got."

"I'd like to check anyways," Dave insisted. "Can you supply me with the details on those messages? The dates and times they were sent, what they said, that kind of thing?"

"I-I guess," Henderson hesitantly replied. "I just wouldn't want this guy to be mad at me."

"We're not going to tell him you're helping us!" McCall laughed before becoming serious once again. "Anyways, I'll get a court order if I have to. I'm not going to give up any chance to catch this wacko. He's killed at least twenty-four people so far!"

"I get to use anything else he sends me?" Henderson asked, starting to give in.

"Absolutely," stated Dave. "But, I'd expect you to let me know when he does contact you. Please understand, Ron, right or wrong, he is a killer and we've got to stop him."

"O.K. I'll let you know if he contacts me again," agreed Henderson, beginning to appreciate the true efforts the cops made. "And I'll try to go easier on you guys in the future!"

"Thanks," McCall grinned. "And I'll stop calling you all those names when I read your articles!"

"I'll stay clear of that one!" Ron grimaced as he rose to his feet. "Unless there's anything else, I'd better get going. I'm doing a radio spot at 2:30. Dave, it's been a pleasure and I think we'll get along!"

"Work on this with me, Ron," replied McCall as he stood to shake the reporter's hand. "And when we get the guy, I'll make sure you have some advance warning!"

"Sir, you can count on my support!" Henderson jovially responded.

He liked exclusives.

## Chapter 28 - Friday, July 26, 1996

The verification of the messages sent to Henderson had proved fruitless.

Dave had contacted Chris on the previous afternoon to bring him up to speed on their most recent leads. Chris had already been aware of the mini-van thing; Eileen had told him when he had got home.

He had been happy however, to learn of the messages to the reporter. Maybe their man would have been less cautious when contacting someone other than the authorities.

He had contacted Henderson, who had proved to be quite cooperative and extremely knowledgeable about PCs and networks. Since it was routine stuff anyways and Carl was not in the best of moods lately, Chris had decided to look after these messages himself this time. But the verifications had yielded nothing; the Vigilante had taken no chances. It was clear in Chris' mind that they were dealing with a very intelligent individual.

\* \* \* \*

The Cayman account was up to $4.3 million.

'$700,000 to go!' thought Carl. 'Then we are gone!'

They could look for him all they wanted after that. The world was a big place with many comfortable, sunny little corners in which to relax incognito.

He had informed his wife that they would have to leave soon as things were becoming a little tense. She was worried that he would get caught but he had reassured her that this would not, could not happen. As he had told her many times before, the fear kept him much too alert for anyone to ever catch up with him.

He still hadn't managed to figure out who was on to him but it didn't really matter anymore. Whoever his antagonist was, by the time he showed up, Carl Denver would be long gone. The remaining $700,000 would be collected by the end of next week.

\* \* \* \*

Harris was amazed at how many people owned Chevy Astro and GMC Safari mini-vans. He had asked Reynolds at DMV for a list of such vehicles registered in the province. However, what he had received was more of a book that a list.

Since he had no idea of the plate number or of the year of the vehicle, the best Reynolds had been able to do was a sort by geographic region. Unfortunately, close to half of the province's population lived in the greater Montreal area. Adding to his pleasure was the fact that Harris had no idea what he was really looking for.

With these discouraging bits of information in mind, he slumped down at his desk and commenced the arduous task of reviewing the long alphabetical list of mini-van owners, searching for God knew what.

* * * *

For more years than he could remember, Gregory O'Shea had dreamt of owning a cottage in the wild and, with time, the dream had become an obsession. In fact, his wife had left him several years earlier because he refused to undertake the slightest activity which had a cost attached to it. No vacations, few restaurants, never a show. He had to save for the future. He had to save for his castle up north, his retirement home. She had finally left him, out of frustration and boredom.

Ironically, her departure had marked the beginning of O'Shea's illegal moonlighting activities. He had been sitting in a bar, a real dive, drinking up a storm and had gotten to talking to a couple of rather crude characters about life, his ex, his dreams and his job.

Although simply amused at first by this plain looking man's drunk blabbering, his audience had become quite interested in his job, or more particularly, in the products his employer manufactured. Soon, they had started asking questions about security, ease of access to merchandise and inventory controls. To their surprise and joy, O'Shea had quite openly informed them that, contrary to popular belief, security and control were very low. Sure, the plant was surrounded by barbed wire fences and roaming guards. But like all systems, his employer's had its flaws; many of them.

Pleased to have someone to talk to, O'Shea had gone on to brag about his rather impressive collection of automatic and semi-automatic weapons, none purchased, all simply taken from work. Pulling these out, he had explained, was easy and, balancing inventory numbers in the system was even easier.

When one of his new 'friends' had suggested that they might be interested in buying such weapons, O'Shea had become uneasy, realizing that maybe he had talked too much. But then, the second individual had started highlighting the value of arms on the street and how there was money to be made. Sophisticated weapons such as those O'Shea had described would be worth a fortune. Just his small collection alone could buy him several acres of woodland and probably even cover some of the building costs of the second home he longed for. It was something to think about.

He had thought about it, practically day and night, for a week. He had to consider that, at the age of forty-nine, he was not getting any younger so, the sooner he could build his castle, the more he would benefit from it. In addition, although he already had a fair amount of capital put aside, it was nothing compared to what he could have if he sold a few guns.

Anyways, he had reasoned, if he didn't do it, somebody else would. In fact, he wouldn't be surprised if some of the people he worked with were already doing it. The plant had more than its occasional inventory short.

He had made his decision. He would fulfill his lifelong dream as well as assure his comfort for his golden years. He had returned to the bar, managed to track down his new 'friends' and, he was in business. His initial clients had introduced him to new ones, and so on and, within no time, the cash had been rolling in beyond his wildest expectations.

Now, three years later, his second home sat on the edge of Lake Sawin, a couple of hours north of the city, nestled among the trees of his 10 acre private wilderness. With its 4,500 square feet of living space, the open-air cottage, equipped with all the possible modern conveniences, was much larger than O'Shea actually needed. But this was his dream, his place.

He spent all of his free time there with never the danger of getting bored. During the summer, he fished from his twenty-four foot boat and roamed the woods on his four-wheeler or mini-bike. When winter came, it was time for the snow-mobile and cross-country skiing on and around his property. Best of all however, he could practice his favourite hobby year-round; shooting his precious firearms, in his private shooting range.

Though not an evil man, Gregory O'Shea did not regret what he had done. He realized that distributing the weapons for profit as he had done was both legally and morally wrong. However, he had come to believe that, in the selfish world we live, one had to look out for oneself. This, he reasoned, is what he had done and it had given him his dream; he had his castle.

* * * *

"When are you going to stop?" she questioned with concern, watching him as he dressed.

Sandy was becoming more anxious as time went by. Although she agreed with her husband's activities, her fear that he would get caught had become constant and she could not bear thinking of living without him. She knew that, one day, he would have to quit, but was no longer certain if he actually realized it.

"Soon," he quietly replied. "Real soon."

"You know how worried I get," she insisted. "I don't want anything to happen to you."

"Nothing will," he stated. "That, I promise."

She sat in silence for a moment, wondering if she should persist or let it go. But she knew that his mind was not easily changed. He would stop when **he** decided no matter how hard she tried to convince him otherwise. They had had this discussion before, many times.

"Will you be back tonight?" she asked hopefully.

"Absolutely! I could never let you sleep alone on a Friday!"

He reached for her, pulling her into his arms to kiss her.

"It's 7:30. I should be back by midnight."

"Be careful, O.K.?" she pleaded, her concern still present.

"I will. I promise," he responded and she knew he meant it. "Time to go."

He walked to the door, then stopped and turned to where she still sat on the bed, staring blankly at nothing in particular.

"Sandy," he called softly.

"Yeah?" she looked up at him.

"I'll stop next week. I just have a few more things to do, for me and for you. Next week, I'll be done. Then, I'll retire."

Without waiting for a reply, none was expected, he turned and headed downstairs.

A moment later, she heard the rumbling of the garage door followed by the mini-van's engine and, he was gone.

* * * *

Watching Frank's house, a half a block away from where he was parked, McCall crouched low in the driver's seat of yet another rental. He still wasn't sure if he should be amused or disgusted by the clerk's suggestion at Thrifty's to open a commercial account to avoid tying up his credit card.

He had followed Frank home at the end of the afternoon, and had been sitting there, and accomplishing nothing, for close to two hours. It was now 7:05 and he was growing angry and frustrated, having no idea how long he would have to wait this time. For all he knew, Frank might be planning to stay home all night, again, but he had to settle this, once and for all.

He started reading a magazine to pass the time, glancing up occasionally. He hoped that none of the residents would report his presence to the cops as he did not want to have to explain what he was doing there. Not yet. He dared to check the time again; 7:28 and still no sign of Frank. He was becoming more and more uneasy with each passing moment. He couldn't stay there all night and began to wonder if he should simply give up and go home. He had already wasted two and a half hours.

Immediately, his thoughts strayed to the previous Friday, the night the slumlord had been murdered. He had been watching Frank that night and had decided to leave, perhaps too early, and had since regretted it. Anyways, he had told Cathy that he might be late; Cathy, his ever-understanding wife, who never said a word about his long hours, who never complained about all night stakeouts.

Such thoughts of Cathy led him to once again reconsider his plans for the evening. What the hell, maybe he should surprise her and show up at a decent hour for once. He was quite aware that he neglected her too much and someday, if he wasn't careful, he might end up losing her.

His mind made up, he reached for the ignition to start the car. He was going home. As he touched the key, he saw Frank's mini-van roll out of the garage and onto the street, heading north, away from him. Swearing, yet relieved, he started the engine and went after Bakes.

\* \* \* \*

Frank Bakes drove across the city in a north-easterly direction while McCall, who had no idea where his subordinate was going, followed blindly along.

With half a dozen vehicles separating them, they were rolling along Bernard Street and approaching Park Avenue. As Frank reached the intersection, the traffic light turned yellow and he stepped on the accelerator, racing across Park as the cars behind him came to a halt.

Not wanting to lose his man, McCall quickly pulled into the right lane but a taxi-cab ahead of him did the same, effectively blocking his path.

"Jesus Fucking Christ!" Dave swore angrily, pounding the steering wheel in frustration.

Helpless, he watched in silent disgust as Frank's Astro made a left turn a few blocks away.

Following several long minutes of impatient waiting, the light was green again and the traffic started to move.

Cutting back into the centre lane, amidst several blasts of angry horns, McCall turned where Frank had and slowed down, desperately searching for the mini-van. As expected however, the vehicle was nowhere in sight. He circled several blocks in the area, in vain, before finally giving up.

He would have to try again another night, he acknowledged, as he headed for home to pay some attention to Cathy.

\* \* \* \*

Evenings at his castle were Greg O'Shea's favourite time, especially in the summer.

On Fridays, he would head north directly from work and was usually there by 7:30. After a couple of beers, he'd fire up the barbecue, cook himself some ribs or a big thick steak and dine on the terrace. By then, nightfall would settle in and he would get a fire going on his small private beach. He could sit by the fire and just listen to nature and watch the stars for hours. That was his routine and this evening was no exception.

With dinner out of the way, he finished loading the dishes in the dishwasher and went back outside, heading down the steps which led from the terrace to the beach.

While the ribs had been cooking, he had prepared the fire and all it now lacked was a flame. Settling into his beach chair, he scanned the lake and woods which surrounded him, taking in the wondrous natural beauty which never ceased to amaze him.

After a moment, he pulled out a pack of cigarettes and extracted one, lighting it with a match. Rather than extinguishing the match afterwards, he flicked it, still lit, into the middle of the carefully assembled pile of wood. The crumpled newspaper caught and the flames quickly began to rise, drawing a satisfied chuckle from O'Shea. He played this little game every week and, most of the time, he succeeded. Once in a while, he had to light another match.

He leaned over to one side and grabbed a fresh can of beer from the cooler. Popping it open, he took a long sip and then stretched back into the chair, sighing in contentment.

"This is the life!" he said aloud. "I could stay here forever!"

\* \* \* \*

Although it was getting quite dark, he found his way easily, having made the trip on several occasions in the past.

It was 9:20, which meant O'Shea would be on the beach, relaxing by the fire. He knew this to be Greg's usual routine, having confirmed it during previous preparatory visits. O'Shea was a very methodical person, a creature of habit, who did not seem to easily deviate from his set sequence of activities.

He pulled into a small natural shelter off the side of the road which he had found on his last trip to the area. It offered the perfect camouflage for his vehicle from anybody who might happen to drive by, although passers-by were few and far between at this time. Turning off the engine, he disembarked and starting quietly making his way through the woods, towards the beach.

\* \* \* \*

O'Shea sat by his fire, lost in his thoughts when the snap of a branch in the woods to his left caught his attention.

"Who's there?!" he called out loudly, rising from his chair.

He could see the beam of a flashlight glittering through the thick brush.

"Sorry if I scared you," apologized a man's voice. "Just let me get out of these damned woods!"

Picking up a piece of firewood which he held as a club, O'Shea took a few steps towards the light.

"This is private property, you know," he informed the approaching intruder.

"I'm sorry, sir," the voice answered. "I got lost."

O'Shea, his guard up, waited nervously for the man to emerge. Following a minute or so of additional crackling, the stranger stepped out from among the trees and onto the beach.

"What are you doing here? This is private property," O'Shea sternly repeated, as he examined his unwelcome visitor.

The man definitely didn't look like a common criminal. Although his clothing was casual, it was obviously of fine quality. Clean cut, he wore a baseball cap and appeared to be in his thirties.

"I-I didn't mean to intrude or trespass," the man sheepishly explained. "I got down here early, when it was light. Came to see some land that's for sale. Started walking around a bit and I lost my bearings. Then it got dark and I was really in trouble."

He glanced nervously at the club in O'Shea's hand. The latter noticed the look and relaxed a bit.

"Whereabouts were you looking at land?" he questioned the stranger, wanting to ensure the veracity of the man's story.

"Down around the Tremblay's place," the intruder replied. "Mr. Tremblay has quite a bit of acreage he wants to part with."

O'Shea knew where the man was talking about; a couple of miles south of his place, along the lake. Old man Tremblay did in fact have a parcel of land he was hoping to sell off, if the price was right.

"Well, you're a little ways off!" O'Shea snickered as he tossed his club back onto the woodpile.

"I-I've been walking for," the man glanced at his watch, "Close to two hours," he sheepishly admitted.

"Well, your safe now!" O'Shea reassured him with a warm smile. "I'll make sure you get back O.K. Name's Greg O'Shea!"

He walked towards the man, extending a friendly hand which the stranger grasped firmly as he introduced himself.

"Ted, Ted Bailey. I'm **really** happy to meet you Mr. O'Shea!"

"Call me Greg, Ted. Listen. Now that your back to civilization, can I offer you a beer?"

"Sure!" Ted gratefully accepted. 'But I don't want to impose."

"Don't be ridiculous!" snorted O'Shea. "My pleasure. I spend most of my time here alone. Divorced, ya see. A little company will do me some good if it doesn't hold you up."

"No, that's fine," Ted answered. "Now that I know I won't be spending the night in the woods, I don't mind staying up here a bit. It's beautiful country!"

"It sure is!" agreed O'Shea wholeheartedly. "Have a seat!"

Gesturing to his chair as he handed Ted a beer, he added, "I'll just get myself something to park my keister on! Be right back."

He strolled onto his dock and unlocked the door of the boathouse. Inside, he moved a few cartons and a cooler to get to the beach-chairs stored behind them. Selecting one, he came back out into the warm night to rejoin his unexpected guest.

"So you're thinking ... Hey, Ted where'd you go?"

As he finished uttering his question, a vicious blow to the back of his head sent him plummeting into darkness.

After tossing the club-like branch into the beach fire, the man lifted O'Shea's unconscious form over his shoulder and started up the steps to the terrace. They would be much more comfortable inside, he thought.

When Greg O'Shea started to regain consciousness, the first thing he noticed was how uncomfortable he felt, though he could not yet quite grasp why. The back of his head hurt like hell and he could not remember where he was.

Cottage, ribs, beach fire ... Wait, a man? He really was very uncomfortable. Although his feet were touching the ground, he felt as if he was suspended upright and his hands and arms were numb. Why were his arms up in the air like that and why couldn't he get them down?

He shook his head and immediately regretted doing so. The pain was tremendous and left him feeling dizzy. He tried to concentrate, attempting to remember what had happened. A man, Ted something, wanted to buy land... beer, boathouse, beach-chairs ... He opened his eyes, but only for a second; the light was too bright. How come it was light? Where was he?

"Welcome back, Greg," he faintly heard a voice call out.

Struggling to clear his thoughts, he tried to open his eyes again, the harsh light only allowing limited success. Squinting through barely raised lids, he could make out a man standing behind the counter, familiar looking, a baseball cap.

"Wake up, Gregory!" The man ordered.

"Where-where am I?" O'Shea asked weakly, still very confused.

"Why, you're in your lovely cottage, Greg," the man responded soothingly.

O'Shea's mind was starting to clear.

"Ted?" he asked, still annoyed by the bright light.

"Well, no. I'm sorry," apologized the man. "I lied about my name."

Fear was now rapidly reviving O'Shea as he realized where he was; his shooting range. Looking up above his head, he saw that his wrists were bound tightly together with filament tape, above the wire cable which ran the length of the tunnel. He was trussed up as a live target!

"Who Are You!?" he shrieked, his eyes wide with terror.

"The Vigilante, at your service!" the man cordially introduced himself.

"W-why are you doing this to me?" O'Shea stammered, trembling. "W-what are you gonna do to me?"

"Two very fine questions, my friend," said the Vigilante, "Both of which merit an answer. First, why am I doing this? Because you are a horrible person. For personal gain, you have stolen valuable and dangerous arms and have sold them. The people you sold these weapons to used them to kill other people. Sometimes innocent people."

He paused for a moment, letting his words sink in before pursuing.

"Now, if you had not sold these arms, I believe that those innocent people would still be alive. Maybe some of them would be enjoying the comfort of **their** fine country homes right now. All things considered, I have no choice but to hold you responsible for their deaths."

"You don't know that!" O'Shea desperately argued. "I-I didn't know what anybody wanted those guns for. M-maybe they were just used for target practice!"

"Wrong," retorted the Vigilante, shaking his head. "On at least one occasion, one of your weapons took the precious life of a young, healthy, expectant mother, as well as that of her unborn twins. The father remains hospitalized as we speak. It's not known when, if ever, he'll pull out of his depressive state."

He stared coldly at O'Shea for a moment before resuming. "Now, as for your second question, sir, what will I do?"

He paused for a few more seconds, gazing at the quivering man suspended fifteen feet away.

"I will kill you, Greg," he calmly stated. "I will try the wonderful weapons you have here and will slowly, but surely, kill you."

He glared at Gregory O'Shea, not at all impressed as the latter burst into tears. The man was crying, not from remorse for what he had done but rather, because he feared for his life. To the end, Gregory O'Shea was a greedy man, thinking only of himself which disgusted the Vigilante.

Closing the heavy door behind him to eliminate any bothersome noise, he systematically started trying O'Shea's wonderful weapons, one by one, until his prospect was dead.

### Chapter 29 - Saturday, July 27, 1996

9:23 a.m. The sky was cloudless, the sun bright and the temperature was already up to 87 degrees in the shade.

Seated on the terrace by the pool, the Barrys shared the morning paper while enjoying a leisurely third cup of coffee, their breakfast dishes still piled on the patio table, pushed to one side. It was, after all, the weekend, a time to take it easy, a time to relax. There was no rush on weekends.

The phone rang, breaking the morning calm, and Chris answered as he continued to scan the paper.

"Hello? Hi, Dave! What's up?"

"We've got another one," muttered McCall, his tone grim.

"Where? What happened?" Chris asked with concern.

"Some guy up at his cottage on Lake Sawin, a couple of hours north. Got shot, a lot. If you can believe it, the gentleman had an underground shooting gallery leading from his basement! Our man used his victim as a target."

"Are you sure it was the Vigilante?" Chris enquired, attracting a curious glance from his wife.

"Yep," Dave replied. "No doubt about that. In his usual helpful style, he sent us a message. That's how we found out. Informed us that the victim, Gregory O'Shea, was a greedy bastard who sold stolen guns. According to our friend, some of those guns were used to kill innocent people and therefore, O'Shea had to die. We got in touch with the provincial police in St-Michel-des-Saints, they went to the scene and gave us a preliminary report. Harris is on his way there now."

"You said he shot the guy?" Chris queried.

"That's right," McCall confirmed. "About fifty times, using O'Shea's own gun collection. Our Vigilante strung him up from the ceiling by the wrists and took shots at him, apparently with several weapons. At least a dozen guns were out of their cases and had been fired. I guess he's really come to believe that 'He who lives by the sword, dies by the sword'."

"Didn't anybody hear anything?" Chris persisted, somewhat incredulous. "Neighbours? I mean, fifty shots!"

"Nope," was McCall's response. "This shooting gallery, it opens up on the basement and extends over a hundred feet underground. Door to get in is soundproof. Walls, floor, ceiling, all concrete. I guess O'Shea didn't want to bother anyone when he practiced. Anyways, we're not talking about a residential district here either. It's all woods, with some cottages over a mile apart. Nice and secluded."

"I see," said Chris, impressed. "Anything you want me to do?"

"Well naturally, for what it's worth, I'd like you to try to trace the message," Dave replied. "Actually, it's the messages. He sent one to Henderson at the **Gazette** as well. I was also wondering if you'd be interested in going down there with me? I could use the company for the drive down and maybe you'll notice something that we don't."

"Sure," agreed Chris. "What time are you leaving?"

"As soon as I can. As soon as you're ready."

"I'm ready," said Chris. "Head on over. In the meantime, I'll get in touch with Henderson and call Carl to have him look into the tracings."

"Great!" McCall replied. "How exactly do I get to your place?"

"Where are you coming from?" asked Chris.

"Dorval. I'm at home."

"Take the 40 to exit 100, the second one for Repentigny. There'll be an Esso to your right at Industrial. I'll meet you there to make things easier."

"Excellent," agreed McCall. "I'll be there in about forty-five minutes."

"No problem," answered Chris. "See you then."

As he cut the connection and laid the phone down, he noticed his wife's amused eyes watching him over her paper.

"What?" he retorted indignantly, pretending not to understand.

"I thought we didn't work on weekends?" she stated, feigning a reprimand.

"This isn't work, my dear," he replied defensively, grinning. "This is my civic duty!"

"Bullshit," she grinned back. "Be careful out there, O.K.?"

"All the time!" he replied with a wink.

\* \* \* \*

Carl was not even frustrated when he located and subsequently erased the transmission records from the Eazy-Com data bank. He still wondered why they kept reappearing as they did. Knowing the system as well as anyone, he had gone over it more times than he could remember, looking for something that he had missed, some subtle clue, but had found nothing.

So, in the end, he had never figured out this elusive message enigma and who, if anyone, was responsible, although he had stopped trying because it really didn't matter anymore. He was on the verge of ceasing his activities for good and would be gone by the end of the week.

\* \* \* \*

With yet an hour to go before reaching Lake Sawin, Chris and Dave rode in silence.

They had chatted for a while, about the Vigilante, then sports and current events, then the Vigilante again. Eventually however, both had grown quiet, each consumed by his own thoughts about this vicious killer on the loose.

"Can I tell you something, Chris?" McCall suddenly asked, seeming hesitant. "I haven't spoken to anybody about this yet."

"Sure. What?" Chris replied, curious.

"It-it's about Frank."

There, he had got it out.

"Frank? Bakes?" questioned Chris, puzzled.

"Yeah, Frank Bakes," McCall morosely replied.

He had started; he might as well go on.

"I'm suspicious of Frank, Chris."

"Suspicious of what?" Chris was still confused. "What the hell are you talking about?"

"I think that Frank may be the Vigilante," McCall bluntly stated.

"What!? Why!?" Chris exclaimed in surprise.

This was not something he had been expecting.

"You're actually the one who got me looking into this," McCall started to explain. "When you talked about how those messages had gotten into our computer, you said maybe a cop had done it. I was sceptical, but, to quote you, 'I couldn't leave a stone unturned'."

He glanced over and noting that he had Chris' complete attention, continued.

"So I started looking into my people's activities since the Vigilante's arrival. Everybody had alibis at the times that some of the murders had taken place. Either they had been at the office or off investigating something with another cop. If I was looking for **one** guilty party, none of them fit the bill. None except Frank. He'd been off duty or off somewhere alone every time the Vigilante had struck. Since I realized this, I've been trying to track him more closely. I started following him when I could but haven't come up with anything for or against him yet."

"I don't want to hurt your feelings, Dave," Chris offered doubtfully. "But what you've told me so far is pretty flimsy."

"I'm not done yet," McCall retorted. "The night Morretto got hit, I called Frank to let him know that Eileen would talk to us the next day. He wasn't home. His wife told me he'd be back late. A few days later I learn that some unidentified cop was in Zack Robert's neighbourhood the night he got whacked. Frank happens to live in that neighbourhood. Then Myers, the slumlord. Frank was off duty. Next, Perry, Giovanni Morretto's assistant; I'm sure that was the Vigilante. The bomb was the same as the one used with Johnny B. Now, who knew about the threats to Eileen? Not too many people, Chris, but Frank did, and he was off that night as well."

"All of this could just be coincidence, Dave," Chris suggested with less certainty. "You mustn't jump to conclusions."

"I haven't arrested him yet," McCall argued. "Like I said, you're the first person I speak to about this."

"Is there anything else?" Chris enquired, intrigued.

"Yup. Last night, I follow Frank again," Dave went on. "He goes home, I wait a couple of hours and he comes out, around 7:30. He drives off and I go after him but I lose him at a traffic light. Now, we were still in town, but the half hour I was tailing him, he was heading north-east. This morning, I find out about this O'Shea. By the way, I don't think I mentioned it but Frank drives a burgundy Chevy Astro."

"Interesting," commented Chris thoughtfully. "What else?"

"That's all I have for now," replied McCall. "Not enough to clear Frank or nail him! This is really screwing me up bad, Chris!"

"I guess! Is this what you had mentioned you were working on?"

"Yup. This is it," Dave confirmed.

Chris fell silent as he mused over this new development. Although far from being concrete evidence, it did hold together so he could understand his friend's concern.

"It could still be all coincidence," he offered encouragingly. "Don't forget that Eileen met Frank and she certainly doesn't seem to think it's him. Plus, the sketch doesn't look like Frank at all."

"Two points which have kept me hopeful," McCall admitted. "Although Eileen didn't see Frank with a hat and shades and, wigs do exist."

They rode quietly for another moment before Chris spoke again.

"Have you decided to go public with the sketch?"

"Nah. I'm still juggling with that one," McCall answered. "I'm still worried that the Vigilante might disappear or go back to Eileen if I do. She's been through enough."

"Yeah," Chris thought aloud. "But didn't one of Morretto's goons see him too?"

"Yep, but he wasn't much help," responded Dave. "When we showed him the sketch, he told us that, with a floppy hat, it could be the guy."

"So, have your artist change the hat," suggested Chris. "Worse thing that can happen is that our friend goes after the bodyguard! Just to play it safe, we can keep an eye on Eileen."

"Not a bad idea," replied McCall, grinning. "It might be worth a try. Maybe somebody will recognize him, and anyways, nothing else has worked so far. I could even give Henderson a call and let him print it. Get him to work for my side for once!"

He shot a glance at Chris and added, "By the way, speaking of Morretto's bodyguards, they've disappeared. Maybe our friend's already gotten rid of them!"

"You think so!?"

"Could be, Chris. Don't underestimate this guy."

Another short pause ensued, broken this time by Dave.

"About the sketch. Every time I look at it, it seems vaguely familiar but I can't figure out why."

"It's funny that you should say that," Chris slowly replied. "When I saw it, I got the same feeling but I just couldn't put my finger on it."

But Chris had put his finger on it. He just wasn't ready to speak to McCall about it yet, needing to work on the computer activity reports generated from Carl's PC before talking. The sketch bore a striking resemblance to Carl.

\* \* \* \*

To describe the scene of Gregory O'Shea's murder as a mess would have qualified as a serious understatement.

The man had died slowly and, without a doubt, very painfully. His arms and legs were riddled with bullet holes and, judging from the vast quantity of blood on the tunnel's floor, it was obvious that many of the wounds had been inflicted prior to death.

The forensics team was on site and had already dusted the weapons for prints but only O'Shea's had appeared. There were no footprints anywhere in the house; the killer had been careful and stayed away from the blood.

Outside, nothing out of the ordinary nor any signs of a struggle had been found. There were embers on the beach, still slightly warm, a beach-chair, an empty beer can, a cooler; nothing particular. Prints taken there also had only served to confirm O'Shea's presence. The woods around the house had also been combed, revealing nothing of interest.

After an hour on the premises, they had seen enough and not found anything which might serve as a clue. Dave granted a ten minute interview to Ron Henderson, who had patiently waited on the sidelines, after which he and Chris headed for home. The Vigilante had eluded them again.

### Chapter 30 - Monday, July 29, 1996

9:34 a.m. "McCall, Homicide," Dave said into the phone, his voice somewhat muffled by a mouthful of doughnut.

"Hey there! What's new on this fine morning?" Chris cheerfully enquired.

"Same old, same old. What's up?"

"I was thinking about our conversation on Saturday, Dave. I was wondering if you wanted a couple of people to do some tailing for you?"

Now that McCall had opened up to his friend about Frank, he did not dislike the idea. Shadowing Bakes himself was growing old at a rapid pace.

"You have people you really trust, Chris?" he asked, lowering his tone. "I want to keep this real quiet until we're sure."

"Absolutely," Chris guaranteed. "You have nothing to worry about. My people don't talk to anyone about their cases, before, during or after. Them's the rules."

"No chance of my man noticing anyone following?" McCall questioned.

"None. You will get nothing but the best," Chris confidently replied. "Hell, Dave! You're gonna want to hire my people once they're done, they're so good!"

McCall smiled. "Thanks, Chris. I don't know how I'd get through this one without you. When can we start?"

"Right now. Fax me a photo, a plate number and a vehicle description. The rest is my problem."

"Give me five minutes and you'll have them," said McCall. "Thanks again, Chris."

"No problem. Later."

Dave hung up the phone, feeling a mixture of both relief and anxiety. Good or bad, they'd know about Frank soon enough. And, in the interim, he would be able to get some sleep.

\* \* \* \*

Although he knew that danger still lurked about, Carl's excitement was growing on a daily basis. He was only $350,000 away from his goal and could practically feel the sun's heat baking him on some tropical beach.

His deeds were nearly done and retirement would be a reality in just a few days.

* * * *

Leaving the office for lunch, Frank Bakes strolled a few blocks away to McDonalds where he had a Big Mac, fries and a Coke. He then wandered around for a while, stopping at Sam's to buy a compact disc, Led Zeppelin II, to add to his collection of old classics. Eventually, he headed back to work, stopping only to buy a pack of cigarettes at a convenience store along the way.

When he arrived at the office, he had been gone just under an hour and did not have the faintest idea that he had been followed during that time.

* * * *

He had two prospects left to settle before quitting.

He had promised Sandy that he would be done by Friday and he was a man of his word. There was therefore little time to waste.

The first prospect was actually one of multiple proportions. His target would be a house, located in the quiet residential north-shore town of Repentigny, just east of Montreal. His goal would be to kill as many of the building's occupants as possible.

Built far back from the street, the large home sat on a 50,000 square foot lot. Mature trees bordered the sides and front of the property and, behind the house, the yard extended close to one hundred feet before dropping sharply to the L'Assomption River below.

Passers-by were often impressed by this prime piece of real estate, with its driveway filled with expensive cars and motorcycles. Strangers to the area wondered who lived there, but local residents knew that it was occupied by several members of the local chapter of the Devil's Delight. Once small and relatively unknown, the motorcycle gang had expanded over the years to become a powerful national force in the world of organized crime.

This one would be easy. Gregory O'Shea had unknowingly made sure of that, for, among his impressive collection of weapons had been half a dozen state-of-the-art explosive devices. Similar to hand grenades, these had the added advantage of a timing mechanism. He had taken them from O'Shea's cottage during his last visit, on the basis that the latter would no longer need them.

He would handle this first prospect tomorrow night. That would leave him a couple of days to settle his final one.

* * * *

Frank Bakes headed directly for home at the end of his shift. Following dinner, he and his wife went for a walk, stopping at the local video store to rent a movie.

Returning home, they watched the film after which Frank's wife went off to bed while he watched a re-run of 'Law and Order' and about half of the 11:00 news before turning in.

Outside, throughout the evening and night, eyes kept watch, alert for any move which might take place around the Bakes residence. If Frank decided to go somewhere, anywhere at all, he would not be going alone.

## Chapter 31 - Tuesday, July 30, 1996

Ron Henderson had been a little uneasy when McCall had offered him the composite sketch for publication.

Since the whole Vigilante saga had started, Ron's articles had always leaned in favour of this 'super hero' killer, who had taken on a personal war against crime. This, in turn, had led to something of a relationship between the reporter and the Vigilante.

However, having now met McCall, Henderson allowed himself to admit that the police were not the bungling idiots he had so valiantly attempted to portray them as. They were hard working men and women with a difficult task at hand, that of controlling crime at all levels of society. And, as McCall had so simply put it when they had recently met, right or wrong, the Vigilante **was** a murderer.

Henderson had solved his dilemma by having the sketch printed on the second page of that morning's paper under the caption **Possibly the Vigilante**. A footnote under the sketch simply mentioned that this was a police artist's portrayal of what the Vigilante might look like, based on descriptions by several witnesses. There was no by-line.

\* \* \* \*

8:42 a.m. Whistling, Carl strolled into his office with coffee in one hand, briefcase in the other and the morning edition of the **Gazette** tucked under one arm.

His usual routine, he set down the coffee, briefcase and paper on his desk then returned to the door to turn on the lights before heading back to his desk and booting his PC as he dropped into his chair.

Removing the lid from the Styrofoam cup, he took a sip of his steaming coffee as he unfolded the newspaper and began scanning the headlines on the front page. Finding nothing of interest, he turned to the second page and suddenly froze. Staring back at him was a sketch of the elusive Vigilante. Although it was not a 35 mm photograph, there were some rather strong, obvious similarities to the facial structure.

Beads of sweat sprouted on his forehead and his breathing became erratic. It was all becoming too much to handle. He just didn't understand what was going on. First the Eazy-Com transmission records which kept reappearing and now, his portrait, or something damned close to it, in the morning paper. Somebody had to know about what he was doing but, if that was the case, why didn't they just confront him? Why do this?

Somebody was trying to drive him crazy.

With trembling hands, he frantically folded the paper, spilling his coffee all over his desk in the process. Cursing under his breath, he hurriedly mopped up the brown puddle with the newspaper and threw the soaking mess in the trash.

He leaned back in his chair, breathing deeply, intent on regaining control. The end was so close, now was not the time to start panicking. Whoever was playing these games with him would not win. He was quitting, retiring in two days, now, maybe sooner.

With fingers flying expertly, he started working the keyboard of his PC. He had only $350,000 to go and he was determined to make it. There was no way he would go down for this. Not after all of his efforts and hard work.

* * * *

3:42 p.m. "Dave, what was that guy's name at CSS?" asked Tim Harris as he sauntered into McCall's office. "The one who traced those messages?"

"Denver. Carl Denver," replied McCall. "Why?"

"Well," answered Harris. "I've been going through this list of Chevy Astro owners and I ran into his name. I thought the name looked familiar, that's all."

"Do you think he has something to do with this?" McCall asked slowly, starting to think.

"No, not really," shrugged Harris. "It's just that we're looking for an angle with this mini-van thing and I've now run into two names of people involved in the case. Denver and Frank. Frank, I'm not worried about. Denver? Hey, I don't even know the guy."

"Tell me something," McCall ventured thoughtfully. "Do you remember what Denver looks like?"

"Sorta, I guess," replied Harris. "About five-ten, 180 pounds, good shape, dark curly hair, sort of a square jaw."

McCall pulled out a copy of the composite sketch.

"Could this be him?" he suggested, sliding the document across the desk to Tim.

Harris studied the drawing for a moment. "From what I can remember, this would need some refining but, yeah, this could be him. Why? Do you know something I don't?"

"No," McCall admitted. "It's just that the sketch reminded me of somebody but I didn't know who. When you asked about Denver, it clicked. Now, you tell me the man drives an Astro, and we already know that he's a computer wiz."

"It ain't very tight, boss," Tim doubtfully replied. "Don't you think?"

"Chris also mentioned a similar murder which took place while he was in Vancouver three weeks ago," Dave added. "Denver was there with him. I know it's farfetched, but it's possible."

"I guess," Harris slowly replied. "Have you spoken to Chris about this?"

"No. Until now, I had never even thought of Carl Denver. But I **will** speak to Chris."

\* \* \* \*

At 5:15 p.m., Frank Bakes left work and headed for home.

He was breathing a little easier in recent days. As time had passed, he had convinced himself that there was nothing wrong with McCall, at least not anything which concerned him. The pressure and frustration of the Vigilante case was probably just getting to Dave.

His wife wasn't home as she was spending the evening with an old friend. He made himself a quick microwave dinner with leftovers he found in the refrigerator, after which he worked a little on the computer and watched some television.

He'd be going out a little later in the evening, but in the meantime, he had some time to kill.

\* \* \* \*

8:22 p.m. Chris was busy at the conference table in his office, a multitude of computer reports scattered before him across the mammoth table. These constituted the complete record of the activity which had taken place on PC number 427 since he had started his monitoring four weeks earlier.

Although Chris had not yet completed his analysis, it was clear that Carl, number 427's user, had been extremely busy in recent weeks, his activities questionable, to say the least. There had been repeated unauthorized access to Eazy-Com in addition to frequent unwarranted programming and systems modifications.

His mind was starting to grow foggy and Chris decided to call it a night. He gathered the numerous reports into a thick, orderly pile which he stored in the safety of his small office vault. Tomorrow, he would complete his analysis, after which he believed it would be time to speak to Dave about Carl.

\* \* \* \*

For the tenth time in twice as many minutes, Frank Bakes checked the time on the antique grand-father clock which stood in the corner of the living room; 8:54.

"Good enough," he decided aloud, tired of waiting and anxious for the evening's coming events.

Turning off the television and VCR, he eagerly started preparing for the night ahead.

\* \* \* \*

9:25 p.m. He was ready, it was time to go.

Picking up the small canvas bag he had packed earlier containing everything he needed, he headed into the garage and was once again faced with having to choose a vehicle. The Vette rarely met the requirements for these expeditions; it was simply too obvious.

Sighing, he tossed the bag onto the passenger seat of the mini-van, climbed in and started the engine. He slid Pink Floyd's 'The Wall' into the CD player as the garage door quietly rumbled open and rolled out to the opening notes of 'In the Flesh'.

\* \* \* \*

To describe what Willy Cobourne felt as boredom as he drove east along Sherbrooke would have been a grave understatement.

The Astro which he had been assigned to tail was two cars ahead of him and easy to keep up with. It was clear that its driver did not have a clue that he was being followed, for Willy had been behind him for roughly fifteen minutes without detecting any sign that his assignment had noticed him.

The mini-van turned north on St-Laurent, as did Willy, staying close enough not to miss any lights but far enough not to be specifically spotted. Shadowing this guy was a joke, offering no challenge whatsoever. The man even respected the speed limits!

The only reason Willy had agreed to do something this routine was because Chris had requested him to. Barry was a very intelligent individual, a man who knew what he was doing and for whom Willy had the utmost respect. If Chris wished to send his most experienced investigator on such a mission, it had to be important.

Stifling a yawn, Willy continued to obediently tail the mini-van.

\* \* \* \*

He pulled alongside the curb on a quiet residential street and cut the engine. Slowly, carefully, he surveyed the area to ensure that it bore no witnesses and, after a moment, he was satisfied that the street and its adjoining properties were deserted.

Not far from where he had stopped was a lot which, for some reason, had always remained vacant. Covered with knee-high weeds near the street, it became somewhat more wooded as it sloped down to the river below. A dirt path, created by the passage of countless neighbourhood kids, cut through the lot and led down to the water's edge.

Stepping out of his vehicle with canvas bag in hand, he headed for the path while continuing to casually scan the surroundings for signs of life.

However, thanks to a slightly cool evening and prime-time television, everybody appeared to be inside.

He quickly made his way down the path and was by the river's edge within a matter of minutes. Heading west along the waterway, he continued to glance around occasionally to make sure he had no company. He was alone.

After three or four minutes, he reached a long wooden staircase which led from water level to the higher ground, some thirty feet above. He checked the time; 10:03; right on schedule. He started up the steep slope, not using the staircase but rather climbing alongside it, using its railing for occasional support. Using the steps would have made the ascent easier, but would also have left him exposed in full view if someone on top happened to come by. He preferred a slightly more difficult task in exchange for the cover offered by the tall weeds and brush growing on either side of the stairway.

As he neared the end of his climb, he slowed his pace, being additionally careful not to make any noise. He reached the top and leaned against the embankment to rest while he mentally reviewed his plans. Especially tonight, there was little room for the slightest error if he intended to fully succeed.

After a moment he was ready to press ahead and carefully raised to a standing position. Peering over the edge of the incline, he slowly scanned the property's rear yard for signs of activity, and suddenly froze. Off to the left, some twenty-five feet away, was a bench which faced the house and seated on the bench was a man.

Although he could not see the gang member's face, the back of his leather vest gave away his identity. Embroidered there was the gang's logo, a smiling devil amidst the flames of hell, above which the words 'Devil's Delight' appeared in a semi-circle of silver. Emblazoned in gold over the gang's name, was another; 'Scorpion'.

Dennis 'Scorpion' Roy was the head of the 'Devil's' local chapter and unofficial leader in the province, this since Henri 'Serpent' Savard had been assassinated several months prior. Rumours were that Roy intended to become 'Grand Chief' for Canada before the year was out, whether the current incumbent liked it or not. This, in turn, had created much violent conflict within the gang in recent months as leadership support varied among its members.

And now, there sat the 'Scorpion', just seconds away from him, relaxed, unguarded and unaware that he was about to die. He scanned the yard again, needing to be certain that he was alone with his prey; nobody.

Silently, he stored his canvas bag securely down amongst the weeds, ensuring that it didn't tumble down the slope. Then, without a sound, he sprang onto the grassy surface, pulling out his knife as he closed in on the man relaxing, without a clue, on the bench.

The last sound that 'Scorpion' heard was the click of an opening blade, a fraction of a second before his life poured out through the massive gash in his neck.

Hoisting the gang leader's lifeless form over his shoulder, he hurried back to the top of the incline. He quickly examined the ground below and then heaved the body over the edge, sending it tumbling halfway down the steep slope where it came to rest, well concealed by the unkempt overgrowth.

Climbing down to where he had left his bag, he took a moment to savour this sudden unforeseen stroke of luck with which he had been served. He would have never expected such a satisfying opportunity, especially not with 'Scorpion'. Even if the house was empty when he destroyed it, he could consider tonight's mission a success. He seriously hoped however, that the house would be occupied. The more of these assholes that died, the better.

He crawled back over the ridge and swiftly made his way along to the west side of the yard where he crouched among the trees while searching for any signs of activity. Although all remained still, he knew that he had no time to lose. He had no idea if 'Scorpion' had some fixed routine which would send someone searching for him when he didn't return.

He crept towards the house along the property's perimeter, taking advantage of the cover offered by the trees which bordered the lot. The lack of security around the place surprised him but he realized that this area really was not gang-war territory.

Once close enough, he scrambled to the rear corner of the house, peering towards the windows for signs of detection, but no-one was in sight. Rushing across the yard, he quickly crawled to relative safety under the home's large elevated wooden terrace.

Wasting no time, he opened the canvas bag, removed a small hand shovel and proceeded to dig alongside the wall of the house. Within a minute, the hole was ten inches deep and large enough to accommodate the first of his six grenade-like devices. He set the timer at ten minutes and pressed a switch, arming the bomb before carefully placing it in the hole. The actual countdown would be activated by radio control once all the explosives were in place. Seconds later, the hole was refilled and he was ready to move on.

He climbed out from under the terrace and hurried to the opposite side of the house. A sunken window well provided an excellent location for his second device and it was in place in no time. He continued on towards the front of the building, peering carefully around the corner for any signs of trouble; still nobody. A number of bushes growing alongside the front wall offered sufficient cover to allow him to set yet another explosive near the main entrance.

Retracing his steps around the back, he returned to address the other side of the dwelling. Two more sunken window wells were available and his devices were quickly installed. He proceeded towards the front of the home once again, on the west side this time, to set his final bomb.

Through a window, a half dozen feet above ground level, he could hear the voices of two, no three men. He smiled; the house was not empty. Quickly, he planted his last explosive in the soft earth of a flowerbed located directly below the window before silently heading back towards the river.

Although the yard remained deserted, he took no chance, dodging among the shadows of the trees as he spanned its length. He reached the top of the incline without incident and scanned the property for a hidden enemy one last time; nobody.

Hurrying to the top of the staircase, he paused only long enough to press a switch on a small remote control transmitter which he pulled from his pocket. 10:00, 9:59, 9:58; the countdown had begun. He rushed down to the river level, using the steps this time.

Six minutes later, he climbed into the mini-van and was rolling within seconds. A few more minutes went by before he heard the low intense rumbling of a massive explosion in the distance behind him.

He turned onto a quiet side street and stopped, reached into the canvas bag on the seat beside him and pulled out his notepad. Flipping it open, he keyed in the appropriate codes to gain access to Eazy-Com. He called the first stored message from memory and quickly read it over.

"Should mention Scorpion," he thoughtfully decided.

After adding a P.S. referring to the gang leader's demise, he clicked 'Address', 'MCC' and 'Send' and his first message was gone. Retrieving the second, he made a similar modification and repeated the simple transmission procedure, sending this one to 'RON'. He then exited the system, convinced that the messages could not be traced and headed for home.

His work was done for the night and it had gone remarkably well. He was particularly pleased that, considering the magnitude and location of his target, nobody had seen him.

## Chapter 32 - Wednesday, July 31, 1996

The headline and by-line appeared on the first page of the morning paper:

### DEVIL'S DELIGHT NO MATCH FOR VIGILANTE
### By Ron Henderson

The message had come in on Eazy-Com at 10:28 the previous evening. In recent days, Henderson had gotten into the habit of checking for Eazy-Com transmissions at the office via his home PC on a regular basis. Last night, his timing had been nothing short of excellent.

He had accessed his office computer at 10:34 and the message had been waiting for him. While he had been reading this privileged information, the phone had rung; it had been McCall, calling to inform him of the explosion.

A half hour later, he had reached the scene, which bustled with frenzied activity. Dozens of cars were parked haphazardly about while hundreds of curious onlookers rambled around the cordoned-off property. Members of the local and provincial police forces kept watch as firefighters brought what was left of the burning building under control.

Several minutes following his arrival, Ron had spotted McCall, who had promised to bring him up to speed as soon as they had something concrete. True to his word, the lieutenant had given Ron an interview at 1:45 that morning while other reporters had been required to wait until an official press conference at 6:00 a.m.

Dennis 'Scorpion' Roy was dead, throat slashed, and four other bodies, badly charred and tattered, had been found amidst the wreckage of the house. As Henderson was already aware, this incident had nothing to do with turf wars with rival gangs or the internal power struggle within the Devil's Delight organization. The Vigilante had claimed responsibility.

Interestingly enough, the killer had completed his messages, both to McCall and Henderson, with the phrase "Just one more to go." Was their man about to retire?

\* \* \* \*

"Good morning, Sonia!" Chris cheerily greeted as he strolled into the office at 8:17 a.m.

"Morning, Chris!" his assistant anxiously replied. "Did you hear that explosion last night!?"

"You better believe it!" he exclaimed. "We were in the yard by the pool when it happened. We didn't just hear it! We felt it!"

"Was it that close to your place?!" Sonia enquired with surprise.

"About a five minute drive," Chris informed her. "Repentigny's not a big town."

"I hope you don't have any damage?"

"No. We weren't that close," reassured Chris. "Apparently, the only real damage was to the house that got bombed."

"Well I'm glad you're all right," stated Sonia with concern. "It's getting that we're not safe no matter where we go! Not even in our own home!"

"Yeah, the world ain't perfect, that's for sure!" Chris ruefully agreed as he headed for his office. "Anything special this morning?"

"Willy's in your office."

"Really? Good. What's the possibility of you getting us a bit of coffee?"

"Already served, sir!" she giggled bashfully. "Willy asked me if I could fetch you guys a pot. He's such a sweetheart!"

"Oh, and I'm not!" Chris snorted playfully as he entered his office.

In shirtsleeves and, as usual, without a tie, Willy lazed luxuriously back in one of the leather armchairs, feet crossed on the coffee table. With a cup of coffee in one hand and a magazine in the other, he looked very comfortable, very much at home.

"Hiya boss!" he grinned as Chris walked in, glancing over the magazine just long enough to deliver his greeting.

"Morning, Willy," Chris chuckled, shaking his head as he headed for his desk to rid himself of his briefcase and jacket.

William Cobourne had joined Walter Olson just a few months after the latter had founded the company some twenty years earlier. He had been a cop with an attitude who, at the age of thirty-five, had been asked to resign from the force.

He had not been asked to leave for having done anything illegal. In fact, Willy had probably been the most honest cop around. He had simply, over a ten year period, managed to get on the wrong side of the vast majority of the people he had worked with, including most of his superiors. When asked to resign, he had complied, but only after slugging his captain, naturally, without the presence of witnesses.

Two days later, he had joined SecurInvestigations as Chief Investigator, then heading a team of two which had since grown to well over one hundred. From day one, he and Walter had never managed to spend more than five minutes in the same room without getting into an argument. However, Willy was excellent at what he did and had remained with Walter ever since and, although neither man would ever admit it, they were extremely fond of each other.

"So, got anything for me?" Chris asked as he dropped into the vacant armchair and poured himself a cup of coffee.

"Report's on the table," Willy sombrely replied, tossing the magazine aside as he looked up at Chris with grave eyes. "Got pictures too, boss. Everything to nail the man."

Chris picked up the envelope from the table and pulled out a sheaf of pages and photographs. He glanced through the pictures and then rapidly read through the written report, a grim expression on his face.

Willy waited quietly for Chris to finish before speaking again. "You gonna go to his boss with this?"

"I don't have any choice, Willy," Chris nodded grimly.

"Too bad," gloomily commented Willy, standing up. 'I've always hated to see a cop go down."

"Yeah, I know," Chris sadly agreed. "But I'm going to have to talk about this. Trust me, it'll be for his own good. Thanks, Willy. You did a great job, as usual."

"Yeah, sure," Willy grunted over his shoulder as he left the room.

\* \* \* \*

8:32 a.m. Carl Denver entered his office to find a Post-it note from Chris on his computer screen:

*Carl,*
*McCall called early this morning. Vigilante has struck again. Check Eazy-Com for transmissions around 10:30 p.m. last night to McCall and Henderson. Thanks,*
*Chris*

Shrugging, he booted the PC and accessed Eazy-Com to verify for records of the message transmissions. Sure enough, they were there.

Wearily, he repeated the process of erasing them, failing to understand why they kept appearing. But this never ending puzzle was really no longer a matter of concern. Tomorrow was retirement day.

\* \* \* \*

It was 11:45 a.m. and Dave McCall sat at a table at Le Mirada, impatiently awaiting Chris' arrival. His friend had called him earlier that morning, urgently indicating that they had to meet to speak about Frank. A CSS investigator had followed Bakes the previous evening and Chris had some unpleasant news to report.

Although Dave had not had any sleep for close to thirty hours, he remained surprisingly alert. There was no doubt that the previous night's events had kept the adrenalin pumping and he was quite anxious to hear what Chris had to say about Frank. He also wished to discuss his concerns regarding Carl Denver, though he realized this might prove fruitless. It all depended on what Frank Bakes had done with his time the night before.

"Which is something I'd know if Chris would only get here," Dave muttered under his breath as he looked up at the restaurant entrance for the hundredth time.

As if responding to a cue, Chris sauntered in and began scanning the dining area in search of McCall. Dave rose to his feet, waving his buddy over to the table.

"Jesus, do you look like shit!" Chris smirked as he slid into the chair opposite McCall.

"Thanks. Wish I could say the same about you!" Dave retorted, glaring down sourly at his rumpled suit. "I should have called you last night and had you join me."

"You should have," Chris agreed, still amused. "I was only five minutes away. And there I was, just wasting my time, swimming and sleeping with my wife when I could have been up with you all night!"

Their conversation was momentarily interrupted by the waitress' arrival to take their orders. Upon her departure, Chris resumed the discussion.

"So tell me about your evening. What else did you do besides chat with reporters and pose for the cameras?"

"I was at the office late last night," recounted Dave, ignoring his friend's humour, "Trying to catch up on some paperwork. Around 10:30, the message from our pal came in on Eazy-Com, telling me about the explosion plus a throat slash in the backyard. I called the locals, they were already on their way then headed on down myself with Tim. When we got there, the place was a zoo."

He paused to light a cigarette from Chris' pack and went on.

"Cars all over the place, lots of curious neighbours milling around, local cops and the QPP trying to control the crowd. Fire trucks were there hosing the place down. Spent the whole night there and didn't find squat, but at least I made Henderson happy. Gave him first run with some information around two in the morning then gave a general press conference around six. Called you around 6:30."

"No wonder you look like shit," Chris commented sympathetically. "What was the final tally?"

"End result is five dead guys, all gang members, including Scorpion, their leader, and one very tired cop. I don't know how my wife puts up with me."

"It's cuz you're such a nice guy!" Chris encouraged with a grin.

"Yeah, right!" grunted Dave. "So, that's the story of my life. What about you? Anything exciting going on? Didn't you want to talk about Frank?"

Chris held off his reply as the waitress arrived with their lunch.

Once she had gone, he hesitantly responded. "Like I told you, I had a guy following Frank last night."

Reaching into his jacket pocket, he produced an envelope which he laid on the table and slid across to McCall.

"My man is good, Dave," he warned, his tone serious. "You've got a full report there and even some pictures of Frank in action. I wish this wasn't true but it is. No doubt about it, you've got enough there to nail him."

McCall tore open the envelope and, feeling slightly nauseous, started looking through the photographs. The first depicted Frank as he entered what appeared to be a motel room. The next was of a woman, most likely a prostitute based on her attire, knocking on the door. Next, Frank opening the door. The remaining photos could have sold as high quality pornography. Chris' man was very good! It was definitely Frank; that could not be argued. The idiot hadn't even had the common sense to pull the drapes!

McCall looked up at Chris, grinning from ear to ear, unable to hide his elation.

Chris bore a similar expression as he spoke. "I guess Frank is not our man!"

"Nope!" laughed McCall with relief. "Based on these, Frank may be **The Man!** but he's not our man!"

"You going to kick his ass?" Chris curiously enquired.

"You're damned right!" McCall replied. "Nothing official cuz he's a good cop, but I'm gonna come down on him all right! Then I'll probably kiss him!"

"So, do you want me to pull my man off," questioned Chris smugly. "Or do you want more pictures?"

"No, this is more than enough," Dave smirked. "I'm sure that Frank will be satisfied with these!"

With the subject of Frank Bakes finally closed, both men fell silent as they turned their attention to their food. Following several minutes of steady eating, Dave resumed the conversation as he pushed his plate aside.

"Now that Frank has an alibi, we need to talk about something else, Chris."

"Sure. What's about?"

"How well do you know Carl Denver?"

"Funny you should bring him up, because I was going to," Chris slowly responded. "To answer your question, not as well as I thought, but I'll explain that after. Why do you ask?"

"Well," replied McCall, "Harris has been looking into owners of Chevy Astros and it turns out that Denver's on the list."

"That's right," Chris confirmed. "I hadn't really thought about it. He usually drives his Corvette."

"What colour's his van? Do you know?"

"Dark grey," answered Chris. "Charcoal."

"O.K." McCall went on. "So Carl owns a charcoal Chevy Astro. Next, we all suspect that the Vigilante is fairly at ease with computers and communication networks. I think you'll agree with me that Mr. Denver is so qualified?"

Chris nodded as the lieutenant continued.

"You remember the sketch, Chris? Who would you say it reminds you of?"

"Carl?" Chris replied questioningly. "So you think it might be him?"

"I know that it's flimsy right now," Dave admitted. "But I think it deserves some looking into."

"I definitely agree," stated Chris with determination. "Remember when I told you that I was working on something, monitoring systems?"

"Yeah, when we played golf?" Dave curiously replied.

"That's right," Chris confirmed. "Well, the monitoring I was doing was at CSS. Since we were looking for someone with strong computer skills, I figured what better place to start than in my own back yard. So I started tracking my brightest people, which included Carl."

He leaned forward, lowering his voice as he continued.

"Now, lately, Carl's been acting strange, he's nervous, jumpy. It seemed to have started around the time we got involved with this case. Then, about a week ago, he starts bitching about how we're wasting our time helping the cops with these Eazy-Com messages. His attitude bothered me, left me with the impression that he had something to hide so I started zeroing in on what **he**'s been doing on his PC."

"And?" Dave anxiously insisted.

"I haven't finished my analysis yet, but I can tell you that he has been doing some stuff that seems a little out of the ordinary."

"Like what?" enquired McCall, the adrenalin starting to flow again.

"It's hard to say right now," admitted Chris. "These reports are a lot of computer code. With the work I did yesterday, I can tell you that Carl **has** been tapping into Eazy-Com and making some systems changes. It may not be related to this case so I don't want to jump the gun. I'm going to have to do some more digging, backtracking into records, to see what those changes were."

"But assuming it's him," McCall queried. "You're suggesting that the guy ran back to his office every time he wanted to send a message? Why not use a PC at home? Wouldn't that be a lot less risky?"

"I doubt Carl owns a computer," Chris explained. "It's not worth it. We supply all our programming and development people with a portable, a notepad. And these are changed or upgraded every six months to keep them on the leading edge. So, to answer your question, no, he wouldn't have to go to the office at all to send his messages. He'd just use the notepad."

"How the hell do you track what he's doing on this notepad?" questioned Dave, becoming confused and frustrated.

"Each notepad is linked to our network via wireless modems, making them simply an extension or terminal of each user's PC at the office," Chris explained. "This means that even if Carl used his notepad, I should be able to find something."

"Even if he erased the message?" asked the lieutenant.

"Absolutely!" responded Chris, growing excited. "The monitoring I've been doing actually records everything that is done on the computer. Anything that's entered or erased; letters, numbers, backspaces, deletes, everything!"

"So we might really have something here!" McCall mused. "How soon do you think you can figure this out?"

"I only really started getting into some detail yesterday," Chris replied. "And a guy like Carl does a hell of a lot on the computer in a day, let alone four weeks!"

He signalled the waitress to indicate the end of their meal as he went on.

"But the sooner I get back to it, the sooner I'll finish. I should have a good idea by tomorrow morning, maybe before that. Come on, let's go."

He rose to his feet and hurried towards the exit, waving to their waitress on the way out while a puzzled McCall trailed behind him to the parking lot.

Once outside, the lieutenant uneasily enquired. "Uh, Chris? Do you always run out of restaurants without paying the bill?"

"Oh, I thought that cops ate everywhere for free," Chris seriously responded before breaking into a smile. "House account, my friend! This one's on CSS!"

"Quite the comedian!" retorted Dave, realizing he had been had. "Thanks for lunch. I'm going home. I haven't seen Cathy in close to two days and I really need some sleep. But I want you to call me as soon as you have something."

"You've got it," Chris promised. "Like I said, this may take a little while but you'll hear from me as soon as I'm done."

\* \* \* \*

5:17 p.m. Following much thought and careful consideration, Carl Denver had made a decision.

This would be his last scam for a while, maybe forever, and an extra $1,000,000 could always come in handy when one retired. This being the last day of the month meant that tomorrow would be the day that financial institutions everywhere made the monthly interest payments to their accountholders.

With the systems layout of Century Bank still fresh in his memory Carl intended to make tomorrow an excellent pay-day indeed.

'One more to go!' he thought with a smile on his lips as he prepared to leave the office for the evening.

\* \* \* \*

    6:48 p.m. Jean Picard finished the long, laborious climb to the third floor and shuffled slowly to the door of his apartment. Setting down the six pack and frozen dinner he had just purchased, he reached into the pocket of his worn jacket in search of his keys.

    Overall, his had been a relatively miserable life. He had not been a hard working man, much preferring laziness over effort throughout the years. His employment history had therefore consisted of drifting from one odd job to another, most of which he had ended up getting fired from. Often, a hiatus of several months had separated his extremely short periods of employment.

    There was one and only one pastime which he had always particularly enjoyed. Jean Picard liked to drink. As he had often joked to anyone who would listen, if drinking was a job, he'd have made it rich a long time ago. Privately however, he had frequently wondered how he would have gotten through the drudgery of life without his sweet alcohol.

    Having been somewhat attractive in his younger days, he had lived with several women over the years, although he had never married. He'd usually stayed with them until they no longer wished to support him and kicked him out. As he had grown older, the women had been harder to come by and he had now been alone for quite some time.

    He had recently turned sixty-five, which meant that the government sent him a monthly cheque for which he had no effort to exert. Although this was the kind of job which suited him best, he wished the cheques were bigger.

    He found his keys and entered the apartment, closing the door behind him and making sure it was securely locked. There had been many break-ins in this neighbourhood in recent years, older people usually being the prey to the young punks.

    He headed into the small kitchen, leaving the frozen dinner on the counter to thaw before turning his attention to his primary interest, the six-pack.

    Ripping open the small carton, he quickly extracted a beer, twisted off the cap and took a long gulp, emptying a third of the bottle. Sighing with satisfaction, he proceeded to store the remaining beers in the near-empty refrigerator. As an afterthought, he pulled one back out before closing the door, this to avoid his having to get back up in five minutes.

    Armed with his two bottles, he shuffled contently towards the tiny living room, taking another healthy sip along the way. As he rounded the corner of the short corridor which connected the two rooms, he froze in his footsteps. A familiar looking man, about half his age, was seated on the old couch in the living room.

    "How are you doing, Jean?" the man asked softly.

    Jean squinted at the man, suddenly recognizing him. "Holy shit! Is that you, boy?"

The man smiled and nodded. "It sure is, Jean. It sure is."

'Whatcha doing here?' Jean asked, the uncertainty clear in his voice. "H-howdya get in here anyways?"

"The door was unlocked, Jean," his visitor replied. "You should always lock your door. There's some bad people out there, you know."

The old man shifted uneasily, still standing. He was certain that he had locked the door.

"Have a seat, Jean," the man invited, motioning to the couch as he stood. "This is your place, after all. Make yourself at home."

Jean obeyed and trudged slowly to the couch, his discomfort growing.

"Y-you're looking good, boy," he commented, making a feeble attempt at small talk.

"I'm doing O.K." the man confirmed. "Got myself a good job, in computers, you know. Nice house, nice cars, wonderful wife. Yeah, I've done all right so far. How about you, Jean? How have you done?"

"This is it, I guess," Jean mumbled with a shrug. "But I'm O.K. I don't need much."

They lapsed into silence, Jean's anxiety increasing with each passing second. He spoke, if only to break the silence.

"I-I'd offer you a beer, but what I got has to last me the night."

"No problem, Jean," the visitor soothingly replied as he rose and started to pace nonchalantly around the living room. "I'm not really thirsty."

Another soundless moment passed before he stopped pacing, standing directly behind the older man.

"Do you remember my sister, Jean?" he questioned, his tone soft, almost nostalgic.

"Y-yeah. Sorta, I guess," Jean stammered, a quiver of fear in his voice.

The small apartment filled with a deathly quiet as the younger man stood motionless behind the couch, wishing to make the elder one suffer. Without a doubt, the old bastard deserved it but, would it change anything?

'Not really,' the younger man thought as he quietly pulled on a pair of latex gloves.

Jean sat stiffly on the couch in silence, staring directly ahead of him. He did not dare turn to look at the man behind him for fear of seeing the hate in his visitor's eyes and confirming his fate.

"Good-bye, Jean," the younger man whispered suddenly as he gently placed a gloved hand on each side of Jean's head, fingers spread across the old man's cheeks.

With a sudden firm and violent twist, he snapped the elderly man's neck with an audible crack. Letting the limp body slump down to one side, he circled the couch and removed the beer bottles still clutched in Jean's hands, placing them on the battered coffee table.

He left the apartment without a sound, closing and locking the door behind him as he went. He descended the three flights of stairs to the street below and was thankful that they were deserted. Naturally, he preferred the absence of any possible witnesses.

Outside, it was warm, the sun was still shining and as he strolled the several blocks to where he had parked, he felt good, at peace. He had no intention to claim credit for this one; there would be no messages. This one was personal in honour of his sister whom he dearly loved.

It was time to retire. His step-father was dead.

## Chapter 33 - Thursday, August 1, 1996

7:12 a.m. Carl was in the office early, ready for Century Bank which ran their interest transfer programmes at precisely 7:30.

Once he had gotten home the previous evening, he had reviewed the required programming changes and was now confident that he could pull this scam off without a hitch. He had been tempted to alter the systems before going to bed but, in the end, had decided to wait until morning to proceed with his modifications. The last thing he needed was for some bright night operator at the bank to discover something abnormal in the systems.

But now it was time, he was ready and in just over fifteen minutes, he would have a total of $6 million in the Cayman account.

His wife was waiting at home, bags packed, ready to go. He planned to stick around the office until lunch, scanning the systems and erasing any unwanted records. Then, he would disappear. Their flight was scheduled for departure at 1:35 p.m.; their tickets and passports were under a bogus name. By the time anyone realized he was missing, they would be long gone.

Carl was very excited, for this was his final day.

* * * *

Exhausted, Chris had finally taken a break at two-thirty in the morning, dropping on the couch in his office for a couple of hours of sleep.

By five-thirty, he was showered, shaved and back to work on his final analysis of the activities which had take place on Carl Denver's personal computers.

At 7:22, he was done and convinced that he had enough evidence.

It was time to call Dave, who was no doubt up at this time. And if he wasn't, Chris was certain that the lieutenant wouldn't mind the call.

* * * *

Dave had been up and waiting for news from Chris since 1:15 a.m. On several occasions, he had picked up the phone and started dialling Barry's number, but had not completed any of the calls, for fear of waking his friend. Anyways, Chris had said he would be in touch as soon as he had something. But what was he waiting for? What was taking so long?

He had endlessly paced back and forth in the living room, the cordless in his hand, waiting for it to ring. At three-thirty, Cathy had come downstairs to ask him what he was up to and why didn't he get some sleep. He had responded with a silly grin and not much else. She had shrugged and stumbled back upstairs to bed, muttering something about 'nuts' on her way.

As he had done many times before in the preceding hours, he checked the time on the clock on the mantle; 7:22. The phone suddenly rang in his hand, startling him.

"Hello?" he whispered, his heart still pounding in his chest.

"Dave? Chris. Did I wake you?"

"Shit, no! I've been waiting for your call all night," replied McCall. "But you just scared the crap outta me!"

"Sorry," Chris chuckled. "Had I known you were up, I'd have asked you to come give me a hand! I've been up working on this all night."

"So?" asked Dave, trying not to sound too anxious. "Anything?"

"Lots," Chris replied with determination. "I'm sure it's him, Dave."

"What have you got!?" McCall insisted, his heart pumping again.

"He's been sending the messages; and erasing them!" Chris excitedly announced. "Transmission times, message ID codes, everything matches! I haven't finished yet, but I definitely have enough for now!"

"What time does Denver come in?" McCall demanded as he headed to the hall closet for his jacket.

"He's in now," Chris replied. "I asked Steve, our morning guard, to let me know when Carl showed up. He came in a little after 7:00."

"I'll be there in half an hour!" said McCall, scrambling into his jacket as he spoke. "Chris, don't do anything. Wait until we get there!"

"Don't worry," Chris promised. "But hurry! This place is gonna start filling up pretty soon. I don't want anybody to get hurt!"

Chris suddenly realized that he was speaking to a dead line. Dave McCall was already on his way.

* * * *

7:27 a.m. Gina Harris rolled over in the bed and shook her sleeping husband.

"Tim, wake up," she mumbled. "Dave's on the phone. He says it's urgent."

Tim sat up in the bed and picked up the receiver as his wife headed for the bathroom.

"Yeah, Dave," he grunted, still half asleep. "What's up?"

"Get your ass out of bed and meet me at CSS in twenty minutes!" ordered McCall from the cell phone in his car. "You were right about Denver! Move!"

Gina returned from the bathroom, curious to know what the emergency was with Dave but she was too late. Her husband was already gone.

* * * *

7:39 a.m. The transmission was complete; Carl had just transferred $1.35 million dollars to the Cayman account. As long as everything went according to schedule, he would be in the air in six hours, forever off to paradise.

Outside, the cloudless sky was a dazzling shade of blue, further accentuated by the brilliant sun which shone through the floor to ceiling windows of his tenth storey office.

'Today will be a beautiful day!' he thought, trying hard to contain his joy.

\* \* \* \*

At 7:54 a.m., Dave McCall drove through the open gate of the main entrance of CSS headquarters, stopping at the lowered barrier by the guardhouse. He was greeted sombrely by the guard who acknowledged that Mr. Barry was expecting him. When he informed the guard that Harris as well as a few other detectives would be arriving shortly, the man responded with a nod. Mr. Barry had given instructions to fully cooperate with the police.

After parking his car in the visitors' area, Dave headed for the building's main entrance. As he neared the doors, he saw Harris pull up, followed by another car with two more of his men.

While he waited for the three to join him, he scanned the street and noted that two other cars, both unmarked, were parked outside the main gate, on either side. He watched as Joanne Nelson got out of one of the cars and hurried over to speak to the guard. Following a brief conversation, the latter picked up a phone and after a moment, hung up, nodding to Joanne. As she returned to her car, the electronically controlled gate silently closed behind her.

A mini-van, with the **Gazette** logo emblazoned on its side, pulled up and parked across the street, some fifty yards from the gate. He recognized Henderson, as well as the photographer who had accompanied the reporter at Lake Sawin and the Devil's Delight bomb scene. The stage was set.

Dave entered the building, followed by Harris and the two others, where they were immediately greeted by Chris who quickly ushered them into a side elevator. They rode up to the twelfth floor, all remaining silent until they were safely into Chris' spacious office.

"He's still in his office, door closed," Chris informed them. "I have Willy Cobourne, a trusted employee, chatting with the department secretary not far from Carl's office. He'll let me know if the man moves. So, how do we do this?"

"First of all," replied McCall, "I'd like to get as many people away from that area as possible. He may go nuts on us. I don't want any hostages or people getting hurt."

"No problem," Chris responded as he picked up the phone and punched a few numbers. "Sherry, is Willy around? Could I speak to him, please?

Thanks. Willy, how many people in the department you're at right now? O.K. I'm going to call Eddie and Joel, and have them block access to the tenth floor. I'll see that the other half of the floor empties. I want you to casually inform the dozen people around you to go get a coffee downstairs and to drink it slowly. You've got five minutes. And Willy, don't bother letting Carl know."

He cut the connection and punched three more digits. "Joel? Chris. Fine, thanks. Listen, is Eddie there? Good. I want you two to get your butts to the tenth and turn away anyone who tries to get onto that floor. Thanks."

He made his last call. "Al, Chris. I want you to get everybody out of your department. Tell them to use the stairs. Tell them to hurry. Tell them to be quiet. I want everyone in the cafeteria in four minutes."

He hung up and looked up at McCall. "Now what?"

With a tight smile, the lieutenant responded. "We wait four minutes and we go."

"I'm going with you," Chris informed him.

"I don't think so. This could be dangerous, Chris," McCall argued. "I'd rather you stayed out of the way."

"That piece of shit's been working for me for five years!" Chris shot back with fire in his eyes. "I even involved him in this case! I intend to see the bastard go down! It's that simple, Dave!"

"O.K." McCall hesitantly agreed. "But you stay clear and let us take care of this. I sure as hell don't want you getting hurt either!"

"Don't worry," reassured Chris. "If it gets crazy, I'll stay out of the way."

Glancing at his watch, he added, "It's time. Let's go!"

\* \* \* \*

Carl suddenly had the strangest feeling that something was wrong.

Usually, even through the closed door, he could hear the hum of activity from beyond. Moments earlier, the faint 'Good mornings' and the muffled chattering of the people out in the office had been present. Now however, everything seemed to have grown deathly silent.

Puzzled, he got out of his chair and headed towards the door of his office to investigate. Before he could reach it however, the door opened and Chris entered, followed by four other men, two of whom Carl immediately recognized; McCall and some other cop who had been at that Saturday meeting in Chris' office. Once inside, they closed the door behind them.

"Morning, Carl," Chris quietly greeted.

"M-morning, Chris. What's going on?" Carl asked nervously, eyeing the four others warily.

"It's over, Carl," Chris responded coldly. "All over."

"W-what are you talking about?" Carl challenged, his voice shaking. "What's over? W-why are the cops here?"

"We've been monitoring what you've been doing on the system for a while now," Chris replied, his tone ominous. "It's all been recorded. The programming changes, the erasing of records, everything. It all traces back to you."

He stared angrily at his subordinate for a moment before going on.

"I'm surprised and disappointed, Carl. You had to know that somebody would catch up with you sooner or later? How could you be so stupid?"

Not bothering to respond, Carl gazed through watery eyes at the five men standing before him and suddenly felt strangely calm. In the back of his mind, he had always known that the possibility of getting caught existed although he had vowed that it would never happen. And now, that time had come. Sadly, he realized that he would not get to retire, at least not the way he had planned.

He had told his wife to leave if he was not home by noon and prayed that she would follow his advice. At least **she** would get to use the money he had diverted to the Cayman account.

He turned towards the window to look outside for it was such a beautiful day. Spread out below him was the city, his home town. In the distance, he could see the St-Lawrence River and the greenery of the Boucherville Islands. He had expected to see this view for the last time today, albeit under different circumstances. He would remember this vision forever.

He thought again of his vow to never get caught and suddenly realized that there was one way out of this. It would not be easy but he had nothing to lose anymore and he had no intention of going to prison.

Turning back towards the office, he bent over to lean on his chair, his hands gripping both armrests firmly. He remained in this position for a moment, breathing deeply, as if to regain his composure. Then, in an instant, he raised the chair high above his head and hurled it at the glass wall which overlooked the city. As the glass shattered, he rushed towards the opening, following the chair's trajectory and plummeting to his death, ten storeys below.

\* \* \* \*

By mid-afternoon, the frenzy of activity which had followed Carl's death had somewhat subsided around CSS headquarters.

The reporters and T.V. crews had all hurried off to be the first to announce the earth-shattering news; the Vigilante was dead. None of their reports or articles however, would have the impact of that of Ron Henderson. His front page story in the morning's **Gazette** would be accompanied by a close up color photo of Carl in mid-air.

Both reporters and the police had attempted to reach Carl's wife but she was nowhere to be found. The Denvers' charcoal Chevy Astro had been located, parked at Dorval International Airport, the stub on the dash indicating an arrival time of 12:29 p.m. However, Mrs. Denver's name did not appear on the passenger lists of any flights having departed that day.

A preliminary search by the police of Carl's Corvette had yielded a well used baseball bat hidden under a tarpaulin in the trunk. Stains on the bat would later prove to be blood, several types of which would be matched to that of a number of the Vigilante's victims.

A search of the Denver home would not produce anything of interest but a detailed analysis of the activity records on Carl's PC would eventually clearly support that the messages had in fact originated from him. It was an open and shut case. The Vigilante was dead.

* * * *

Chris slumped wearily in the chair behind his desk, exhausted by the day's events and from lack of sleep. It was 3:27 and he would be going home soon. He just needed to accomplish one more task before leaving.

Flipping open his notepad, he keyed in a series of codes and quickly got to work. Several minutes later, he was done and ready to go.

He packed his briefcase and left his office, pausing only long enough to inform Sonia that he would take the next day off. He then headed for home and his charming spouse.

## Chapter 34 - Friday, August 2, 1996

The clerk returned to his desk accompanied by George Fullerton, manager of the Royal Bank in Georgetown, Grand Cayman.

"We seem to have a bit of a problem, Mrs. Denver?" suggested Fullerton with a polite smile.

"I'll say we do!" she snapped. "I want to withdraw $5,000 and this one says I can't. Something about a $10,000 minimum balance requirement. What's going on?"

"We do insist, Mrs. Denver, that our account holders maintain at least a $10,000 balance. That is where your account now stands."

"There's six million dollars in that account, mister!" she hissed. "All I need right now is five thousand!"

The smile having disappeared, Fullerton referred to a computer monitor nearby as he stiffly replied.

"Transfers of funds totalling $5,992,546.87 were made late yesterday afternoon. The proper identification codes were given, everything is in order. Might I suggest that you speak to your husband, Madam. In the meantime, if you require some money, you may close your account. Good-day, Mrs. Denver!"

\* \* \* \*

Across Canada, the administrators of a number of reputable charities were pleased to discover that generous donations from an anonymous donor had been made to their respective accounts.

### Chapter 35 - Saturday, August 3, 1996

Accompanied by Cathy, his wife, Dave McCall pulled into the driveway of the luxurious Barry residence and examined the property in awe.

Like everything else about Chris, the man's home was impressive. Surrounded by an ornamental wrought iron and concrete block fence, the property was a carefully planned masterpiece, with its beautifully manicured lawns, exotic flowers and decorative trees and shrubs. A miniature waterfall cascaded alongside the wide expanse of steps which lead to the main entrance of the house, a large modern structure of brick, aggregate and glass.

As they ascended the steps, Dave continued to feel somewhat uncomfortable with Chris' invitation. If anything, **he** should have invited Chris to dinner, not the other way around. Without Barry's help, the case might have never been solved.

"I shouldn't have accepted," Dave muttered as they reached the door.

"Stop being silly, Dave," Cathy scolded. "You get along great with Chris and I'm sure we'll have a wonderful time."

"I guess," her husband conceded as he rang the bell.

A moment later, the door opened and they were greeted by an extremely attractive woman.

'Impressive wife!' McCall thought, flashing his best grin.

"Hi!" she greeted them with a warm smile. "You must be Dave! It's so nice to finally meet you, I've heard so much about you! Come on in. Chris is out back, lazing by the pool."

"This is my wife, Cathy," introduced Dave as they entered the foyer of the spacious home.

"It's a pleasure to meet you, Cathy!" their host replied, extending a friendly hand. "I'm Cassandra Taylor, Chris' wife. But you can call me Sandy. Everybody does."

# BOOK # 2

# THE CONSULTANT

A novel by
**Claude Bouchard**

### Prologue - Tuesday, January 7, 1997

"Who the hell is this!?" demanded the voice on the other end of the line.

"Never mind who I am," George replied, his voice a wavering whisper. "Just listen. Quality Imports. Got it? That's all I can say. Quality Imports. Check it out."

He quickly hung up the phone and sat in the darkness of his office, breathing deeply, fighting back the urge to vomit. After a moment, his shaking subsided and the churning in his stomach slowed. He realized that this was dangerous but also knew that he had done the right thing.

Standing, he began to pace back and forth as he continued his deep breathing in an attempt to regain his composure. He started feeling ridiculous and began to relax. There was no reason to worry, he reasoned, he was alone. Anyways, nobody had the slightest idea that he was aware of anything.

Feeling better, he picked up his briefcase and left his office, heading for the main entrance. As he walked by the door leading into the warehouse, he paused then stopped. He had to look again. It was silly because he had seen what he had to see but he felt drawn, as if by some powerful, invisible magnet. He set down his briefcase and, following a moment's hesitation, opened the door.

The warehouse was dark but he had been without light for some time now and his eyes had grown accustomed to its absence. Quickly, he made his way to the rear receiving area where he had seen the cases an hour before.

As he picked up the crowbar he had used earlier and started to pry off the cover of the first wooden case, he could feel the adrenalin pumping through his system once again. The lid came off more easily this time and he leaned it off to one side against the racking. Although this time he knew what to expect, he experienced the same gut wrenching feeling he had felt an hour ago when he had first discovered the cocaine.

At least, he believed it was coke. The shipment came from Columbia and, according to the labels and paperwork, was supposed to be coffee. Though he was far from being a drug expert, he was certain that the contents of this case alone were worth several million dollars on the street.

As he stared in awed horror at the rows of powder filled plastic bags before him, the warehouse lights suddenly came on, bathing the cavernous room in harsh light.

"Good evening, George," a familiar voice greeted from behind him.

He turned to find himself faced by four men, two of whom, like him, were executive managers of the company. The other two, whom he recognized as warehouse employees, were armed with what appeared to be automatic weapons which they pointed directly at him.

"Greg! Wayne! What's going on?" George nervously exclaimed, for lack of something better to say.

"Well," responded Wayne, the company's Director of Operations. "What's going on seems to be that Georgie is not minding his own goddamn business! What do you think, you stupid fuck!"

"Listen," pleaded George, shaking all over again. "Whatever you guys do with your spare time is your own business! Just let me go and I promise I won't say anything. I swear!"

"You sure of that, Georgie?" enquired Wayne with a warm smile. "I can't let you go unless you're sure of what you're saying."

"I swear it, Wayne!" promised George, sweat streaming from every pore of his body. "I won't say a word! Hell, I'll even quit if you want! I won't even show up tomorrow!"

Wayne gazed at him thoughtfully for a few seconds then pulled a handgun equipped with a silencer from under his jacket.

"You got that right, dude!" he grinned as he calmly pulled the trigger four times.

"Was that absolutely necessary?!" whined Greg, Director of Finance, as George's body slumped to the floor.

"Greg, sometimes I wonder why the fuck I ever involved you in all of this!" Wayne snarled in exasperation. "What were we supposed to do? Believe the schmuck and let him go?! You just better pray that he didn't speak to anybody about all of this!"

Turning to one of the other two, he continued. "Bring his car out back and get him out of here. Dump him and the car in some tough neighbourhood somewhere. Hopefully, the cops will think it was a mugging or something."

"Do you think he might have spoken to somebody?" Greg questioned uneasily as he watched the body being dragged away.

"He can't have been on to us for long so, I doubt it," Wayne replied with his usual overconfidence. "But if he has, I'm sure they'll understand that their best bet is to shut the fuck up!"

## Chapter 1 - Wednesday, January 8, 1997

Walter Olson signed the last page of the thick, legal-sized document and slid it across the boardroom table to Chris Barry.

Although he knew its contents by heart, Chris allowed himself several minutes to scan the agreement one last time and then also apposed his signature.

The deal was complete. CompuCorp was now majority shareholder of CSS Inc., having acquired all of the shares owned by Walter Olson and Chris Barry.

Founded by Walter Olson some twenty-five years prior, CSS' original *"raison d'être"* had been to offer security and investigative services to the business community at large.

Nine years ago, in a time of difficult markets and falling revenues, Chris Barry, now Executive Vice-President and Chief Operating Officer, had joined the firm and rapidly turned it into a leader in the field of computer security. The company had gone public after three years and had continued to expand ever since. Revenues of the preceding year had slightly exceeded $3 billion and conservative forecasts for the current year were for a 15% increase.

Of the one hundred million outstanding shares, which were currently trading at $16.25, Walter, the firm's president and CEO, held 40%. In addition to a generous salary and a variety of other perks, Walter had awarded Chris with a number of stock options over the years, in recognition of his contribution towards the company's success. Today, this translated in Chris' owning 20% of the firm.

Having turned sixty during the preceding year and satisfied with his accomplishments, Walter had decided that it was time to retire. To ensure a serene retirement, Walter felt it necessary to completely exit the business world and invest his profits in fixed income vehicles, thus eliminating the stress related to the volatility of the stock markets.

His only concern with his decision had been Chris and how the latter would react to it. They had worked extremely well together for nearly a decade and had grown extremely fond of each other during that time.

To Walter's surprise, when he had announced his intentions, Chris had agreed wholeheartedly, even indicating that he also was at a turning point in his life and wished to take it easy for a while and enjoy life with Sandy, his wife.

CSS had been approached with merger propositions on several occasions in recent years and when word had gotten out that the company was for sale, offers had begun pouring in.

Recognizing the firm's current value and future earnings potential, CompuCorp had come in with the best bid, offering CSS shareholders $28 cash per share. Walter and Chris had accepted and were now both much wealthier men.

"Are you sure you won't change your mind, Chris?" asked Jeff Sanders, CEO of CompuCorp. "With Walter out of your hair, you could really make CSS work!" he added with a smile.

"Nope," Chris replied without hesitation, shaking his head. "I appreciate the vote of confidence but Walter's the one who really built this company. I just helped keep it profitable over the last few years. He's decided to turn the page and frankly, having worked with him for close to ten years, I really feel that I'm entitled to a well deserved break!"

"Do you bastards want me to leave the room so that you can continue your goddamn conversation!?" demanded Walter in mock anger, now $470 million richer.

"No, stick around," answered Chris with a smirk. "I'm a rich sonovabitch now and you ain't my boss anymore. I think it's time you heard what I've really got to say about you!"

"Unappreciative, little punk!" Walter grinned, ending the playful exchange.

"Well, if you change your mind, Chris, let me know," said Sanders. "I have no doubt that we can find a place in our organization for you."

"Thanks," Chris responded. "But thirty-five is not a bad age to retire and I'm sure my wife and I can find something to do to pass the time, at least for a little while."

\* \* \* \*

Chris finished collecting the various documents laid out on the boardroom table before him and walked through the door into his spacious adjoining office. Walter, who was already seated in one of the comfortable leather armchairs in the corner and sipping a Chivas, neat, looked up as Chris entered.

"Are you sure this is what you want, kid?" he questioned, not certain if Chris had made the right decision.

"Harry, I'm gonna turn thirty-five in March," Chris patiently replied. "I just signed a contract that will put $560 million in the bank in my name. That's a profit of $235 million with what I consider little or no effort. Yep, this is what I want."

"What are you gonna do now?" pursued Walter, still not convinced.

"To start," laughed Chris. "I'm gonna get a **real** good night's sleep. Then, I will have frequent sex with my wife, which we both thoroughly enjoy, travel, mow the lawn, do crossword puzzles, read and paint. Hell, I might even write a book! That's always been something I wanted to do."

"After that," pressed Walter. "What are you gonna do if you get bored?"

"You worry too much, Walter," Chris chuckled, shrugging his shoulders in exasperation. "After that, if I really get bored, I'll find myself some work to do. You know, freelance. I'll become a consultant."

## Chapter 2 - Thursday, January 9, 1997

Employed by the federal government's Ministry of Defence, Jonathan Addley's official title was Director of Police Relations and, although he allotted a small portion of his available time to the duties related to this title, this was not his true function.

He was in fact responsible for a small, yet elite division, the existence of which was known by very few. Though it had no official name, it was sometimes referred to as Discreet Activities and it worked in tight collaboration with similar organizations of other countries. The purpose of this covert network was to supply whatever help it could to ensure the security and well-being of the member countries' citizens.

In so doing, Discreet Activities was open to solving problems at all levels and often dealt with issues that might otherwise be looked after by the police at the municipal, provincial or federal level. In fact, as often was the case, such authorities were actually investigating criminal activities which this clandestine team decided to handle. However, when the division became involved, it always did so without the official knowledge of these law enforcement agencies.

The staff of the Canadian team consisted of little more than a handful of people, carefully recruited by Jonathan. None of them however, were on the government payroll, at least not as salaried civil servants. Rather, when their services were required, they were paid from the government's coffers as consultants.

Their assignments usually consisted of tasks which required high levels of discretion as well as actions that could not be carried out by the customary law enforcement agencies. Each member of the team knew well that in the event of an assignment going sour, their government would not back them up as doing so would be admitting that the network actually existed. They were on their own, but were handsomely compensated for this risk and their efforts.

Though Jonathan did not often recruit new members, he remained constantly on the alert for possible candidates, which were a rare commodity in his line of work. He finished reading the confidential file entitled "Christopher Barry" and leaned back in his chair, reminiscing on how he had come to learn of this new potential recruit.

It had been late morning towards the end of September of the previous year and he had been sitting and chatting in the office of his personal friend and professional ally, Nick Sharp, RCMP Director for the province of Quebec.

Nick was one of the few people who were more closely aware of Jonathan's covert activities and the two occasionally helped each other out when possible.

As they had chatted, their conversation had been interrupted by a knock on the door.

"Sorry to bother you, Chief," apologized Arty, one of Nick's officers, coming in and closing the door behind him. "I've got a lady out there who insists on speaking to the person in command."

"What about?" asked Nick.

"Won't say," Arty shrugged. "She just says that she has something of vital importance to discuss with someone high up."

"Of vital importance?" Nick scoffed. "Is she a crazy one?"

They had their share of nuts coming in off the street to supply information about enemy spies with master schemes or aliens from other planets.

"Nope," Arty shook his head. "She's well dressed, good looking, a little agitated, but I don't think she's crazy."

"Alright," Nick sighed. "Show her in."

As Arty left the room Jonathan rose from his seat but Nick waved him back to the chair.

"Stay," he suggested. "Just in case she **is** a wacko, I may need you for protection! Seriously, you're a senior government officer so you can hear what she has to say. Plus, I was hoping you'd buy me lunch so, stick around!"

As Jonathan laughed and dropped back into his seat, the door opened once again and Arty entered, followed by an attractive woman in her early thirties. She did seem agitated, her nervousness displayed by her wan smile and her abrupt, rapid movements.

The two men stood to greet her as she moved into the office.

"This is Chief Sharp, ma'am," Arty announced before leaving the room, closing the door on his way out.

"How do you do, Miss...?" enquired Nick, smiling warmly as he extended a hand.

"Mrs." she corrected uncertainly, not responding to the handshake. "Mrs. Denver."

For some reason, the name seemed vaguely familiar.

"Well, Mrs. Denver, I'm Nick Sharp and this is Jonathan Addley," said Nick as he sat back down. "Mr. Addley's with the Ministry of Defence. Have a seat, please."

As she lowered herself into an armchair, she eyed Jonathan suspiciously and asked, "Does he have to be here?"

"I was told that you wished to speak to somebody high up," answered Nick with a serious smile. "Mr. Addley is about as high up as they get. You have nothing to worry about."

"O.K." she hesitantly replied. "I just want to be careful with who I talk to."

"Quite understandable," Nick replied soothingly, wondering if she **was** mentally imbalanced. "Now, how can we help you Mrs. Denver?"

She stared at both men, the uncertainty clear in her eyes, then took a deep breath and spoke.

"Before I say anything, I want you to promise me immunity and, if required, protection."

"Immunity and protection from what?" queried Nick, his curiosity mounting.

"What I have to talk about concerns a major murder case in Montreal, which was solved a couple of months ago," she responded, hesitating before adding, "The killer is still on the loose."

Nick leaned forward slightly in his chair. Denver; the name became more familiar although he still couldn't pinpoint exactly why. Maybe this lady wasn't crazy after all.

"What killer, ma'am," he asked softly.

"Immunity and protection," she insisted, a little more confident. "Then I'll talk."

Nick glanced at Jonathan who gave a slight nod. He was also curious as to what this lady had to say.

"O.K. Mrs. Denver," Nick accepted. "I'll presume that you aren't guilty of some hideous crime and, on that basis, I'll agree to your request. However, until you tell us more, I can't promise you anything specific."

"I haven't really done anything wrong myself," she nervously explained. "M-my late husband did some things with computers though, that I was aware of. That's the extent of my guilt."

"Well, that sounds tame enough," reassured Nick. "I'm sure we can overlook that in exchange for something concrete about a murder."

"Murders," she corrected. "Alright, I'm going to trust you gentlemen. Frankly, I've got nothing to lose, nowhere to go and I'm scared as hell!"

She took a deep breath to calm herself and plunged ahead. "Are you familiar with the Vigilante?"

Denver! Carl Denver! It all came back to Nick. Two months earlier, Carl Denver had committed suicide when cornered by the police. For a period of seven months, the Vigilante had been active in the Montreal area, killing a variety of criminals which the system had either failed to penalize or never caught up with. Approximately thirty victims had met their fate before the authorities had finally zeroed in on Denver.

From what Nick could remember, the evidence in that case had been airtight. Denver was the Vigilante and he was dead. His wife had disappeared on the day of his death.

"You are Mrs. Carl Denver?" Nick stated more than asked, staring at the woman before him.

"Yes," she replied with pride. "And my husband was innocent. Carl never hurt anybody. He hated violence."

"Mrs. Denver, I realize that this is difficult for you to accept," Nick sceptically insisted. "But from what I know about the Vigilante case, the evidence was rather clear. One of the murder weapons, a blood stained baseball bat, was found in your husband's car. Blood tests matched with some of the victims. Computer records showed that he had sent and erased messages to the police on Eazy-Com."

"Carl was framed!" she retorted emphatically.

"Then why did he kill himself when the cops went to him?" Nick shot back.

"The money," she quietly replied.

"What money?" asked Nick, somewhat puzzled.

He did not remember anything about money being involved in the Vigilante case.

"Carl was a computer genius," Mrs. Denver replied, less proud. "He had been skimming money from a variety of sources for a while; banks, trusts, brokers, that kind of thing. On the day that he died, we were planning to disappear. I did. He died. We had six million dollars accumulated in an account in the Cayman Islands."

"So you're saying," Nick spoke slowly, "That your husband killed himself because he thought he was getting busted for the money scams?"

"That's the only thing that makes sense," she nodded, tears welling up. "Carl was not the Vigilante. He rarely went out alone and we were together on many of the nights that murders took place. On several occasions, we were even out to dinner. Credit card slips were signed by Carl. Check it out. You'll see Carl was not the killer!"

"Do you have any idea who the killer might be?" Nick gently enquired.

"No, not really," Mrs. Denver shook her head. "It was someone who discovered what Carl was doing with the money, but I don't know who."

"How do you know that?" probed Nick.

"Carl and I had agreed that, no matter what, I was to take the plane and leave. I did and made it to the Caymans. When I tried to access the cash, the account had been cleaned out. The killer is still out there, my husband is dead, I'm broke and wanted by the cops. I'm scared, gentlemen. I will do what I can to help you but you must help me."

"We're going to have to check all of this out, you understand," Nick informed her. "But if what you're telling us is true, yes, we will help you, Mrs. Denver. We have a witness protection programme we can get you into. You have nothing to worry about."

"What happens now?" she asked helplessly. "I had left, and returned, under an assumed name. I don't have anywhere to go and like I said, I'm broke. The only money I do have is in the bank under my real name. I'm not real comfortable in going there or going back home."

"And we wouldn't want you to do that either," answered Nick. "We have a few places, safe-houses, where we keep witnesses from time to time.

We'll set you up there until we can work things out. Don't worry, you'll be comfortable and in complete security."

He picked up the phone and punched a few numbers. "Arty, we have a guest here for our Lake Brome residence. I'd like you and Sammy to drive her down there. Thanks."

He replaced the receiver in its cradle and smiled at Mrs. Carl Denver. "We're all set. All you have to do now is relax and let us do our job. I'll let you know if you can do anything else to help."

"Thank-you," she murmured gratefully and rose to her feet as Arty opened the office door to escort her out.

Once she had gone, Nick glanced at Jonathan and feigning surprise, exclaimed, "Oh, are you still here!?"

Grinning, Jonathan replied, "Yep. Just didn't have much to say. You asked all the right questions so why should I interrupt?"

"So? What do you think?" asked Nick.

The lady's story had been quite believable but he didn't know quite what to make of it.

"I think she's telling the truth," Jonathan answered with conviction. "Once we start checking, everything will pan out."

"We??" enquired Nick, now his turn to grin.

Smiling widely, Jonathan replied, "You know how my mind works, Nick. I followed the Vigilante case closely enough and was pretty impressed by the guy. Honestly, I was disappointed when it ended. Not because they had caught up with him, mind you, although I did consider the man was actually doing society a favour. What really bothered me was that he ended up not being as smart as I had given him credit for. Now, to find out that he's not gone, it's not over, that he got away clean as a whistle?! Now, I'm proud of him again!"

"So, you're thinking recruit?" asked Nick, although it was not really a question.

"You never know," Jonathan admitted. "Let me work on this for a bit and save you some man-hours."

"Be my guest," Nick invited. "I much prefer spending your budget over mine!"

"Speaking of which," replied Addley. "I believe that I'm supposed to buy you lunch. Let's go."

During the months which had followed the initial meeting with Mrs. Denver, Jonathan, with the help of a few consultants, had quietly begun digging into the Vigilante case. They had been quickly able to confirm that Carl Denver's wife had spoken the truth as Carl's whereabouts could be clearly established on many occasions when murders had taken place.

This had led Jonathan to review the entire Vigilante investigation with two major questions in mind. Who was the actual killer, and why had the money which Denver had electronically skimmed never been questioned, never even been an issue?

As Jonathan had continued to search for answers, one name had strangely kept popping up; Chris Barry, Executive Vice President at CSS, Denver's employer. Barry had worked closely with the police on the case and, by monitoring Denver's PC activities, had been the one to discover the latter's Eazy-Com message transmissions and subsequent erasures. If this was actually what had transpired, why hadn't Carl's money scams been uncovered? These had all been accomplished with the use of the computer, hadn't they? And according to Mrs. Denver, Carl had performed several of his tricks during the weeks which had preceded his death. Police records indicated that Barry had been monitoring Denver's PC during that period of time.

Verification of Barry's financial records had confirmed that he had not taken the cash unless it had been diverted to some confidential account. This, Jonathan doubted as the guy was filthy rich as it was. It was not as if he needed an additional six million.

The investigation reports had mentioned the possible involvement of a mini-van in the Vigilante crimes and Carl Denver owned a Chevy Astro. Interestingly enough, although this was far from solid evidence, DMV records indicated that Barry had owned a Chrysler Town & Country at the time. In addition, though it had no bearing in the case, both men had coincidentally also owned Corvettes. Barry had since replaced both vehicles.

It was when Jonathan decided to look into the past that things, however still fragmented and inconclusive, became more promising. Through birth records, he had come to discover the identity of Barry's parents.

His father had died when Chris was very young, leaving Mrs. Barry to see to the upbringing of her son and daughter, alone. She had taken on employment as a cashier with a major supermarket chain where she had remained until a few years ago, when she had retired. Group insurance records indicated a Jean Picard, common-law spouse, as her beneficiary, a number of years earlier.

When attempting to establish the whereabouts of Mr. Picard, Jonathan had learned that the gentleman had been murdered a few months prior, the time of death coinciding with the end of the Vigilante's activities. Police records indicated that Picard had had a history of domestic violence which included complaints submitted by Mrs. Barry. She had eventually left the man, bless her heart.

The past of Chris Barry's wife, Cassandra Taylor, had also proved somewhat interesting. At the age of seventeen, she had witnessed the murder of her father during a fouled hold-up at the family-owned convenience store. Those responsible, three unidentified teenagers, had never been caught. As chance would have it, Cassandra and Carl Denver had both grown up in the same neighbourhood and, although she was a couple of years older than he, both had attended the same high school.

Jonathan had paid Carl's mother a visit to try to find out more about the supposed Vigilante and his earlier years. He had heard her speak of a quiet, studious boy, beyond reproach, except for those hoodlum friends of his, Mike and Eddy. When he had later attempted to track these gentlemen down, Jonathan had discovered that both had since been murdered, one as recently as last July, in Vancouver. Verification had quickly shown that Barry, as well as Denver, had been on the West Coast at the time.

Jonathan knew that he did not have anything close to a foolproof case against Chris Barry. In fact, what he had was really nothing more than a lot of bits and pieces which could all be attributed to coincidence. However, he also had a gut feeling and such feelings had proven more often right than wrong in the past.

He had just learned that Mr. Barry had recently opted for a very early retirement, having sold his interest in CSS Inc. Considering that the gentleman was about to have much more free time on his hands, Jonathan felt that the time was right to get together with Chris to discuss the past and, possibly, the future.

## Chapter 3 - Friday, January 10, 1997

Officer John Riley turned right off De Lorimier onto Logan and immediately saw the turquoise Plymouth Sundance, still parked in the same spot.

He had first noticed the vehicle two days earlier and had written a ticket for parking by a fire hydrant. The previous day, he had seen the car again and called in the plate number to verify if it was stolen, which it wasn't. He had added a second parking ticket to the first.

He pulled up behind the automobile and climbed out of the warmth of his cruiser to investigate further. Although the abandoned car's windows were somewhat frosted from the cold, he could see inside well enough and noted nothing of interest. The parking tickets remained in place under the wiper blade, indicating that the vehicle had not yet been moved. He tried the doors but both were locked, as was the trunk. Returning to his patrol car, he called in to dispatch.

"Kelly? Riley. Listen, you want to check on plate number TIN 147? Turquoise Plymouth Sundance, a couple of years old. I'd like a name and address of ownership. The car's been abandoned. Let me know when you find something. In the meantime, send a tow truck to the corner of Logan and De Lorimier to pick this thing up cuz it's been here for over two days. Thanks. Over."

As he set down the transmitter, he gazed at the abandoned car and suddenly noticed something which he had not earlier. Several brownish-red, elongated spots could be seen on the license plate, as if someone had splashed a few drops of paint or stain.

Climbing back out into the bitter cold, he hurried over to get a closer look and, though he wasn't certain, those stains could be blood. Several more similar spots were splattered on the car's bumper.

Determined to find out more, he went to the trunk of his cruiser and pulled out a crowbar. Returning to the Plymouth, he jammed one end of the crowbar under the lid of the trunk and, with the help of his two hundred fourteen pounds, popped the trunk open like a bottle top.

The body inside was frozen solid, thanks to Montreal's sub-zero January weather. He searched the corpse for identification and quickly found a wallet in an inside pocket of the man's suit jacket. As he looked into the wallet for I.D., the portable transmitter-receiver attached to his coat collar crackled.

"52-10, do you read me?" called Kelly's voice.

"Yeah," Riley grimly replied. "I read you."

"I've got that ownership information you wanted on the Sundance."

"Let me guess," interrupted Riley, "George Robinson, 6240 Rosemont Boulevard."

"That's right," responded Kelly. "How did you know?"

"I found his driver's permit in his wallet," answered Riley. "I asked for a tow truck before. You better send a meat wagon too because this guy's definitely dead."

## Chapter 4 - Monday, January 13, 1997

Chris Barry sat at the large crescent-shaped desk in his corner office on the twelfth floor of the CSS building. It was a sunny day and he was admiring the view, watching the sun's reflections as they bounced off the expanse of snow covered ground and trees in Maisonneuve Park across the street below.

He knew that he would miss this place but he was due for a well earned break. He estimated that he had put in excess of thirty-five thousand hours in the rebuilding of this company over the last nine years and felt he now deserved some free time to truly enjoy life with his precious Sandy. Vacations over the years had always been interrupted on a daily basis with phone calls, faxes and decisions to be made. It would be nice to travel with only leisure activities in mind for a change.

The buzz of the intercom broke into his reverie.

"Chris, there's a Jonathan Addley down at the gate who wants to see you. Says he's with the Ministry of Defence. Steve says the I.D. looks official."

"O.K. Sonia," replied Chris. "Let him in. I'll see him."

A visitor would be a nice break in the monotony as this was Chris' last week and he didn't really have much to do. The people from CompuCorp had collected pretty much all the files of current and potential contracts, leaving Chris and Walter with little to occupy their final hours with the firm.

Following several minutes of waiting, the intercom buzzed again.

"Mr. Barry, Mr. Addley is here to see you," Sonia's voice formally announced.

"Thanks," Chris acknowledged. "Be right there."

He crossed the wide expanse of white oak flooring to the door leading to the tasteful reception area which also served as Sonia's office.

Seated in one of the comfortable visitors chairs was a man in his early forties who did not resemble any of the government bureaucrats Chris had met in the past. Of medium height and build, this man looked fit, tough and determined. Chris had a strange impression that his visitor would have felt right at home in a camouflage suit, tracking enemy snipers in a jungle somewhere. As he approached, he had a weird feeling that his guest was sizing him.

"Mr. Addley," greeted Chris with his usual charming smile.

"Mr. Barry." Jonathan jovially responded, standing as he reached for his host's extended hand.

"Can I offer you something to drink?" offered Chris, gracious as always.

"If you can find a cup of coffee somewhere, that would be great," accepted Jonathan.

Chris glanced at an already nodding Sonia and grinned. He would definitely miss her once he was gone. She deserved to have her picture by the definition of 'Administrative Assistant Extraordinaire' in any dictionary.

"What can I do for you?" Chris curiously enquired, ushering his guest into his office.

"I was hoping you and I could discuss a little business," answered Jonathan as Chris gestured for him to sit.

"You might not be aware of this, Mr. Addley, but CSS has been sold to CompuCorp. I will be leaving the company at the end of the week so I'm probably not the best person to speak to. Perhaps I can refer you to someone over there?"

"No, Mr. Barry," Jonathan confidently replied. "You really are the person that I want to speak to."

"Sure, fine," Chris shrugged. "And call me Chris. Formality and I don't get along very well!"

"O.K., Chris it is!" smiled Addley. "You can call me Jonathan."

They paused for a moment as Sonia entered the room with a complete coffee service. Once she had gone, Chris did the honours and they resumed their conversation.

"Now then, back to my original question. What can I do for you?" Chris asked.

Jonathan eyed Chris intently for a moment before answering. His in-depth study of the man over the last three months had clearly indicated that Chris Barry was a highly intelligent man and this first personal contact did not lead Jonathan to believe any differently. It was in Barry's eyes; blue as ice; intense, brilliant eyes. Jonathan sensed that Chris was not one with whom to play games. His best bet was to play it straight; sort of.

"Chris, I'm gonna tell you a story that I'm putting together," Jonathan started. "Maybe it's fiction, maybe not. I don't know. I'd like you to listen to the story and when I'm done, we can discuss it if you wish. Sound fair?"

"Hey, it's not like CompuCorp left me with a whole lot to do!" laughed Chris. "I've got time. Tell me a story!"

"O.K. Here it goes," Jonathan went on. "There's this kid who's brought up surrounded by violence in the streets and at home. He's a smart kid and grows up to be very successful. But the violence he saw and endured during his younger years left him with scars that he has to deal with."

He paused for a sip of coffee then continued.

"To add to his pain, the young lady he has married was witness to her father's murder. The only way he finds to help the healing process is through violent acts of vengeance. He therefore becomes the Vigilante and makes people pay for their crimes."

"Interesting," Chris nodded approvingly. "Go on."

"Being a very intelligent and calculating man, our man plans his deeds well and never gets caught, never leaves a trace. He doesn't intend to go on forever, but he must ease the hurt. Most of his victims are personally unknown to him and are simply part of his therapy. But there are a few people, four to be exact, who must die for the healing to be complete. Three of them are those have caused personal pain to his wife by taking the life of her father. Able to identify them, her decision at the time was to make them pay some day herself. As destiny would have it, she has since married our hero, who is willing and able to handle this task for her. Two of these individuals die. The third is reserved for later."

Jonathan went for another sip of coffee, watching Chris closely for any signs of stress. Detecting nothing of the sort, he pressed on.

"The fourth person is his mother's lover from many years before. This man's crime is not obvious but it probably relates to domestic violence. His death is justified and necessary for our hero to complete the healing process."

"So our man kills his mother's ex-lover?" Chris requested clarification.

"That's right," Jonathan nodded. "We now come back to the third murderer of our man's father-in-law. Planned or destiny, I don't know, but he ends up employed by none other than our hero. In the end, this poor soul is framed for the rash of murders and commits suicide, leaving everyone to believe that the Vigilante is dead. What do you think of my story, Chris?"

"It's an incredible story, Jonathan," Chris admitted, impressed. "It is violent at times but it has a happy ending. **Is** this a true story, Jonathan?"

Jonathan eyed his host intently as the latter spoke, searching for signs of nervousness or panic. What he saw however, was a calm man, definitely relaxed and composed.

"Quite frankly, like I said, I don't know," answered Jonathan. "What do you think, Chris?"

"It could be true," Chris reasoned. "It definitely sounds plausible. Is that where the story ends or does something else happen?"

Although he really had nothing more to base himself on, Jonathan was now convinced that Chris Barry was the Vigilante. Why else would the man have listened to him and be willing to pursue this strange conversation. He had to make a decision, as he had done in the past with other recruits. Was Barry stable enough to warrant continuing the process or was he some psychopath presently in remission? Jonathan gazed thoughtfully at Chris for a moment and decided that this was probably the most solid candidate he had ever interviewed. He could continue.

"There is more to the story, Chris," Jonathan replied. "A witness comes forward, claiming the innocence of the dead, supposed Vigilante. This brings a special agent to discreetly investigate the case all over again and he discovers that what the witness says is true. Many of the murders occurred while the supposed Vigilante's presence could be vouched for elsewhere. The agent continues to dig and eventually finds the person he believes to be the true Vigilante who, of course, is alive and well."

Chris smiled, thoroughly entertained. "This really is a great story, Jonathan! What happens next?"

"The agent meets with the Vigilante. Now, you must understand that the agent heads an obscure department of the government, which is unknown to the public. This department is responsible for what we might call clandestine activities aimed at the betterment of the country and its allies."

"Wow! Isn't that a very important person to have investigating a local murder case?" asked Chris, amused, "Especially a case which is already officially solved?"

"Well, the agent's objective is not to catch the Vigilante," explained Jonathan with a smile. "The agent is responsible for recruiting new members for this secret department."

"Sure, that makes sense," chuckled Chris. "Jonathan, this is great! Are you telling me that the agent wants to hire the Vigilante to work for the government?"

"The agent is impressed with the Vigilante and believes that his talents could be a definite asset to his department and to the country."

"But what if the Vigilante is not interested?" enquired Chris, suddenly pensive. "What happens then?"

"Nothing," Jonathan replied. "Disappointed, the agent goes away to find recruits elsewhere."

"What about blackmail?" Chris probed on, "Any chance that this agent might try that route with the Vigilante? You know, to convince him to join the team?"

"Not worth it," Addley shook his head. "Those who join the team must be fully devoted. Also, as I mentioned, very few are aware of this department's existence so the agent couldn't just come forward to make the Vigilante story public. Doing so might put the department's secrecy at risk."

Chris nodded thoughtfully and asked, "What about the witness? Couldn't the witness try to make the whole thing public?"

Again, Addley shook his head as he replied, "All that the witness needs to be told is that following an investigation, the authorities were unable to discover the true identity of the Vigilante. To ensure her safety however, she will be kept in the witness protection programme indefinitely."

**She!** No doubt Carl's wife, thought Chris.

He smiled as he spoke, "And you're certain that she will keep quiet?"

"She has no idea who the true Vigilante is," Jonathan answered, realizing his slip-up, too late. "All she knows is that he is not dead. She will keep quiet. Her main concern is physical and financial survival. That will be supplied."

"Well, Jonathan," said Chris, standing to indicate the end of their meeting. "I like your story. It's got promise."

"Thanks, Chris," Jonathan replied, also rising to his feet. "Listen, would you mind thinking about the story for a bit and giving me a call. I haven't nailed down where it will go from here. Maybe you can make some suggestions?"

He pulled a card from his jacket pocket which he handed to Chris. All that appeared on the card was a telephone number.

"I'll think about it," Chris nodded. "I'm about to have a lot of free time on my hands so, who knows? Maybe I can help you out."

"Excellent! I'm sure you could be really helpful," said Jonathan. "Sir, I appreciate your hospitality and, hopefully, we'll be talking soon."

He shook his host's hand and then headed for the exit. As he reached the door, he stopped and turned.

"By the way, Chris, that witness who came forward; would you think that she could be in any danger?"

"Nah, I doubt it," Chris replied with a reassuring smile. "From what you told me, she doesn't really know anything and hasn't done anything wrong. I'm sure that she's not in any danger whatsoever!"

* * * *

Nick Sharp was scanning through the New Activity Report which the computer spewed out on a daily basis. The report was a compilation of data entered into the National Police Information Network by officers at the local, provincial and federal levels and contained thousands of pieces of information regarding new cases, leads on open cases and solved cases. Though information regarding cases anywhere in Canada was available on request, the system was programmed to automatically generate only data related to cases within a geographic area defined for a specific RCMP division. For Nick, this represented the province of Quebec.

As he glanced through the pages, he happened upon a name which seemed familiar; Quality Imports. Quickly, he read the details of the new case, a murder which was being investigated by the Montreal police; body found in the trunk of a car; shot four times in the chest; victim's name, George Robinson; age thirty-one; five-seven, one hundred fifty-eight pounds; male, Caucasian, brown hair and eyes, single; Director, M.I.S. for Quality Imports.

He picked up the phone and punched in a few numbers. "Arty, remember that call you got last week? Some guy was telling you to check out some company? Yeah, that's the one. What was the name of the company? Quality Imports?! Are you sure? Well, I'm just going through the Activity Report and it seems that the locals found a body on Friday, in the trunk of a car. The guy's been identified as George Robinson, employed by Quality Imports. Yup, strange coincidence. No, that's all right. Let me make a few calls. I'll let you know if I need anything else."

## Chapter 5 - Tuesday, January 14, 1997

As Jonathan Addley climbed into his comfortable, government supplied automobile the cell phone in the breast pocket of his jacket started to vibrate.

"Yeah," he spoke into the phone as he closed the door and started the engine.

"How's it going, bud!?" enquired Nick Sharp's familiar voice.

"Hang on a second," replied Jonathan, pausing to activate the scrambler system. One could never be too careful with cell phones. "O.K., I've got the scrambler going now. To answer your question, it's going pretty good. What's up?"

"Jon, we got a call last Tuesday, anonymous, telling us to check out Quality Imports, some import firm in the Laval industrial park. Arty, who got the call, brought it to my attention and did some routine checks on their financial status, customers, bank records, that sort of thing. Everything looked kosher. Now, yesterday, I'm going over the New Activity Report and there's this new murder the locals are looking into. Victim turns out to be the M.I.S. Director for Quality Imports. The preliminary M.E. report this morning estimates the time of death as somewhere between last Tuesday night and Wednesday morning."

"Interesting coincidence," replied Jonathan thoughtfully as he drove amidst the morning traffic. "What can I do to help?"

"Well, I've got a feeling that the call Arty got and this murder are related. But, we can't just go busting in there, we have no grounds to do so. Neither would the municipal police if I told them about this. I was wondering if this might be a little project you'd want to think about. Maybe you can get one of your snoops in there, just to look around."

"The guy was in charge of M.I.S.?" asked Jonathan, his ever-active mind switching to a higher gear.

"Yup. That's what the report says," Nick answered.

"O.K. Let me think about it. I have a possible new recruit who happens to be somewhat knowledgeable with computers. This might be a good testing ground for him if he's interested. Leave it with me. I'll get back to you."

* * * *

"CSS, Good afternoon."
"Good afternoon," said Jonathan. "Chris Barry, please."

"I'm sorry, sir. Mr. Barry is no longer in our employment," the receptionist sadly replied.

"Oh really?! I thought he was remaining until the end of the week?"

"Well, technically, he is, sir," the receptionist informed him. "But he has decided to take the last few days off."

"I see," responded Jonathan. "Can you put me through to his secretary?"

"One moment, sir."

He waited as the connection was made and, following a couple of rings, someone responded.

"Chris Barry's office, Sonia speaking."

"Good afternoon, Sonia. Jonathan Addley. I met with Mr. Barry yesterday morning."

"Yes, Mr. Addley. How are you?"

"Fine, thanks. I understand that Chris decided to leave early?"

"Yes, unfortunately," Sonia confirmed.

"I discussed a project of possible interest with Chris when we met and he's supposed to get back to me. However, I may need his help sooner than I had originally anticipated so I'd have to speak to him. Do you know if I can reach him at home?"

"I don't think so," Sonia answered carefully, always the discreet secretary. "I believe he and his wife went skiing for a few days."

"Do you happen to know where?" Jonathan hopefully enquired.

"Unfortunately not," replied Sonia.

"O.K. Thanks for your help. If Chris calls, can you ask him to get in touch with me as soon as possible? He has my number."

"Absolutely, Mr. Addley."

"Thanks, Sonia. Bye."

Jonathan cut the connection and punched in a few numbers. "Hi, Shirley. Jonathan. I'm looking for a Chris Barry who's gone skiing for a couple of days. I'm presuming he's stayed relatively local. Can you try to get a handle on where he might be and let me know? I need to speak to the gentleman. No, don't leave a message. Just let me know where he is if you find him. Thanks."

Shirley Tompkins was responsible for all travel and lodging arrangements for the personnel of the Ministry of Defence and she was an ace. If Chris Barry was booked in a hotel or resort somewhere, anywhere, she would find him.

## Chapter 6 - Wednesday, January 15, 1997

Chris reached the bottom of the slope, coming expertly to a halt, and turned to watch Sandy finish her descent. It was hard to believe that this was only her second season; she skied like a pro. But then again, she had had the opportunity to practice.

Her school schedule last winter had been such that she had no classes on Mondays and Fridays and, after her first taste of skiing, she had quickly fallen into the habit of getting her studies out of the way by Sunday. This had allowed her additional practice of the sport for fifteen consecutive Mondays the previous year.

She approached him at a rapid pace, stopping at the last moment and making sure to spray him considerably with the snow from her skis in the process.

"Sorry!" she apologized with an impish grin as she leaned over to kiss him.

"Yeah, right!" he laughed, wiping snow from his cheek with a gloved hand. "Want to go for a last run?"

"I think I'd rather call it a day," she prudently decided. "This **is** our first time this year and I'm already under the impression that I'm gonna hurt tomorrow."

"Chicken!" her husband taunted with a smile.

"Yup!" agreed Sandy. "Go on, tough guy! Just don't complain tomorrow when you wake up stiff all over! I'll go take a shower and limber up. Meet you in the bar in forty-five minutes?"

"Deal," he said, kissing her again before heading off to the chair-lift.

As he approached the chairs, he reasoned that he too was starting to experience some muscular pain.

"Maybe she's right," he thought. "Shouldn't overdo it. We will be here for another two days."

He changed direction and headed for the lodge where the bar was located, a cold rum and coke being his next objective. After shedding his skis and poles, he entered the cozy bar and made his way to a small table by the fireplace. Within moments, he was comfortably seated, contently sipping his objective.

"How are you, Chris?" a vaguely familiar voice asked from behind him.

He turned towards the voice and smiled in surprise at the man standing there.

"Jonathan! What a pleasant surprise. Have a seat."

"Well, I don't want to barge in on you," Addley politely replied.

"Come on. Have a seat," Chris insisted, pushing a chair back with his foot. "You didn't go to the trouble of finding me just to say hello, did you?"

"Guess not," Jonathan grinned as he settled into the chair.

"So what's up?" queried Chris, leaning back comfortably.

"I was wondering if you had a chance to think about the story we discussed?"

"Yeah, a little," Chris nodded. "The way I see it, your hero might be interested in the agent's proposition. His wife however, is not sure if he should do it or not."

"I see," replied Jonathan, his expression thoughtful. "Say an opportunity came up for our hero to try his hand at this new line of work. A little job that would probably turn into nothing, a testing ground, so to speak. Do you think he might be willing to give it a shot?"

"I'd say it would depend on what exactly the job was," Chris answered, obviously interested. "Have you determined that?"

"In fact, I have," admitted Jonathan. "Let's say the cops get a call, anonymous, telling them to look into a company. Let's call it Quality Imports. Shortly after, a man is found dead in the trunk of his car. He turns out to be the M.I.S. manager for the very same company. Now our hero, who happens to be a computer wizard, offers his services to this firm. They're in need of a computer guy and he has a reputation for being the best. They accept his services and he's in. Once inside, he can snoop around to see if anything wrong is going on."

"That's it?!" exclaimed Chris, nodding approvingly. "I think that would work, Jonathan. Our hero could probably convince his wife to agree to his doing something like that."

"Good," said Jonathan. "One thing I don't believe I had pointed out when we spoke the other day. Due to the sensitive nature of the activities carried out, our hero would have no official government backing. Only a handful of people know that this department even exists."

"So if our hero gets caught doing something nasty, he's on his own?" Chris slowly suggested.

"That's right," Addley explained. "In the sense that no government official would step in and say, 'It's O.K., he was working for us'. Now, this doesn't mean that no support is available to our hero if he found himself in a jam. I should also mention that he would be handsomely compensated in return for this element of risk."

Chris considered this for a moment before replying. "As long as our hero is aware of these conditions, no problem."

"Excellent!" said Jonathan, rising to his feet. "You're really helping me with my story. I'll be in touch."

As he turned to leave, he stopped and looked at Chris. "By the way, remember the guy who was framed as the Vigilante? Say he had embezzled a large amount of money. What do you think would have happened to that money afterwards?"

Chris shrugged with a grin. "I don't know. How about if it was transferred by our hero to a number of worthwhile charities?"

"I like it," Jonathan chuckled. "We'll go with that!"

"Who was that?" questioned Sandy, motioning towards the departing man as she joined her husband at the table.

"That, my dear, was my new friend, Jonathan," Chris replied.

"Coincidence?" she asked.

"Nah," Chris shook his head. "The world ain't that small. He tracked me down to offer me a trial run. Just to see if I'd like this kind of work."

"I don't know, Chris," Sandy worriedly replied. "This could be dangerous."

"It could," he admitted. "But somebody's got to do it."

"But does it have to be you?"

"It doesn't have to be," Chris quietly responded. "But it could."

"You want to do this, don't you?" said Sandy, more a statement than a question.

"It seems intriguing, that's for sure," Chris acknowledged.

"How well does it pay?" Sandy asked.

Chris laughed as he replied. "Apparently well, but I don't know specifically. Would that really make a difference considering our financial situation?"

She shrugged and was silent for a moment. "You promise you'll be careful?"

"All the time!" he reassured her. "Now, let's enjoy our vacation. It seems that I'm going back to work soon!"

### Chapter 7 - Monday, January 20, 1997

Although almost two weeks had gone by since George Robinson had died, Charles Peterson, owner and president of Quality Imports, was still shaken by his M.I.S. Director's tragic end.

George had been with the company almost since it had been founded ten years earlier so, not only had Charles lost a friend, he had also lost the only person who knew the entire systems layout. Never having developed the slightest interest for computers, Peterson had always counted fully on Robinson, who had literally built the firm's information systems. The two programmers and computer operator were doing their best to keep up with the workload but George had been a hands-on manager and the true backbone of the M.I.S. department. Charles knew that he had to find a solid replacement quickly but had no idea what he was even looking for.

A knock on the door brought him out of his miserable reverie.

"Mr. Peterson, there's a Mr. Chris Barry at the reception area who would like to see you," announced Crystal, his secretary. "He says he can help us with our M.I.S. problems."

Chris Barry. The name sounded familiar.

"Did he say where he's from?" asked Peterson, trying to remember where he had heard the name before.

"He says he was with CSS until the recent takeover by CompuCorp," Crystal replied.

That's why the name rang a bell. He had read about the acquisition in the papers. Barry was the guy who had put CSS on the map!

"Sure, Crystal," Peterson responded, suddenly curious and excited. "I'll see him. Send him in."

While he waited for his visitor to arrive, he pondered as to why Barry was here to see him in the first place. For one, no recruiting activities had yet been initiated; getting over the shock of George's murder had required some time. Secondly, Barry was a king in the world of business. Why would such a man be interested in helping a small firm like Quality Imports? He could have stayed with CompuCorp and become CEO within a couple of years but, according to the papers, Barry had refused to remain with the company, opting for a very early retirement instead.

The door opened and Crystal ushered their visitor in.

"Mr. Peterson, pleasure to meet you!" greeted Chris with his usual charm.

"The pleasure's all mine, Mr. Barry! Please have a seat. Coffee?'

"No, thanks," Chris declined. "But you go ahead if you want some."

"I have enough to keep me up nights without adding caffeine to the mix," replied Peterson with a wan smile.

He nodded to his secretary who left the office, closing the door behind her.

"I understand that you're here to offer your services, Mr. Barry?" Peterson continued. "Frankly, I'm flattered but also a little puzzled, a man of your stature."

Chris smiled and explained. "I've been on a diet of eighty hours of work per week for the last ten years. I felt I needed a break so my initial intention was to stop working when our company was acquired. I presume you've heard about the CSS acquisition?"

Peterson nodded and Chris went on.

"Now, I've come to realize that you don't put in eighty hours per week unless you enjoy working. This being the case, I've also realized that quitting cold turkey is a lot harder than I thought it would be. Therefore, in order to allow myself a less painful withdrawal, I've decided to offer my services on a contract basis to whoever might be interested."

"O.K. I understand that part," acknowledged Peterson. "Now, could you explain what suddenly brings you to my doorstep?"

Chris took on a more serious air as he answered, "I have a few friends who are with the police and one of them told me about your M.I.S. Manager's untimely death. I saw a possible opportunity for the two of us to help each other to our mutual benefit. I hope that doesn't sound too cold or disrespectful."

"I guess not," Peterson shrugged his shoulders. "I mean, you didn't know George so it makes it much easier for you to look at the whole thing from a business perspective. And, I definitely do need help with my computer department. I don't know or understand a damn thing in that area. George put together all of our systems; accounting, payroll, inventory control, everything. The problem is that documentation wasn't George's strong point. He had everything in his head."

"Well, I'd be open to analyzing your systems and putting together the documentation for you," offered Chris. "Like I said, I'm looking for a little contractual work, not a full time job. While I do that, you could look for a full time replacement. I could also help you with the technical side of the recruiting if you want."

"I guess I'd be a fool to refuse," Peterson nodded thoughtfully. "I'm just not sure that I can afford you, Mr. Barry, a man of your expertise."

"Don't believe everything you read in the papers!" Chris warned with a grin. "I'm not that good! Make me an offer, Charlie. I'm not doing this to get rich."

"Seventy-five hundred a month?" suggested Peterson hopefully.

"That's fine," Chris replied.

"Then we've got a deal, Mr. Barry!" Peterson exclaimed, extending his hand as he stood.

"Great!" said Chris as he rose to shake Peterson's hand. "One last thing. You'll have to drop the 'Mr. Barry' stuff and call me Chris. I don't function well under formality."

"Sure, Chris," Peterson agreed. "And you can call me Charlie."

Chris grinned, "I already did!"

* * * *

Having agreed to assume his duties the following morning, Chris drove his new Pathfinder out of the Quality Imports parking lot and, within minutes, was cruising eastbound on the 440, away from Laval's industrial park. He picked up his cellular phone and punched in the most recent speed dial number he had created.

"Hello," answered a voice after two rings.

"Good morning," greeted Chris. "This is your co-author."

"Hang on a second," replied Jonathan, activating the scrambler. "O.K. We can talk now. What's up?"

"Just wanted to tell you that there's been some progress with our story," Chris announced. "Our hero has managed to obtain temporary employment with that firm we had talked about."

"Excellent!" exclaimed an impressed Jonathan. "When would he start?"

"I figure we might as well have him start tomorrow," Chris replied.

"That soon?! That's great! Let me know how the story develops. By the way, Chris, we never mentioned anything about what this job might pay. Don't you think that might be appropriate?"

"The way I see it, money is not our hero's major concern," Chris responded. "He's financially at ease and has no doubt that he will be properly compensated for his efforts."

"Fine," Jonathan laughed. "Keep in touch."

Chris cut the connection, inserted Melissa Etheridge's 'Never Enough' CD into the player and, as 'Ain't it Heavy' started blaring through the speakers, headed home to Sandy.

## Chapter 8 - Tuesday, January 21, 1997

"Ladies and Gentlemen," Charles Peterson called out to open the brief meeting. "I would like you all to meet Mr. Chris Barry. As some of you may be aware, Chris was the driving force behind CSS until its recent acquisition by CompuCorp and is also somewhat of a computer genius. He is currently in semi-pre-retirement and has graciously offered to help us document our computer systems following our recent tragic loss of George. I trust that you will all appreciate his presence and join me in welcoming him in his temporary stay with us. I also hope that you will do what you can to help him in any way possible."

A murmur of "Hi's", "Welcome's" and nods of greeting emanated from around the boardroom table.

Seated to the immediate left of Charles Peterson at the head of the table, Chris rose to his feet to address the group.

"I'd like to thank Mr. Peterson for his overly flattering introduction. I know very little about your business but I do know computers to some extent and will do my best to put together the appropriate documentation so that your next M.I.S. guy can get a head start. I know that I'm gonna need everybody's help on this and just want to thank you in advance for any support you can give me."

He paused to clear his throat then went on.

"Now, everybody knows who I am but I have no idea who you all are. If nobody has any objections, I'd ask everyone to introduce themselves. With a little luck, I'll remember a couple of names and look less like an idiot in the days ahead!"

Following a round of chuckles and smiles, the man seated to Peterson's right gave Chris a friendly wink as he spoke.

"Wayne MacKinnon, Director of Operations. Pleased to meet you, Chris!"

"Hey, Wayne," Chris replied.

"Greg Pierce," the small bespectacled man next to Wayne announced, almost uneasily. "Director of Finance."

"Nice to meet you, Greg!" Chris responded, smiling at the obvious accountant.

One by one, the remaining individuals seated around the table introduced themselves while Chris studied each face, making mental notes to remember who was who.

"Well, I thank everybody for their words of welcome and I promise not to be shy if I need a hand," said Chris once the process was over. "Now, if you'll excuse me, I'll go sit quietly somewhere and try my best to figure out what the hell I've got to do!"

## Chapter 9 - Wednesday, January 22, 1997

By the end of his second day at Quality Imports, Chris had managed to accumulate enough information about the firm as well as its employees to create a starting ground for his investigation.

The company had been founded by Charles Peterson ten years earlier, who still owned eighty percent of it. His directors of operations, finance and sales each had a five percent share. The remaining five percent now belonged to the estate of the late George Robinson, but would be purchased back by the company, this according to regulations in the charter stipulating that shareholders had to be employed by the firm.

Charles had indicated that, as per past practice, this block of shares would eventually be awarded to George's successor, once merit had been established. He believed that managers tried harder when they owned a piece of the pie and, the success his business had known thus far appeared to fully support his theory.

Prior to becoming his own boss, Charles Peterson had been the purchasing manager for Roosevelt's, a major textile importer and distributor. At the age of forty, he had been informed that, due to rightsizing, one of the popular management trends of the time, his services were no longer required.

On the following day, Charles had rented a small office and with the help of his already established contacts overseas, had founded Quality Imports and gone into direct competition with his previous employer. Within six months, he had turned his one man operation into a flourishing business with two dozen employees, including the best sales people from his former employer. A year later, he had acquired Roosevelt's, which was by then on the verge of bankruptcy, having lost a number of key accounts.

As things progressed, Peterson's firm had moved into the importation of other products ranging from mini-blinds and athletic shoes produced in Asia to coffee beans from Columbia. Today, over three hundred were employed.

The business itself was quite simple. Having established a reputation for low prices and a rather wide (and ever growing) distribution base, Quality Imports was able to purchase an impressive variety of products at high volume, hence, low cost. Prices were marked up only enough to cover expenses and provide a modest profit on a per item basis. However, what the company lost in margin was more than made up for in volume.

A quick look into the firm's financial records indicated that it was healthy, generating a profit of approximately $5 million per year. Of this, 10% was distributed to its handful of shareholders as dividends, proportionate to their percentage of ownership in the company while another 20% was distributed to the firm's remaining population in the form of profit sharing bonuses. The end result was an efficiently run organization where everyone pitched in to improve service and reduce operating costs.

When comparing the company's financial records to its banking and investment records, Chris could not identify anything that seemed out of the ordinary. There did not appear to be any large excesses of cash or other assets in comparison to the company books. A first glance clearly indicated that the firm was on the up and up and not involved in any illegal or fraudulent activity.

But just because the cops had been advised to look into Quality Imports didn't mean that the company itself was involved in any wrongdoing. It could very well be some of the players within the organization who required investigation. To this effect, Chris had easily extracted the names, addresses, social insurance numbers and bank account information from the company's payroll system. With this information in hand, he would be able to run some checks on each individual to see if anyone might be involved in any underhanded activities.

He glanced at his watch and was surprised to see that it was nearly 7:00. He tossed a couple of reports, which he hoped to look at after dinner, into his briefcase and headed towards the side door where he was parked.

As he walked past the glass-walled reception hall at the front of the building, he noticed an Econoline, followed by a Jaguar, turn into the parking lot. He stopped and watched as both vehicles headed towards the west side of the building and rounded the corner, out of sight.

Intrigued, Chris hurried to the side door, on the east side, and quietly exited. He was pleased to note that the parking area on this side of the building, which was reserved for visitors, was not illuminated. As he unlocked the Pathfinder, he casually scanned the area but saw no-one. Satisfied that his presence had not been detected, he started the engine and quickly left the grounds, heading east, away from the side of the building where the two vehicles had gone.

A quarter mile further, he turned right and at the next intersection, turned right again. By driving another quarter mile, in the opposite direction now, he found himself in front of a warehouse located immediately behind the Quality Imports facility. He pulled into the shelter of a recessed shipping dock and, leaving the truck, rapidly headed towards the rear of the warehouse on foot.

At the back of the lot, some seventy-five feet behind the building, were several piles of skids which would serve well as an observation point. Thankful for the early evening darkness, he crept across the open space to the welcome cover of the skids, confident that he had not been seen.

A hundred feet away were the Jaguar and Econoline, parked by an open door of the Quality Imports' shipping area. One man, unknown to Chris, appeared to be keeping watch, concentrating his attention towards the front of the building, apparently not expecting any intruders from behind.

A muffled shout was heard from inside and the watchman moved to the elevated shipping dock where another man had appeared with four wooden cases on a hand truck. One by one, the obviously heavy cases were transferred into the Econoline. As soon as the fourth case was loaded, both men climbed into the van and drove off.

As Chris watched on, two other figures suddenly appeared in the still open doorway and these, he did recognize; Wayne and Greg, Directors of Operations and Finance. Greg appeared nervous, glancing furtively about, twitching and pacing back and forth. He muttered something, which Wayne responded to with a laugh and a shake of the head.

The latter reached inside and the lights went out as the huge door began to descend. As Wayne jumped off the four foot dock, Greg gingerly climbed down the short steel ladder affixed to its side, drawing another head shake and laughter from his colleague. They hurried to the Jag and climbed in, Wayne in the driver's seat, and, seconds later, sped off into the night.

Chris checked the time; 7:08. From start to finish, their little visit had only taken eight minutes. He wondered what could be important enough to bring four men here on a Wednesday night in January for such a short stay? Maybe the variety of products imported by the company was wider than he had been told.

He was starting to believe that he would truly enjoy this job. He returned to the Pathfinder and headed home to Sandy.

## Chapter 10 - Thursday, January 23, 1997

"I'm gonna have to find out what's in those boxes," Chris informed his lovely wife as they chatted over breakfast.

"It's guns or drugs," Sandy confidently guessed. "What else could it be?"

"Stolen art, bacterial weapons, I don't know," Chris responded, shrugging his shoulders. "But you're probably right; guns or drugs."

"So these guys are probably dangerous."

It was a statement, not a question.

"I'll be real surprised if they're not," admitted Chris, knowing where this was going. "Yes, my love. I'll be careful!"

"Is there anything I can help you with?" Sandy offered, ignoring his last comment.

"Actually, I think there is," Chris replied. "Peterson is paying me to document his systems so I'm gonna have to start working on that if I want to stick around. Which means I won't have time to do some other stuff. I copied some information off the payroll system to run a check on everybody working there. What I'm looking for is anything that would indicate someone living much beyond their means."

"Like a shipping clerk with a yacht and condo in Maui?" Sandy playfully suggested.

"Yeah, anything like that," Chris replied with a grin. "Think you can handle it, kiddo? There's about three hundred people to look into."

She knew exactly how to go about digging into other people's lives through the computer. She had seen Chris do it hundreds of times during his Vigilante days.

"Piece of cake, Mr. Barry!" she replied confidently, leaning over to kiss him. "I was trained by the best!"

\* \* \* \*

"That new guy, Barry, he makes me nervous," stated Greg.

He was seated in Wayne's comfortable office along with Wayne and Bryan Downey, Director of Sales.

"Ah, Jesus, Greg!" retorted Wayne in disgust. "Your goddamn grandmother makes you nervous!"

"I just don't like having some unknown person digging around here, that's all!" Greg shot back. "I have this strange aversion to spending many years in prison."

"What **do** we know about this guy?" Bryan quietly enquired, as usual the mediator between these two extreme personalities.

"He was EVP at CSS," Wayne arrogantly replied. "He's a computer genius, semi-retired, filthy rich. He just wants to do a little contract work as a bridge between working constantly and doing nothing at all. Christ, I can understand the guy! He's what, maybe thirty-five? He's just trying to slowly withdraw from the workforce. I see no reason to worry about him."

"Is there any danger of his finding anything out?" Bryan pressed.

"No fucking way!" answered Wayne, annoyed. "He's here to document our systems! He's not gonna **find** anything on our systems!"

He stopped suddenly and stared at Greg, his eyes narrowing. "I trust you weren't stupid enough to set up our records here, were you?!"

"Of course not!" Greg shot back, indignantly. "It's all on my PC at home. Sometimes I access the files from here through Eazy-Com but nothing is recorded here!"

"So then, what's to worry?" challenged Wayne. "All he can find out is that Quality Imports is a well run, profitable business. All the transactions are kosher, all the suppliers real. Everything is under control, guys."

"Hey, I'm comfortable," Bryan retorted defensively. "I'm just making sure that Greg isn't worrying about something concrete!"

He turned towards the fidgeting accountant. "Relax, Greg. I'm sure Barry won't be a problem."

"Alright, if you say so," Greg doubtfully replied, forever uneasy. "I just don't want any more screw-ups."

\* \* \* \*

It had been a while since Chris had done any systems analysis and he was quite enjoying himself. Maybe he would seriously consider taking on a couple of free-lance contracts per year as a hobby.

Peterson had settled him in the late George Robinson's office, where he was currently busy reading lines of code and drawing a flowchart.

"So, how's it going so far?" questioned a voice from the doorway.

"Good, Charlie. Good," he replied to Peterson. "Maybe your man wasn't keen on documenting what he did but he was a damn good programmer. Real clean work, no patches or plugs; just straightforward and logical."

"I'm happy to hear that," said Peterson. "I just wanted to see how you were doing. Let me know if you need anything."

"Sure thing. I do have question for you while you're here. Do you operate on multiple shifts?"

"Nope. Day shift only, eight to five," Peterson responded. "Volume's not high enough yet for extra shifts but we'll get there."

"Any special orders sometimes that someone might come back to look after in the evening?" Chris persisted.

"Not really. Maybe a little overtime on busy days but normally, when we lock up we do so for the night. Why?"

"Well I noticed that some of the inventory control programmes had some cut-off times worked into them, probably to ensure proper stock levels," Chris explained. "I haven't finished going through them yet so maybe some other programme lines compensate. I'm presuming that further into the programme, I'll run into some code that sets off the running of back-up jobs. In any case, I was just concerned that entries made after a cut-off time might not record in the system."

As he had hoped, Chris could see that Peterson had no idea what he was talking about. In all fairness, Charlie **had** admitted that he knew squat about computers.

"All I know," repeated Peterson with a look of confusion. "Is that we've only got one shift; eight to five. That's it."

With that, he turned and walked away.

Chris held back a smile as he watched the departing man and murmured under his breath, "And that's all I wanted to know. Thanks, Charlie!"

## Chapter 11 - Friday, January 24, 1997

With cup in one hand and computer print-out in the other, Chris returned from the coffee machine, reading as he went along.

"Good morning, Mr. Barry!" a familiar voice called out as he walked by the reception hall.

He stopped and turned towards the voice, breaking into a warm smile as he identified the speaker.

"Lieutenant McCall!" he exclaimed with exaggerated formality, tucking the printout under one arm to extend a hand.

Chris and Dave McCall had worked closely together several months earlier on the Vigilante case and had grown quite fond of each other. It was Chris's guidance which had led Dave and his team from the Special Homicide Task Force to the late Carl Denver, the supposed Vigilante.

"**Captain** McCall to you, sir!" Dave McCall barked in insult as they shook hands.

"Well, excuse me!" Chris jokingly retorted. "How the hell am I supposed to know when you don't keep in touch! So you made captain. Good for you! When are you gonna head the force?"

"Next year," Dave replied with a grin, "One step at a time. So, how have you been?"

"Fine, great!" answered Chris, gesturing towards a hallway. "Come on in to my office for a few minutes."

"So, what the hell are you doing here?" queried Dave once they had settled into Chris's temporary quarters. "I thought the papers said you had retired?"

"Well, I realized that it would be best to ease out of the labour force," Chris explained. "So I decided to do a little contract work here and give this place a hand until they find a new M.I.S. Manager."

"Yeah, well as you may have guessed, I'm here to talk about the last M.I.S. Manager," Dave sombrely said. "You're aware of what happened?"

"Uh-huh," Chris nodded. "The top cop looking into this? Is this a major case?"

"Nah. It's probably just a mugging gone bad," Dave responded. "I just have less and less time to get out on the street so, every once in a while, I pick a routine investigation and handle it myself. Just to keep my blood running. Did you know the guy?"

"Nope," replied Chris. "I didn't even know this company until about a week ago when an acquaintance mentioned it. I saw an opportunity for Quality and I to help each other to our mutual benefit. I made a proposition and Charlie Peterson agreed to it so, here I am."

"Well, good for you," said Dave as he glanced at his watch; 8:57. "I'm gonna get out of your hair cuz I have an appointment with Peterson at nine. Listen, give me a call. You and I have to get together real soon. We've got a lot of catching up to do and, from what I read in the papers, now you can really afford to buy me dinner!"

"You shouldn't believe everything you read in the papers," responded Chris with a smirk. "I'm just a poor soul trying to get by!"

"My heart bleeds for you!" laughed Dave as he left the office.

* * * *

Dave's meeting with Charles Peterson had proved to be a waste of time and effort and, although this was what he had been expecting, he had to follow up on all possible leads. Unfortunately, murder investigating was a business of trial, error and luck, not at all an exact science.

Peterson had described the late George Robinson as a quiet, friendly individual who, though not socially active, got along well with everybody. Originally from Calgary, he had moved to Montreal about ten years ago and had joined Quality Imports less than a week later. His sole passion was computers and they occupied most of his waking hours.

He had no immediate family, being an only child and having lost his parents in an automobile accident five years earlier. Peterson, who truly did not believe that George had any enemies, attributed his employee's untimely demise to simply being at the wrong place at the wrong time.

To date, nothing had indicated anything different to Dave and he was inclined to agree. Unfortunately, in this day and age, there were lots of nasty people out there.

As he drove across the Des Prairies River on highway 15, with George Robinson's useless death on his mind, his thoughts strayed to the Vigilante. Maybe they should have left him alone. He **had** been supplying a valuable service to the population at large, making the world a safer place for its honest citizens.

Although Dave recognized that the man had been a criminal, he couldn't help but feel some respect for him and for what he had undertaken. Dave himself had often had to fight off the urge to pull out his gun and blow some punk away. Knowing that they were back on the street before one even finished the paperwork was, at the very least, goddamn frustrating. But the law was the law and they had to play by the rules.

He allowed his mind to wander again as he drove and Chris Barry popped into mind. He was surprised, yet happy to have seen Chris. Shortly after the solving of the Vigilante case, he had been promoted and the size of his task force had been increased. Unfortunately, murder was a growing business.

At about the same time, CSS had been put up for sale so both he and Chris had ended up with very busy fall schedules and little time for social activities. He would make a point of getting together with Chris in the near future however, as he truly enjoyed the man's company. He chuckled suddenly as he realized that what had created occasions for them to see each other thus far were murders. He'd have to warn Chris to stay away from such events lest he want to be considered a suspect!

* * * *

"So like I was saying, Mr. Johnson, we realized that we had too much space for nothing. That's when we built this wall to cut off our warehouse from this side of the building and sectioned off this side into smaller storage areas. Most of our clients are local businesses who need occasional space for temporary overstocks."

"Well, this will do just fine," said Chris, nodding approvingly as he peered out towards the rear of the building through the windows of the office above the storage area. "You see, the mini-warehouses I saw were just too small. My parents have been living overseas for a number of years and now, my father has retired and they're moving back here. While their house is being built, they're gonna fulfil a lifelong dream and go for a trip around the world for a few months. In the meantime, they're shipping all their stuff here, including a car, and I have to put it somewhere until the house is ready. Plus, there's some furniture they bought, so on and so forth. Bottom line is, I need a place to stick it all and this would be perfect!"

"It's available if you want it," replied Tony Bradley, owner of the building located directly behind Quality Imports. "You can take one closer to the front if you want. Like you saw, they're all pretty much the same."

"No, I'd like this one," insisted Chris. "I might use the office occasionally and this one has windows. I like to see outside."

"Your call," Tony shrugged indifferently. "They all cost the same; a thousand a month."

"That's fine. Three months should be all I need. Is cash O.K.?"

"Sure!" agreed Tony with a huge grin. "Cash is great!"

"Excellent," said Chris, pulling out his wallet and starting to count. "There you go, Mr. Bradley; three thousand. I'll let you know if I need it longer."

"Hey, you're welcome to stay as long as you want, Mr. Johnson!" exclaimed Tony, admiring the wad of bills he clutched tightly in his fist. "And if you need anything else, don't be shy! I aim to please!"

## Chapter 12 - Saturday, January 25, 1997

Chris put away his breakfast dishes in the dishwasher, being careful not to make any noise which might wake Sandy. She had worked late on some research for him the previous evening and deserved her sleep.

He poured himself another cup of coffee and headed downstairs to his workshop. He was nearly finished working on the equipment he needed and planned to go install it at his newly rented warehouse later that day.

After starting up 'Cracked Rear View', the first CD by 'Hootie and the Blowfish', he resumed his work on the modified video cam he had clamped to his work bench. Fifteen minutes later, the few remaining connections were complete and the transmitter was in place, set to the proper frequency. All that remained to be done was the testing.

He picked up a stopwatch, started it and placed it in front of the camera lens. After turning off the CD player, he headed for the garage, choosing the Lexus 400SC for his little ride. The roads were dry and at 6:45 a.m. on a Saturday, he figured he could speed a bit with little risk of getting pulled over.

Within minutes he was on the 40 heading west and then north on the 640. Twenty minutes later, he was approaching the Quality Imports building, heading west again, this time on the 440. He pulled out his cell phone, called a number stored in memory and gazed down at the Sony Watchman on the seat beside him.

Following a few seconds of static, the tiny picture cleared and he could see the stopwatch ticking away back at home. Twenty-four minutes, thirty-seven seconds. He punched a second memory number on the phone and the screen went blank.

At Chomedey Boulevard, he crossed over the 440 and headed back east. As he approached Quality Imports, from the west this time, he looked at his watch. Five minutes had gone by since his last transmission. He recalled the first memory number on the phone and the miniature T.V. screen came back to life. Thirty minutes, three seconds. He smiled with satisfaction as he called yet a third number from memory, this one aimed at turning off his little network altogether.

At 7:39, he rolled the Lexus back into its spot in the garage and hurried to his work shop. He pressed the rewind button on the video cam and listened to the whirring sound of the tape. It stopped after fifteen seconds or so. Smiling with satisfaction, he pressed the play button. As the image of the stopwatch appeared on the camera's small view-screen, he leaned forward to verify its time recorded on the videotape. Twenty-four minutes, forty-three seconds. He watched the recording for the next five minutes until it ended; at thirty minutes, five seconds. He smiled again and headed upstairs for another cup of coffee and the morning paper.

* * * *

"Good morning, sir!" yawned Sandy as she shuffled into the dining room where Chris sat, reading the paper.

"Well, it's about time!" teased Chris, tossing the paper aside. "I've been up for hours, I'll have you know!"

"Yeah, so?" Sandy replied as she leaned down to hug him from behind. "That's cuz while **I** was doing **your** work, **you** were sleeping!"

"Oh yeah!? Well you better have something good for me!" retorted Chris with mock sternness, heading for the kitchen to get her some coffee.

"If you're not satisfied, boss," she called out with a sly smile, "You can hold off on those sexual favours I crave for!"

"And risk a complaint to Employment Standards," he snorted, returning to the dining room. "Not a chance, lady!"

"What a relief!" Sandy sighed as he handed her a cup of coffee. "Thanks. Now sit down and I'll give you my report."

"Great! What did you find?"

"Three of the top boys at Quality seem to be doing extremely well financially," she proudly started, referring to a computer printout she had brought down with her. "Wayne, the operations guy, has been buying real estate for a couple of years now. Mostly apartment blocks, commercial buildings, that kind of thing. Places that generate income. He owns well over twenty million in rental properties, in addition to several extremely expensive homes which are either occupied by members of his family or used for recreation. He currently has no mortgages or loans outstanding."

"Maybe he's just a sound financial planner," kidded Chris. "What else?"

"Greg, your Director of Finance, lives pretty conservatively. One house, nice, based on the price, but not extravagant; his real money's into investments; stocks, bonds, mutual funds. He's also worth a lot more than what he gets paid at Quality; many millions more."

"Who's the third?" asked Chris, not surprised about the first two.

"Bryan Downey," replied Sandy, "Director of Sales."

"I've only met him once, briefly," admitted Chris, "On my first day when Peterson introduced me to everybody."

Sandy continued. "He seems to be a flashy one; a number of properties, all apparently for his personal use. One is his main residence in Laval-sur-le-Lac. He also has condos in Vancouver, Palm Beach and Santa Barbara and villas in Oahu, Phuket and Maracaibo. He seems to like big toys because he currently owns nine expensive cars, three boats including a sixty foot yacht, not to mention a helicopter."

"Jesus, I've got to get myself a full-time job at this place!" exclaimed Chris with a playful air. "Anybody else?"

"The supervisor of the receiving department earns $36,000 a year and is living in a quarter million dollar home and driving a sixty thousand dollar car. The two lead hands in receiving both have comfortable properties, fully paid for. One also has a second residence in St-Sauveur while the other has an eighty thousand dollar yacht parked at the Oka Marina. These guys earn $26,000 a year so I guess they must do a lot of overtime!"

"Anybody else seem shady?" Chris enquired.

"Not from what I could dig up. If anyone else is involved, they're not getting paid much or they're doing a much better job at hiding the extra cash. You've got addresses, makes of cars, names of boats, everything in here."

She slid the computer report across the table to him.

"Well, I must say Ms Taylor, you've done some excellent work!" commended Chris, standing and reaching for his wife. "I don't know how I'll ever repay you!"

"Think a little," Sandy replied as she removed her oversized sweatshirt, revealing her firm naked body underneath. "I'm sure something will come up!"

\* \* \* \*

After a memorable morning with Sandy, Chris had reluctantly switched his mind back to the task at hand and headed to his warehouse behind Quality Imports. Before leaving, he had made a few last minute adjustments to some of the hardware he would be using and he was anxious for a final test.

Although Tony Bradley had assured him that nobody went into the rented warehouses, Chris had changed the locks on both the shipping dock and walk-in doors and had also installed door alarms for good measure. He did not want anybody nosing around.

His observation camera was now in place in the second floor office window from where one had an excellent view of the shipping doors at Quality Imports where he had seen Wayne and company the previous Wednesday. It was time to see if the whole thing worked.

He pulled his cell phone from his pocket and retrieved a number from memory. The 'record' light on the video cam came on but the usual whirring of the tape could not be heard; so far, so good. He punched another number on the phone and listened to the ringing while waiting for a reply.

"Hi, gorgeous!" answered Sandy back at home.

"Hey there! So, you got your breath back?" he enquired teasingly, referring to their morning together.

"Just barely," she laughed. "But I should be in shape for another round when you get back!"

"Whoa, sweetheart! Gimme a break," he groaned. "Don't forget, I'm a retiree!"

"O.K., I'll wait til tonight," she conceded with a chuckle. "By the way, the VCR started just before you called. What I can see is the back of a warehouse with an occasional car driving by on the highway in front. I presume that's what you wanted?"

"Yes! Great!" Chris replied. "I'm just about done here. I'll see you in a little while."

"Be careful," Sandy responded. "Bye."

He had been bothered with having the tape in the video cam. First of all, it limited the recording time to eight hours which would have meant having to show up at the warehouse much more frequently to change the tape, therefore increasing the risk of being seen. Secondly, if somebody did get into this place, they could easily grab a possibly valuable tape.

To overcome these problems, he had installed a receiver on the VCR at home, hoping that the image would transmit properly via the cell phone network. It worked. Basically, his system was simple. He had set a switch and transmitter in the video cam which was activated by phone. One frequency started the camera and transmitted the signal to the receiver installed in the VCR. Another frequency also sent the image to the screen of his Sony Watchman. A third simply turned off the whole network. Ingenious! He could now track the questionable activities of some of his new co-workers in relative safety.

He'd look into the possibility of setting up another camera inside the Quality warehouse but recognized that that would be risky. He wouldn't want anybody to spot it and he certainly wasn't interested in having anybody walk in on him during the installation. He would have to think about that one carefully.

Pleased with his accomplishments thus far, he left his warehouse, locking the door securely behind him and arming the alarm system with a remote control he produced from his jacket pocket. He quickly crossed the paved yard and moved onto the property of his temporary employer, towards the second leg of his journey.

Satisfied that he was alone after having walked the perimeter of the building, he entered by his usual side door, pausing only long enough to enter his security code into the alarm control pad. As he started his tour of the premises, he turned on his cell phone and pressed the appropriate keys, activating his surveillance camera. His Watchman came to life, displaying the empty yard by the shipping doors.

Within fifteen minutes, he had completed his visit of the front section of the building, having concentrated his attention on the offices of Wayne, Greg and Bryan. He moved on to the warehouse area, waiting a moment for his eyes to adjust to the low illumination. Not quite certain of what he was looking for, he started to wander slowly through the aisles, keeping his eyes open for anything of interest.

As the minutes went by, he became engrossed in his search, poking into boxes and crates, amazed by the variety of merchandise stored in the place. He sauntered into another aisle where he noticed a number of familiar looking wooden cases. Maybe he'd get to find out what had been in the ones he had seen on Wednesday night.

Examining the first crate, he noted that it was securely nailed shut. He went back to a wrapping station he had passed two aisles earlier and returned with a small crowbar. As he got to work on the case, the warehouse was suddenly flooded with light.

"Holy shit!" Chris muttered under his breath, pulling the Watchman from his jacket pocket and staring at the screen while he fumbled for his cell phone.

A black Maxima was parked below the shipping dock. He pressed the appropriate keys and the screen went dark. He'd have to be less stupid in the future. For now though, he had a problem to solve and he had no idea where his problem was or if he was alone. He couldn't hear any conversation which he hoped meant he was dealing with one person only.

He concentrated for a moment, thinking back to Sandy's computer report which he had scanned before leaving; Black Maxima. One of the receiving lead hands, Rick something. That might come in handy if he came face to face with the guy.

He considered his options and decided that, if at all possible, he preferred to just get the hell out for now. It was too early in the game to get caught snooping around.

He started backing up slowly towards the side aisle, listening for any sound which might indicate the visitor's whereabouts. He felt something against the back of his leg and realized, too late, what it was. The crowbar clattered to the concrete floor, its metallic jangle, without a doubt, the loudest noise that Chris had ever heard.

Footsteps rapidly approached along the central aisle and Chris started towards them, crowbar in hand.

"Who's there?" he demanded in a loud, firm voice as he rounded the corner.

Rick, some fifteen feet away, stopped in his tracks as this somewhat familiar looking man appeared before him wielding a crowbar.

"Who the fuck are you?!" Rick nervously asked, keeping his distance as he pointed the small pistol he held at Chris.

"Chris Barry. I'm working on the computers until they find a new guy. You're Rick, right?" Chris asked, relaxing his stance a bit as he lowered the crowbar.

"Yeah, that's me," Rick replied, also relaxing slightly. 'What are you doing here?"

"My wife and I got into a fight," Chris responded, grinning sheepishly. "I figured I'd come in and work a little while she blows off some steam."

Rick snickered and seemed more at ease. "What were you snooping around back here for?"

"I was in my office and I saw a car go by. When I didn't see it come back, I came to make sure everything was O.K."

Rick, visibly relaxed now, took a few steps towards Chris. 'I'm sorry, Mr. Barry. I just wasn't expecting anybody here. I thought somebody had broken in."

"Seems like you would have done O.K. even if that had been the case," suggested Chris, gesturing towards the gun.

"Oh, shit! Sorry, Mr. Barry!" Rick exclaimed, tucking the small weapon into the back of his pants. "We've had some problems here before. One of our guys got beat up pretty bad. That ain't gonna happen to me."

"Good for you, Rick. Good for you," said Chris encouragingly. "Listen, if everything's under control, I'll get out of your hair and get back to work. It was nice to meet you!"

"Sure, Mr. Barry, nice to meet you too."

The two men shook hands and headed their separate ways, Chris towards the front offices and Rick to the back of the warehouse.

Chris hurried to the side door by which he had come in, entered his security code and exited. He moved quickly towards the rear along the east side of the building, activating his camera as he went. The Maxima was still visible on the screen but Rick was nowhere in sight. He rounded the corner, scanning the area to make sure no chance witnesses were present but the place was deserted. As he approached the next corner, he slowed his pace and looked at his screen, smiling as he saw himself.

He waited for a moment and saw Rick appear with cardboard box in his hands, heading for the Maxima as the trunk popped open. As Rick leaned forward to load the carton into the car, Chris moved in swiftly and silently behind him, the crowbar raised high. He swung it down forcefully, delivering a solid blow to the back of Rick's skull. He quickly flipped the unconscious man into the open trunk, pausing only to retrieve his victim's car keys and gun before closing the lid.

"Sorry, Rick," Chris murmured softly. "I didn't want you to tell your friends I was here and, I was curious to find out what you guys have in those boxes. Let me get you somewhere more comfortable so you can sleep. You and I can talk later."

## Chapter 13 - Sunday, January 26, 1997

Chris strolled up to the door of his rented warehouse, disarming the alarm with the remote control as he approached. He had parked a couple of blocks away, as he had done the previous day, to avoid having his vehicle spotted. He unlocked the door, wondering how his guest was this morning. He hoped Rick had slept well.

He had been angry at himself yesterday for his carelessness and had sworn that nothing similar would happen again. But in retrospect, he was happy with how things had turned out and how easy it had been.

He had driven the Maxima around the block and brought it to his warehouse. The pull-out ramps installed within the loading dock had made stashing the car child's play. He had pulled Rick's still unconscious form out of the trunk and, with the help of a roll of filament packing tape and a support post in one corner, had ensured that his visitor would be no trouble.

Rick was awake but still in the position Chris had left him, seated on the floor and securely taped to the post behind him. He glared at Chris as the latter approached to check if his wrists and ankles were still properly bound.

'Good morning, Rick!" Chris cheerfully greeted. "Did you sleep well? Silly me; how can I expect you to answer me with that tape on your mouth?!"

He bent over and, with a swift jerk, ripped off the tape, causing Rick some obvious discomfort.

"You goddamn motherfucker!" Rick bellowed, trying to rub his painful face on his shoulder.

"I'm standing here, completely free and mobile," Chris stated calmly, "While you're sitting there, totally helpless and vulnerable, taped to a pole. I suggest you be careful how you talk to me, Rick. Understand?"

"Fuck you!" screamed Rick. "You don't know who you're dealing with, asshole. You're a dead man!"

"Rick, Rick, Rick. You just don't seem to realize who's got the big end of the stick here!" Chris muttered, shaking his head. "How can you threaten me? You're not being logical. Think, man! Think!"

"They're gonna kill you," Rick insisted. "You're gonna regret the day you decided to fuck with them!"

"Who's gonna kill me, Rick?" enquired Chris, obviously not shaken by his prisoner's threats.

"Fuck you, you son of a bitch!" Rick shot back. "You'll find out soon enough. I ain't stupid enough to give you a lead."

"Are you talking about Wayne and Greg?" Chris suggested. "Or do you mean Bryan? Oh, I know! Maybe you're talking about Bob, your boss, or Matt, that other little shit that works with you!"

Rick's face paled noticeably as the various names were mentioned, drawing a smile from Chris. Barring the verifications that Sandy had made, Chris had nothing specific linking these individuals to any criminal activity. Any one of their comfortable financial positions might have been explained by an inheritance, a lottery or a rich parent. Rick's initial reaction however, seemed to confirm the involvement of the named parties.

"So which one should I be worried about, Rick?" Chris continued. "Are they all killers or just some of them? But maybe they're not into murder. Maybe that's your job. Maybe you're the guy who shot George."

Rick's body stiffened and the fear was apparent on his face.

"Bullshit! I didn't do it!" he blurted out. "And there's no way you could prove that I did!"

"I'd have to disagree with you on that," Chris smoothly replied. "I've got your gun and a boxful of coke. The cops have a dead body. Put everything together and it fits. You're in for life."

"The cops'll see it ain't my gun that did it," Rick argued, doing his best to seem confident.

"Oh come on, Rick!" Chris snorted in disgust. "How stupid are you?! Do you think the cops give a fuck if it's the right gun? They'll know you were into some kind of shit. So what, maybe you didn't kill George. Somebody's gotta pay. They take your gun and shoot a few rounds into a side of beef. Then they pull out the slugs and replace the ones they had taken from George's body. Bingo! Dead body, your gun, your slugs, your murder!"

"Th-they can't do that!" Rick cried out. "That's, that's wrong!"

"That's life, Ricky-boy!" Chris responded with a laugh. "There's got to be a guilty party."

"Well, I don't buy it," Rick spat out defiantly, another attempt at courage. "The cops can't pin George's murder on me and you're still in really deep shit! That's all I got to say."

Chris sighed, shaking his head as he pulled up a chair. He sat down and stared at his guest for a moment before speaking.

"I want you to listen very carefully to what I have to say because it's important. There are only two people who know where you are right now; you and me. That's it. There's also nobody else who knows or even suspects that I had anything to do with your disappearance. So your threats on my life don't impress me. In fact, they're starting to really annoy me."

He paused for a few seconds, continuing to stare at the younger man with cold, unblinking eyes. He believed he now had Rick's full attention.

"Now, you've mentioned a few times that I don't know who I'm dealing with. Well, I'll let you in on a little secret, my friend. **You** don't know who **you**'re dealing with. You said you didn't kill George and Rick, I believe you. I don't think you ever killed anybody because you wouldn't have the balls to do it. Now me, on the other hand, I've killed people; many times. Sometimes I beat them to death with a baseball bat. Other times, I slashed their throats. Once, I had this guy suspended by his wrists and used him for target practice. I must have shot him fifty times with his own guns! Oh, and another time, there was this pusher who sold crack and smack to little kids. I tied him up and injected him with the biggest goddamn overdose you ever saw. So, you see, I **have** killed before. I know how to do it and I do it well. I could easily do it again."

Another short pause allowed his words to clearly sink in.

"Do you know what kind of people I killed, Rick? I'll tell you. My victims were criminals; the nasty kind; murderers, rapists, wife-beaters, pushers, that kind of thing. Do you realize Rick, that you and your friends fit that category? You guys are just the kind of garbage that I used to eliminate as a hobby! That's who you're dealing with, Rick."

The hard look previously on the young man's face had been replaced by one of petrified fear. He obviously believed what his captor had said and began to visibly tremble, despite his sturdy restraints.

"W-w-what are you gonna do with me?" he stammered in a quivering voice.

"Who killed George, Rick?" Chris asked, his tone quiet, serious, deadly.

"They're gonna kill me, man!" Rick pleaded.

"Believe me, my young friend," said Chris, almost gently. "That is not your primary concern right now. Who killed George?"

"Jesus, man! Can't you give me a break?" cried Rick, now sobbing.

Chris responded with a cold, hard stare, saying nothing.

"He's gonna fucking kill me, man!" Rick screamed. "And it'll be on your fucking head! Wayne did it! Wayne shot George cuz he found some coke!"

"Who was there when Wayne shot George, Rick?" continued Chris, unmoved by his prisoner's emotions.

"Me, Greg and Matt," Rick muttered between sobs.

"Who dumped the body?"

"Me and Matt got him into the trunk of his car. Then I drove it into town and Matt followed me. I parked and took off with Matt. But we were just following orders from Wayne. You gotta believe me!"

"I believe you so far, Rick. You're doing good. Keep it up. Now tell me about this little business you gentlemen have going. How does it work?"

"I don't know much," Rick admitted.

The answers were flowing freely now.

"Me and Matt, we're like gofers, errand boys. We receive the stuff, do deliveries, that kind of thing. Wayne pays us five thousand a month, cash."

"Who's supplying the stuff? Where's it coming from?" enquired Chris, happy with Rick's cooperation. It made the job so much neater.

"I don't know who. It comes from Asia, Columbia, places like that," answered Rick, hopeful that his helpful attitude would play in his favour. "Bob, our supervisor, tells us when a shipment comes in. Matt and I look after those pallets and put the merchandise in the overstock area. Then, in the evening, we all come back and take the stuff out and put the merchandise back into the proper locations."

"Wait a minute," interrupted Chris. "Explain that to me in a bit more detail. What merchandise?"

"The stuff comes in with other stuff we import. Like, say we get some coffee. Well, there'll be some coke packed into the middle of the crates. Mini-blinds come in from Asia and have heroin stashed in the bottom rail of each blind. That kinda thing."

"Impressive," commented Chris, nodding thoughtfully. "You guys must have somebody at customs working for you?"

"I guess," replied Rick, actually starting to relax. "I know that for those shipments, we don't use the same broker that we use for the regular stuff we import."

"Who do you use for these special shipments?"

"Rapid Forwarders. Our contact there is Andy. I've spoken to him a few times. I don't know his last name."

"Anything else of interest that you might want to tell me?" asked Chris, convinced that the kid had played straight. He surely wasn't the mastermind behind this operation.

"No. Nothing that I can really think of," Rick replied emphatically. "Like I said, I don't know much. It's not like I'm running this thing. I'm just an employee."

"Does Peterson have anything to do with this?"

"Shit man, no way!" Rick responded, actually breaking into a smile. "Old man Peterson thinks grass is hard drugs. I've seen him fire guys a couple of times on the rumour that they smoked dope. He'd freak if he ever found out!"

"Well, I think you've given me all the information you could. You see, Rick? Wasn't it easier this way, with you cooperating?"

"Yeah, except that now I'm a dead man!" Rick replied sullenly. "I'm gonna have to disappear. And if Wayne ever gets a hold of me, he'll kill me."

"Don't worry about Wayne, Rick," Chris said with a soothing smile. "He'll never get a hold of you. I'll make sure of that. I'm gonna help you disappear so well, he'll never be able to get to you."

"Can I keep the drugs I took?" asked Rick hopefully. "That would at least give me some cash to start off."

"Yeah, Rick. O.K. You can take some of the coke. Anyhow, I promise that you won't have to worry about any future financial problems!"

### Chapter 14 - Monday, January 27, 1997

"Come on in, Bob," invited Wayne from where he sat behind the large desk in his office at Quality Imports.

Also present were Greg Pierce and Bryan Downey.

"Close the door behind you, Bob. Have a seat."

The silence which ensued quickly made Bob, Quality Imports' receiving supervisor, uncomfortable.

"Can somebody tell me what's going on?" he asked after several seconds, not having the faintest idea why they wanted to see him in the first place.

"Where the fuck is Rick, Bob?" demanded Wayne in an accusing tone.

"How the hell should I know?!" Bob retorted, suddenly feeling persecuted.

"Well, he's your goddamn employee and he's not fucking here!" Wayne shot back angrily. "I figured you'd have some goddamn idea of what the fuck your employees are doing!"

"What the hell is going on?!" asked Bob, glaring at the three other men.

"What the hell is going on?!" mimicked Wayne in a surly tone. "I'll tell you what the hell is going on! That little bastard was supposed to pick up four keys of coke here and deliver it on Saturday. He never showed up for the delivery and our client is not happy. Now, we can't find the little prick anywhere and the coke is gone. That shit's as pure as you can get, Bob. Once cut, it's worth over a million on the street!"

"Rick wouldn't do something like that!" Bob defensively argued, having been the one who brought Rick into the business. "He knows what crossing us could mean."

"He knows what crossing us could mean," repeated Wayne sarcastically. "A million bucks can encourage a twenty-five year old punk to do a lot of stupid things, asshole!"

"He's not at home?" Bob queried, scrambling for a logical explanation.

"I tried to call him a few times Saturday night when I found out that he hadn't showed up for the delivery," Bryan dejectedly responded. "We called again yesterday and Wayne went over to his place. His car wasn't there and neither was he."

"Maybe he had a wild weekend with one of his bimbos," Bob hopefully suggested.

"He has four kilos of snow, Bob," growled Wayne in frustration. "Why would he pick up the dope and then decide not to deliver and party with a broad instead?"

"Have any of you considered the fact that maybe he got arrested?" asked a sweating Greg Pierce. "He might be spilling everything he knows to the cops right now!"

Silence filled the room as everyone realized that Greg's suggestion was a definite possibility.

"W-we would have heard something on the news," said Bryan unconvincingly.

"Yeah, right!" snorted Wayne in disgust. "Whenever the cops bust a punk with a million dollars of blow, they automatically call the reporters to make sure anybody else involved gets tipped off nice and proper! You ain't too bright sometimes, Bryan!"

"Hey, fuck you, Wayne!" Bryan retorted, pouncing from his chair towards the other man. "I ain't the one letting high school drop-outs run around with four kilos of coke!"

"Gentlemen, please!" cried Greg in exasperation. 'I don't think this is the time to argue about your levels of stupidity! We've got to figure out what happened to Rick! In the meantime, we should assume the worst and presume he was arrested, which means, let's shake our ass and get whatever fucking shit we have here, out of here!"

Greg's use of profanity was practically non-existent. When Greg started swearing, he was serious.

"Greg's right," stated Wayne, his tone more controlled. "Bob, you go have a serious talk with Matt. See if he knows anything. And I do mean **anything**. And go over to Rick's place again. Get inside and check it out. Greg, what's our current inventory?"

"The four keys was all the coke we had left. The next delivery is Wednesday, twenty-five kilos. We have half a dozen keys of heroin but Bryan has three of those sold. Another shipment will be in on Friday; ten kilos."

"O.K." said Wayne, thinking furiously. "Bryan, call our guy with the Aces of Death. Tell him we'll get him three keys of horse for the same price we had agreed on for the four keys of coke. That's a great deal for him and it'll clean out our inventory here. I'd like you to deliver it personally cuz he was really pissed off with Rick's no-show on Saturday. If we get in with these guys, we can really start moving some shit. Talk to him about the stuff we have coming in this week. I want it out of here as soon as it gets in. We're gonna have to play real careful until we find out what happened to Rick."

\* \* \* \*

Wayne paced back and forth in his spacious office, consumed with frustration, anger and, especially, fear. They had to find Rick and until they did, keeping the business going could be extremely dangerous.

The timing for this could not have been worse. Although they had done very well since they had started importing drugs a few years ago, they were now on the verge of making some really big money. The Aces of Death had a strong hold on the drug trade throughout Quebec and had solid ties with two major biker gangs in Ontario which controlled the market there. Combined, these two provinces held close to sixty percent of the country's total population of close to 30 million, which was not a negligible customer base. Wayne's contacts in Asia and South America had informed him that production was now running to perfection so they could supply whatever volume he required. As it was, the Aces of Death organization was currently looking for one supplier with the capacity to cover their entire needs. Everything had seemed perfect.

A light tapping at the door broke into Wayne's thoughts.

"Excuse me, Wayne," said Chris Barry. "You got a minute?"

"Sure, Chris, sure," Wayne forced a smile, gesturing towards a couch in the corner. "Have a seat. We haven't really had a chance to chat much since you joined us. I've been pretty busy. Sorry."

"No need to apologize," Chris responded reassuringly. "I'm no stranger to heavy workloads and busy schedules."

"What can I do for you?" asked Wayne, settling into an armchair across from Chris.

"Well, actually," replied Chris, looking a little troubled. "I wanted to tell you something that might be of interest to you. Maybe it's nothing but I thought you should know."

"Sure. What's up?" asked Wayne, feigning interest.

"Saturday afternoon, my wife and I were out shopping and on our way home, we happened to drive by here so I stopped to show her the place."

Wayne leaned forward in his chair, his interest in what was being said suddenly much more genuine.

Chris continued. "We came inside and I was showing Sandy my office when I saw a black Maxima drive by towards the back of the building. We continued the tour and just as we walked into the warehouse, the lights came on. I went to the main aisle and called out and one of the guys from receiving, Rick, he said his name was, came walking up the aisle towards us. When he recognized me, he relaxed a little but he seemed nervous the whole time we chatted. He asked me what we were doing here and I explained and introduced my wife. I asked him what he was doing there and he told me that a customer needed a rush order and you had asked him to get it. His story was plausible but, like I said, he really seemed nervous and that left me wondering. When he saw that we were turning back towards the offices he seemed relieved and hurried back towards the shipping area. My wife and I left the building and I walked over to the west side to look down towards the rear. I could see the Maxima parked by the shipping dock and they were putting a box in the trunk."

"They?" Wayne interrupted, sounding concerned. "Rick wasn't alone?"

"Well, I thought he was when I saw him inside but there were two guys with him at the car. I didn't want them to see me and think I was spying on them so I headed back to the other side where I was parked. As I was getting ready to leave, I saw the Maxima pull out onto the road and take off. They seemed to be in a hurry, which made it seem even stranger."

"I see," said Wayne with a stern look on his face. "Something's definitely wrong here, Chris, because I never called Rick about any special order. I wonder what they took?"

"I couldn't tell you," Chris ruefully replied. "I was pretty far so all I can say is that it was a cardboard box, not too big."

"Hey, don't worry about," Wayne reassured him. "We'll check the inventory to try to find out what's missing. This might explain why he didn't show up this morning."

"Oh really?!" Chris exclaimed. "Do you have anything valuable enough that somebody would abandon a job for?"

"Well, we do import some electronic components that could be worth a couple of bucks," Wayne explained, obviously angry. "If he found a market for them and has been taking stuff for a while, it might be worthwhile."

"Wouldn't somebody have noticed an inventory short?" enquired Chris.

"Yeah, I guess. Eventually," admitted Wayne. "But some of this stuff is only used by a few customers who aren't very good at forecasting. They don't order often but when they do, it's in massive quantities and it's needed for yesterday. So we stock up heavy and it sits in our warehouse for a few months until suddenly, it all goes at the same time. Until that order is placed, we wouldn't know that anything was missing unless we did a physical count and we only do those once a year, in October."

Chris nodded in understanding. "So Rick might have been stocking up for a couple of months by now."

"It's possible," replied Wayne in frustration, "The little bastard! I better not get my hands on him!"

"Well, anyways, that's what I wanted to tell you," Chris said as he stood. "Let me know if I can help you with anything. I'd be interested in knowing what happened to Rick when you find him."

"Sure thing, Chris," Wayne agreed.

He stood and extended a hand.

"Thanks for the info. I'm sure that what you saw on Saturday will help. By the way; those two guys you saw with Rick. What did they look like? Did you recognize them as some of our other employees?"

"No, I'm pretty sure of that," Chris replied decisively. "They looked kinda rough if you ask me. You know, like bikers maybe, that kind of thing. There again, I was pretty far so I wouldn't be able to give a great description. But they seemed to be wearing blue jeans and leather jackets and both had long hair. One had a beard."

"O.K., good. That might be helpful. One last thing; did you talk to Charlie Peterson about this?"

"Nah," Chris replied with a wink and a smile. "You know how those top guys are. They blow everything out of proportion and make mountains out of nothing. You're the operations guy; you're the one I came to!"

"You're a good man, Chris!" said Wayne, winking back. "And a good judge of character. You've got Peterson down pat! Thanks again. I'll keep you posted."

He waited until Chris had closed the door on his way out before picking up the phone. He punched in a few numbers and waited impatiently, swearing under his breath until someone picked up.

"Bob. Rick was here on Saturday with two biker types. Barry happened to be here, showing the place to his missus and he saw them loading a carton into the Maxima. Find that little cocksucker and bring him to me! I will personally show him what happens to little bastards who try to rip us off!"

\* \* \* \*

"I still don't think Rick would have tried to steal the coke," Matt stated determinedly as he and Bob drove through the streets of St-Eustache to Rick's home. "And if he did, we sure as hell ain't gonna find him sitting around his place."

"Listen, Matt," replied Bob in an annoyed tone. "He picked up the four keys on Saturday and disappeared. He was with two guys when he went to the warehouse. He knows better than to bring somebody to the warehouse. He ripped us off! I know we're not gonna find him sitting at home but Wayne said to check, so we check."

They drove the few remaining minutes in silence. As they turned the corner onto Rick's street, they were surprised to see the black Maxima parked in the driveway of their co-worker's residence.

"Well I'll be a sonovabitch!" Bob muttered under his breath. "The asshole **is** home!"

He parked a few houses away and they proceeded warily on foot, examining Rick's house as they approached but noticing no apparent activity.

"You got your gun?" asked Bob in a low voice.

"Y-yeah," replied Matt in a quivering voice.

He found the drug running exciting and profitable but the recent murder, and now this, was somewhat less appealing.

"Well, don't use it unless you have to," warned Bob. "I don't want the neighbours calling the cops about gunshots."

They reached Rick's residence and slowly crept up the driveway, still looking for any signs of movement inside or out, but saw none. As they moved on to the front door, they noticed the weekend's accumulation of flyers and local newspapers sticking out of the mailbox. Maybe Rick wasn't there after all.

After glancing around for possible witnesses, Bob grasped the door handle, slowly depressed the latch and gently pushed inward. Offering no resistance, the door opened; it was unlocked. He looked nervously at Matt, uncertain of what to do next or what to expect inside. The house might be empty or this could be an ambush. They stepped quietly into the vestibule and closed the door behind them.

"Now what?" Matt mouthed soundlessly.

Bob pulled a revolver from his jacket pocket while thinking of an action plan. Finally, deciding that indicating their presence might be interpreted as a wish to avoid confrontation, he called out softly.

"Hello. Is anybody home? Rick, are you here? It's Bob and Matt. We were worried about you."

They listened for any sounds of movement, anything which might indicate somebody else's presence, but heard nothing.

Bob motioned Matt forward, barely whispering, "Slowly."

They crept silently ahead, searching frantically for any sign of activity. As they moved past the wall which separated the living room from the vestibule, Bob turned his head and gasped. Sprawled on a couch was Rick's dead body, a syringe still protruding from his arm.

"Oh, fuck, man!" mumbled Matt. "I'm gonna be sick!"

True to his word, he made a serious mess on the thick pile carpet.

"Get a hold of yourself!" hissed Bob. "Come on. Let's check the rest of the house. There may still be someone here!"

They continued their painstakingly slow search, which was interrupted on two occasions by Matt's additional bouts of nausea, but found the house to be void of other occupants. Their search complete, they went into the kitchen, both badly in need of a drink. After draining a first beer, Bob picked up the phone to call Wayne.

"Yeah, it's me," he grimly announced as he popped open his second beer. "We found him. The asshole overdosed. He's still got a needle stuck in his arm. Yeah, at his place. Car's in the driveway, the front door was unlocked. Nope, we didn't find it yet. We'll look a bit more to see if it's around or if there's a bundle of cash stashed somewhere but I ain't promising anything. Yeah, I figured that's what you'd want us to do. We'll get rid of him. I don't know where but I'll make sure nobody finds him for a while. Don't expect us back today."

He hung up the phone and looked at Matt who was sitting at the kitchen table, still in a daze.

"Finish your beer and get your act together, boy," Bob said with a smirk. "We've got ourselves a body to make disappear!"

* * * *

Chris lay sprawled comfortably on a couch in the den watching the T.V. screen with an amused smile. He heard the shower stop upstairs and a moment later, smelled her light soapy perfume as she entered the room behind him.

"Don't try anything you might regret!" he playfully warned. "I know you're there!"

"Well, with the line of work you've chosen, Mister," she replied sternly. "You sure as hell better!"

She leaned over him from behind the couch and with his assistance, slowly crawled over its back, all while delivering a rather passionate kiss.

"What are you watching? A cop show?" she asked as she snuggled up against him, clad only in a large towel.

"Something like that," he responded, his attention now equally divided between the screen and her inviting body beneath her scanty attire. "It's my surveillance tape from this morning. Their morning started with a 'Where the hell is Rick?' discussion, followed by my bullshit story to Wayne. You see those two? That's Bob, the receiving supervisor on the left. The other guy is Matt, the second lead hand. They were on their way to find Rick."

"How do you know all this?" asked Sandy, knowing that her husband would have an intelligent explanation.

"While I visited Quality on Saturday, I happened to plant a few mikes in Wayne's, Greg's and Bryan's offices. Secondly, since the phone system is linked to the mainframe, it was pretty easy to set up a recording and monitoring system this morning. Let me zap this a bit. O.K. Here we go. There's one of Bryan's toys, as you put it; a Mercedes 42D SEL. That's him getting out of the car. Now, you see that box he's carrying? That, my dear, is 6.6 pounds of high quality heroin which he's going to deliver to the Aces of Death."

"My God!" Sandy cried in alarm. "Chris, do you really think you should mess with these guys? I mean, Jonathan did tell you that you were on your own!"

"No, no, no," Chris soothingly disagreed. "All Jonathan said was that if I got caught doing something illegal, he couldn't vouch for me. If I need some help, I can call him and he'll send another consultant."

"So call him," Sandy said with a pleading undertone.

"I will, if and when I need help. Right now, I'm just setting things up. Anyways, you know I like to work alone."

She gave him a scolding stare which initiated a quick comeback.

"But as soon as I need help," he promised with a grin, "I'll call Jonathan."

"You're such an asshole sometimes!" she stated with a pout, bringing her knees under her chin and exposing more than her thighs in the process.

"Yes I am," admitted Chris, moving in on the exposure. "But I hope you'll always love me anyways."

"Always," she moaned as she leaned back and shifted her thoughts to the matter at hand.

### Chapter 15 - Tuesday, January 28, 1997

Clad in fish-net stockings, leather jacket, mini-skirt and bra-less under her tight sweater, the sexy young blonde strutted up to the main desk of the St-Eustache police station.

Gazing at her in awe as she approached, Sergeant Robert Savard wondered if he should ask for her hand in marriage, simply invite her over for sex, arrest her for prostitution or offer assistance. After seriously considering his second option, he opted for the last.

"How can I help you, miss?" he gallantly enquired, staring at this vision of loveliness.

"My boyfriend's missing," she replied a matter-of-factly.

"I see," said Sergeant Savard, making a valiant effort to concentrate on the serious nature of the business at hand. "Did you and your boyfriend have a fight, Miss, uh?"

"Rousseau," answered the bombshell. "Louise Rousseau. And no, Ricky and I didn't have a fight. Ricky and I get along really great."

'I'm sure you do. I know I would!' thought Savard before asking, "What makes you think he's missing, Miss Rousseau?"

"Well, Ricky and I saw each other Friday night and he said he'd call me on Saturday, but he didn't," she whined. "He does that sometimes but usually, he calls the next day to explain how he got tied up with some business. But Sunday he didn't call and yesterday either."

"Maybe he's just been really busy, Miss Rousseau," Savard replied sympathetically, starting to realize that God might have sacrificed this one's brains for her heavenly looks.

"No!" Blondie disagreed. "I called him at work yesterday and again today but they told me he's not there! I went over to his house but he's not there either, but his car is. Ricky loves his car. He wouldn't go anywhere without it and if he did, he'd at least put it in the garage."

"When **did** you last see Ricky, Miss Rousseau," asked Savard, uncertain if she was just wacky or if her concerns were truly founded.

"Friday," she repeated. "When I went to his house, I checked around and all his clothes and stuff are still there. He just disappeared and I'm worried."

"O.K." Savard gave in, figuring her statements at least deserved some looking into. "What's your boyfriend's name?"

"Ricky, Richard Beauchamp."

"His address and phone number?"

"327, Landry. 472-1289."

"Age?"

"I'm not sure," she giggled. "About twenty-five, I guess."

"Can you describe him?"

"Well, he's pretty cute," she replied with a shy smile. "Blonde hair, usually tied in a ponytail. Well built but slim. He's about five, nine and weighs, I guess, around a hundred sixty pounds."

"O.K. We'll see what we can do," said Savard, writing a case number in the appropriate box on a witness information card. "Could you complete this for me? If we find anything, or need more information, we'll be able to get in touch with you."

"Sure!" she responded, flashing a killer smile at the young, handsome cop. "Don't hesitate to call!"

'At least, if this turns into nothing,' thought Savard, 'I'll have her name and phone number.'

She completed the card and, after another heart-stopping smile, left with a hip swaying stride that caused heads to turn and kept Savard hypnotized until she was out of sight.

Once she had gone, he returned to reality and the routine of entering the data he had just collected into the National Police Information Network.

\* \* \* \*

Greg finished re-reading his entry and, satisfied with what he had written, saved the text on his home PC and logged off from Eazy-Com. He had neglected his journal for the past few days which was something he did not like doing.

He had started writing it four years ago, the very day that Wayne had first proposed the smuggling of drugs along with the company's legal shipments. At first, Greg had thought Wayne was kidding, but his colleague had quickly demonstrated how serious he really was. Contacts had already been established with drug suppliers as well as with some of the firm's regular suppliers. Customs brokers and officers interested in some additional cash had been identified and approached. The network had already been established. All that had been required was a little investment of time and cash and their new business was born.

Greg had never imagined being involved in any kind of illegal activity. He had difficulty jaywalking without troubling his conscience. However, the financial possibilities of Wayne's proposition had been overwhelming. No legal investment, no matter how lucrative, could generate an equivalent return and, Greg loved money. That was what had drawn him to the field of finance in the first place. He had accepted to go into business with Wayne and had started his secret journal.

His journal was an insurance policy for him and it was therefore important that he keep it constantly up to date. It contained a complete description of all their activities, down to the smallest detail; dates, names, quantities, amounts; it was all in there. If he ever got busted, he would be certain that everyone went down with him. In fact, Greg sincerely believed that the information in his journal could win him complete immunity and a new identity. Should something ever happen to him, such as an untimely demise, a letter addressed to his lawyer would be found in his safety deposit box. It contained instructions and appropriate passwords allowing access to his journal.

"Yes," Greg thought with determination as he watched the main menu reappear on the computer screen. "If anything ever goes wrong, many people are going to pay!"

\* \* \* \*

From the comfort of his office, Chris watched his computer screen go blank for a fraction of a second, followed by the reappearance of the main menu. He pressed a few keys and the image generated by Greg Pierce's PC disappeared from the monitor, to be replaced by the lines of code he had been working on earlier.

"Works like a charm!" he breathed to himself, proud of his programming capabilities.

All the PCs within the building were linked to the mainframe, thus allowing them to double as terminals. Thanks to this network, tapping into the PCs of any of his suspects was made relatively easy. With a little bit of programming, he had established a monitoring system which recorded the activity taking place on their computers at any given time. As an additional gadget, he had foreseen a flashing icon, which he could turn on or off at whim, which informed him of any such activity. He could then link on to the PC in question, his screen becoming a double of the other computer's monitor.

Greg had just been unknowingly kind enough to create the opportunity for Chris to test the system and, it worked. Chris, with growing interest and amusement, had read Greg's words as they were being produced. The man kept a diary! And Chris could only guess that it would provide some extremely interesting reading.

He would have to visit Greg's home computer shortly and he was certain that doing so would prove to be a very easy task. After all, not only did he have the address, he also had the passwords.

\* \* \* \*

Bryan strolled into Greg's office to find Wayne, Bob and, of course, Greg, waiting for him.

"Sorry I'm late," he apologized as he closed the door. "You know how it is in sales; work, work, work, work!"

"Yeah, yeah, sit down," grunted Wayne, not the biggest fan of Bryan's bubbly, salesman nature. "This shouldn't take very long. I just want us to get into the habit of having a quick daily chat for the next little while. I don't like it when things don't go smoothly and I want us to keep each other informed of what's going on. O.K.?"

All heads nodded in agreement as he continued.

"First thing I want to talk about is the Aces of Death. How much do you trust these guys, Bryan?"

"As much as you can trust a bunch of fucking bikers!" Bryan chortled. "Listen. They're pushers, pimps and murderers. But they're also the major channel of distribution for our dope, especially for the volume we'd like to move. We've done a couple of deals with them so far and they haven't tried to screw us. I think they're comfortable that we can deliver what we said we could and they love the quality of the shit so far. Plus, they're completely removed from the importing of the stuff which they definitely like. So, to answer your question, I trust them enough to keep on doing business with them and to become filthy rich in the process."

"All right," replied Wayne, unable to disagree with his colleague's logic. "Let's just be real careful with these bastards. Rick was supposed to deliver to our friend 'Diamond Jimmy' on Saturday. He showed up here with two guys that looked like bikers and the next thing we knew, Ricky was dead and we had lost a bunch of snow. I don't want that to happen again."

"Yeah, we'll keep our eyes open," Bryan agreed before turning his attention to Bob. "While we're on the subject of Rick; what's the status with our dead little friend?"

"It's all been taken care of. Matt and I drove up north, way up, to dump the body. We took him into the woods and buried him. Believe me, it was no easy task. The ground's goddamn frozen this time of year!"

"Well, a little sweat won't kill you," chided Bryan. "It's about time you did some of the dirty work."

"What the fuck is that supposed to mean?" Bob fumed, rising from his seat.

"Oh, Jesus Christ! Sit down!" ordered Bryan, not the least bit swayed by the other man's aggressive reaction. "I'm just saying, Bob, that we've all done our share of crap; Wayne, Greg, Rick, me, even Matt. We've carried enough shit with us to do life if we'd got caught. When did you ever make a delivery, Bob? Never! You got your cushy job inside, away from any danger!"

"It was never planned that way, Bryan," said Greg quietly in Bob's defence. "I'm sure Bob will do more if we need him to."

"Well I hope so," Bryan muttered. "We've gotta share the risk is all I'm saying."

"And I'm doing my share!" Bob stated defiantly, staring coldly at Bryan for a moment before going on. "Now, about Matt; we're gonna have to keep an eye on him. He's pretty fucked up since we found Rick yesterday. I think the events of the last few weeks might be too much for him to handle."

"Well, he better **learn** to handle them!" growled Wayne. "We're paying that little fuck lots of bucks to handle **anything** that happens! Keep a close eye on him and if he shows any signs of cracking, let me know. We don't have time for this kind of crap! Anything else?"

"One last thing," Greg spoke up, "About Saturday when Rick was here. Don't you find it strange that Chris Barry just happened to be here to see him? I'm still not comfortable with having him around."

"Peterson hired him to document the systems," Wayne responded in a slow, strained voice. "That's what the man is doing. I've seen some of the stuff he's put together so far and frankly, he's damn good. For the first time in years, I understand how some of our systems work. Stop worrying, Greg. Barry's just a nice guy doing his job. Leave it alone!"

\* \* \* \*

In his office, Chris removed the tiny earpiece and returned it to his jacket pocket.

'Wayne, my friend,' he thought with a smile. 'I thank you for your kind words and your vote of confidence.'

He accessed Eazy-Com and linked up with his computer at home. He had to learn more about the Aces of Death and one of their members, Diamond Jimmy. He was certain that he could find some useful information in the databases from his recent 'Vigilante' days.

Quickly finding what he was looking for, he read for a few minutes, taking an occasional note when pertinent. Once done, he tapped into Greg Pierce's home computer to pursue his research and, after forty-five minutes, he felt he had gathered enough knowledge to go ahead with his plan.

He pulled his cell phone from his jacket pocket and keyed in a number. It was time to set up a meeting with Diamond Jimmy.

\* \* \* \*

Diamond Jimmy sat at his usual table near the rear exit of *'Scandale'*, his favourite strip joint, when he saw the man come in and slowly make his way towards him. He discreetly signalled a fellow gang member at the bar and unobtrusively felt under his jacket for the gun strapped to his side, releasing the safety.

Chris reached his table and asked in a low voice, "You Diamond Jimmy?"

"Who the fuck are you?"

"I'm Bob," Chris answered, sitting down, "A friend of Wayne and Bryan. We spoke this morning."

"I've heard your name before, Bob, but I ain't never seen you," explained Diamond Jimmy. "I like to be sure who I'm talking to."

"I can show you some I.D. if you want," Chris offered, reaching for his wallet.

Diamond Jimmy grinned as he replied, "I.D. ain't worth shit to me! I could show you cards that make me Frank Sinatra! Tell me more about Wayne and Bryan and your organization."

"We don't like talking too much about our organization," Chris responded. "When you talk too much, the wrong people can learn things they shouldn't. We're interested in doing business and you're testing us. One of our delivery boys fucked up last Saturday and you didn't get your blow, four keys. Bryan offered you three keys of smack instead for the same price. We got more coke coming in on Wednesday and a delivery from Asia on Friday. Bryan told you about those too."

He looked calmly at Diamond Jimmy with a slight smile, waiting for the latter to respond. He could tell that he had convinced the man.

"Alright, what do you want from me, Bob?"

"Like I told you this morning, the four keys of snow which didn't happen on Saturday are now available," Chris replied. "Are you interested?"

"You wouldn't be here if I wasn't," Diamond Jimmy answered.

"Good," replied Chris, nodding.

"You got it with you?"

"It's close by."

"Go to the bar and have yourself a drink," said Diamond Jimmy. "When you're finished, go to the can, second stall. You'll find your part of the deal. After, head for the McDonalds one block north from here. In the bathroom, there's a broom closet. Leave the stuff there, just behind the door. Then have a coffee or something and wait until someone asks you for a cigarette. Understand?"

"No problem," agreed Chris, standing. "Nice doing business with you."

"Sit down, Bob," Jimmy ordered. "I ain't done yet."

Chris returned to his seat, gazing calmly at the biker as the latter continued.

"You were real clear that I shouldn't talk to Wayne or Bryan about our little meeting, right?"

"That's what I asked," Chris replied slowly, feeling slightly uncomfortable for the first time.

"That tells me that you're ripping off your buddies to do a little personal business," stated Jimmy with a grin. "Am I right?"

"Yeah, I guess you are," Chris nodded uneasily.

"Don't worry, Bob. I didn't tell your little friends but, silence has a price."

"How much?"

"Twenty percent off what we had agreed to this morning," the biker informed him. "Is that O.K.?"

"I guess I don't have much choice," Chris shrugged as he rose to his feet.

"No you don't," Jimmy smiled. "And Bob, don't try anything stupid. If you do, we're gonna kill you. Have a nice evening."

## Chapter 16 - Wednesday, January 29, 1997

As was his usual routine, Nick Sharp started the day with a hot cup of coffee while scanning through the New Activity Report; burglaries, rapes, muggings, drugs, missing persons; same old, same old.

He started to turn a page of the report when something caught his eye; Missing person; Richard Beauchamp, 327 Landry, St-Eustache, long blonde hair, five nine, one hundred sixty pounds. Reported missing by Louise Rousseau, friend and Quality Imports, employer.

"What the fuck is it with that place?" he muttered to himself, wondering if Jonathan had had a chance to look into to it.

He reached for the phone and dialled his covert colleague's number.

"Hey, bud! Howya doing?" he asked, waiting the usual few seconds for Jonathan to activate the scrambler.

"Fine, Nick," replied Addley. "Sorry I haven't had a chance to call recently. I've been busy catching up on some of the work that goes with my official title."

"No problem, Jon," Nick reassured him. "I got a quick question for you. Remember when we talked about Quality Imports a couple of weeks ago? You told me you'd see if you could look into it. I was just curious to know if you had done anything with it."

"As a matter of fact, I did," Jonathan responded. "I've had somebody working on it for a week now but I haven't heard anything from him so far. Why do you ask?"

"The N.A. report has something about a missing person this morning and guess where he works."

"Quality Imports," Jonathan replied, more a statement than a question.

"Yup, Quality Imports. Like I said, I was wondering if you were looking after that place and thought you might be interested in this information."

"Don't worry, Nick. It's in capable hands. I'll get in touch with my guy though, just to see how it's going. Thanks for the call."

\* \* \* \*

Chris cruised along the 440, heading west while enjoying the impressive lead guitar from Pink Floyd's 'Comfortably Numb'. As he drove past Industrial Boulevard, his usual exit, the phone rang, interrupting his listening pleasure.

"Chris Barry," he answered.

"Good morning, Chris."

"Well, good morning to you, Jonathan."

"I tried to reach you at the office but was told you weren't in yet."

"Yeah, I have a little errand to run this morning; something to do with our story. To what do I owe this pleasure?"

"Nothing really particular. I just hadn't heard from you recently and was wondering how you were doing."

"I'm doing great, Jonathan! Never better. I've been working on our little project and it's really coming along!"

"That's good to hear, Chris. Listen, I heard that somebody where you work was recently reported missing. Do you know anything about that?"

"Absolutely!" Chris beamed. "I know everything about it."

"O.K." said Jonathan. "I wanted to make sure you were aware. If you need any help, Chris, don't hesitate to call. I've got other consultants I can recommend and even I have been known to be handy on occasion. I don't want you to get into any trouble."

"Don't worry, boss," Chris replied reassuringly. 'If I need help, you'll be the first one to know."

\* \* \* \*

As they had agreed the previous day, Wayne and his cohorts assembled for their daily meeting, this time in Bryan's office. Once all were seated, Wayne started the conversation.

"So, gentlemen, anything new to report?"

"Two things," Greg answered, addressing Bob and Bryan more particularly. "First of all, Wayne and I had a quick discussion yesterday about Rick's disappearance and thought that it would be a wise move to bring it to the attention of the police. We felt that it was something we would have done if we hadn't been aware of what happened to him."

Both Bryan and Bob nodded in agreement.

"Secondly," Greg went on. "The coke we were expecting today came in, as scheduled. We all agreed the other day that we get it the hell out as soon as possible so can everybody stick around tonight so that we can unpack this stuff?"

He was answered with more nods from the others in the room.

"So, Bryan," Wayne spoke up. "You might as well give Diamond Jimmy a shout and see if we can move this through him. Don't sound too pushy. I don't want him to start thinking we got problems or have him looking for discounts. But I do want to get rid of this shit quick."

"Don't worry," Bryan replied confidently. "He said that they were looking for a volume supplier with quality dope. That's what I'll show him we are; nothing more, nothing less."

"Anything else?" asked Wayne, accepting the short silence which ensued as a no. "Good. We'll meet in the warehouse at five-thirty."

\* \* \* \*

Dave McCall sat at a table at Le Mirage on St-Martin Boulevard, waiting for Chris. He had had some business to attend to at Laval's central police station earlier that morning and had called Chris to invite him to lunch.

The purpose of their getting together was twofold. For one, Dave enjoyed Chris' company and, barring their brief encounter the previous Friday, they really hadn't had a chance to chat since late September. Secondly, Dave had gone through the new activity report early that morning and had learned of the disappearance of one Richard Beauchamp, employed by Quality Imports. Not one to leave much to coincidence, Dave planned to ask Chris if the latter had noticed anything strange going on at his current place of employment. Chris was a very intelligent and observant man and might have spotted some oddities.

"You invited, ergo, you pay!" said the familiar voice from behind him.

"Ah, no wonder the poor get poorer!" Dave sighed, rising to greet his friend.

Like school children, they talked up a storm throughout the meal, pausing only to stuff an occasional bite of their jumbo smoked meat sandwiches or fries into their mouths. To hear them, one would have thought that they were two childhood friends who had known each other forever. The fact was the two men had met just a little over six months ago but an immediate chemistry had formed. Their wives had also become close friends after having met towards the end of the summer and they now saw each other on a regular basis.

They finished emptying their over-filled plates and, thoroughly stuffed, leaned back in their chairs to attempt digestion over a cup of coffee.

"There's a little business I was hoping to talk to you about while we're here," said Dave, "Something about Quality Imports."

"Sure. Shoot." Chris responded, curious of what his friend had to say.

"We have a reporting system that generates daily data about all sorts of crimes across the country," started Dave. "All law enforcement agencies are linked to it. I was looking over today's report this morning and there was a mention of a Richard Beauchamp who's gone missing. The guy worked for Quality Imports. Have you heard anything about it?"

"Well, I did hear that the guy hasn't show up for work since Friday," replied Chris, obviously trying to remember what he had heard. "Seems to me, it wasn't the first time this kind of thing happened. I think somebody said that the kid was suspected of having a drug problem. I've only seen him a couple of times myself. He worked out in the warehouse, shipping or receiving. I don't spend much time back there."

"You don't think his disappearing has anything to do with Quality Imports?" Dave queried.

"Why would I think that?" Chris asked, puzzled. "Do you think there's a link between him and that murder?"

"I don't know," Dave admitted. "And it probably is just coincidence. I mean, people skip out on jobs everyday, right? I just noticed the thing on this guy because the name Quality Imports was in the report. Seeing as I had a contact in the place, I thought I'd ask."

"Well, I haven't seen anything weird going on but I can keep my eyes open a bit more if you want," offered Chris. 'You know, go take a walk around every once in a while. Maybe I'll see something."

"Sure, you can do that but don't go out of your way. I don't want you getting yourself into any trouble on my account!"

"Don't worry!" Chris laughed. "I'm a big boy. I can take care of myself!"

\* \* \* \*

Bryan had spent most of the day working his real job and making official company sales. By 3:00 p.m. however, he felt that if he wanted to swing a rapid deal with the Aces of Death, he'd better give Diamond Jimmy a call. He keyed in the now familiar number to the biker's phone and waited for a reply which was not long in coming.

"Yeah," Diamond Jimmy gruffly answered.

"Jimmy, Bryan. Howya doing?"

"Getting richer by the pound!" replied Jimmy, laughing at his own joke. "What do you got for me?"

"As expected, it snowed today. The forecast was accurate."

"We talking quality?" enquired Jimmy.

"The best, Jimmy! Same as the stuff you should have got last weekend," Bryan replied.

"That I finally got yesterday!" Jimmy grinned over the phone. "O.K.! We're talking some fine shit!"

"W-what do you mean, Jimmy, yesterday?" Bryan asked slowly as his stomach tightened.

"Your man, Bob, cut a quiet deal with me," Jimmy laughed proudly.

"Bob sold you the four keys?" asked Bryan, fighting to control his anger. "Why didn't you call me?"

"Easy, Mister Manager!" Jimmy warned. "I don't have to call nobody, understand? Somebody comes to me with a solid proposition, I do business! He gave me a better price than you do. You're lucky I even told you about this!"

"Why tell me this now?" questioned Bryan, still fuming.

"Cuz I don't approve of double-crossing little pricks," Jimmy chuckled. "So, you still wanna do a deal?"

"Absolutely, Jimmy," Bryan answered, swallowing his ego, "Same quality, same supplier; twenty-five kilos."

"Alright! Big time!" exclaimed Jimmy, apparently impressed with the quantity. "Give me the night to work out the cash and call me in the morning. I think that we're gonna do some fine business together. I won't even ask you for a discount like I did with Bob! Later, Mr. Manager!"

Bryan slammed down the phone and stared blankly about, breathing deeply in an effort to control his rage. They had questioned to what extent the Aces of Death could be trusted and, in the meantime, one of their own was screwing them right under their noses!

After a moment, he picked up the phone and punched in Wayne's extension. They would need to have a little chat with their partner, Bob.

* * * *

Chris moved quietly into the warehouse, checking the time as he sauntered amidst the rows of high racking; 5:17.

He walked around casually for a few moments until he was satisfied that he was alone, then headed to the last row of racking and climbed the sixteen feet to the top to settle into his little niche among some boxes. He was certain that they wouldn't find him here. Earlier, he had verified the merchandise within these boxes to make sure it was only what it was supposed to be. He sat back and waited, ready to observe.

* * * *

Wayne pulled the heavy door to the utilities room shut and securely locked it.

"Well, that's it boys," he announced, turning towards the others. "Now all we gotta do is get rid of the crap," he added, looking at Bryan.

"Jimmy said he'd be getting back to me tomorrow," Bryan answered confidently. "We're talking about a bigger load of cash this time but don't worry. This will all be gone in less than twenty-four hours."

"I hope so," Greg pitched in worriedly. "I don't like the way things are going lately. And I still don't trust these bikers. They're probably the ones who did Rick in."

"We don't have any proof of that, Greg," Bryan replied impatiently. "For all we know, Rick overdosed himself and some of his buddies took off with the dope. Whatever happened, I have a gut feeling that it had nothing to do with the Aces of Death."

"Could be," said Greg doubtfully. "But I still think we should be really careful."

"Greg, we're dealing with millions of dollars of smack and coke," Wayne spoke in a condescending tone. 'Of course, we should be really careful! Come on, let's get out of here."

* * * *

As the double garage door glided silently upwards, Bob rolled his black Jeep Grand Cherokee slowly up the driveway and pulled in next to the white Corvette convertible, his summer car.

After cutting the engine, he climbed out of the 4x4 and headed up the five steps leading into the living quarters of his luxurious home, pausing only long enough to step out of his overshoes at the top of the staircase. As he headed towards the kitchen for a beer, he proudly admired his spacious abode, pricelessly decorated by expensive professionals.

"Who says crime doesn't pay!" he laughed aloud to the empty home.

He reached the kitchen, tossed his coat on a chair and was on his way to the refrigerator for a beer when the doorbell rang.

"Who the fuck is that!" he muttered, changing direction as he glanced at the clock on the stove; 7:47 p.m. "Probably some little punks selling goddamn chocolate bars for school again!"

He opened the front door to find Wayne and Bryan standing there.

"Hey guys!" he exclaimed in surprise. "Come on in."

He stepped aside to let them enter, closing the door behind them.

"So, what brings you here?" he curiously asked. "Is something wrong?"

"We had something to discuss with you, Bob," replied Wayne, his tone serious. "And we didn't think it was appropriate to talk in front of Greg and Matt. You understand, don't you?"

"Sure, guys. Sure," Bob agreed, unsure of the topic of discussion. "Have a seat. I was just getting myself a beer. You want one?"

"Yeah, Bob. A beer would be nice," Bryan agreed. "Why don't I get them for you. You have yourself a seat."

Their host did not appear to be armed and Bryan certainly did not want to give Bob an opportunity to grab a gun somewhere.

"Yeah, alright," Bob responded hesitantly, growing uneasy. "You know where the fridge is. Go ahead."

He turned to Wayne as Bryan went into the kitchen. "What's going on, boss?"

"Just a little situation we need to talk about, Bob," Wayne replied smoothly. "What do you say we just wait for Bryan?"

Within a moment, Bryan returned with three beers which he passed around to the two others. After each man had opened his bottle and taken a healthy gulp, Wayne resumed the conversation.

"So, Bob? What have you been up to lately?"

"What do you mean?" asked Bob, perplexed. "I don't understand your question."

"Well, then I guess I'll be a little more specific," Wayne became impatient. "What did you do last night?"

"Last night? Nothing special," Bob responded, becoming annoyed and somewhat frightened. "What the fuck is going on, guys?!"

"I had a chat with Diamond Jimmy this afternoon," Bryan stepped in. "About the coke we just got. He told me that you delivered four kilos of cocaine to him yesterday!"

"What!? That's bullshit!" exclaimed Bob incredulously, starting to rise.

"Sit down, you asshole!" ordered Wayne, drawing a silenced pistol. "Why would Jimmy say that, Bob, if it wasn't true?"

"H-how the fuck should I know!" Bob cried, staring in horror at the handgun pointed at his head. "I don't even know the guy!"

"Jimmy was quite specific," Bryan resumed. "He clearly mentioned that it was the dope we fucked up with last weekend and that you called him to cut a deal. Wayne and I were figuring that maybe you had found the coke at Rick's place and decided to make yourself a bit of extra cash? We're thinking you might have even whacked Rick to get your hands on the blow!?"

"Wayne! Bryan! Come on!" pleaded Bob, sweat starting to glisten on his forehead. "We've been in this together since the beginning. Why would I do something stupid like that for a few hundred thousand? I'm making fine money as it is!"

"Well, then. Answer my fucking question! Where were you last night, Bob?" enquired Wayne, his tone soft, but deadly. "Prove to us that you weren't with Jimmy."

"Jesus, Wayne! I was here watching television!" Bob cried, now sweating profusely. "This Jimmy asshole is up to something! I never delivered no coke!"

"Bryan, why don't you look around a bit," suggested Wayne, apparently unimpressed thus far with Bob's arguments. "See if you find anything interesting. I'll keep an eye on our host here."

* * * *

Still quietly hidden in his elevated hideaway above the warehouse floor, Chris checked the time; 7:45 p.m. The others had been gone for over fifteen minutes now and his Sony Watchman continued to display an empty parking lot.

He climbed down the racking and hurried to his office in the front section of the building to get his briefcase. Returning only minutes later, he quickly headed for the door of the utilities room. Having learned from experience, he kept a close eye on his miniature T.V. screen while he got to work.

As long as the door lock did not give him too much trouble, which he did not believe it would, he'd be on his way to a relaxing evening with Sandy by eight o'clock.

* * * *

"Why don't you get Jimmy over here?" insisted Bob, confused, angry and scared. "At least the cocksucker will have to say it to my face that I brought him the goddamn coke!"

"You said it yourself, Bob. Jimmy doesn't know you," Wayne quietly explained. "If that's the case, why the fuck would he make up a story and tell Bryan that some idiot he doesn't even know scammed us and sold him some coke? It just doesn't make any sense, Bob. You tried to screw us and you got caught! It turns out that this biker bastard can be trusted more than one of our own!"

"Call the fucker!" Bob screamed hysterically. "I didn't do anything! He's goddamned lying! Get the fucking scumbag over here!"

"I'm trying to establish a working relationship with the Aces of Death," Wayne replied softly. "If I called Jimmy and even suggested that I doubted what he told us, I don't think he'd appreciate it. I still don't see why he would tell Bryan that you were there if you weren't, Bob. It's that simple."

"Hey, Wayne!" Bryan called excitedly as he hurried down the stairs from the second floor. "Look what I found in old Bob's bedroom closet!"

He carried a brown leather satchel of a kind familiar to both him and Wayne. To date, the Aces of Death had always delivered payment in such satchels.

"What's this, Bob?" asked Wayne with an unpleasant sneer.

"Th-that's not mine!" stammered Bob. "I don't know what that is!"

"Open it," Wayne ordered Bryan and the latter complied.

"You just better pray that this ain't full of cash, Bob!" Bryan smirked as he pulled open the zipper atop the bag.

After briefly glancing at its contents, he turned the open satchel upside down, dumping the stacks of bills in a pile on the floor.

He turned towards Bob with a knowing grin, pausing a few seconds before speaking. "Somebody's been a very bad boy!"

"This is a set-up, guys," Bob pleaded in a quiet voice, tears streaming down his cheeks.

"I just can't see how that can be," replied Wayne, just as quietly.

"Good-bye, Bob," he added with finality as he raised the silenced revolver and repeatedly pulled the trigger.

\* \* \* \*

As he had hoped and expected, the lock to the utilities room had proved to be of little challenge to Chris and, within no time, his tasks were done for the night.

He left the building and casually strolled to his Pathfinder which he had parked a few blocks away. As he started the engine, he looked at the clock in the dashboard. 7:59 p.m. He smiled as he pulled away from the curb. He had promised Sandy that he'd leave the office by eight.

## Chapter 17 - Thursday, January 30, 1997

"Boy, do you guys look like hell!" stated Greg, examining Wayne and Bryan as he entered the latter's office.

Glancing around the room, he added, "Where's Bob?"

"Bob's no longer part of the organization, Greg," Bryan grimly informed the accountant. "Bob's the reason that we look like hell."

"What are you talking about?" asked Greg, suddenly feeling queasy. "What's going on?"

"Bob's the one who had the four missing kilos of coke," explained Wayne in a tired voice. "The idiot tried to screw us and went and sold them to Diamond Jimmy. Jimmy mentioned it to Bryan so we paid Bob a visit last night. He denied everything but we found three hundred thousand dollars stashed in his closet. I guess he hadn't had time to go to the bank."

"Where's Bob now?" asked Greg sullenly, although he already had somewhat of a clear idea.

"Up north," answered Bryan. "Sonovabitch kept us up until three this morning. He was right about digging holes in the frozen ground. It ain't easy."

"Does Matt know about this?" Greg questioned, trying to remain calm.

"Not yet," Wayne grunted impatiently. "I'm gonna talk to him later."

"Because they were together when they went to Rick's place," Greg worriedly pointed out.

"You think Matt was in on this?" Wayne asked thoughtfully.

"I'm not saying he was," replied Greg. "I just know that Bob was ice fishing at Saint-Anne-de-la-Perade over the week-end. He dropped off some of his catch at my place on Sunday night when he came back so, I figure the only time he could have gotten hold of the coke is on Monday."

"I'll talk to Matt," said Wayne in an angry, quiet tone. "The little bastard better not have anything to do with this!"

"How are we going to explain Bob's disappearance?" Greg nervously questioned.

"Right now, everybody thinks that he's gone on vacation," Wayne explained. "I said he called me last night and told me that he had a sudden opportunity to go to Mexico real cheap with a girlfriend."

"What are you going to say in two weeks' time?" persisted Greg, clearly unhappy with this latest development.

"We'll deal with that when the time comes!" Wayne exploded with more than a hint of exasperation. "Maybe the stupid fuck will decide to stay in Mexico!"

Bryan broke in, intent on changing the subject.

"In the meantime, we have more urgent matters to attend to. I spoke to Diamond Jimmy earlier and Wayne and I are going to do the deal this morning. This is it, Greg. If you thought we made good money so far, you ain't seen nothing yet! We'll be coming back today with over 1.5 million goddamn dollars! And this will be the first of many!"

"Well, that's some good news," Greg listlessly muttered, his expression hardly brightening. "I just hope things start improving. These last few weeks have been getting to me. You guys be careful, O.K.?"

"Don't worry," Wayne confidently responded. "Nothing can go wrong this time! Just wait and see!"

\* \* \* \*

Wayne and Bryan hurried across the busy, icy downtown street towards 600 de Maisonneuve West, their thirty pound briefcases not making the task any easier. They bustled into the spacious lobby of the upscale office building and boarded an elevator to the fifteenth floor.

"You sure you got the address right?" growled Wayne in his usual antagonizing manner.

"You're a real pain in the ass, you know that?" Bryan shot back. "Yeah! I got the address right! You didn't expect to do this kind of deal in the bathroom at McDonalds, did you?!"

Before the argument could progress any further, they reached their floor and the elevator doors opened.

Falling silent, they exited and examined the central lobby in search of their destination. To their left were the offices of some actuarial firm. To their right, the floor-to-ceiling oak doors were tastefully set with a discreet brass name plate:

**MURRAY, SOMMERS and GREEN**
**Attorneys at Law**

"Big time!" whispered Bryan, impressed as he pulled open the massive door and walked into the expensively furnished reception area.

The lovely young receptionist looked up at them with a smile as she spoke.

"Good morning, Gentlemen! How can I help you?"

"Morning," gruffly answered Wayne. "We have an appointment with Allan Sommers."

She scanned a page of a heavy leather bound volume on her desk and replied, "Mr. MacKinnon and Mr. Downey, I presume?"

"You presume correctly," beamed Bryan, always the charmer with pretty young ladies.

"If you gentlemen would follow me," she invited as she rose. "I'll show you to Mr. Sommers' office. Mr. Sanchez has already arrived."

More than happy to comply, they followed her down a hallway to the door of a corner office. She knocked lightly and waited obediently for an acknowledgement before opening the heavy door.

"Misters MacKinnon and Downey are here to see you, sir," she announced before stepping aside to grant them entrance.

Wayne and Bryan entered the huge office, impressed by its obviously expensive decor and furnishings.

"Thanks, Nancy. That will be all," Sommers dismissed her from behind his mammoth desk. "Gentlemen! Come on in! I believe you have already met Mr. Sanchez."

On this occasion, Diamond Jimmy Sanchez hardly looked like the head of the Aces of Death which he was. Wearing an Armani suit, his long hair pulled back tightly in a ponytail, he could easily have been mistaken for a lawyer or at least, a very rich client. But, of course, he was in fact, the latter.

"Nice suit, Jimmy!" said Wayne with a grin.

Smiling back, Jimmy replied, "Thanks, Mr. Manager. Maybe one day, you can buy yourself one just as nice! Let's make some business!"

"Gentlemen," Sommers spoke on cue. "There's coffee and anything you might like to drink at the bar. The attaché case on the table is for you. If you want to make yourselves comfortable and verify Mr. Sanchez's part of the deal, he and I will go into the next room and make sure your merchandise is satisfactory."

With that, he picked up the two briefcases his guests had arrived with and followed Diamond Jimmy into an adjoining conference room, closing the door behind him.

"This is great!" Bryan gushed once they were alone. "This is how to do business!"

"It sure beats the piss smelling bathrooms that Jimmy usually deals in," admitted Wayne, giving in to the excitement. "Yep, Bryan, this is how it'll be from now on! Let's get us some coffee and get to work. We got ourselves a shit-load of money to count!"

Twenty minutes after Diamond Jimmy and Sommers had left the office, the latter opened the door and addressed Wayne and Bryan.

"Gentlemen, could you join us for a moment," he announced sombrely. "We appear to have a slight problem."

"You're fucking right, we got a problem!" Diamond Jimmy could be heard bellowing from the other room. "We got a big fucking goddamn problem!"

The two men followed Sommers into the adjoining conference room where the twenty-five bags of coke were separated into two distinct piles on the table. Diamond Jimmy sat in one of the huge leather chairs in one corner of the room, his feet propped up on the table. There was no doubting the rage on his face.

"What's going on?" challenged Wayne. "What problem do we have?"

"You fuckers trying to screw me!" hissed Jimmy. "That's the problem!"

"Those," Sommers said quietly, pointing to the smaller of the two piles, "Are powdered sugar."

"What the fuck!" Bryan exclaimed. "Bullshit! We tested every bag last night! What is this, Jimmy?"

"What the fuck is what?" snarled Jimmy, "You saying that I'm trying to rip you off, you fat motherfucker?! I'll throw you out the fucking window!"

"Calm down, Jimmy!" soothed Wayne. "Nobody's accusing you of anything. Just let us see the bags. I want to know if they've been tampered with."

"What the fuck are you talking about, man?" accused Jimmy, a vicious look in his eyes. "I thought your network was perfect!"

"It is, Jimmy," Wayne hastily assured. "This is just a minor internal problem that you're already aware of and we've already started to address it."

"You better finish addressing it!" Jimmy shot back. "If this kind of shit happens again, you're a dead man!"

Angered by the threat Wayne retorted, "Don't worry about our end of the business! And from now on, you want to deal with us, you talk to me or Bryan! Nobody else! This kind of crap like you did with Bob is what creates problems like this!"

"You want me to deal with you exclusive? That's fine," Jimmy snorted. "But don't make it like your problems are my fault. Keep your guys and your shit under control! Your guy called me Tuesday morning and told me he had the dope. I said fine and we set up a meet. I ain't guilty! I'm just a businessman!"

"What time did he call you on Tuesday?" asked Bryan, suddenly curious.

"Who the fuck cares!" the biker arrogantly replied, "Around eleven-thirty, maybe. Why?"

Wayne shot a furtive glance at Bryan. They had been with Bob and Greg most of Tuesday morning and all four had gone to lunch together afterwards. Maybe Bob had made the delivery but he certainly hadn't made the call.

"Just trying to see how the bastard set it up," Bryan replied with a shrug.

For a moment, he considered questioning further but figured Diamond Jimmy was pissed off enough as it was. Any more digging would serve to confirm the doubts the biker already had about them and would vastly increase the risk of losing the Aces of Death business altogether.

Apparently thinking along the same lines, Wayne changed the subject.

"Anyways, right now we've gotta get this fake coke thing sorted out. And believe me, this won't happen again."

\* \* \* \*

Chris concentrated his efforts that morning on his documentation work for Quality Imports.

As far as the drug ring went, he believed that he already had enough information to bring the whole thing down. Greg's complete diary to date had been copied on disks which were now safely stored in a safety deposit box. These were accompanied by tapes of pertinent conversations which had taken place since he'd installed his surveillance equipment as well as records of telephone and Eazy-Com communications.

He had contacted Jonathan and was meeting him for lunch to discuss the progress of their story. In Chris' opinion, the next step was to deliver this information to the police and let them 'legally' dismantle the drug importing network and he was certain that Jonathan would agree.

"Bother you for a minute?" Charles Peterson asked, entering Chris' office.

"Sure, boss. What's up?"

"The local Chamber of Commerce is holding one of those 'exchange business cards' cocktails tonight, from five to seven. My staff and I always attend and I was wondering if you wanted to join us; might give you the opportunity to build some contacts for some future freelance work."

"Sure. Why not," agreed Chris, wanting to make his effort to be part of the team. "Where's this thing taking place?"

"At the Sheraton, just up the road."

"No problem, Charlie. I'll be there."

\* \* \* \*

Wayne and Bryan rode in silence on the way back from their meeting with Diamond Jimmy. He had agreed to buy the coke they had, eighteen kilos, the seven bags of sugar being their problem. Upon their departure, Jimmy had re-emphasized the fact that they had one last chance. Any further screw-ups would cost them dearly.

"Maybe it wasn't Bob," Bryan stated softly, breaking the silence. "Maybe we killed him for nothing."

"Yeah, well it's a little late to figure that out!" snarled Wayne, fixing his gaze on the traffic ahead.

"But if it wasn't Bob, who could it be?" worried Bryan. "Matt?"

"I don't think Matt's got the balls or the brains to try to screw with us," Wayne replied. "Anyways, why would he rip off the coke and leave the money at Bob's? Where's the gain?"

"Maybe he and Bob were in this together," suggested Bryan. "Maybe Matt called Jimmy while Bob was with us. That would give Bob an alibi if we caught on to anything afterwards."

"I don't know," Wayne responded doubtfully. "Granted, they're not the smartest people I've ever met but it's a damn flimsy plan. I mean, if either one delivered the coke to Jimmy, they'd have to realize that he could identify them afterwards. Logically, if you ripped off some dope, wouldn't you go sell it to somebody other than your regular customer? I would. It doesn't make sense, Bryan. I'll have a chat with Matt, but something's wrong. I think Bob was set up and, so were we in the process. Somebody wanted us to kill Bob."

"Who?" asked Bryan, the anxiety in his voice apparent.

"Probably the same person who switched the coke for sugar," Wayne replied in a deadly tone. "This fuck is trying to play with our heads! I don't know who it is, but when I find out, I'm gonna rip his heart out!"

\* \* \* \*

Chris walked into Moe's and spotted Jonathan seated at a small table in the bar.

"Hey, bud!" he chanted as he slid into chair across from Addley.

"Greetings to you, sir!" replied Jonathan, extending a hand over the table. "I must say, I'm happy you suggested we get together. I haven't heard very much from you since we started this little project which is not how I usually like to work with my consultants."

"Don't take it personally, Jon," Chris apologized. "I'm pretty independent by nature. You asked me to look after something, so I did. No sense bothering you every other day if I had nothing to deliver, right? Today, I have something for you."

He proceeded to recount, in fine detail, the events of the preceding week, from his witnessing Greg and Wayne's visit to pick up the wooden cases, to this morning's conversation where Wayne and Bryan had informed Greg of Bob's untimely passing.

After having spoken for an hour, during which time Jonathan had not uttered a sound, Chris concluded his report with a slight grin.

"That's what I've been up to, boss. How do you like my story?"

"It's definitely a good story, Chris," approved Jonathan, impressed by the progress his new recruit had made in just over a week. "Any suggestions as to where it goes from here?"

"I think that enough information has been accumulated to dump the whole thing on the police and have them handle it." Chris suggested. "They'll have names, dates, places, financial records, everything."

"Does that fit with our hero's regular pattern?" Jonathan queried with a smile. "Wouldn't he have some kind of internal drive to eliminate these assholes himself?"

"I've retired from my Vigilante days," Chris quietly replied. "I'm healed, remember? I'm willing to help my country, for a fee, but I've realized that I can't single-handedly wipe out crime. Bottom line, it's no longer my job, Jonathan."

Addley nodded thoughtfully, now convinced beyond a doubt that Chris was as sane as they came. His violent past had existed for reasons which

Jonathan could understand but Chris had completed his therapy and was now at peace. Enough had paid for his pain according to his terms.

"You're absolutely right, Chris," Jonathan stated. "We definitely have enough for the cops to take over. When can you get the disks and tapes to me?"

"I'll get everything together tomorrow and we can meet somewhere on Saturday. I'll give you call."

"That will be fine," answered Jonathan, waving at the waiter for the check. "I just want to say that you've done some incredible work. I hope that you'll consider taking on some other contracts in the future. It would be a shame to let your talents go to waste."

"I'm too young to completely retire," replied a smiling Chris. "I don't plan to go for any full-time jobs, but you can consider me as a free-lance consultant!"

\* \* \* \*

"You wanted to see me?" asked Matt from the door of Wayne's office.

"Yeah, I did," Wayne responded, looking up from the report he was reading. "Come on in, Matt. Would you close the door behind you?"

"Sure, boss," Matt replied, complying with his superior's request before having a seat. "What's up?"

Matt was generally a nervous individual who did not function well under too much pressure. Wayne was therefore certain that if Matt knew anything, he would crack in no time.

"We've had a few problems that I need to bring you up to speed with," announced Wayne, almost kindly.

"What kind of problems?" asked Matt.

His usual worried look appeared but he did not seem uneasy.

"Yesterday, we discovered that Bob was the one who had stolen those four keys of coke on Saturday," stated Wayne, eyeing Matt carefully.

"What!? That's impossible, Wayne!" exclaimed Matt. "Bob wasn't even in town on Saturday! He was gone ice fishing!"

"So I've heard," replied Wayne. "Maybe he came back for something."

"No, Wayne!" insisted Matt. "A few of the guys out back were up there with him. They were joking around and talking about their trip on Monday morning when we got in. I'm sure Bob was up there for the weekend!"

"O.K. then. Maybe he grabbed the coke on Monday when you guys went over to Rick's place," Wayne suggested, still intently watching his subordinate.

"No way!" Matt argued. "I was with him the whole time!"

"Are you sure, Matt?" questioned Wayne. "This is very important."

"Wayne, I tell you there's no way that Bob could've found the coke and taken it without my knowing," Matt insisted, "Absolutely not!"

"Then, is there any way that he might have taken it and that you **were** aware of it, Matt?" enquired Wayne, staring at the young man through narrow eyes.

"What!?" shouted Matt, jumping from his seat, his expression a mixture of fear, disbelief and anger. "Bob had nothing to do with that coke disappearing and neither did I!"

"Calm down, Matt, and sit down!" commanded Wayne, knowing that the younger man spoke the truth. "I had to check. Relax. I believe you."

Matt returned to his chair, breathing heavily, clenching and unclenching his fists with rage and frustration.

"What did you do with Bob?" he asked sullenly, staring blankly at the floor.

"Listen," said Wayne with a tone of finality. "An important customer told us Bob sold him the coke. We went to talk to Bob about it and found a big pile of cash. Everything fit. We had to take care of Bob. End of story!"

"You killed Bob," Matt slowly mumbled, in a daze. "But you killed him for nothing!"

"Maybe we did, maybe we didn't," replied Wayne, not willing to admit his error. "Regardless, we have to move on. We can't change anything."

"Well, I think it's wrong," Matt announced with a sudden strength in his voice. "Don't you understand!? You killed Bob for nothing!"

"Let's just get one thing straight, you little bastard!" Wayne hissed angrily. "We're all in this together! Do you understand?! That means we stick together and, if we have to, we go down together! You think about that real carefully, mister, because if I start getting the impression that I can't trust you anymore, Bob is gonna be the least of your worries! Got it? Now, get the hell outta here! I've got things to do!"

* * * *

"What can I get you, sir?" politely enquired the barman at the Sheraton Hotel.

"White rum and Coke, please," replied Chris.

"Here you go, sir."

"Thanks."

"Thank-you, sir!"

Drink in hand, Chris rejoined Paul Anderson, President of Andernet Communications, to resume their conversation. Peterson had been right about this Chamber of Commerce cocktail. In just under an hour, Chris had established three contacts with whom his consulting services showed definite promise.

"As I was saying," resumed Anderson. "The direction our firm is heading in is definitely an area where your knowledge and expertise could come in handy..."

As Anderson spoke, Chris noticed Tony Bradley, his warehouse lessor, enter the reception hall at the far end. Suddenly oblivious of what Anderson was saying, Chris watched as Bradley greeted a few acquaintances. The latter apparently asked a question to which one of his buddies replied by pointing to the bar located behind Chris and Anderson. Bradley smiled, turned and headed directly towards them.

As if suddenly remembering something, Chris stared at his watch and exclaimed, "My God! Look at the time! Paul, you'll have to excuse me! I have an appointment downtown at 6:30! I have your card. I'll give you a call."

With that, he rushed off to a nearby exit, hoping that Bradley would not see him. He made it safely to door and quickly left the hotel, cursing himself for his renewed stupidity.

This game was nearly over. Now was not the time to make such careless mistakes.

* * * *

As Tony Bradley approached the bar, he caught a glimpse of Chris heading towards an exit.

"Hey, Mr. Johnson!" he called out just as Chris was going through the doorway.

He hurried after Chris, but could not see him anywhere in the lobby beyond. He re-entered the hall and went to the bar to get himself a drink.

"Howya doin, Tony!" Wayne heartily enquired, sauntering up to join the warehouse owner.

He had witnessed Chris' sudden departure as well as Bradley's subsequent pursuit.

"I saw you running out there and thought you were leaving."

"Nah," Tony explained. "I was just trying to catch up with this guy I rented a warehouse to last week. Mr. Johnson. You know him?"

"Johnson? Johnson?" mused Wayne, deep in thought. "Don't believe I do. What's he look like?"

"Did you see the guy that walked out just before I did?" asked Tony.

"Blonde fellow?"

"Yeah, that's the guy," replied Tony. "That's Johnson. So, you know him?"

"Nope. Can't say that I do," answered Wayne, a slight smile on his lips. "He looks familiar though. What kind of business is he in?"

"Couldn't tell you," was Bradley's response. "All I know is that the guy rented one of my mini-warehouses to store some stuff and paid me ahead, three months, cash. My kinda guy!"

"I guess!" agreed Wayne with a knowing chuckle. "I just can't remember where I've seen him. Maybe I saw him roaming around your place."

"Could be," Tony answered. "He took the last warehouse in the building; the one that gives right by your yard."

"Yeah, that must be where I saw him," nodded Wayne. "Well, I'm gonna mingle. Catch you later, Tony."

\* \* \* \*

Chris settled back in the couch to watch Letterman with Sandy. Although the show was generally good every night, this evening's programme would be particularly appealing as the musical guest was Melissa Etheridge, of whom both Chris and Sandy were major fans.

As Letterman started his monologue, the phone rang.

"Who's calling at this time?" asked Sandy as Chris reached for the cordless on the couch beside him.

"Hello. Hello?!"

The line went dead.

"Guess they didn't want to talk to me," shrugged Chris, tossing the phone back onto the couch.

"Unknown name, unknown number," stated Sandy, verifying the call display screen on the phone's base.

"Either a wrong number or one of your lovers!" quipped Chris.

"Probably one of my lovers," agreed a smiling Sandy.

\* \* \* \*

Wayne cut the connection on his cellular phone and looked up at Bryan.

"Well, Mr. Johnson is home, so let's check out his warehouse."

They climbed out of Wayne's Jag and crossed the rear yard of Quality Imports towards the neighbouring warehouse building.

"How do you plan to get in there?" asked Bryan as they approached the door to Chris's warehouse.

"Our friend, Mr. Bradley, has an incredible love for money!" Wayne smugly replied. "I rented the key to Barry's warehouse for the night for two hundred bucks. Another hundred bought me Bradley's promise to shut up!"

He finished speaking as they reached the door and, after scanning the area to make sure they were alone, attempted to insert the key into the lock.

"Sonovabitch!" he muttered under his breath.

"What's the matter?" asked Bryan.

"Either Bradley screwed me or that bastard Barry changed the fucking locks!" Wayne hissed through clenched teeth.

He hurried over to the doors of the next two warehouses and verified the locks.

"The others are Weisers," he fumed as he returned. "This is a Medeco."

He peered at the key in his hand and added, "This key's a Weiser. Barry changed the locks!"

"So, genius! Now what?" taunted Bryan.

"We go get a ladder and break a fucking window on the second floor!" Wayne shot back. "That's what, asshole!"

## Chapter 18 - Friday, January 31, 1997

It was 6:48 a.m. when Greg pulled into the parking lot of the Ste-Rose Diner. Getting up early was not one of his favourite sports, and doing so to have breakfast with Wayne and Bryan did little to render the activity more pleasurable. However, Wayne had sounded serious when he had called the previous night, or rather, very early that morning, and Greg had promised to meet them for breakfast at 6:30. At least, he had the satisfaction of arriving late.

After parking his car in the closest spot he could find, he hurried through the morning's bitter cold and entered the restaurant.

"Those bastards better be here!" he muttered to himself, searching the dining hall for his two associates.

"Greg! Back here!" he heard, then saw, Wayne calling and waving from a booth in the rear corner.

He reached the table and was greeted with Wayne's "You're late!" as he slid into the booth.

"I'm early enough!" he grunted back, signalling a waitress by pointing to his coffee cup. "What's so goddamn urgent that it couldn't wait until a reasonable hour at the office?!"

"We've got a problem," Bryan glumly announced.

"Yeah! Well, it seems every time we talk lately, we've got a problem!" Greg whined. "What is it this time? Your friend Jimmy rip us off with the coke?"

"No," Bryan answered, realizing that they hadn't told Greg about that problem yet. "But that deal didn't completely pan out. Someone switched part of the shipment on us. Seven keys were powdered sugar when we delivered to Jimmy. He was not a happy man."

"Holy shit!" whispered Greg, his grumpy disposition changing to one of fear. "You think it was Bob?"

"Actually, we're pretty sure that it wasn't Bob, or Matt," Wayne informed him, "In fact, we probably whacked Bob for nothing."

"Oh, great!" Greg buried his face into his hands. "Then, what's going on? Who's doing this?!"

"We think it's Chris Barry," Wayne hesitantly responded. "You were right, Greg," he added, not allowing his accountant friend the pleasure of saying 'I told you so!'

"What led you geniuses to believe that Barry might not be trustworthy?" enquired Greg, his tone heavy with sarcasm.

"Yesterday, at the cocktail party, I saw our neighbour, Tony Bradley, running after Barry," answered Wayne, ignoring Greg's shot. "Only, Tony knew our friend by the name of Johnson. It seems that Mister Johnson rented one of Tony's mini-warehouses to store a bunch of stuff. Now, it turns out that the warehouse in question, which happens to overlook the back of our building, is empty. Anyways, now it is. Until last night, this was stored in there, right by the window that gives on our yard."

He placed a video cam on the table before him.

"The bastard's been filming us?!" whispered Greg incredulously.

"It would seem so," Wayne nodded. "When we got into his warehouse last night, the camera was running. The only thing is, there was no tape in it. It's probably got some kinda transmitter set in it or something."

"Jesus Christ!" Greg swore, visibly shaken. "Do you think he knows we're onto him?"

Wayne was unable to hold off a grin. "Well, if he was filming last night, he'll know as soon as he looks at the tape. The sonovabitch changed the locks on the doors so we couldn't get in with the keys I got from Tony. We get a ladder and Bryan climbs up to the window on the second floor. He trying to see something inside and has got his face pressed up against the glass. He notices a small red light glowing right inside and suddenly realizes that he's got a camera lens about six inches from his mug. He nearly fell off the ladder! I never thought somebody Bryan's size could move that quick!"

"Yeah, yeah! Real funny, asshole!" muttered Bryan. "Next time you go up and we'll see how you do!"

Turning his attention to Greg, he continued. "We think that Barry might have bugged our offices and phones. That would explain how he knew about the dope, the deliveries, so on and so forth; which means, we don't talk at the office anymore until we fix this guy."

"And how do we plan to go about that?" Greg asked, once again wishing he had never gotten into this business.

"Presuming that he hasn't seen last night's tape yet, he'll be in the office this morning," Wayne hopefully replied. "If that's the case, we'll invite him to lunch and stash him somewhere until we figure out what to do."

"But what if he has seen the tape?" Greg insisted. "What then?"

"Then we'll go over to his place and have a chat with him there," Wayne quietly stated. "Either way, this piece of shit is not going to fuck us up! We've come too far to have some righteous ex-executive take us down!"

"What if he's not in this alone?" an ever-worrisome Greg pushed on. "What if he's a cop or something?"

"Oh, Jesus-Christ, Greg!" Wayne retorted in frustration. "The guy's a well-known Montreal businessman whose been building his career for years. He's had his picture in the papers dozens of times in the last five years. All of that was just a set-up for some cop?! Come on! Get real!"

"I guess you're right," Greg uneasily admitted. "It's just that things have been pretty screwy over the last three weeks and I'm getting really nervous!"

"Relax, Greg. Take it easy," soothed Wayne. "We've identified the problem. Now we'll fix it and everything will go back to normal. Don't worry so much."

\* \* \* \*

"Good morning, gorgeous!" Sandy greeted her husband as she joined him in the kitchen. "You're up bright and early."

"Yep. Got things to do, people to see," Chris replied, leaning back to kiss her. "Going to visit a friend of Jonathan's this morning. Apparently, the guy's got a fancy set-up to edit and copy videotapes. I can probably get what's important on one cassette."

"Are you getting everything to Jonathan today?" asked Sandy, anxious for her husband's spy adventure to end.

"Nah. More likely tomorrow," answered Chris. "I want to review the whole thing one last time before I deliver. I want to make sure my face or name don't appear anywhere in any incriminating fashion. What are you up to today?"

"Cathy's picking me up and we're heading downtown for lunch and a little bit of shopping. You need anything?"

"Nothing comes to mind," Chris responded with a smirk. "Anyways, you should start going easy on the spending. Don't forget that I'm no longer permanently employed!"

"I promise to buy only what's on sale!" laughed Sandy.

\* \* \* \*

"The bastard's not coming in!" Wayne announced to Greg and Bryan.

They were standing in an open area of the shipping department, relatively comfortable that they were safe from bugs.

"Maybe he's just late," suggested Greg hopefully.

"No such luck," Wayne sneered. "I spoke to Peterson. Barry called him earlier to say that he had some personal business to attend to. Maybe he'll come in this afternoon but he said not to expect him."

"So, now what?" asked a nervous Greg, sweat starting to trickle down his back.

"So now, Bryan and I will pay Mister Barry a visit," Wayne replied. "I told Peterson that we would be visiting customers all day. Greg, you stay here. If anything strange happens or if Barry shows up, call us."

"I don't like this," muttered Greg, wringing his hands. "It's all gonna blow up in our faces!"

"Not if we move fast," Wayne insisted impatiently. "Just stay calm and keep your eyes open! We'll fix this. Let's go, Bryan."

\* \* \* \*

A few years earlier, Sandy had taken up oil painting as a pastime. Since, her easels remained installed in permanence in one corner of the sunroom, with never less than two canvasses in the making. It was a hobby which she truly enjoyed and she often picked up brush and palette as soon as five or more minutes of free time became available.

Cathy was to pick her up around 10 o'clock and it was only 9:45. With fifteen minutes ahead of her, she headed for the sunroom to pursue her latest masterpiece. No sooner had she entered the room than the doorbell rang.

"Cathy's early," she said aloud as she returned to the front of the house to greet her friend.

She opened the door and was startled to find herself faced by two gentlemen, both who looked vaguely familiar.

"Yes, can I help you?" she asked, trying to remember where she had seen these men before.

"Is Mister Barry home?" queried Bryan, pleasantly enough.

"No," replied Sandy, suddenly wary of the two individuals standing before her. "Unfortunately he's not. If you want to leave your names, I'll be sure to let him know you dropped by."

"Where is he?" demanded Wayne, not as pleasantly as his counterpart.

"He's not here!" retorted Sandy, raising her tone. "Now, if you gentlemen will excuse me, I'm busy!" she added as she started to close the door.

With a swift gesture, Wayne straight-armed the door, slamming it open and causing Sandy to jump back in astonishment.

"Not so fast, lady!" he snarled, moving inside, followed by Bryan. "We ain't done talking yet!"

"I don't know who the hell you think you are!" screamed Sandy, regaining her composure. "But you better get the hell out of here!"

"Shut up, bitch!" growled Wayne as Bryan closed the front door behind them. "Now, where the fuck is Barry!"

"I don't know," Sandy coldly responded, hiding her fear. "He must be at work."

"No," replied Bryan in his annoyingly pleasant voice. "If he was there, we wouldn't have had to come over here and bother you sweetheart, now, would we?"

"W-well, then I can't help you," stammered Sandy, suddenly recognizing her visitors. "If he's not at work, then I don't know where he is."

"O.K." sneered Wayne. "Then, here's what we're gonna do. Let's the three of us go for a ride. Later, if you remember where Chris is, you can let us know. Get your coat Mrs. Barry. It's cold out there."

\* \* \* \*

"McCall, Homicide," Dave answered the phone.

"Hi, hon," said Cathy, his wife. "Sorry to bother you."

"No problem. What's up?"

"Well, I'm parked outside at Sandy's and Chris' place," Cathy replied with concern. "Sandy and I were supposed to go shopping together but nobody's home."

"You sure it was today?" asked Dave.

"Of course I'm sure!" answered Cathy. "I spoke to Sandy yesterday afternoon. I tried her cellular but it's not on. Do you have Chris' number with you? I'd call him to make sure everything's all right."

"Yeah, hang on a second," her husband replied, digging into his briefcase. "Here we go. You can reach him at 668-1245 at work. I'll give you his cell phone too; 352-3310. If anything's wrong, let me know."

"I will," Cathy promised. "Thanks. Love you, and be careful. Bye."

\* \* \* \*

Chris was quite impressed with the video equipment made available by Sonny, Jonathan's acquaintance. In just over two hours, he had managed to edit a week's worth of videotapes onto one cassette, thanks to Sonny's miniature audio-visual recording studio.

He was rapid-viewing the final cassette, that from the previous night, when his cell phone rang.

"Hello," he replied, his eyes glued to the images moving at high speed on the monitor before him.

"Hi, Chris," he heard Cathy McCall's voice on the line. "How are you?"

"Fine, Cathy, fine. Yourself?"

"Doing O.K., thanks. Chris, do you know where your lovely wife is?"

"I thought you two were going to spend Dave's and my hard earned money?" Chris jokingly replied. "Why? Where are you?"

"In your driveway," Cathy answered. "Sandy doesn't seem to be home."

"That's strange," Chris responded, puzzled. "I know she didn't forget that you were going out together because she talked about it this morning. Maybe she just went out to run a quick errand."

"Probably," agreed Cathy. "I'll wait a bit. If you hear from her, you can reach me in my car."

"O.K.," Chris replied, a little concerned. "Let me know if she doesn't show up."

"I will. Don't worry. Bye."

Chris flipped the phone shut and laid it down on the counter beside him, looking away from the video monitor for a second or two. As he returned his attention to the screen, he had the impression of having caught a glimpse of a face just before the image disappeared, to be replaced by the hissing snow of an unrecorded tape.

He pressed the rewind button and, sure enough, the face appeared again, but only for a fraction of a second at such a high speed. Curious and anxious, he hit the play button on the control panel before him and the tape began playing normally. He could see the deserted back lot of Quality Imports and not much else.

But wait! He detected a slight movement in the darkness at the bottom of the screen. He re-winded again and resumed his viewing at normal speed. He could vaguely make out two men walking in the dark towards Quality Imports, apparently coming from Bradley's warehouse. As they moved into the light of the Quality building, Chris easily recognized Wayne and Bryan.

As he watched, he saw Wayne enter the building's shipping area and return with a ladder which he handed down to Bryan. The latter hurried back towards Bradley's building, followed by Wayne and soon, both men were out of the camera's scope.

Several seconds later, a few dull, metallic clanking sounds were heard, followed by the sudden close-up appearance of Bryan's pudgy face, inches from the camera lens. No more than another half-minute went by before the sound of breaking glass could be heard, after which, the image completely disappeared.

They had discovered him, or at least his camera! But how? Probably thanks to Tony Bradley, although Chris didn't really hold the warehouse owner responsible. It was his own stupidity that had led to his being found out.

Anyways, it didn't really matter. He'd get everything together and make his delivery to Jonathan today. If required, he and Sandy would spend the weekend safely out of town.

Sandy? Where was she? It was not like her to be late for an appointment. She had too much respect for people.

His stomach tightened as he grabbed for his phone and speed-dialled their home number. No answer. He tried her cell phone but got the network's message centre indicating that the user was currently not available.

Was it possible that they had gotten hold of Sandy? He'd never forgive himself if something happened to her, especially if it was a result of his own carelessness.

He decided to call Cathy back, hoping that Sandy had since arrived. As he flipped open his phone, it rang, startling him.

"Hello?" he answered.

"Hi, Chris," Sandy's voice sounded strained.

"Hi! Where are you? What's the matter?" he asked, both relieved and concerned.

"She's with some friends, Mr. Johnson!" Wayne's familiar voice chided, making Chris feel nauseous.

"You're making a serious mistake, Wayne," Chris responded, his voice deadly quiet.

"No! You made a serious mistake, Barry!" Wayne shouted into the phone. "We weren't looking for any trouble. This is your fault. You fuck with us, you pay!"

"Listen to me very carefully, Wayne," Chris continued softly. "Take very good care of my wife. It will make your death much less painful."

"Chris, Chris, Chris," taunted Wayne in a soothing tone. "You're really not in any position to make threats right now. Don't worry about your dear little wife. She's just collateral. Nothing'll happen to her as long as you're a good boy. Now, I just wanted to let you know that she was with us. I'll call you back later. In the meantime, be a smart boy. O.K.?"

With that, the line went dead.

Chris stared at the phone in his hand, breathing deeply to ease the churning he felt inside. After several moments, having somewhat regained his composure, he punched in Cathy's number and waited impatiently for her to pick up.

"Yeah, Cathy? Chris. Listen, Sandy just gave me a call. She wasn't feeling well and decided to go to the clinic. No, nothing serious. Don't worry. Yeah, I'll have her call you. Sorry you drove out for nothing. No, I don't think we can make it this weekend. I'm gonna be really busy. Listen, I have to go. I'll ask Sandy to call you later, O.K.? Once again, sorry. Bye."

\* \* \* \*

At 5:26, Dave McCall pulled into the driveway of his Dorval home, trying to remember the last time he had left work at a reasonable hour. Smiling, he climbed out of the car and headed into the house, looking forward to a complete weekend off with Cathy.

"Hi, hon!" he called from the foyer as he peeled off the apparel necessary for Montreal winters.

"Hey there!" exclaimed Cathy, coming down the stairs. "This is a pleasant surprise!"

"Yup," replied Dave. "And if all goes well, nobody's gonna kill anybody over the weekend and you'll have to endure me for the next two days!"

"I think I can manage that," she murmured, placing her arms around his neck and kissing him.

"So, did you and Sandy have a good time?" asked Dave as they moved into the kitchen.

"Actually, we didn't go. Sandy wasn't feeling well and was gone to the clinic when I got there. Chris got back to me to let me know after I called him."

"Anything serious?" enquired Dave, concerned.

"I guess not," Cathy shrugged. "At least Chris didn't think so. He said that Sandy would call me back but I haven't heard from her. I'll give her a shout tomorrow."

"If they're up to it, maybe we can get together."

"Well, I suggested that to Chris but he said he'd be really busy this weekend," Cathy replied. She hesitated a little, then added, "Chris sounded strange when I spoke to him, Dave. He seemed distant and anxious to get off the phone. I had the impression something was wrong."

"You just worry too much, Mother!" Dave kidded. "He was probably just worried about Sandy."

"I guess," Cathy doubtfully replied. "I just had a feeling that there was a problem."

"We'll talk to them tomorrow and you'll see, everything will be all right. Now, let's get something to eat. I'm starving!"

\* \* \* \*

He pulled on some black jeans and a sweat-shirt, also black, found his running shoes and put them on. He moved downstairs to the hall closet where he pulled out his black leather jacket. Black leather gloves and a baseball cap completed his outfit.

He headed into the dining room where the apparatus required for the evening lay on the table. As he reviewed the items one last time, he wondered if his true intention had ever been to retire from his violent activities. If so, why had he kept all this equipment? Souvenirs?

He completed his inventory check and was comfortable that he had everything he might need. The two handguns went on his person, the .357 Magnum in the holster strapped under his right arm, the other, a tiny .22, into a small discreet pocket within his jacket. The switchblade went into a zippered pocket on the left leg of his jeans. The rest; tape, rope, wire snips, and a few lock picking devices, went into a small gym bag.

He knew that he wouldn't have to worry about an alarm system. He had checked that afternoon and the home he was planning to visit was linked with Pro-Tek Systems. A little computer hacking had ensured that the system would be properly dysfunctional.

He headed towards the garage, pausing only to pick up the new baseball bat he had purchased that afternoon, cash.

He started up the Pathfinder and rolled down the driveway, heading for his destination. As he reached the street, the phone rang on the seat beside him.

"Hello?"

"Chris!" greeted Jonathan's voice. "I hadn't heard from you today so I was wondering what was going on? Are we still on for tomorrow?"

"No," was Chris's blunt reply.

"No! What do you mean, no? What's the matter, Chris?"

"This thing has become personal, Jonathan."

"Personal?!" exclaimed Jonathan, angry and bewildered. "Chris, what the hell is going on? Have you lost it? I thought the 'Vigilante' had retired?!"

"They found me out and took Sandy, Jonathan," Chris stonily replied. "It's become personal."

"Ah Jesus!" Jonathan muttered in disgust. "I'm sorry, Chris. When did this happen?"

"This morning around ten. They called me and told me to lay off. They're supposed to call me back but I don't know when."

"Why didn't you call me, Chris?" Jonathan reproached. "I can help! You know that! I've got a whole team if we need it!"

"This is personal and I intend to make these bastards pay, Jonathan," Chris coldly stated. "You've got to understand that."

"I understand, and believe me, they'll pay! I'm not suggesting that you let us take over, Chris. I'm telling you, let us help. Let **me** help!"

Chris was silent for a moment before responding. "I'll think about it. Right now, I've got an errand to run. I'll give you a call when I get back."

"Are you sure, Chris? Don't bullshit me!"

"I'll call you, Jonathan," Chris promised. "Some time tonight. Maybe late but I'll call."

"All right, Chris," Jonathan sighed. "Be careful."

"I will. Thanks, Jon."

\* \* \* \*

Matt poured himself another healthy dose of vodka, splashing some on the counter in the process, but not caring. What was this? Drink number five, number six? It didn't matter. What mattered was the numbness. At least the nausea was gone and the buzz felt good. But he still wished he had never gotten into this.

Sure, at first, and for a while, it was a blast. He was important, he had money, his friends admired him and he was respected at the clubs and restaurants he frequented. Life in the fast lane! Mister Big Shot! That was all fine and nice until they shot George. And everything had turned to shit since. Now it was kidnapping on top of the drugs and murders. And Wayne, the genius, had no idea who Chris Barry even was or what he knew. The guy might be a goddamn cop! And to top it all, they were now holding Barry's wife at his, Matt's, cottage in St-Sauveur!

Feeling another bout of nausea coming on, Matt went for the vodka again, not bothering with a glass this time. The burn felt good and his stomach settled once more.

As he put the bottle back down, the phone rang, startling him. He hoped, prayed, that it wouldn't be Wayne. At least, with half a bottle of vodka and a few snorts of coke in him, he'd have a good excuse not to go if they asked him to head to the cottage that night.

"Yeah?" he mumbled into the phone, the drugs and alcohol really starting to take their toll.

"Hello, Mister Shaffer, please," asked the voice on the phone.

"Listen, bud!" slurred Matt. "This is the third time I tell you! There's no fucking Mr. Shaffer here! Understand?!"

"I'm sorry to have bothered you, sir," the voice apologized. "I promise I won't call again."

\* \* \* \*

Outside Matt's house, Chris flipped his phone shut and pulled the wire snips from his gym bag.

"Just wanna make sure that you won't call anybody either, you little piece of shit!" he breathed as he severed the home's phone line.

He crept along the shovelled patio and up the steps leading to the elevated terrace from where he had a view of the kitchen inside. As he watched, he saw Matt sitting at the dining room table beyond, apparently preparing a line of coke.

"I better get in there soon," he muttered as he crawled back down the steps. "Bastard's gonna kill himself without any help!"

He headed for a pair of french doors located at patio level and peered inside at what seemed to be a game room of sorts; pool table, bar, big screen T.V. A quick examination of the lock confirmed that this would be his point of entry. As long as Matt remained in the upper section of the split-level house, he wouldn't hear a thing.

He got to work on the lock and, within ten seconds, felt the bolt slide back. Pushing the door in no more than half an inch, he reached into the gym bag, pulled out an aerosol can of lubricant and quickly sprayed the hinge areas of the door. He'd been careless enough in recent days; no more.

Moving soundlessly into the dark room, he headed toward a dimly lit corridor atop a short flight of stairs. Upon reaching the top step, he looked down the hall to his left, towards the kitchen and dining room. He could see Matt, back to him, still sitting at the table, still playing with his little pile of white powder.

He crept slowly, silently, one step at a time, praying for the floorboards to remain quiet under the thick carpet as he approached his unsuspecting prey. He reached Matt just as the latter bent forward for a snort. As the young man regained his original position, he felt something cold and hard press into the back of his neck.

"Do not make any sudden moves, Matt," Chris ordered in a gentle voice. "If you do, I will blow your throat out. Nod slightly if you understand."

The nod was barely perceptible.

"Good. Now, I want you to bring your arms down along the sides of the back of your chair. Slowly, that's good. You and I are going to get along great, Matt; real rapport."

He proceeded to heavily tape Matt's wrists to the top of the chair's rear legs.

"Now, your feet, Matt. Great! I don't even have to tell you what to do! You're a natural! There you go. All taped up!"

He walked into the kitchen and closed the vertical blinds.

"Wouldn't want the neighbours peeking in on us," said Chris, winking at Matt as he pulled out a chair and sat down. "Now, let's you and I have a little chat, O.K.?"

Matt nodded, his eyes uncertain.

"I guess you know who I am, Matt? You've seen me around the warehouse, haven't you?"

Matt nodded again.

"You can answer me, Matt," encouraged Chris, lightly patting the young man's cheek. "You can talk. I want you to talk, O.K.?"

"Y-yes sir," Matt mumbled.

"Good, Matt. Good. And you can call me Chris. None of this sir bullshit; I don't function well under formality. Now, what should we talk about? Do you have any ideas?"

"N-no, Chris."

"No?! Well, here's something we can talk about. Why don't you tell me where you cocksuckers are holding my wife. Let's start with that, Matt."

"I-I don't know where she is. They didn't tell me. They just said that I should stay home and wait til they called."

"Wrong answer, Matt," Chris barked, his tone much colder. "Try again."

"I swear, Chris!" Matt insisted, suddenly feeling strangely sober. "Wayne called me and told me that they had grabbed your wife and that he'd call me later! That's all I know!"

Chris leaned across the table, his face inches from his prisoner's. "Are you sure you don't know anything else, Matt?"

"I swear, man! If I did, I'd tell you!"

"Let me think about that, Matt," Chris mused as he picked up his roll of filament tape, cutting off a six inch strip.

"W-what are you doing?"

"I need a bit of peace and quiet while I think," Chris explained as he applied the tape firmly to Matt's mouth.

He paced around the room for a moment before turning back towards the young man.

"Maybe you're telling me the truth, Matt. But, maybe you're not. You see, I have a hard time believing little, motherfucker, drug pushing, murderer, pricks like you. So I have to be convinced that you're not lying to me."

He turned and moved into the kitchen where he began opening drawers from which he selected several cooking utensils. Matt watched, his terror mounting, as Chris turned on the two front burners of the gas range and proceeded to place the variety of knives, forks, spatulas and other cooking tools in the flames.

"This," said Chris approvingly, holding up a potato masher before placing it on the burner, "Can be a lot of fun! You've got some nice stuff here, Matt. Nothing like heat resistant handles on cooking utensils. I hate burning myself. Don't you?"

He examined his lay-out on the stove and, satisfied, returned to his chair facing Matt.

"We'll let those heat up for a few minutes, get them nice and hot! In the meantime, you might want to think real hard about where my wife is."

\* \* \* \*

As Chris approached his home, he noticed a dark Acura Vigor parked in the driveway, close to the house and facing the street. He slowed and watched, waiting for the signal. Two quick flashes of the headlights, followed by a pause; then three longer flashes. As he pulled into the driveway, he activated the automated garage door and signalled the driver of the Acura to back into the three car garage. He followed, pulling in between the Acura and his Lexus.

"Greetings," said Jonathan as he got out of his car. "How are you holding up?"

"O.K. so far," Chris sombrely replied. "I'll be a lot better when Sandy's back and I've taken care of these bastards!"

"Don't worry, Chris," Jonathan responded in a determined tone. "That'll be **real** soon. Have they contacted you again?"

"Nope. Not yet. And that's got me worried."

"Don't be," reassured Jonathan. "They're still trying to figure out their next step which I'm sure is not real clear in their minds right now."

"Well, let's get going," replied Chris. "Because I'm pretty clear what my next steps are gonna be!"

They moved into the house from the garage, pursuing their conversation as they went along.

"So, how did your errand go?" Jonathan asked, not knowing exactly where Chris had been but certain that it was linked to the whole affair.

"Exactly as planned," responded Chris with fire in his eyes. "Now I know where they're holding her and I have a pretty good idea who's there."

"Who'd you visit?" enquired Jonathan.

"Matt, one of their gofers," answered Chris, "The one who was still alive."

"Was?" Jonathan raised an eyebrow. "Nobody saw you?"

"No. Being careless is what got Sandy involved in this thing. I'm not careless anymore."

"Good," said Jonathan. "What's next on your agenda?"

"Greg Pierce, the accountant," Chris replied. "I'm gonna visit him to make sure we have his complete journal. Then I'll make sure that he doesn't interfere with the rest of our week-end plans."

"When are you going to see him?"

"Early in the morning," answered Chris. "After that, you and I head up to Matt's chalet in St-Sauveur."

"Who's going to be there?"

"As far as Matt could tell me, Wayne and Bryan are up there," replied Chris. "They've also asked their friend, Diamond Jimmy, for some help. They should have four members of the Aces of Death guarding the place. Matt was supposed to drive up there in the morning but, unfortunately, he's not gonna be able to make it."

"So we'll have to move quickly," stated Jonathan. "Before they find out what happened to Matt. Are you sure that Matt told you the truth about where they're holding Sandy?"

"Yeah," Chris nodded. "I convinced him that if he didn't play straight with me, I'd hurt him really bad. He even gave me the blueprints of his St-Sauveur place. I'm sure that he told me the truth."

He stood up and stretched as he looked at the clock on the wall. "It's quarter to one. I'm going to catch a couple of hours of sleep. Make yourself at home and holler if you need anything. The guest room is the first door to the right upstairs when you want to get some sleep."

"I'm fine for now," Jonathan replied. "I treated myself to a little nap while I was waiting for your call. I'd like to see the information you collected, if you don't mind, and I might have a few calls make."

"Second door to the right upstairs is my study," offered Chris. "There's a phone, PC, fax and anything else you might need. You'll find two boxes on the table in the corner. Everything's in there, including seven kilos of cocaine. Enjoy yourself. I'll see you in a couple of hours."

## Chapter 19 - Saturday, February 1, 1997

Greg turned over in his sleep, trying to escape the annoying sound, but it persisted. He awoke to realize that the phone was ringing. As he sat up in his bed, he squinted at his watch and swore.

"Hello!" he growled into the phone.

"Greg! Where the fuck is Matt?" shouted an angry Wayne on the other end of the line.

"Jesus, Wayne! How am I supposed to know?" retorted Greg. "It's not even goddamn five o'clock! I was sleeping!"

"Yeah, well, get up!" ordered Wayne. "I told that little bastard to stay home until I called him. Now there's no answer. I want you to get over to his place and make sure everything's O.K. I don't trust that little scumbag! I think he's really starting to lose it and I don't want him running to the cops! Call me back once you know what's going on."

With that, the phone went dead in Greg's hand.

"Goddamn Jesus fucking Christ!" Greg shrieked as he climbed out of bed and started getting dressed to go to Matt's place. "This is gonna have to end soon!"

\* \* \* \*

Chris approached Greg's residence which was located just a few blocks from Matt's, where he'd been the night before. As he turned onto the accountant's street, he spotted the latter's Buick Roadmaster pull out of the driveway and speed away. He accelerated a little and proceeded to tail the large car. It quickly became obvious that Greg was on his way to Matt's, where they arrived within a matter of minutes, Greg parking in the driveway while Chris stopped half a dozen houses away to watch.

Greg climbed out of the car and hurried to the front door of the attractive home, clearly unaware that he had been followed. He rang then pulled a key from his coat pocket, unlocked the front door and went inside, closing the door behind him. Less than a minute later, the door was thrown open and Greg rushed out, barely managing to make it down the five steps leading to the driveway before falling to his knees and vomiting what was left of his prior evening's dinner.

He remained on his knees for a few seconds, breathing heavily, before standing up again, unsteadily. With an air of panic, he glanced wildly about, trying to determine if anyone had seen him. Barring an unoccupied Pathfinder parked further down the street, the area was deserted.

He stumbled hurriedly back up the steps to close the door, not bothering to lock it, and rushed back to his car. He backed out of the driveway and headed back for home as quickly as he could without squealing the tires. In his frenzied state, he did not notice the Pathfinder leave the curb to follow him.

\* \* \* \*

The small conference room at the RCMP Quebec Division office in downtown Montreal slowly and quietly began to fill at 5:25 a.m. Ten people had been summoned and there was no doubt that all would show up.

There was little conversation as they arrived. Most were not scheduled to work that day and those who were, were only slated to start somewhat later. The eve being Friday, some had barely had time to fall asleep when the call had come.

Although the meeting had been called for 5:30, three of the participants had still not arrived at 5:35. At 5:37, one rushed in, looking like he had not even had the chance to get to bed from the night before. They had stressful jobs and liked to unwind on their nights off. Another arrived a moment later, the dishevelled hair indicating that some slumber had been attained, but the dark glasses highlighting that the previous evening had been demanding.

As was always the case when such a meeting was called, the last arrival was Nick Sharp, Director of the Quebec Division, RCMP, and caller of the meeting. Such tardiness was not of his usual nature and only occurred at these special meetings. He recognized that in such circumstances, these people were doing more, much more than they had signed up for when joining the force. They were the best he had and all dropped their personal schedules and lives without a word whenever required. He therefore always made sure that everyone was present before joining them at these meetings, allowing them the impression that none were late.

At 5:39, he entered the small conference room, greeting the ten seated around the cigarette scarred table as he closed the door.

"Good morning, ladies and gentlemen! I thank you all for being here on such short notice."

An array of nods, mumbles and grunts were offered in response.

"Good!" Nick continued with a smile. "I can see that everyone's fully rested and raring to go!"

This time, a medley of grunts, chuckles and mutterings emanated from around the table.

"Alright! Let's get rolling. A friend has supplied me with some very interesting information," Nick informed them, using the opening line he always used at such meetings. "In summary, we're dealing with some people who've been importing smack and coke from Thailand and Columbia using an honest import company as their means and cover. The Aces of Death have become their main client in recent weeks so we'll finally have a chance to get a crack at those bastards!"

Murmurs of approval were pronounced from the rapidly wakening group.

"As in the past, we've been lucky enough to have a shit-load of data dumped onto us," Nick went on, "Without having to spend months following, investigating and tracking down a bunch of low-lives. So now, we have to shake our asses and put together some solid case files and investigation reports real quick! I trust that none of you had any major plans for the week-end?"

A combination of shrugs, moans and blasphemies came as response to the rhetorical question.

"No wonder I like working with you guys so much!" Nick exclaimed. "As usual, the information that's been supplied is in its raw form. Some of it will have to be modified a little to make it stick. This story has to stand up when we're done with it if we want to cover for my friend out there. I've already got some points that we'll need to fine tune and he'll be getting back to me with some last minute details over the next day or two; Andy, John, Sue, Lisa and Gary, everything's in those two boxes."

He paused to light a cigarette before continuing.

"There's a dozen pages of notes in the top box that map out quite nicely how this whole thing might have taken place. Base yourself on that. If you have any questions, let me know. Now, go and write me an incredible story! Arty and the rest of you, stick around. We've got some visits to coordinate."

\* \* \* \*

Greg sat in his study, working feverishly on his journal. He'd had enough with the whole thing and had made a decision. Everything was falling apart and, in addition to possibly getting busted soon, his dying had now become a real possibility.

As soon as he completed this final entry he would take his precious journal, go hide somewhere and contact the cops. Once they promised immunity, he'd deliver, testify and disappear. He could definitely afford it financially and, since his wife had left him, he had no ties to hold him back.

He completed his entry and proceeded to save his document. Following the usual crunching of the hard drive, he was surprised to see the screen suddenly go completely black for a couple of seconds before turning bright red.

"What the fuck!" he muttered under his breath, dumbfounded.

He hoped that nothing was wrong with his computer. He hadn't backed up his data in quite a while and now was not the time for his journal to become inaccessible. He tried hitting a few keys but generated no reaction from the machine. As he was about to attempt to reboot the system, bold black letters began to appear on the red screen.

**IT'S OVER GREG!! YOU AND YOUR FRIENDS HAVE GONE TOO FAR. DON'T THINK YOU CAN DO**

**ANYTHING WITH YOUR JOURNAL. IT'S GONE. NOW, YOU MUST DIE. YOU SAW WHAT HAPPENED TO MATT. THAT WAS NOTHING. HE WAS JUST A JUNIOR IN YOUR OPERATION. NOT YOU. YOU'RE ONE OF THE BIG BOYS. THAT MEANS YOU REALLY GET TO SUFFER AS YOU GO. IN A VERY SHORT WHILE, YOU WILL WISH THAT YOU HAD BEEN ARRESTED AND THROWN INTO PRISON FOR LIFE. GETTING SODOMIZED EVERY NIGHT BY A DIFFERENT SLIME BAG WOULD BE PARADISE COMPARED TO THE TORTURE I WILL MAKE YOU ENDURE!! I WILL TEND TO YOU SOON (SOONER THAN YOU THINK).**

As each word appeared, painfully slowly, letter by letter, Greg read the message with growing terror. Although he had emptied his stomach in Matt's front yard, he found himself retching uncontrollably. Sweat poured out of every pore of his body and within a matter of moments, his clothes were soaked through. Glancing down for an instant, he had the faint realization that he had urinated in his pants.

The message finally finished printing itself on the screen, glaringly taunting the accountant. Greg stared back, in a daze.

After a minute or two, he reached down to the lower drawer of his desk, pulling it open in a slow, mechanical fashion. He absently pulled out the .38 Special which Wayne had given him two years earlier, stuck the barrel into his mouth and pulled the trigger.

\* \* \* \*

After making sure that he had in fact copied the final version of Greg's journal, Chris snapped his notepad closed and slipped it back into his duffel bag.

Quietly, he climbed the stairs leading from the basement of Greg's home to the first floor. As far as he could determine from Greg's steps earlier, the study would be at the back of the house, off to the left. He headed in that direction, gun in hand, alert for any possible danger, although he didn't expect any. He had heard the shot a moment earlier.

Before actually reaching the room, he could see through the open door that Greg would present no immediate or eventual threat to himself or anyone else. The man had, wisely, literally blown his brains out.

Chris leaned over the dead accountant's body and rebooted the PC. Only a few seconds were required to confirm that he had in fact erased the journal from the hard drive.

"Bye, Greg," he said softly as he headed for the basement door by which he had entered. As he descended the stairs, he could hear the phone begin to ring upstairs.

* * * *

"Jesus Christ! Stupid motherfuckers!" Wayne screamed hysterically, throwing the cordless phone across the room. "Where the fuck are those assholes!"

"Calm down, Wayne! Jesus!" snapped Bryan, his tone exasperated. "Maybe they went to get something to eat! What the fuck is your problem?"

"I told that idiot, Matt, that I would call," Wayne hissed impatiently. "And I asked that other goddamn moron to call me once he had checked in on Matt! That ain't that complicated, Bryan! Why didn't they call? Something's wrong. I know it."

"I'll go check," Bryan decided, lifting his bulky form from the couch. "I'm getting tired of sitting around here anyways, seeing as you don't want me to party with our little friend upstairs."

"We don't touch her until we've figured out exactly what to do. Understand?" commanded Wayne. "Once we get our hands on Barry, you can do whatever you want with her. Not before!"

"Yeah, yeah. I know," Bryan rolled his eyes, having heard the speech several times already. "The more I wait, the sweeter she'll be! Anyways, I'm gonna go see what's up with Greg and Matt. And don't worry. I'll call."

* * * *

Andy Kovac had never dreamed that working as a clerk for a customs broker would prove to be such a lucrative position. And to think, four years earlier, he had come so close to quitting this dead-end job.

That had been right before Wayne had showed up and offered to pay a handsome salary for very little work. Just a little merchandise coordination at the warehouse until the proper customs inspectors came along. That was it. And the nice thing was, his wife didn't even know about it. That meant that he got to spend all the extra cash on his greatest passion; sex with the hottest call girls in town; sometimes a nooner, other times, the always reliable 'night out with the boys'.

Last night had been particularly interesting, he thought as he stepped into the shower. With his wife gone to Vancouver to visit her sister, he had been able to hire not one or two, but three lovely and very nasty ladies to cater to his needs, right in the comfort of his own home. It had been expensive but, God, it had been worth it! He was surprised that he could even stand up this morning.

As he continued to think of the previous evening and the three women still sleeping in his bed, he found himself getting excited again. He looked down at his now semi-aroused penis and smiled.

"I'm so proud of you!" he chuckled, now convinced that he'd be in shape for another round of fun and games.

As if in response to his desires, he heard someone come into the bathroom.

"I don't know who you are," he called out over the shower curtain. "But I've got one stiff cock here that needs some attention!"

The shower curtain was pushed aside and he found himself staring at a very large gun, held by a very large man. Two uniformed officers stood in the background.

"Don't look that stiff to me, Andy!" said Arty Hubbard of the RCMP. "Anyways, you're not really my type. I prefer long legs and breasts. Get your clothes on, Andy. We're going downtown. You're under arrest for conspiring to import illegal narcotics into the country. You have the right to retain and instruct counsel..."

\* \* \* \*

Richie 'Butch' Boulanger was only nineteen but he had already killed several times, even before the Aces of Death had asked him to do so to prove he was worthy of being a member. And he had proved it beyond the shadow of a doubt.

It was not simply that taking a life did not bother him. He actually enjoyed doing it. 'The ultimate power trip', he had bragged to others. Some of his associates thought that he was just a little too crazy. However, all treated him with respect and few dared to confront him when disagreements arose. It was thanks to Richie's fearless qualities that Diamond Jimmy had selected him as one of the four guards to help out Wayne and Bryan.

\* \* \* \*

Jimmy had not been happy when Wayne had called but the quality of the dope these idiots were supplying him with warranted a little patience towards their inexperience in the field of illegal narcotics. He just hoped that they would improve with time.

Actually, what Jimmy was really banking on was that Wayne et al. stay in business just long enough for the Aces of Death to develop the direct contacts with the suppliers in Asia and Columbia. After that, Wayne and his little friends would become expendable. After that, they would become useless.

\* \* \* \*

Richie had been assigned to guard the sector to the east of Matt's St-Sauveur residence, located halfway up one of the numerous wooded mountains in the area.

Standing several hundred feet from the building, the biker had a relatively good view into the forest which spanned below him. To his left, through a clearing in the trees, he could catch a glimpse of the road which wound steeply upwards. A little to his right was a rather deep ravine which pretty much guaranteed that no intruders would arrive from there. Up the slope behind him, the roof of the large country home he was protecting could be seen protruding above the top of the multitude of evergreens which crowded the terrain.

He carefully scanned the woods before him, looking for any signs of activity below; nothing. As he turned his head, carefully scrutinizing the landscape, he sensed, rather than saw, a slight movement by the ravine to his right. Slowly, he crept forward, attempting to make as little noise as possible with the frozen snow underfoot.

As he approached, he felt for the grip of the silenced .22 Beretta Minx tucked in the small of his back. Before he had time to withdraw the weapon, a man's head suddenly appeared over the top of the ravine some fifteen feet away. Initially startled, the man then broke into a smile and finished his climb over the edge.

"Wow, you scared me!" the intruder exclaimed, standing and brushing some snow off his black jeans and leather winter jacket.

"This is private property, buddy," Richie warned, remaining alert as the stranger took a couple of steps forward.

The man stopped, giving Richie a puzzled and troubled look before replying.

"Well, yeah. I know. This is Matt's place. I'm Matt's neighbour. I live in the next house down the road. Is there a problem?"

"No. No problem," answered Richie, relaxing a little, not feeling highly threatened by some neighbour maybe twice his age. "Some punks broke into Matt's place so he asked us to keep an eye on it."

"Not too much damage, I hope?" enquired the obviously concerned man as he moved a couple of steps closer.

"Nah, not too much," Richie responded as he leaned against a tree and dug into a pocket for his cigarettes. "Busted some windows and stuff. Nothing serious."

"Well, that's good to hear," the man replied with relief, now standing just a few feet from Richie. "It's getting that we're not safe anywhere anymore. This kind of stuff used to be reserved for the city and now they come out here to rob us!"

"Uh, yeah. Right," yawned Richie, becoming bored with this righteous conversation. "Listen. There's gonna be few of us watching the place for a couple of days so it's probably best that you keep off Matt's property for a while. Wouldn't want one of us to take you for a punk, right?"

"Yeah, sure, I understand," the man responded earnestly. "I do some rock climbing and the ravine here is a good spot to practice. But I'll stay out of your way. You be sure to tell Matt to call me if he needs anything. Tommy's the name."

"Sure. I'll do that," Richie chuckled as he turned away to head back to his observation point.

The six inch steel blade plunged through his back into his heart so quickly that he barely had time to feel the pain before dying.

"One down," breathed Chris as he began dragging the dead biker's body the short distance to the ravine.

* * * *

"Good morning! Who's going to Disney World?!" asked Gene Fennell as he sat down at the breakfast table.

"We are!" chorused his four kids aged five to ten.

"You bet you are!" he beamed proudly at them.

Looking over at his wife who was busy preparing breakfast, he asked, "Bags all ready?"

"Yup," she replied, glancing up at him and flashing a smile. "Once we've got these little monsters fed, we'll be ready to go."

"We've got lots of time," said Gene amidst several anti-monster protests emanating from around the table. "It's only nine o'clock. Flight's at 12:10."

As an inspector for Canada Customs, Gene Fennell had considered that he earned a relatively decent living with his annual salary of $46,268. This, naturally, had excluded the additional perks in the form of contraband merchandise seized from ignorant tourists returning from trips abroad. However, with four kids to raise, a mortgage and two cars, month-ends came quickly and savings, or other luxuries, had not been easy to come by.

This had been the case until Wayne MacKinnon had come along four years ago. Gene had met MacKinnon while carrying out an inspection at Rapid Forwarders, a local customs brokerage operation. They had been introduced by Andy Kovac and the three had ended up going to lunch together. That was when Wayne had put forth his proposal to Gene, outlining the complete drug import scheme to him.

At first, Gene had not believed the man and once he had realized that Wayne was serious, he had been shocked. However, MacKinnon was proposing some serious money for simply overlooking certain shipments of merchandise and Gene had ended up telling Wayne that he would think about it.

That night, he had brought up the subject with his wife who, after a moment of thought, had replied that they didn't open every single parcel, crate or container when they carried out an inspection. Why not just avoid opening those loaded with dope? It was easy money. Money for vacations, stuff for the kids, retirement.

He had contacted Wayne the next morning and suggested the possibility that shipments be identified somehow to ensure that they not be tampered with. This would allow Gene to open only appropriate crates and keep his paper work kosher. Wayne had agreed, thinking that this was a splendid idea, and they were in business.

Gene finished the remains of his coffee and backed away from the kitchen table.

"I'm just gonna hop over to Bill's next door and give him our keys."

Grinning mischievously at his children, still in their seats, he added, "You guys go wash up and go to the bathroom because we're leaving soon. Those who aren't ready are gonna have to stay here!"

He laughed as he watched the four of them scramble off. As he started to rise, the front doorbell rang.

'Must be Bill saving me a trip,' he thought, heading for the door and opening it.

Standing on the front porch were two officers of the RCMP.

"Yes? Can I help you?" Gene asked, surprised and puzzled by these unexpected visitors.

"Are you Gene Fennell?" one of the officers asked in a serious tone.

"Y-yeah, yes I am. What seems to be the problem, officer?"

"Mr. Fennell, you are under arrest for conspiring to import illicit narcotics into the country..."

\* \* \* \*

Nick Sharp had a reputation of being an honest, experienced cop. The honest part, he had earned over the years by clearly demonstrating that he played by the rules and treated people fairly. The experience had also come with time, time during which he had learned that one couldn't always go by the book 100%. Occasionally, one had to slightly circumvent the system, if only for the sake of expediency.

To this effect, Nick had developed a number of contacts over the years who could discreetly tap a phone line or conveniently turn off someone's electricity for a while. Occasionally, such acts were required urgently and no time was available to get approval through the appropriate channels and, on those occasions, Nick sometimes took advantage of his contacts.

Naturally, Nick never highlighted the fact that such requests were made by the force and no obvious attempt was ever made to use evidence collected by improper means.

On this particular day, considering the schedule that Jonathan had laid out, Nick judged that he had to bend the rules a little. In fact, his intended action was of such a minor nature that he did not even have to consciously decide to make the request.

Picking the phone, he dialled the number of Keith Schmidt, a close friend employed by Bell Mobility, a cellular carrier.

"Keith! How goes it? Fine thanks, but busy as hell. Listen, you got a pen and paper handy? Good. I'm gonna give you a few numbers that should experience technical difficulties real soon. Yeah, three or four hours will be fine. Thanks, bud. I owe you one!"

* * * *

Bryan's Mercedes veered wildly into the driveway of Greg's home and came to a screeching halt.

Despite his portly stature, he was up the steps and banging loudly at the door within seconds. Not able to wait for a reply, he headed frantically to one side towards the rear yard, scanning the building for anything unusual.

As he reached the back of the house, his heart sank as he noticed the opened basement door at the far end swaying slightly in the wind. In a frenzy, he hurried over and entered the house, horrified by what he might find but knowing that he had look.

Halfway up the stairs, it dawned on him that if Greg had received a visitor as had Matt, the visitor in question might still be in the building. Cursing himself for his carelessness, he slowed his pace and pulled out the small pistol he carried in his jacket. He reached the first floor and proceeded hesitantly forward, his heart jumping at every sound.

He prayed that Greg wouldn't be there, that he wouldn't find another massacred corpse as he had at Matt's. He shuddered as he thought of Matt, the image of the battered body covered with burn marks still clearly etched in his brain.

He reached the living room at the front of the house but found it empty. He moved back through the dining room and into the kitchen; still nothing. He glanced into the bathroom as he passed it but everything seemed in order. Continuing down the short hallway, he noticed that the door leading to Greg's study was firmly closed. Grasping the doorknob, he turned it, ever so slowly, until it would turn no more.

After a moment's hesitation, he decided that, if someone was in there, the element of surprise would be more effective than a slow announcement of his arrival. Slamming the door suddenly open, he jumped a step back as he raised his gun in self-defence.

He had nothing to worry about however, for Greg was alone. Alone, slumped in a chair before his computer, his brains splattered on the ceiling, walls and floor of the room. Bryan stared for a moment, as if in a trance, breathing heavily to fight the nausea. In a daze, he returned the gun to his pocket and headed to the front door.

Once into his car, he backed slowly out of the driveway and started his return trip to St-Sauveur, driving carefully, respecting speed limits. He hoped that no neighbours had seen him at Matt's or Greg's. Things were rocky enough as they were.

He suddenly remembered that he was to call Wayne to let him know what he had found. Picking up his cellular phone, he dialled the number to Matt's cottage up north but realized that the phone was no longer working. This was turning out to be a really lousy day.

\* \* \* \*

Cathy McCall wandered into the dining room where her husband was reading the morning paper.

"So? Sandy feeling better?" Dave absently asked, glancing up from his reading.

"Couldn't tell you," his wife replied. "There's no answer."

"Therefore, she must be feeling better," he concluded, returning his attention to an article about the never ending saga of Canadian unity.

"I guess," said Cathy doubtfully, unable to shake the strange feeling that something was wrong.

\* \* \* \*

Pierre Tardif gathered with the other three plain-clothes RCMP officers at the main entrance of the luxurious condominium complex in Old Montreal.

"There's only one door in the back so you can cover that, Bobby. Jim, once we go in, block the garage door with the car, just in case he tries to use that as an exit. Paul and I will go up and invite the gentleman to join us for a little chat. All set? Let's do this!"

As the two others hurried off to their posts, Pierre and Paul entered the large entrance foyer and headed to the doorbell console located to one side. Pierre proceeded to press the buttons of dozen different apartments and stepped back to wait for a response. Within seconds, the intercom started emitting a staticky chorus of "Hello?, Oui?, Who is it?". However, at least one person responded by pressing the door button, allowing both men access into the building. People were so naive of the security they paid so dearly for.

They headed to the sixth floor and searched the hallway until they found apartment 619. They could hear the faint sounds of a television or radio coming from inside. Pierre knocked on the door as they positioned themselves on either side of it, each with his hand on the grip of his revolver resting in its unsnapped holster.

From within, they heard the sounds of a couple of dead bolts sliding back before the door opened to the extent allowed by the security chain.

"Yes?" asked the attractive blonde through the three inch opening. All she wore was a rather thin silk bathrobe and, although it was just past nine in the morning, Pierre could smell alcohol on her breath.

"Mrs. Sommers?" he enquired, giving her a friendly smile.

"That's right," she confirmed with a faint slur. "What can I do for you?"

"Is Mr. Sommers home?" Pierre politely requested. "We would need to speak to him."

"No, he's at the office," she sneered, pausing to take a solid pull from the glass in her hand. "**Working** with that little whore secretary of his!" she added with a sarcastic laugh.

"I see. Sorry to have bothered you, Mrs. Sommers," Pierre apologized.

"Oh, no bother," she responded in a husky voice as she looked him over. "Maybe you want to come in for a drink or, **something**?"

To emphasize the **something**, she shifted her weight a little and raised one knee slightly, exposing quite a lot of firm thigh as a result.

"Ah, as appealing as that invitation sounds, I can't this morning," replied Pierre, flushing, "Maybe some other time."

"Anytime!" she replied throatily, licking her lips before closing the door.

\* \* \* \*

Blade stood on the west side of Matt's St-Sauveur residence, carefully scanning the hillside above him. It was damn cold but he was tough and could endure anything. After all, he was an Ace of Death.

Quite frankly, he didn't really understand why they were helping these two misfits out; a couple of assholes in suits! But Diamond Jimmy had requested that it be done, so here he was.

Blade was a small man, barely five feet, four inches tall, with an impressive weight of one hundred sixteen pounds, fully clothed. He had grown up in a tough neighbourhood however, where he had been required early on to compensate for his lack of size. By the time he turned thirteen, he had already earned his nickname and it had stuck ever since.

He couldn't see, nor hear anything out of the ordinary in the woods around him. He wondered why he and the other gang members had to freeze out here while the two idiots in suits got to stay inside with that sweet looking dame. Because Diamond Jimmy requested it, he reminded himself once again.

He continued to survey his assigned area, confident that if anybody managed to attack the house behind him, it would not be from this side.

\* \* \* \*

"I thought you said we had a lot of work to do?!" complained Nancy, her annoyance genuine.

"We do!" snickered Allan Sommers, ignoring her tone as he squeezed her buttocks with both hands. "I just think that we need a little break. I have to clear my thoughts!"

"But we just got here, Allan!" his secretary whined, though she knew that her protests were futile.

"And not a moment too soon!" he cooed, sliding one hand under her sweatshirt and fondling her breasts. "Now, why don't you get out of those clothes and have a chat with my friend down here! Come on, baby! You know what I like!"

"You're the boss," Nancy sullenly gave in.

She obediently removed her sweatshirt, exposing her delightful twenty-four year old body. As she began to pull down her tight fitting jeans, the door of the office suddenly burst open, startling both she and Sommers.

"Who the fuck are you?!" Sommers bellowed angrily, fumbling to re-zip his pants while Nancy scurried behind the desk, trying to hide her half naked body.

"Pierre Tardif, RCMP," the first man informed him, holding out a shield and I.D. card for Sommers' inspection. "This is my partner, Paul Landry."

"Yeah?! Well this is a private office, gentlemen!" snarled Sommers, "And we're busy right now so you'll have to leave. Call for an appointment on Monday if you need to see me!"

"Sorry, Mr. Sommers," insisted Pierre. "No can do. You're under arrest for conspiring to import and distribute illegal narcotics..."

"What! Under arrest! Illegal narcotics!" interrupted Sommers, incredulous. "This is ridiculous!"

"Mr. Sommers, you represent a gentleman by the name of James Sanchez, don't you?" asked Pierre. "Otherwise known as Diamond Jimmy?"

"Uh, yes, Mr. Sanchez is one of my clients," responded Sommers uncertainly, taken aback by the question. "But I don't understand what that has to do with your ridiculous accusation of drug trafficking!"

"We have a witness who's testified that this office is used for narcotics transactions and storage," Pierre explained.

"This is outrageous!" Sommers nervously argued. "This is a law office! Not a goddamn drugstore!"

"Listen, Mr. Sommers," Paul Landry spoke soothingly. "We're just doing our job, acting on a tip from a witness. We were told that there was some cocaine stored here right now. Do you mind if we look around? If we don't find anything, that'll take a lot of credibility out of the witness's testimony."

"You want to search this place?" responded Sommers, gaining back some confidence. "Go right ahead. Search the fucking place! You won't find anything! But let me warn you right now! You haven't heard the last of this!"

Having received consent, the search began and silence ensued safe for the sounds of Paul Landry opening the drawers and doors of the various pieces of furniture in the room. Within moments he had completed his search and had found nothing.

"What's back there?" he asked, pointing to the door behind Sommers' desk.

"Conference room," snapped Sommers, now fully composed. "Go for it. Search that too! It'll just cost you more when I sue you guys for false arrest, harassment, invasion of privacy and defamation of character!"

Paul moved into the conference room and continued his search while the others remained in the main office. After a moment or two, he appeared in the doorway with a strange look on his face. He stared at Sommers as he spoke.

"Would you come in here, Mr. Sommers?"

Sommers rose from his chair, his look of uncertainty having returned, and walked into the conference room.

"Would you like to explain what those are, Mr. Sommers?" Paul demanded, pointing to two bags of white powder on the conference table.

"I-I don't know w-what those are!" Sommers stammered. "They're n-not mine! W-where did you find them?!"

"In those binders," Paul replied, pointing to two large empty binders, also on the table. "Excellent hiding place, Sommers. I nearly missed them, right there, out in the open in the bookcase."

"So, this whole drug thing is outrageous, Sommers?!" challenged Pierre, stepping in. "Then what the hell is this?!"

He reached over and picked up the two bags which he tossed at Sommers.

Instinctively catching the bags, the latter pleaded. "These aren't mine! I've been set up! You've got to believe me!"

Dazed, he dropped the bags back on the table as Pierre approached and proceeded to handcuff him. "Mr. Sommers, you are under arrest for possession of illegal narcotics."

Sommers' eyes suddenly narrowed as rational thought superseded the shock of the last thirty seconds.

"**You** set me up, you motherfucker!" he screamed at Paul Landry. "You brought that shit with you, you bastard!"

"Get this guy outta here!" ordered Pierre, signalling Bobby and Jim, who stood at the door of the main office.

The two officers escorted the screaming, handcuffed lawyer out of the office and down the hallway towards the bank of elevators. Pierre walked out of the conference room to find the young lady still cowering in the corner behind Sommers' desk. She had since put her clothes back on and appeared extremely frightened.

"What's your name?" he asked gently.

"N-Nancy...Tessier," she replied in a tearful voice.

"O.K., Nancy. Do you know anything about Mr. Sommers being involved in drugs?" Pierre continued.

"N-not really," she stuttered with fear. "I-I n-never saw any drugs but some of h-his clients are g-gang m-members. I s-see their pictures in the p-papers sometimes."

"Don't worry," said Pierre. "You haven't done anything wrong. But we might need you to testify about what happened here today. What did you see?"

"Y-you guys came in and found some drugs in the conference room?" she answered hopefully.

"That's right," Pierre responded, smiling slightly. "Did Mr. Sommers give us permission to search his office?"

"Yes he did," she replied, her expression brightening. "And the conference room."

"Good girl," Pierre nodded. "And Nancy. When we arrived, as far as I'm concerned, you were sitting in a chair writing notes or something while Sommers spoke!"

*  *  *  *

From his natural hideout, offered by a series of conifers oddly growing in a circular formation, Jonathan had been observing the guard posted on the west side of the St-Sauveur residence for forty-five minutes. During this time, he was confident that he had established the small man's informal patrolling routine.

After four or five minutes of careful scrutiny from his central watch point at the base of a large oak, the biker would stroll to his right several hundred feet, past where Jonathan sat, nearly to the gravel road which snaked up the incline. He would then return, past his oak tree, walking some four hundred feet to the edge of a deep ravine which horse-shoed around the rear of the property. There, he would scan the portion of the ravine visible to him for several minutes before returning to the foot of the large oak tree to recommence the process.

Satisfied, Jonathan waited for the guard to remake his way to the ravine, absently playing with a length of strong but thin nylon rope in the interim. Within a few minutes, it was time and he quickly and stealthily made his way to his chosen point of attack; the large oak tree.

Blade returned from the ravine and settled once again at the foot of the big tree. He was getting bored and cold. He wished the stupid fucks inside would bring him a cup of coffee or something. After all, he was protecting them! The least the bastards could do was show a little consideration. God, it was cold.

He wondered if the cold would bother him less if he was stoned and decided to find out. Anyways, nothing was going on, and if something did happen, it wasn't the fact that he'd have smoked a joint that would change anything. A good old THC buzz actually sharpened one's senses, he had always believed.

He pulled a joint from his cigarette pack and lit it, sucking the heavy smoke deeply into his lungs and holding it for several seconds before exhaling. He smiled, already feeling the effect after one toke. It was grass, Thai, but its quality and potency surpassed that of any hash he'd ever done, even Kashmir or black Columbian. He pulled in another lungful of the wonderful smoke, holding his breath until he'd counted to thirty. He chuckled to himself and leaned his back against the large tree, content. Getting stoned, he decided, definitely helped ward off the cold. He took another hefty toke and chuckled again.

Several feet above Blade's head, the trunk of the mammoth oak tree branched off rather symmetrically into four massive limbs. Sometime in the past, a prior owner of Matt's property had begun building a tree house, using the four large branches as the natural foundation for the structure. For reasons unknown, construction had ceased once the floor had been completed, rendering the tree house into simply an observation platform, some eight feet off the ground. It might not have served much purpose in the past, but on this day, Jonathan thanked its builder, whoever and wherever he was. For today, the platform, on which Jonathan was now perched, was a gift from heaven. Its existence almost made the task at hand too easy.

Below him, the small man had lit a joint a few minutes earlier and, judging from his almost continuous, quiet chuckling, was obviously quite stoned; another gift from heaven.

Ever so slowly, Jonathan raised himself to a kneeling position, praying for the old grey boards not to creak. They didn't. The Lord was generous today. He inched to the edge of the platform and soon could see the small man, his head, just a few feet away.

His rope ready, he tossed the noose quickly, expertly, landing it perfectly around his target's head. With a forceful, upward yank, he jerked the small biker's body a couple of feet off the ground. Although he'd heard the unmistakable crack of the neck snapping, he held on, keeping the body suspended until it stopped twitching. He then lowered it slowly, intent on avoiding to make any unnecessary noise.

After descending from the tree and ensuring that the guard was in fact dead, he picked up the body and hurried quietly through the woods, away from the house. Several hundred yards further, a cluster of pine trees supplied appropriate cover for the corpse.

He dumped the body and returned towards the house, erasing his tracks as he went. He hoped Chris was getting along as well as he was.

* * * *

Thai Airlines' Flight 835 in from Hong Kong landed right on schedule at Phuket International Airport; 8:17 p.m., local time.

The variety of tourists disembarked from the 747 onto the runway and climbed into the bus which would drive them to the airport terminal, a walking distance away. Hans Fritz had been here often in the past and had always found amusing, this bus ride which lasted all of thirty seconds. His theory was that the airport authorities had purchased the bus in haste when the airport had been built and were too proud to admit their error. Therefore, any traveller arriving was required to board the bus for a half minute trip, a process which sometimes took as much as fifteen minutes from start to finish.

Hans had remained close to the door inside the bus and was one of the first to go through customs and immigration.

"Passport and declaration, please," barked the stout customs officer with the mock sternness such public servants display worldwide.

Without a word, Hans complied with the man's request.

"The purpose of your trip, Mr. Fritz?" demanded the man as he examined the passport.

"Mostly business, I'm afraid," replied Hans with a warm smile. "I am here to help export some more of your lovely pearls."

"You are staying how long?"

"Only two days, unfortunately," answered Hans, his tone one of disappointment.

"Please try to visit our beaches," suggested the officer, dropping the tough facade. "Have a nice stay."

"Thank-you. And I will try to visit your lovely beaches but, as they say, business before pleasure."

He strolled into the small terminal, searching for a familiar face and they saw each other at the same time. Neither had ever met before but they had each been faxed photos of the other and they knew of each other's reputation through the grapevine.

"Mister Fritz, I presume," she said as she approached with an extended hand.

The photograph had not done her justice. To say she was gorgeous would have been an understatement.

"Miss Tahashi, a pleasure!" he replied, taking her small but firm hand in his and shaking it warmly.

"Call me Kim, please. And I will call you Hans," she proposed, flashing a heavenly smile. "Come. I have a Jeep waiting outside."

They left the terminal in silence, each evaluating their first impression of the other. Once settled into the Jeep with Kim at the wheel, they headed south on highway 402.

"So, you are the famous Jeweller," stated Kim, concentrating on the narrow winding road.

"Infamous, perhaps!" Hans chuckled. "And you are the famous Teacher. What brings a Japanese English teacher to Phuket?"

"I was actually here for a week of vacation when I received the call," she replied. "I had flown in from Tokyo last night. How long will you be here?"

"A couple of days only," he sighed. "I was due to make a trip shortly to visit some suppliers so it will be done. You're staying at Le Méridien?"

"Yes I am. And you?"

"The same," he said. "Perhaps once we're done, I could have the honour of buying you dinner?"

She smiled before replying. "I have already reserved a lagoon-side table at Pakarang for 10:30. I trust that that gives us sufficient time?"

He looked at his watch which read 8:47.

"Yes, my dear. More than enough time."

\* \* \* \*

"I'm worried about Sandy and Chris," Cathy stated, interrupting her husband's reading once again. "I call and there's no answer. When I try their cell phones, I get the message service."

"They could be gone shopping, skiing, you name it," Dave replied, a touch of exasperation in his voice. "Honey, what's the matter with you? So what, they're not home? You know Chris and Sandy. They're always on the go!"

"Sandy never called me back yesterday!" retorted his wife, her tone equally impatient. "That's not like her. Don't believe me if you don't want to but something is wrong, Dave!"

"Cathy!?" he called as she stormed out of the dining room.

Receiving no response, he shrugged and returned his attention to his newspaper. One thing was certain. She would not disturb his reading for a little while.

\* \* \* \*

The building had existed on the outskirts of Phuket City for about ten years. One hundred feet wide and about sixty deep, it housed the operations of a clothing manufacturer and employed seventy-five locals who worked for the pittance wages often customary in many Asian countries. T-shirts and other sportswear were the major product lines, mostly produced for export to Europe and the Americas.

Although the operation was profitable, in recent years it had become a cover for a much more lucrative business. For within the two-storey building's high barn-like roof was probably Asia's most highly advanced heroin refining laboratory. Few people were aware of its existence as access to this part of the structure was well concealed and the lab itself was perfectly sound-proofed.

On evenings and weekends, a guard was posted at both the front and back of the building as an extra precaution. Vandalism and theft did occur occasionally in the area, so the presence of these individuals was not viewed as uncommon by the odd passer-by. Most watch-shifts however, were uneventful, leaving the guards with little to experience barring boredom.

Unfortunately, this would not be the case for the two men on duty on this particular evening.

Prasop really did not enjoy working on the Saturday night shift. Although the job was never exciting on any given night, having to be there on Saturdays was frustrating in addition to being boring. Saturdays were, after all, party nights when the young ladies went into the bars and loosened up. But a job was a job and more importantly, the boss was the boss. He also had to consider that this particular employment allowed him access to the 24 Hours Bar, where the tough guys socialized. This gave him special status which served to impress the majority of available young ladies.

As he sat on the old wooden crate which served as his chair, he heard a dull thud come from his right. Standing up, he took several steps in the dirt parking area which spanned the rear of the building. Searching the darkness, he saw nothing. He started to turn back when another similar sound occurred. Turning sharply towards the noise, he withdrew his revolver and moved cautiously forward, peering into the night. Another thud came, a little more to the left this time, the sound of a stone hitting the packed earth.

He continued to advance, slowly, searching the night in vain. Another one, this time to his right. Adrenalin pumping, he moved quickly in that direction, advancing a dozen yards before stopping to listen. Motionless, he stood there, straining to hear anything out of the ordinary. Nothing. He scanned the area, turning slowly until he had completed a full circle. Still nothing. He remained in this spot for several minutes, continuing to circle, searching for the cause of the unusual disturbance, completely unaware that this would be his last Saturday night.

Past the parking area behind the building was a ditch, overgrown with a variety of weeds, brush and shrubs. It offered excellent cover although Ron Singer hoped none of it was vegetation of a poisonous kind.

Upon his arrival, he had been disappointed to see the guard seated on a wooden box, his back leaned against the wall of the structure. With no cover close by, the element of surprise became non-existent. As time had gone by, his disappointment had grown as he realized that the man did not even leave his post to patrol the area. Ron had come to the conclusion that he would have to draw the guard out if he wanted to settle this assignment that night.

Banking on the hope that the guard was not too bright, he found several stones, large enough to create an audible sound upon landing. These, he proceeded to toss, one by one, to attract the other man's attention. By the fourth stone, the guard stood less than fifteen feet away, frantically searching for the source of the noises. After several minutes, he seemed to relax and decided to head back to the comfort of his wooden crate.

Only seconds were required for Ron, an expert in this type of activity, to silently cross the short span separating them. The garrotte swung swiftly, perfectly around the Asian's neck, his death, almost instantaneous.

Ron dumped the body into the ditch and headed towards the front of the building to see if his brother Mike needed any assistance.

\* \* \* \*

Arnie Schwartz had always looked for ways to make an easy buck. He was generally lazy and thus, strongly believed in the concept of getting as much as possible for the least effort. He didn't hide this fact and often boasted that this was the main reason why he had gone to work for the government. Decent gains for little effort.

He particularly enjoyed working as a customs officer, not for the job itself but rather, for the side benefits it offered if one was smart enough to take advantage of them. Loads of seized merchandise were poorly accounted for and there for the taking. So Arnie took, a lot, for personal consumption as well as for sale to others.

Eighteen months ago, he had been enraged to learn that he was being transferred to warehouse inspection duty. Recognizing that such a transfer would put an end to his profitable secondary business, he had argued with his supervisor but, to no avail. It was transfer or leave, due to personnel reductions.

Grudgingly, he had transferred to warehouse inspections, where he had begun his new duties; inspecting random commercial shipments imported into the country. The job wasn't bad, definitely not tiring, although Arnie saw little possibility of maintaining his sideline. At least, his partner, Gene Fennell, was a good guy who liked to listen to Arnie's anecdotes about long-term borrowing of seized merchandise.

At the end of his second week in his new position, he was having lunch with Gene, when the latter proposed an opportunity to Arnie which made his former sideline seem like pocket change. Arnie had willingly agreed to participate in Gene's 'narcotics overlooking' activities and had been financially content ever since.

The shrill shrieking of the phone amplified the ringing in his head. He had suspected that he would suffer from a hangover in the morning but had not expected anything like this. He rolled over, hiding his face from the light with a pillow as he desperately grasped for the phone.

"Yeah?" he groaned, hoping to hell it was an emergency.

"Arnie?!" a woman's voice cried. "They came to get Gene, Arnie! You've gotta help!"

"What the fuck!" Arnie muttered, confused as he sat up in bed. "Who is this? What the hell is going on?!"

"This is Lisa Fennell, Arnie. Gene's wife," the shaky voice replied. "About forty-five minutes ago, they came to get Gene! I've been looking for your number everywhere! You've got to help, Arnie! Please!"

Gene? Lisa Fennell? Gene Fennell. His partner. He was starting to understand. A little.

"O.K. Lisa. Calm down! Who came to get Gene? What's going on?"

"The police, Arnie!" Lisa sobbed, breaking down again. "It said RCMP on their jackets and on the cars! You've got to help, Arnie! They arrested Gene! Because of the drugs! We were going on vacation! They took him away! Please!"

"Take it easy, Lisa!" ordered Arnie, no longer concerned with his hangover. "Arnie will take care of everything. Just relax. I'm gonna hang up now cuz I have some calls to make. Don't worry. I'm gonna fix this, O.K.? Now, don't call me back cuz I don't want to tie up the phone. I'll let you know what's going on. Don't worry."

With that, he slammed down the phone and scrambled to get some clothes on. As he hurriedly tied his shirt, he peered through the partially opened vertical blinds to the street below. Nothing. But he had to hurry. If they knew about Gene, they knew about him. Or, they would soon.

He praised himself for his silly habit of keeping cash handy. Rushing into the storage closet of his second storey condo, he pulled out his stash and counted; $4,700. That would cover him for several days. He'd make some withdrawals from cash machines but he'd have to be careful. The cops would trace that. Credit cards would be iffy too. At least he had something to start with. Now, the priority however, was to leave. The cops could show up any second.

Running into the entrance hall, he jammed his feet into his untied running shoes as he frantically pulled his ski jacket from the closet. He bolted from his apartment, not bothering to close the door behind him and headed for the parking garage, two levels below.

RCMP detectives Eric Levesque and Daniel Samson were approaching the Belanger Street building in Anjou where Arnie Schwartz resided when a candy apple red Mustang GT roared out of the inside parking, swerving wildly to avoid colliding with their vehicle.

"That's him, Eric!" Daniel exclaimed. "Red Mustang GT! That's Schwartz! Go!"

Levesque threw the gear shift of their Taurus in reverse and backed out of the entrance with tires screaming. Down the hill, they could see Schwartz's vehicle turn right on the red at Langelier, narrowly missing an approaching pickup truck.

"He's going for the Met," predicted Samson, referring to the Metropolitan, Montreal's elevated throughway.

With sirens blaring, they took pursuit of the red Mustang, both vehicles running through three other red lights before engaging onto the westbound Met.

Here, Schwartz opened up the powerful engine of his automobile, quickly increasing his speed to ninety miles per hour as he dodged in and out of the Saturday morning traffic.

"We're not gonna have to catch this guy," muttered Levesque as he hesitantly increased his speed on the icy road. "He's gonna kill himself!"

As if his words were a command, the Mustang suddenly went out of control as it swerved to avoid a car coming up an on-ramp ahead. Recent heavy snow, followed by a sudden drop in temperatures had turned the sides of the elevated highway into dangerous jump ramps. Several cars had already gone off the road in the last week.

The Mustang spun two perfect three-sixties before projecting itself a dozen feet above the level of the road where, for a fraction of a second, it seemed to hang in mid-air. Then gravity took effect, violently pulling the car to its smashing end, twenty-five feet below.

Several minutes were required for Levesque and Samson to make it down to the site of the crash. By the time they got there, a crowd had formed and an ambulance was already on the scene. The driver of the Mustang, the detectives were informed, had died on impact.

\* \* \* \*

The road which ran in front of the clothing manufacture and into Phuket City dropped into a steep hill a quarter mile past the building. Mike and Ron Singer had parked their vehicles at the bottom of this incline and proceeded on foot, Ron heading for the rear of the structure while Mike cut through the field across the road.

After ten minutes of hiking through the tall weeds, he had found himself directly ahead of the building, a hundred yards away. Here, he had settled comfortably and begun observing the rather mundane activities of his eventual victim.

Looking at his watch, he acknowledged that it was time to go and began retracing his steps towards the vehicles. Once hidden by the top of the incline, he cut across to the road and turned back towards the building. As he reached the top of the hill, he slowed his pace, incorporating a slight irregular stagger to his walk as he headed towards the guard.

Tridhosyuth tensed a little as he watched the figure approaching in the darkness. Although the man was alone, he seemed to be speaking, mumbling to himself. Every once in a while he walked slightly out of step as if unsure of his balance.

"Crazy drunk tourist!" Tridhosyuth cursed under his breath, rising to his feet.

"Hello, there!" the foreigner called out, his accent unmistakably American. "Do you speak English?"

"A little," the guard responded. "This private area. You go away."

"Sure, sure!" the American slurred, stopping in his tracks and holding up both hands. "I ain't looking for trouble. I'm just a bit lost."

"Where you go?" asked Tridhosyuth, willing to help the drunk leave.

"Well, a bunch of us took a little bus from the hotel to town, ya know," the man explained, wavering slightly. "We had a few drinks in a bar and I went out to get some air, ya know. Started walking but I sorta lost my bearings."

"Town? Phuket City?" asked the guard, confused by the American's language. "You go there?"

"Yeah, Phuket City!" laughed the drunk, take a few steps forward. "Downtown, ya know, where I can take the bus."

"Phuket City, downtown, that way," answered Tridhosyuth, pointing in the direction from which the drunk had come.

"Well, goddamn! I was headed the wrong way!" the drunk guffawed, totally amused by the situation. "Thanks a bunch! You're a good man!"

As the guard returned to his seat, the American turned away and staggered a few steps, stopped and turned back again.

"Oh, by the way," he said, the drunken slur gone. "Thanks for letting me get so close."

With expert precision, he fired the silenced handgun which he inconspicuously produced, hitting Tridhosyuth twice in the forehead and once in the heart.

"You've made my job so much easier!"

*  *  *  *

From a small natural shelf four feet below the edge of the ravine, Chris had been watching the guard at the back of the St-Sauveur chalet for the better part of a half hour.

This one might prove to be difficult. For one, there was little cover near the man, making a surprise attack unfeasible. The lack of cover also made the guard and the surrounding area much more visible from the house, should anyone decide to glance outside. Chris' biggest concern however, was the man's sheer size; at least six-four and probably close to three hundred pounds. Thoughts of a possible one on one combat with this gorilla made him shudder.

The guard started one of his patrol walks again, as he had done a half dozen times so far. Chris pressed himself into the recess under the edge of the ravine, once again holding his breath and covering his nose and mouth, lest the steam of his breath give him away. Above his head, the giant's boots crunched past in the snow. Chris waited, still not clear on how he would eliminate the man.

*  *  *  *

A few minutes before reaching Patong Beach, Hans climbed into the back of the mini-van and, reaching under the seat, pulled out the twenty inch long case which had formed the bottom of his carry-on bag. Opening the case, he quickly assembled the various components and was ready in no time.

"How do you get that through the airports?!" Kim asked curiously from the driver's seat as she watched him in the rear-view mirror.

"Most of it's plastic," Hans proudly replied. "I made it myself. A talent I've acquired over the years."

"Plastic!" Kim exclaimed, intrigued. "Won't it melt?"

"Yes," Hans grinned. "Single use only. Sort of like those disposable tourist cameras!"

"What about the shell?" persisted a curious Kim.

"I make those too. They look like a can of deodorant, even on close examination. I carry them in my suitcase!"

They ceased their conversation and both donned nylon stocking masks as they rolled onto the main strip of Patong Beach. Kim slowed the vehicle and pulled onto the left side of the road, stopping directly in front a short side street lined with a half dozen bars on either side. At the end of the street, directly facing them, was the 24 Hours Bar.

Known and avoided by the locals as a fraternizing spot for the tougher crowd, it was actually an exclusive club for a group of organized criminals specializing in the refining and subsequent exporting of heroin.

With the mini-van barely stopped, Hans pulled open the sliding side door and climbed out, weapon in hand. He took several steps forward as he raised the cylindrical shaped object to his shoulder, paying no attention to the awed onlookers. Coming to a halt, he dropped to one knee, looked through the sight and, following a slight pause to ensure proper aim, pulled the trigger.

With a roaring whoosh, the rocket seared down the street and through the open doors of the 24 Hours Bar. A fraction of a second, which seemed like an hour, went by with no result. Then, as if by magic, the building seemed to expand as it exploded into flame, leaving none of its occupants as survivors.

Hans smiled at the shocked witnesses through his nylon mask, waving as he quickly, yet casually strolled back and climbed into the already moving mini-van.

"That went well," commented Kim, pulling off her mask as they sped out of the village.

"Indeed it did!" agreed Hans, looking at his watch. "I do believe we'll have time to dump this van **and** have a drink at the bar before dinner!"

* * * *

In frustration, Jonathan observed the guard on the wide front porch of Matt's Laurentian hideaway. In forty minutes, the man had left the porch once, to saunter down the driveway to the road. Only once! No checking the woods on either side, no quick walks along the road to search for suspicious vehicles. He just stood on the damn porch!

After careful consideration, Jonathan made up his mind. He would have to get a hold of Chris before attempting to get rid of this guard. Between the two of them, they'd have a better chance. Silently, he made his way among the trees towards the back of the house.

\* \* \* \*

Followed by a Jeep, the small closed-box pickup truck rolled into the parking area behind the building, coming to a stop before the large shipping/receiving door. Ron Singer climbed out and, with the help of a set of industrial metal cutters, snipped the two heavy padlocks which secured this entrance. After opening the door, he returned to the truck and drove it into the building, parking it in the center of the empty shipping area. He hurried out, closing the large door behind him before joining his brother in the Jeep and they drove off in the direction of Phuket City, their task nearly complete.

After a couple of minutes, Ron pulled a small remote control device from his pocket, much like those used to activate car alarms. He calmly pressed a button and returned the object to his pocket. From a few miles behind them came a huge orange glow, immediately followed by a deep rumbling which could be both felt and heard.

Their task was complete.

\* \* \* \*

Bull, due to his size and appearance, was generally presumed to be a rather unintelligent individual. As many had unfortunately learned over the years however, he wasn't completely stupid.

He had caught a glimpse of the man hiding on the edge of the ravine almost twenty minutes earlier. He knew that the intruder had not been there very long because he had looked down into the ravine along the length of his watch area as little as fifteen minutes before spotting the man.

He hadn't made any moves yet, believing that time could an excellent ally. When one played it one's way, a little time could conveniently lull an adversary into a false sense of security. But as Bull returned from the east side of the house, he decided that his adversary must be sufficiently lulled.

"Don't make any sudden moves, Mister!" he ordered in a surprisingly soft voice. "Or I'll blow your fucking brains out!"

Considering the barrel of the shotgun aimed at his head from some six inches away, Chris felt compelled to comply with the man's request.

"Get up here. Now!"

Chris climbed over the edge as the ape backed away a couple of feet.

"Listen, I don't know what the problem is and I'm not looking for any trouble. I'm just rock climbing. That's all."

"Yeah?" sneered Bull. "Why you been sitting on the ledge for twenty minutes watching me?"

"W-well," Chris stammered, his mind racing.

The bastard had known he was there!

"W-when I saw you with the gun, I got scared. I-I didn't want to make any noise and end up getting shot. Come on! I live in the house down the hill. I practice climbing here all the time! Matt doesn't mind!"

"What's your name, Mister?" asked the giant, apparently brighter than his counterpart whom Chris had met earlier.

"Paul. Paul Wessell," Chris replied convincingly.

"O.K. Paul," Bull said with an unfriendly smile. "Show me some I.D. Show me something with the name Paul Wessell on it and I'll let you go home."

"I-I don't have my wallet with me!" argued Chris, starting to really worry. "I was out climbing in my backyard, for Chrissakes!"

Bull tightened his grip slightly on the shotgun as he spoke. "Empty your pockets, Mister. Real slow. Cuz I don't think you're no Paul Wessell. I think you may be the bastard these fuckers inside are scared of!"

Speechless, Chris stared at the ape and started to tremble. Slowly, he reached into a side pocket of his jacket and pulled out his wallet. As he held it out to Bull, it dropped from his badly shaking hand.

"Thought you had no wallet, Paul!?" Bull chided. "Pick it up!"

'Thank-you!' Chris thought as he crouched down, bending forward towards the wallet.

With sudden force, he lunged forward, closing the short distance which separated them. His left shoulder smashed into the huge man's stomach, just below the rib cage, causing an audible cracking sound. Reaching up into the air, he grabbed desperately for the guard's gun and, miraculously, found his hand wrapping around the cold steel of the double barrel. He jerked violently, sending the rifle flying high and then clattering down into the ravine.

At that moment, he felt the gorilla's hands reach under his armpits and straighten him back to a standing position, as does a child with a rag doll. He stared into the giant's eyes and could see that he had caused him pain. Unfortunately, it had been too little pain; much, much too little.

The hands quickly slid from his armpits to his neck and suddenly, his feet were no longer touching the ground. He kicked the ape in the ribs as the latter held him suspended by the throat. The kicks seemed to have little effect safe for encouraging the giant to squeeze Chris's neck a little harder. He could no longer breathe and was starting to lose consciousness.

'I love you, Sandy,' he thought sadly, realizing that he was about to die and would never see her again.

His vision was growing extremely hazy and he was starting to hallucinate. It was like watching a movie in which he had a central role. He could see his feet dangling above the ground, the gorilla's angry smiling face, Jonathan behind them pointing a gun. It was all so dreamlike.

He crashed to ground suddenly and was aware of severe pain as something extremely heavy fell on top of him. He was confused and his neck hurt really badly, but he could breathe. The pressure was gone from his throat, he was lying on the ground under some dead-weight and he could breathe.

"Come on, Chris!" Jonathan's voice whispered hoarsely in his ear. "We gotta get out of here! Anybody looks out those windows, it's all over!"

With the added luxury of oxygen, Chris's thought process was returning back to normal at a rapid pace. He sat up, pushing the ape's body off him as Jonathan pulled. Definitely not less than three hundred pounds.

Two holes were clearly visible on the left side of the man's head. The other side, where the bullets had exited, was a mess. They rolled the heavy body a few feet and watched it tumble and slide down the side of the deep ravine, then hurried off for the cover of the woods, waiting to be clearly out of sight and earshot before speaking.

"Thanks!" rasped Chris, massaging his bruised neck.

"All in a day's work," replied Jonathan with a quick smile as he replaced the two missing bullets in his silenced pistol's magazine. "One to go!"

* * * *

Along the north shore of Laval spanned Mille-Iles Boulevard, named after the river which stretched the length of that side of the island. The area near Autoroute 25, in the eastern part of Laval, was sparsely developed residentially, home mostly to farms and woods.

If one drove along Mille-Iles Boulevard, east of the 25, one eventually saw a large fenced-in area located between the road and the river. Barbed wire lined the top of the fence and surveillance cameras were visible around the property. Seated several hundred feet from the road was a large two storey residential structure which was regularly patrolled by guards clad in blue jeans and leather jackets. This was the headquarters of the Aces of Death and the home of Diamond Jimmy Sanchez.

As is the case with most such gangs, the Aces of Death made little effort to hide who they were or what they did. What the public, and even police, knew was not a problem. The main thing was to ensure that nothing could be proven in a court of law. Keeping at least one step ahead of justice was the name of the game.

This was a concept that Diamond Jimmy was well aware of and he had built his residence accordingly. Very few trees or any other type of cover could be found on the grounds. Motion sensors were strategically hidden all over the property and pressure detectors, able to detect any weight in excess of twenty-five pounds, had been systematically buried under the vast lawns. From dusk till dawn, powerful halogen spots washed the entire property in their harsh light. Naturally, the house itself was equipped with a security system rivalling that of the Royal Canadian Mint and, at any given time of the day or night, the surveillance centre was manned by no less than four highly trained technicians.

No surprise attacks or ambushes from other gangs, nor raids from the cops would take place here without the headquarters' occupants being well aware.

This, of course, was information that was known by the police, which allowed Nick Sharp to plan the RCMP visit to Diamond Jimmy's fortress accordingly.

Since this was a major operation which would surely become public knowledge, it was to be played strictly by the book. By 8:30, Nick's file preparation specialists, with the help of Greg's journal and other data which Jonathan had supplied, had put together a sufficiently convincing dossier of 'past' surveillance operations and informant evidence for Nick to officially use. With it, he quickly obtained the required authorization to set his plan in motion, which included cutting power, phone service, water supply and gas. The operation, scheduled for ten o'clock, would also require an army of some fifty officers.

Today, they would bring down Diamond Jimmy and the Aces of Death.

\* \* \* \*

The rented helicopter left the airport at Bucaramanga and headed southwest, into the mountains towards Málaga. At the stick was Wild Billy Harrelson, ace chopper pilot and a veteran from the Vietnam War.

Contrary to many of his peers from Nam, Billy had not returned angry at the government or suffering from post-traumatic stress disorder, although he would have had every reason to do so. He had not agreed with the war and had lost his right leg fighting it. However, the army had taught him how to fly a chopper and Vietnam had given him the opportunity to really learn how to maneuver such a machine.

Upon his return and following his convalescence, he had started a helicopter ride business in Hawaii, offering the ultimate thrill to the ultimate thrill-seeker.

He also did some 'consulting' work on the side. Today was a consulting assignment.

Seated next to Billy was Freddy "Guns" Mager, also a Nam veteran and long time friend. Freddy was the one who had introduced Billy to the 'consulting' a few years earlier, a career which he himself had embarked in immediately after the war. Three or four assignments a year were sufficient to keep him overly comfortable financially, allowing him much leisure time which he spent travelling the world on "Victory", his sixty foot yacht.

Neither man was worried about today's mission. They had both been involved in others, much more complex.

As Freddy often said, "Every once in a while, they throw in an easy one. Ya know, bonus money!"

\* \* \* \*

At precisely 10 o'clock, all utilities were cut to the headquarters of the Aces of Death. At the same time, a heavily armoured tractor trailer smashed through the main gate at break-neck speed and rushed towards the building. As it veered sideways in front of the house and screeched to a halt, side panels on the trailer slid open, letting out dozens of officers in full protective gear.

In the meantime, a second identical vehicle was also emptying its cargo of manpower, these men quickly taking position around the perimeter of the property outside the fence.

Inside the house, Diamond Jimmy was in a basement room, commonly referred to as the "lab", with a couple of subordinates. This room was generally used to test, cut, weigh and repackage narcotics, hence its name.

Having chemically tested the coke for its purity and composition, Jimmy was sitting at a glass covered table, preparing a line for a "physical" test. As he leaned forward to snort the white powder, the windowless room went completely dark.

"What the fuck!" he bellowed as the battery-powered emergency lights came on, filling the room with an eerie glow. "Goddamn fucking Hydro!"

Several seconds later, the power returned, accompanied by the low distant rumble of the large gasoline powered generator located in the garage. At that moment, the door of the room burst open and one of his guards on duty rushed in.

"Jimmy! We've got a fucking problem!" he breathlessly exclaimed. "A fucking raid! They got two trucks full of cops surrounding the goddamn place! They busted through the front gate! They got a fucking army!"

"Jesus Christ!" screamed Jimmy in frustration.

He turned to the two in the lab. "Dump the shit! Burn it! Now!"

He hurried out of the lab while the two started loading the bags of coke in the high intensity gas incinerator foreseen for just such an occasion. He preferred to lose eighteen kilos of cocaine than spend an equivalent number of years in jail.

Unfortunately, when the power had gone out, the gas had been cut as well.

\* \* \* \*

"We'll be there in about five minutes," shouted Wild Billy over the roar of the chopper's engine.

Guns Mager nodded and climbed into the open cargo space in the back to set up his equipment.

As one might guess, Guns had earned his nickname due to his passion for firearms of all kinds. As a child, he had started by making his own slingshots and by the age of seven, had easily convinced his father, a hunting fanatic, to buy him a pellet rifle. He'd gone on his first hunting trip at eight and by the time he'd turned ten, he was already known as **the** gun expert in his county.

Not only was he an exceptional shot, he was also a walking encyclopaedia on any and all subjects related to firearms, big or small. He started designing and building his own guns before becoming a teenager, a hobby which he had maintained and perfected since.

The weapon of the day was one of his creations and its functioning was actually quite simple. In fact, it was actually a large scale model of a compressed gas pellet gun; very large scale. A three foot length of two and a half inch pipe served as the barrel which was mounted on a five pound canister of compressed carbon dioxide. Appropriately modified hand grenades replaced the pellets and six could be loaded in the ammunition dispenser at a time. Pulling the trigger released a sudden measured burst of gas into the barrel which projected the grenade.

It was accurate to one hundred feet and with Wild Billy as his pilot, Guns knew that they'd come in much closer than that.

\* \* \* \*

"This is the RCMP," Nick Sharp's voice echoed metallically through the bullhorn in the cold morning air. "We have the property surrounded. We have a warrant to search the premises. If we're not granted access, we will use force to enter the building."

Lowering the bullhorn, he turned to François Duguay, Regional Commander of the Quebec Provincial Police. "We'll give them a minute to respond. If they don't open up, we break in."

\* \* \* \*

"You got that shit burning?!" demanded Jimmy as he rushed back into the lab.

"Yeah, just started," replied his subordinate. "Fuckers cut the gas too! Had to use the backup tanks."

"Bastards!" hissed Jimmy, staring at the incinerator as it turned a fortune of coke into nothing. "We have nothing else in here?"

"Nope," assured his lackey. "They'll find a few guns but that's it."

"Fucking waste of taxpayers' money!" Jimmy muttered. "I'm gonna make these cocksuckers pay someday!"

\* \* \* \*

The helicopter came over the last ridge and their target was in sight. Two buildings; a barn, which was really the cocaine processing lab, and an old farmhouse used for sleeping and eating. Behind these structures was a small landing strip for the planes that flew the coke out of the area. A half dozen

Jeeps and pickup trucks were parked haphazardly around the buildings, indicating that several people were on the premises. A lone guard, armed with an automatic weapon, rose from his seat by the barn entrance as the helicopter approached.

Playing with the throttle, Billy started sporadically increasing and decreasing the revolutions of the engine. This, combined with the erratic swaying of the chopper, left a clear impression that the machine was experiencing mechanical problems.

As they came down into the clearing before the buildings, Billy waved the guard frantically back, and the latter seemed more than happy to comply.

With the helicopter no more than a half dozen feet from the ground, Billy suddenly swung the machine sideways, exposing the open cargo door. Mager fired off three rapid shots with a handgun, hitting the guard on all counts.

Dropping the pistol, he turned his attention to his grenade launcher, taking aim at a window of the barn. He pulled the trigger four times, proudly observing each of his projectiles make their way into the old wooden building. After all, it was barely thirty feet away.

The chopper swung 90 degrees and Guns expertly delivered the two remaining grenades through a window of the farmhouse.

Billy opened the throttle and the helicopter quickly rose as it turned before speeding off back over the nearby hills, leaving a series of massive explosions in the background.

From start to finish, the operation had taken twenty-three seconds.

"See! What'd I tell ya!" shouted a grinning Guns as he climbed back into the front seat. "Bonus money!"

*  *  *  *

"Chief!" called out the officer as he ran over to Nick Sharp and François Duguay.

"They've got a fire going!" he said, pointing towards the roof of the building.

Looking up, they could see the heat haze accompanied by light smoke shooting out of a chimney.

"Bastards are burning their stash," Nick commented with a smile.

"Poor Jimmy," replied François. "This is really gonna turn out to be a lousy day for him!"

Nick nodded as he raised the bullhorn to his lips.

"This is your last chance. Open the door or we will come in by force."

He waited a few seconds, then nodded to an officer already seated in a small but powerful armoured tractor which had been lifted out of the trailer. The diesel engine rumbled and the machine began rolling forward, its pointed, plough-like front aimed at the main door of the house. A dozen officers quickly fell in formation behind it.

With the tractor no more than ten feet from its target, the door suddenly opened and a voice called out from within.

"O.K. We ain't looking for no trouble! You guys want to come in and fuck up our morning, go ahead!"

Through the bullhorn, Nick replied, "I want everybody in the house to assemble in the living room, arms spread, up against the walls. You have one minute. Then we're coming in."

He signalled his officers who quickly approached the building, lining up along its walls on either side of the entrance.

"At least they're cooperating," François murmured approvingly.

Nick turned to him and with a grim smile said, "My friend, don't trust these fuckers for a second. If you do, you're dead! Let's go."

They walked to the front door, preceded by a dozen officers with weapons drawn, and entered the large house.

The living room, to the left, was surprisingly well decorated. Apparently Diamond Jimmy insisted on comfort. As requested, the occupants, fourteen in all, were lined along the walls, although none had assumed the desired position.

"All right, gentlemen," Nick addressed the group. "You know the routine. You've all been there before. Hands against the wall and spread em."

With a lazy nonchalance, all but one of the gang members complied, some chuckling, others exaggerating the requested spread-eagled stance.

The non-complier approached a step with hands spread. He was Shaun "Chains" Wilson, the undisputed second-in-command of the Aces of Death.

He stared coolly at Nick as he spoke.

"Before we go any further, I'd like to know who the fuck you are and I wanna see your fucking warrant!"

Nick eyed Chains for a moment, then walked up to him until their faces were a half inch apart.

"I'm RCMP Chief Nicholas Sharp, you little piece of shit. Now get yourself against the wall real quick or I'll blow your fucking brains out!"

He leaned the barrel of his withdrawn Colt .45 against Chains' right temple as added incentive. Following a fiery ten second stare, the gang member stepped back and slowly moved to the wall. Nick gestured and a number of his officers began frisking the bikers while others went off to explore the rest of the house. Quickly, the pile of compulsory switchblades grew in the middle of the carpeted floor.

Scanning their prisoners, Nick's stomach tightened as he realized that his main objective was not present.

"Where's Jimmy Sanchez?!" he demanded.

In response, Jimmy strutted in from the next room, apparently having been simply waiting for his cue.

"Howya doin, Nicky-boy?!" he smirked as he dropped on a nearby sofa.

"Up against the wall, Sanchez," Nick ordered.

"Come on, Nick!" Jimmy sneered as he leaned back into the couch. "You think Jimmy is stupid enough to walk in here armed when such important guests come to visit?!"

"Up!" commanded Nick, motioning with his revolver. "Don't screw with me, Jimmy!"

"Chief's got a rock up his ass this morning, boys!" Jimmy stated loudly as he rose and moved to the wall. 'O.K. Chief. Search me. But don't play with my balls too long. I don't go for that shit!"

Quickly and expertly, Nick frisked the gang leader, amidst the hoots and jeers encouraged by the gang leader's comments.

"Now, Chief," Jimmy resumed as he returned to the couch. "Let's get down to business. I wanna see your fucking warrant. Now!"

Nick reached into an inside pocket of his vest and pulled out a folded document, tossing to Sanchez. The biker scanned the piece of paper for a moment, scowling as he read.

"Reasonable reason to believe major quantity of illicit narcotics on property?!" he said incredulously, looking up at Nick. "What is this shit! Who's your informant, Nicky? Because he's fulla crap! You ain't gonna find squat in this place! Nothing! I just might sue you fuckers for harassment!"

Nick stared hard at Jimmy for a moment before turning to François.

"Anything on any of these guys?" he asked.

"They all had switchblades," François replied. "Those aren't legal. Two guns. A little grass, hash and coke."

"Possession of illegal weapons and drugs," mused Nick, staring once again at Jimmy. "Take them in. All of them! We're pressing charges."

"What is this garbage, Sharp?!" argued Jimmy from the couch. "Why you fucking with us like this? You're gonna bust my guys for knifes and grass? You won't have time to start the fucking paperwork, they'll be back here! Why don't you fucking leave us alone!?"

Nick gazed at Jimmy without answering, waiting for the other gang members to be handcuffed and led from the house. After a moment, they were alone.

"You're wasting everybody's fucking time, Sharp!" Jimmy snarled, his anger obviously growing. "You ain't gonna find anything in this fucking place! Understand?!"

"That's where you're wrong, asshole," Nick replied calmly, almost gently.

He reached into his bulky protective vest, pulled out two one kilo bags of cocaine and tossed them to Sanchez. François, who had re-entered the room in the interim, came forward, throwing another bag on the couch. A third officer came in from the dining room holding two additional bags.

"You see, Jimmy," Nick continued softly. "You're wrong, asshole."

Stunned, Jimmy stared at the five bags of coke as he quietly muttered, "Motherfuckers!"

Looking up at Nick, he suddenly screamed, "MOTHERFUCKERS!!" as he pulled out a revolver from between the cushions of the couch.

Long before he ever had time to get the gun clear, all three officers raised their weapons in response, firing five shots in total. Thirteen minutes after the raid had commenced, it was over and Diamond Jimmy Sanchez was dead.

* * * *

Alex "Kid" Wilson stood on the porch of the St-Sauveur residence, still fuming at having to be there. That was thanks to his brother, Chains, the high and mighty second in command, who had volunteered him for the job.

"The exposure will do you good, Kid", the senior Wilson had said. "You've got to do a job once in a while or the other guys won't respect you."

The other gang members had stood around with smirks on their faces.

Alex enjoyed being in the gang for several reasons; status, drugs, women, money. He just didn't like having to work to obtain these lifely pleasures and being Chains' little brother usually got him excused from the lowlife tasks.

Recently however, some of the other members had started bitching that the "Kid" was riding for free and this was quickly becoming unacceptable. Everybody had to do their share. This was why Kid now stood on this porch, enjoying the pleasures of the sub-zero winter.

At least he had gotten the porch. He'd made that clear as soon as they'd arrived. There was no way he'd go stand out in the woods and freeze his balls off!

As he mulled over his frustration, he noticed a man rush clumsily among the trees near the road and hide behind a massive pine. After a few seconds, the intruder dashed again, moving another ten feet, to the cover of a large rock. He raised his head a foot above the rock, looking towards the house for several seconds before dropping back into hiding. He resembled a young child playing war games, badly. Even when he attempted to hide, he was clearly visible to Kid.

Taking hold of the rifle he had slung over his back, Kid crept cautiously off to the left, taking a circular path to approach the unwelcome visitor from behind. Within in a minute, he had covered forty yards and could now clearly see the man, still crouched behind the large rock. He approached quietly, thinking of the glory coming his way. The "Kid" would show those assholes what he was made of. He would single-handedly bring this job to its conclusion.

He reached the intruder from behind just as the latter was once again attempting to peer towards the house over the rock. Pressing the gun barrel into the back of the man's neck, Kid spoke in a quiet, sure tone.

"Get up real slow, motherfucker. Real slow."

The stranger stood up, instinctively raising his hands above his head.

"Turn around, asshole!" ordered Kid, backing away a couple of steps. "Watcha looking for?"

"Uh, n-nothing," stammered Jonathan. "Just looking, that's all."

"Looking for what?" Kid demanded. "Looking how you can get inside that house, maybe? We've been waiting for you, mister!"

He finished his sentence, oblivious of his impending fate. From behind, Chris, armed with a heavy club improvised from a fallen limb, swung at the gang member's head. Death was immediate, the blow so forceful that Kid's body literally lifted off the ground and was projected a half dozen feet away where it slammed into a large maple tree.

"Thanks," said Jonathan as he moved towards the lifeless form.

"I owed you one," responded Chris, scanning the area to make sure they had not attracted any attention.

"Where did you learn to hit like that?" asked Jonathan, examining the messy wound on the dead biker's skull.

"Years of practice," Chris replied.

\* \* \* \*

Bryan drove through the village of St-Sauveur, feeling strangely calm. He would be back at Matt's chalet in a little under ten minutes, five if he hurried. But he was in no hurry.

He had respected the speed limit during his hour long drive, although he could have easily driven faster with little risk of getting pulled over, just by following the Saturday morning traffic; city dwellers rushing to the multitude of ski centres available to them all over the Laurentians. People whose prime concern was to get out there to breathe fresh air and pack in as many runs as they could in one day; people who read about drug traffickers and murderers in the papers and found such things horrible. He had been surrounded by such people on the drive down and had found it quite comforting, being amongst the normal, generally good people. He had not been in any rush to part company with them.

The cellular phone still wasn't functioning. He'd tried it several times on the way down but to no avail. The battery was fully charged but he couldn't get a signal. He chuckled to himself as he thought of Wayne who was probably freaking out by now, waiting for a call. Well, Wayne wouldn't have long to wait now before finding out what was going on. Bryan would be there in a few minutes and he'd bring his friend up to speed.

He wasn't sure what Wayne's next plan of action would be. All he knew was that if it wasn't absolutely brilliant, he was hopping a plane and getting the hell out. He had more than enough to retire on and frankly, he was growing tired of the cold Quebec winters.

\* \* \* \*

"Yeah, well, no doubt about it," Jonathan confirmed as he stood from Kid's body. "He's definitely dead."

"We're gonna have to dump him somewhere," said Chris as he surveyed the area. "He's too visible from the driveway and the road."

"I'll look after that," Jonathan replied, nodding. "You go and check out the house. I'll join you as soon as I can."

He picked up the dead man's rifle, slinging it by its strap over his right shoulder then hoisted the corpse over his left. He had noticed a rather deep ditch which ran alongside the road and ended just across the driveway and was certain that their latest victim would be comfortable there. As he moved off, Chris headed through the thick woods towards the house, and Sandy.

\* \* \* \*

Bryan drove up the hill, the last stretch of road before reaching the cottage. As he came around the bend, he thought he caught a glimpse of some movement behind a cluster of thick evergreens. Suddenly, it dawned on him that Barry might be here. After all, with the way Matt had been mutilated, it must have been to make him talk. A cold shiver gripped his body as he realized that he was quite possibly in extreme danger.

He slowed the vehicle as he pulled out his small .22. He wouldn't die without a fight.

\* \* \* \*

Having made his way around to the west side of the house, Chris examined the building from across the fifteen foot clearing which obviously served as a parking area. He found what he was looking for, just as the blueprints had indicated; a four foot square door leading to the basement. Its usual purpose was to facilitate the bringing in of firewood. Today however, it would serve nicely as his point of entry.

\* \* \* \*

The driveway leading from the road to Matt's chalet did not run in a straight line. Rather, it zigzagged around a number of mature trees which the original owner had wished to preserve. The added benefit was intimacy as one could not really see the house from the road through the multitude of trees.

This landscaping, and the cover it offered, pleased Jonathan as he hurried across the driveway towards the ditch on the other side, loaded with the guard's body.

A sudden glint of light through the trees down the hill, followed by the rumble of an engine caught his attention. Someone was coming!

As he reached the edge of the ditch, he glimpsed the approaching silver grey vehicle through an opening amongst the heavy pines. Hurriedly, he heaved the corpse off his shoulder, catapulting it into the ditch. With barely time to turn around, he saw the Mercedes veer slowly into the driveway and come to an abrupt stop, the driver staring at him.

He approached the car, holding the rifle across his chest, the picture of an alert guard.

"Sorry, private property, Mister," he informed the driver through the partially lowered window.

"Who the fuck are you?!" demanded Bryan, his small .22 concealed just below the bottom of the window, his finger on the trigger.

"Ice!" Jonathan coldly replied. "Now, who the fuck are you?!"

"I'm staying here for a few days!" Bryan shot back.

"Are you Bryan Downey?" asked Jonathan, his tone slightly less aggressive.

"Y-yes. Yes I am," responded Bryan, relaxing a little.

"Can I see some identification, Mr. Downey," continued Jonathan. "Jimmy told us to be real careful about who we let in."

"Sure, sure," answered Bryan as he slipped his gun into his jacket pocket and pulled out his wallet. "There you go."

Jonathan gave the driver's permit a cursory glance and handed it back.

"Thanks. Sorry if I came on strong, Mr. Downey. Jimmy gave us strict orders."

"No problem," Bryan reassured him. "Better safe than sorry. What happened to the other guy that was here?"

"Jimmy sent me to replace him," replied Jonathan. "They needed him back in town for something."

"Well, good," Bryan grinned. "He was a little too much of a snot nose whiner for my taste! No problems so far this morning?"

"No sir!" Jonathan answered. "We've got things under control."

"Excellent!" approved Bryan. "You guys keep up the good work!"

"Yessir, Mr. Downey!" replied Jonathan. "You've got nothing to worry about."

\* \* \* \*

Chris scrambled across the clearing to the relative safety offered by the elevated porch which ran along the west side of the house. He quickly got to work on the lock of the firewood door but suddenly froze, straining to hear.

Sure enough, as he listened, he detected the sound of tires crunching over the frozen snow, accompanied by the rumble of an engine. He pressed himself into the corner under the porch steps, breathing into his coat to avoid making steam.

The sounds grew louder and the car suddenly appeared, stopping no more than a half dozen feet away. From where Chris sat, he could see the front left side of Bryan's Mercedes, including the first half foot of the driver's door. He had no idea if the driver, presumably Bryan, could see him.

Being careful to move as little as possible, he withdrew the heavy revolver from the holster strapped under his right arm and waited. He hoped he wouldn't have to use it for now, but had no intention of getting shot himself, at least not without a fight.

The car door opened, the driver disembarked and swung the door back shut. He took a few steps forward and stopped, scanning the woods which surrounded them. It was Bryan. Apparently satisfied with what he saw, he turned and walked back, out of sight. Within seconds, Chris heard the man's footsteps climb the staircase over his head, a key insert into a lock and the creak of hinges as a door opened and then slammed shut.

Chris breathed deeply for a moment, realizing that he had been instinctively holding his breath then returned his attention to the task at hand.

* * * *

"Where the fuck were you!" bellowed Wayne as Bryan entered the house. "I asked you to fucking call!"

"Wayne, go screw yourself!" Bryan tiredly responded, hanging his coat on a peg by the door. "Give me a fucking break! Matt and Greg are dead, O.K.?! I saw their fucking bodies, not you! I tried to call you but my goddamn phone isn't working anymore! I need a drink!"

He stomped over to the bar and poured himself a healthy tot of scotch as Wayne slumped heavily into the couch.

"The bastard killed them!" Wayne murmured softly, shocked by this latest unfavourable turn of events.

"Yeah, the bastard killed them," Bryan mimicked. "And judging from the condition of Matt's body, he was obviously tortured, so now the bastard probably knows where we are!"

"Jesus fucking Christ!" Wayne cursed. "What about Greg?"

"I'm not sure if someone killed him or if the little twerp committed suicide," answered Bryan. "I found him sitting at his computer with his brains blown all over the room and a gun in his hand."

"We're gonna have to get outta here," decided Wayne.

"And then what?" challenged Bryan. "Where we gonna go from here? What's the big plan, Wayne?!"

"I don't know yet!" Wayne shot back. "Let me think. Maybe Jimmy can help us out."

"Well, I'm seriously considering catching a plane and getting the hell outta the country!" Bryan informed his partner. "I've got enough to live on."

"Yeah, but you can have more, Bryan! Much more!" replied Wayne with conviction. "Let me think a little. I'll figure something out."

"You better think quick, my friend," Bryan decisively warned. "And it better be good. Otherwise, you're on your own!"

* * * *

Chris had studied the blueprints which Matt had been good enough to provide him with and had a clear image of the house's layout imprinted in his mind.

Although the shades which covered the basement windows were quite opaque, enough daylight filtered in from the sides to render his flashlight unnecessary. Considering the absence of light, he was relatively certain sure that nobody lurked in any corner.

If Matt had told the truth, and Chris was confident that he had, the only people on the property were Wayne, Bryan and the four guards; and, of course, Sandy. Since the four guards had been taken care of rather permanently, there remained only two to deal with.

He quietly and cautiously began to explore the basement, a task which would consume little time. Most of it was actually one big room, the game room in which he currently found himself, equipped with a pool table, bar, fireplace, sound system and so on. A small complete bathroom could be found in one corner towards the back of the house and the furnace room, in the other corner. Sandwiched between these two rooms was a cold room.

Considering the fact that it was windowless and had a heavy, locking door, it made an ideal place to imprison someone. Chris hoped that Sandy's captors had also believed this. Getting her safely out of the building would make the remainder of the tasks of the day so much easier.

He reached the door and gently turned the knob, praying for it to be locked but, to his dismay, it wasn't. Barring a variety of bottles, jars and the like, the room was empty which meant that Sandy was upstairs somewhere.

He'd just have to go up there and get her.

*  *  *  *

"So? Have you come up with your master plan?" demanded Bryan.

His patience was wearing thin following several minutes of pacing and two hefty scotches.

"I haven't really been planning anything," admitted Wayne. "But I have been thinking about something."

"Well, why don't you share those thoughts," suggested Bryan, his sarcasm far from subtle.

Ignoring his colleague's tone, Wayne explained, "When we discovered that Barry was on to us, I was worried that he was working with the cops. Now, I'm really not so sure that he is."

"Why's that?" enquired Bryan, vaguely interested.

"Because the cops haven't shown up here," Wayne reasoned, "Even though Barry knows where we are. Because Matt and Greg are dead. I don't think Barry would have killed them if he was working for or with the police."

"Yeah, but we snatched his wife," reminded Bryan. "Maybe that made the guy go nuts."

"Maybe," Wayne responded doubtfully. "But presuming that Barry is the one who's been screwing with us all along, which we both believe he is, why did he kill Rick? Why did he set up Bob? Why did he switch the coke on us? We hadn't grabbed his wife then. No. I don't think the cops are in on this at all. I don't know what motivated the bastard to screw with us, but I'm sure it's just him and us."

"O.K. Great," accepted Bryan, puzzled. "So what's the point?"

"Point is, my friend, that I knew we would eventually have to deal with this guy and that his missus would serve as the bait. I just wasn't clear on when because I didn't know who was involved in this. Now I'm clear."

"And?" asked Bryan, still not quite following.

"If the cops aren't in on this, then the only problem is Barry," Wayne explained with a pained expression. "If he's gone, then nobody knows about our activities anymore."

"What about all these dead bodies?" questioned Bryan, not quite enthralled with Wayne's thoughts.

"What bodies? There's really been only one body so far. George. Who says Rick and Bob are dead? They've simply disappeared. Maybe they've been ripping off Quality Imports. We could short the inventory to support that theory. As far as Matt and Greg go, one was murdered and the other committed suicide. Hell, we had nothing to do with that! We were up here since Friday afternoon. We've got people in the village here that could vouch for that. All we have to do once we've taken care of Mr. Barry is keep our noses clean for a couple of months. Then we just pick up right where we left off!"

Both men stared at each other for a moment. Bryan had to admit, the way Wayne explained it made a whole lot of sense; definitely plausible.

"O.K. What's our next step, then?" asked Bryan.

"We get that little bitch down here," snarled Wayne, "And the three of us will call her husband to suggest he get his butt over here real quick!"

\* \* \* \*

From downstairs, Chris could hear the muffled voices of a discussion taking place on the main floor. As best as he could determine there were two people involved and both were male. The sounds of the conversation seemed louder when he moved towards the front of the house, leading him to believe that Bryan and Wayne were in the living room. That was good. The staircase leading up to the first floor was at the back of the house.

He started up the steps, slowly, one at a time, a small can of WD-40 ready for the hinges of the door on top. He wondered where Jonathan was. Considering Bryan's arrival without any evident panic, he figured that Jonathan had managed to make things appear normal. He hadn't known Jonathan for long but was confident that the man would be there if he needed him.

\* \* \* \*

Jonathan kept watch on the front porch, glancing inside on a regular basis. Wayne and Bryan were in the living room, deep in conversation, with the former doing most of the talking. There was no sign of Chris yet and Jonathan had no idea what his most recent consultant intended to do. However, Chris had clearly established that he was quick on his feet, able to rapidly evaluate a situation and react accordingly. Whatever he determined to be the appropriate action, Jonathan would be ready to back him up.

* * * *

Sandy was seated on the brass bed, her right wrist securely handcuffed to the railed headboard. Although she had no idea what fate the coming hours reserved for her, she felt strangely calm. Regardless of what happened to her, she knew that her captors would pay. Pay and suffer. Her husband would see to that. Her husband was the 'Vigilante'.

The door to the second floor bedroom suddenly swung open and Wayne strolled in, keys in hand.

"Come on, sweetheart," he smiled, unlocking the cuff at her wrist. "It's time to call hubby!"

"Fuck you," she calmly responded. "I'm not doing anything to help you."

His smile turned to a nasty grimace as he spoke.

"You're not in any position to make decisions, bitch! Now, get your sweet ass downstairs or I'll throw it down!"

He grabbed her wrist and pulled her roughly from the bed, propelling her from the room and down the stairs. Into the living room, he pushed her onto the couch before picking up the cordless phone which he shove in her face.

"Call!" he ordered.

She gazed at him with a slight smile then spit at him in response.

"You little cunt!" Wayne screamed, raising a hand to strike her.

"I wouldn't do that if I were you," warned Chris, his voice a deadly monotone.

Both Wayne and Bryan spun around in surprise to find Chris standing at the entrance of the hallway which led to the back of the house. The hole in the barrel of the .357 Magnum he held seemed large enough to walk into. Bryan threw a glance at his jacket, hanging far away on the peg by the side door, thinking of his gun in the pocket.

"Don't try anything stupid," Chris ordered, turning his attention to the man for an instant.

Wayne, taking advantage of the slight diversion, pulled a revolver from behind his back and pressed its barrel to Sandy's head.

"Who's gonna shoot first, Barry?" he growled. "Who's the first to die?"

"My guess would be Mr. Barry," came Jonathan's voice from the front door, where he stood with his rifle trained on Chris's chest. "Put down that cannon real slow, Mister Barry. Real, real slow."

"Who the hell are you?" blurted Wayne, somewhat confused by the sudden appearance of this stranger.

"Ice," replied Jonathan as he took a step forward, his unblinking eyes fixed on Chris. "Jimmy's best, Mr. Mackinnon. Now, Mister Barry, I ain't gonna ask you again. Get that gun down on the floor or I'll blow your fucking heart out!"

He took another step into the room as he raised the rifle butt to his shoulder, assuring better precision of his aim. Chris stared at him for a few seconds and then, slowly began lowering the gun, admitting defeat.

"Well, Chris," Wayne smugly taunted, lowering his revolver from Sandy's head. "Guess you're not that bright after all!"

Turning to Jonathan who now stood no more than three feet from him he added, "Kill him."

Chris froze, his gun now down to waist level, as Jonathan grinned. "You got it, boss!"

With an unexpected swing, Jonathan whipped the barrel of his rifle into Wayne's face, sending the man reeling and his revolver clattering across the floor, safely out of reach. Losing his balance from the blow, Wayne fell and immediately found himself pinned to the ground by a rifle barrel leaning heavily into his throat.

"Everything O.K.?" Jonathan called out as he stared down at Wayne.

"Fine," replied Chris, his heavy handgun aimed directly at Bryan who, stunned by the sudden turn of events, remained very still.

"Good," said Jonathan, stepping back a few feet from Wayne. "Mr. Mackinnon, please roll over on your stomach and spread your arms and legs wide. Don't try anything stupid or I will kill you."

Wayne silently obeyed.

"Good boy," Jonathan continued. "Now, Mr. Downey, please come over here and lay down on your stomach next to your friend, same position."

A nervous Bryan abided by the request without a word.

"Thank you," Jonathan politely said.

He reached into a pocket of his leather jacket, extracted a small aerosol can and crouched down near the two men's heads.

"Night, boys!" he pleasantly chanted as he quickly sprayed them to sleep.

Standing, he turned to Chris and Sandy who were already in each others arms.

"Why don't you two take a break and get reacquainted. I'll entertain our hosts in the meantime!"

\* \* \* \*

Wayne and Bryan awoke within seconds of each other, their state of mind, a bit foggy. Each was propped up against and securely taped to one of each of the two oak support beams which ran from floor to ceiling between the living room and dining area.

As they regained their senses, they became aware of someone standing before them. Looking up, they recognized Chris, which quickly brought them completely back to reality.

"Gentlemen, nice to have you back," said Chris, his smile charming but his gaze deadly. "I couldn't leave without saying goodbye."

The two stared up at him but uttered no reply. The several layers of tape covering their mouths prevented them to do so.

"While you were sleeping, I had a chat with my wife," Chris continued. "I was quite interested in knowing how you gentlemen had treated her during her stay. Although she was understandably frightened by the whole ordeal, she has assured me that you did not harm her and, for that, I extend my thanks."

He paused for a moment, looking from one man to the other, before pursuing.

"Over the years, I have earned the reputation of being honest and straight-forward, a man of my word. I promised you no pain if you didn't harm Sandy and I will keep my promise."

Turning towards the dining table behind him, he pointed to a small digital clock which read 10:43.

"At precisely eleven, this clock will transmit a signal. We have placed explosives in strategic locations in the house, armed with detonators which will be triggered by the signal. The explosion will be so massive, gentlemen, that your death will be instantaneous. I promise you will feel no pain."

With these as his final words, he stepped through the front door to join Sandy and Jonathan, who waited in the Jeep Grand Cherokee which Jonathan had conveniently obtained for the day's activities. They drove off, heading south for home.

As they embarked onto the Laurentian autoroute, they heard and felt a sudden rumbling in the distance behind them. The clock in the Jeep's dashboard read 11:00.

## Chapter 20 - Sunday, February 2, 1997

Dave McCall awoke at 6:15, which was considered sleeping in by his standards. He quietly climbed out of bed, careful not to wake Cathy. They had gotten in late the night before, following a lovely dinner and an evening of dancing which Dave had proposed in order smooth over the previous morning's silly spat.

He padded to the kitchen to get the coffee going, used the bathroom and then headed to the front door for the morning paper. Due to their evening out, he had missed the news and he liked to keep abreast of current events.

He returned to the kitchen to get some coffee before settling down to read. As he dropped the paper on the table in passing, the front page headline caught his attention. Any articles related to crime naturally piqued his interest and he forgot about his coffee as he started to read.

### RCMP CRUSH DRUG IMPORT RING AND "ACES OF DEATH"

by Ron Henderson

Following months of intense investigation, the RCMP, assisted by officers of the QPP, closed in on a major narcotics importation and distribution ring yesterday, announced Nicholas Sharp, Director of the RCMP detachment for the Province of Quebec.

Thanks to tips from informants and a series of surveillance operations which spanned a period of some eighteen months, an undercover team, headed by Sharp, was able to confirm cocaine and heroin imports from Columbia and Thailand.

The masterminds behind the complex import network are suspected to have used their employer, Quality Imports of Laval, as the cover and means to their operation. Unbeknownst to Charles Peterson, owner and president of Quality Imports, the drugs were allegedly included within regular shipments of merchandise brought into the country by the company.

Also suspected to be involved in the drug import scheme were two customs officials, one employee of Rapid Forwarders, a local customs broker as well as legal counsel to the infamous "Aces of Death" motorcycle gang which is also alleged to be involved, handling the distribution of the narcotics.

Having accumulated sufficient evidence to crack the network, the authorities proceeded with a series of raids yesterday morning during which dozens were arrested and sizeable quantities of illicit drugs and weapons were seized. Two died, including Diamond Jimmy Sanchez, head of the Aces of Death.

Interestingly enough, of the six Q.I. employees suspected to be overseeing the narcotic imports operation two have not been seen for several days while the bodies of the other four were found yesterday at various locations.

Data obtained from the personal computer of Q.I.'s Greg Pierce, who was found dead at his Laval home from an apparent suicide, indicates that relations with the Aces of Death had grown more than tense following several shipments of phoney cocaine to the bikers. It is suspected that a war may have developed between the two groups. This is supported by the discovery of six bodies in St-Sauveur late yesterday morning following a powerful explosion at a cottage, owned by Matthew Roth, also employed by Q.I., whose badly mutilated body was found in his Laval home.

Of the six bodies found in St-Sauveur, four were known members of the Aces of Death. The other two were Wayne MacKinnon and Bryan Downey, both employed by Q.I. and allegedly involved in the narcotics import scam. Police suspect that the deaths were the result of an attempted settling of accounts between the two groups.

A neighbour to the Roth cottage in St-Sauveur informed police that he saw a black Jeep Grand Cherokee leave the residence shortly before the explosion occurred. Police suspect that the vehicle was that of Robert Rivard, also employed by Q.I. and presumed to be involved in the drug operation. Rivard, according to Peterson of Q.I., is on vacation in Mexico since Thursday, although authorities have not been able to locate him to date, nor find any record of his leaving the country. Police suspect that Rivard may still be in the area, accompanied by Richard Beauchamp, also of Q.I., reported missing since Tuesday.

Dave put down the paper in a daze. Maybe Cathy had been right. Maybe something had happened to Chris or Sandy. He swore to himself for not having listened as he rushed to the phone. Frantically, he punched in the Barrys' home number, waiting impatiently as it rang.
"Hello?" answered Chris's sleepy voice.
"Chris! You're home!" exclaimed Dave, surprised, but pleased.

"Where else would you expect me to be this early in the morning?" mumbled Chris. "What time is it?"

"Nearly six-thirty," Dave sheepishly replied. "Listen, I'm sorry if I woke you. I was just worried about you guys since I learned what was happening at Quality Imports."

"What? What's happening at Quality Imports?" asked Chris, still sleepy and obviously confused. "What are you talking about, Dave?"

"You can read about it in the paper. Sorry I woke you, Chris," Dave apologized. "Go back to sleep and give me a call later, O.K.?"

"I will go back to sleep," Chris agreed with a yawn. "But since I have you on the phone, why don't you people come over for dinner tonight?"

"Well, if Sandy's not feeling well," Dave started.

"Sandy has never felt better," Chris interrupted. "See you later. Goodnight!"

Dave replaced the receiver in its cradle as Cathy padded into the kitchen, yawning.

"Who are you talking to at this hour?" she asked, squinting in the light.

"Chris," replied Dave, grinning. "And for your information, he and Sandy are fine, just like I told you!"

* * * *

Chris and Sandy were comfortably seated in the den watching television when the doorbell rang.

"You sure you're O.K. with this?" Chris asked as they headed towards the front door. "You have your story straight?"

"It's a little too late now anyways, wouldn't you say?" his wife replied sweetly before opening the door to greet their dinner guests.

"Hey there!" they chorused as they ushered Cathy and Dave in from the cold.

A round of hugs and kisses took place during which Cathy complimented Chris on how elegant he looked wearing a turtle-neck sweater.

"It's to hide the hickeys Sandy gave me!" he kidded, thinking of the bruises left by the gorilla's attempt at strangulation less than thirty-six hours earlier.

"So I guess you're feeling better?" an ever-concerned Cathy asked Sandy as the latter took her coat.

"I'm great!" reassured Sandy. "It was just a temporary thing, something that didn't agree with me. Come on. Let's go to the kitchen and let these two catch up on sports and stuff."

"I was worried about you," Cathy persisted as they walked off, "Especially when I couldn't reach you yesterday."

"Oh, we were visiting with some acquaintances of Chris' up north yesterday..." were Sandy's words as the two women departed, causing Chris to involuntarily smile.

"What's so funny?" asked Dave as Chris motioned his guest towards the den.

"Women and how they worry," Chris candidly replied.

"Tell me about it!" stated Dave as Chris tossed him a beer from the fridge at the bar. Although, I have to admit that when I read the paper this morning, I was concerned."

"Yeah, quite a story," Chris agreed as they relaxed into a couple of comfortable leather easy chairs. "I spoke to Peterson earlier and he's quite shocked, poor guy. I'm gonna give him a hand to keep the place running until he gets himself some replacement management."

"You think this might affect his business?" Dave enquired. "You can't consider that this was the best kind of free publicity a company can get!"

"I asked Charlie about that," Chris responded. "He told me that he's already received calls from a number of larger clients offering help, sympathy and their full support. No, I don't think that this is gonna hurt him."

Dave remained quiet for a moment, hesitant to even ask the question. Finally, he mustered up the courage and simply blurted it out.

"Chris, you had **no** idea that any of this was going on? I mean, I know you were just there for a couple of weeks, but still! Didn't you notice anything out of the ordinary?"

"Can't tell you more than you already know," Chris shrugged nonchalantly. "I was just a consultant."

The two men fell silent as they turned their attention to the news on the television, first watching a report on the bombing of a farm in Columbia, followed by another from Thailand regarding an explosion at a clothing manufacture and the destruction of a bar known to be a criminal hang-out.